girl
friends

Holly Bourne is a bestselling author. Alongside her writing, Holly is passionate about gender equality and is an advocate for reducing the stigma of mental health problems. She is also an ambassador for Women's Aid, working with the charity to spread awareness of abusive relationships.

Girl Friends is her third adult novel.

Also by Holly Bourne

How Do You Like Me Now?
Pretending

holly bourne

girl friends

HODDER &
STOUGHTON

First published in Great Britain in 2022 by Hodder & Stoughton
An Hachette UK company

1

Copyright © Holly Bourne 2022

A CIP catalogue record for this title is available from the British Library

Hardback ISBN 978 1 529 30157 1
Trade Paperback ISBN 978 1 529 30158 8
eBook ISBN 978 1 529 30159 5

Typeset in Plantin Light by
Palimpsest Book Production Limited, Falkirk, Stirlingshire

Printed and bound in Great Britain by Clays Ltd, Elcograf S.p.A.

Hodder & Stoughton policy is to use papers that are natural, renewable
and recyclable products and made from wood grown in sustainable forests.
The logging and manufacturing processes are expected to conform
to the environmental regulations of the country of origin.

Hodder & Stoughton Ltd
Carmelite House
50 Victoria Embankment
London EC4Y 0DZ

www.hodder.co.uk

For my girls.

Thirty-one

If I'd known Jessica was going to turn up unexpectedly after all this time, I would've worn a different outfit.

Though it's not as if that would've stopped her looking better than me, and no outfit could rescue my general limp appearance that day. I'd woken up to a vibrating notification from my period tracking app: *'Warning – you may be experiencing PMS symptoms today'*.

'What is it?' Ben had asked, in a voice thick with sleep.

I'd kissed his creased face and handed over my phone.

He read the screen and smiled. 'Thanks for the heads-up. I'll get my panic room ready.' He cradled my head and kissed me quickly on the lips, before returning my phone and rolling out of bed to get ready for work.

I grinned as I listened to him sing in the shower, shifting to lie in the leftover warmth of his sleeping body. I inhaled his scent on the pillow and couldn't imagine any PMS capable of breaking through my Ben-induced oxytocin.

My boyfriend emerged dripping in a towel, looking both cute and sexy. 'How are you feeling about tonight?'

'It will be fine,' I sighed. The thought of the upcoming evening curdled the edges of my good mood. 'It's not like I sell out *every day*.'

'You're not selling out,' Ben repeated for the twentieth time. He leant over to kiss me, sprinkling me with drops of shower water. 'Remember, Fern, some days you just need to do your job and pay the rent.' He glanced at the time on his phone to check he wasn't late. 'If this "author",' he made air quotes with his fingers, 'says some stupid things, then that's on her, not you.'

'Stop being so nice to me if you're now going to dare leave for work when you're so naked and brilliant,' I groaned.

He laughed into my mouth as he kissed me, and I felt positively sickened by my own happiness.

'I've got to go.' Ben gave me a final kiss, before straightening up, and pulling a shirt and trousers over his damp body. After he'd finished brushing his teeth, he appeared in the doorway with a breakfast bar in his hand to eat on the bus. 'See you later, gorgeous. Message me when the event's over. You're going to smash it.' He picked up my phone, which still had the warning up. 'When you look at the PMS dark side, careful you must be,' he said in a Yoda voice.

I couldn't help my smile. 'You're ridiculous and I love you.'

'You too. Oh shit. Late. Always, always late. Right. Gotta go.'

When the front door clicked behind him, I sank again into the glorious smell of his pillow.

*

Of course, it didn't take long for the app to be proved correct. My best friend, Heather, messaged me to say she wouldn't be able to make it that night as she'd been given a last-minute late shift at the clinic. I dropped my toast peanut-butter-side down, spilt legions of coffee over my notes for that evening, and couldn't get through Week Five of my Couch to 5k app. After I showered off the sweat from my failed run, I found my body had swollen like proven dough. My chosen outfit, which had looked fine a week earlier, now taunted me with its clinginess. Despite my shower, my hair still had a greasy sheen to it, and hung lankly around my shoulders. I tried curling it, but burnt my neck – flinging my GHDs onto the carpet, and calling them *'a self-satisfied pair of cunts'*. These 'cunts' proceeded to singe our landlord's acrylic carpet in retaliation, and, it was just as well I hadn't applied make-up yet, as I actually rage-cried for a full minute.

By the time I left for the event, I'd masked my low mood and oestrogen levels with red lipstick, and arranged my hair so it covered my GHD hickey. I wore an old and reliable black, long-sleeved jumpsuit and had gold heels I'd change into when I got to the venue. I was pelted with long strings of rain as I ran to the bus stop, soaked by the time I reached shelter. I checked my appearance using the selfie mode on my phone, and admitted defeat. This was just going to be a ball-ache of a day, with the event still to come.

'At least no one you know is coming,' I reassured myself, as the bus hissed its way around the corner, splashing the bottom of my jumpsuit with puddle water.

★

'Fern, you made it. Oh my God, isn't the weather terrible?' Gwen, the bookshop's event manager, met me with the standard publishing industry two air kisses.

'February is a very determined month,' I said, while my umbrella dripped onto her brogues. 'Oh no, I've made you wet. Sorry.'

She waved her hand. 'Don't worry. Right. Sit down. Can I get you anything? Tea? Coffee? Wine? Stacy isn't here yet.' Gwen checked her watch as she clattered over to a laden table and started putting food I'd not asked for onto a paper plate. She checked the time again as she dumped freshly cut melon onto my palm.

'Oh, right. Thank you. Umm, Stacy's just posted an Insta story on her way here. She's on her way from the hairdresser. Stuck in traffic by all the rain.'

Gwen twitched. 'Oh, yes. OK. Have you seen the queue outside? They've arrived so early. They're all going to be soaked.'

'I'm sure they're too excited to care.' I pushed a watermelon slab into my mouth to stop me making a sarcastic comment.

'Shall I show you the stage set-up? I know you've done this loads of times before, but can't hurt to go over it, can it?'

I sensed it was to ease her nerves rather than mine, but nodded, and followed her scuttling through the corridors out onto the giant empty stage. Stacy was too big for her events to fit into a bookshop, so they'd hired out a theatre. Gwen and I stepped out into the blinding lights, while a technician paced around the stage, clapping at different moments. A jolt of nerves went through me. So many people would be witnessing this damn carry-on. Stacy's publishers had done a paid partnership with *Gah!*, the website I worked at, and wanted me to chair the event to give her autobiography credibility. From what I'd been told, we couldn't afford to turn down the advertorial, and I was stuck pretending to like a book I'd thrown across the room seven times the previous weekend.

'It's dangerous and outdated . . . nonsense, I don't think Stacy's ever met a psychologist,' I'd told Ben – both before and after lunch, and twice more before bedtime. 'And yet *Gah!* are splashing it all over their homepage for a whole *week*.'

He'd laughed and lowered his lips onto my eyelids. 'And just think, out of all the chairpersons they could've chosen to peddle such misinformation, they chose you.'

I stared out at the ocean of space. 'That's a lot of seats,' I said.

Gwen grinned. 'It sold out in an hour, did I tell you? One of the quickest we've had. Do direct them to buy the book at the beginning *and* the end. So many people forget.'

'Of course.'

'Shall I show you the *Gah!* stand?'

'The *what*?'

She led me past a side table dwarfed by the wobbling piles of Stacy's book. Hulking hot-pink hardbacks towered towards the high ceiling, and, just past it, was a sorrowful-looking table with the *Gah!* banner above it, loaded with some promotional key rings I doubted anyone wanted.

'That's your table. It will be nice for you to be able to chat to people afterwards.'

'Oh great,' I said, immediately furious at my editor, Derek, for not telling me about this part of the evening. Nobody mentioned me having to loiter around some stand afterwards.

Gwen's phone went and she leapt on it, her eyes wide with relief. 'Stacy's here,' she told me, as if Beyoncé had just arrived. 'Quick.'

'Can you BELIEVE this weather,' Stacy bellowed to everyone, rushing into the green room with her tiny publicist, knowing she didn't need to introduce herself. 'I spent so long getting my hair perfect, and all for what? Oh my God. It makes you want to kill yourself. Whoops. Bad joke. You know me! Hey, do you guys have a phone charger I can use? Cheers.' Stacy snatched a lead from Gwen's twitching hands, then spied the snacks. 'Oh, cakes, yummy. Is this all for me? How sweet.'

We all hovered and watched Stacy eat a cupcake, while I wondered when I should introduce myself. The young influencer had clearly made a 'book launch outfit' mood board at some point after googling *what writers look like*. Gone was her usual array of erratic, revealing clothing. Instead she'd poured herself into a crisp white shirt with skinny tie, dark blue jeans, heels, and gathered her hair into a professional ponytail, topped off with prescription-free large-rimmed glasses. 'Wow. Watermelon too. Oh, this is great.' She pulled out her phone. 'Look. Everyone outside is so excited.' Stacy fell down a social media rabbit hole, and it was now slightly weird she hadn't said hello to anyone. I coughed, to alert her publicist, who was also buried in her phone. She looked up, and I saw the obvious effort it took her to pretend enthusiasm for me.

'You must be Fern! Oh my. Lovely to meet you.' She launched herself up and air-kissed me.

'Nice to meet you too. How's it been going?'

'Oh crazy. Just crazy! We found out today we hit the best-seller list though. After only three days of sales.'

'That's wonderful.'

'So much thanks to you and *Gah!*, of course.'

'We were so happy to support Stacy.'

Stacy, behind us, held up her phone, and started filming a video to post. 'This, ladies, gentlemen, and everyone in between . . . is what a green room looks like,' she said, narrating herself without a whiff of self-consciousness. I sucked my stomach in as the lens swept over me, pretending I didn't know I was being beamed to over four hundred and fifty thousand followers.

'Stacy? Are you free for a second? I'd like you to meet Fern, your amazing chair.'

The influencer stood up to shake hands. 'It's great to meet you.' She smiled with the full-wattage, as if I was one of her fans. 'Fern, was it?'

Her publicist filled her in. 'Fern's the mental health editor of the *Gah!* website. And she founded the *Hold On For Tomorrow* project. You know? That blog post that went viral a few years ago, encouraging people to post reasons to stay alive? She started that.'

I watched Stacy's expression as she realised I was, actually, quite relevant. 'Oh my God, of course that was you! I *loved* that project! I knew I recognised you from somewhere. We must take a photo. Hayley, could you?' She tossed her phone to her publicist and smooshed her face against mine. Awkwardness reigned my body as I tried to pose in a way that didn't make me look as if I was trying to *get down with the youth.* I was highly aware of my eye wrinkles compared to Stacy's smoothly made-up face. One of her many 'youth privileges', like being able to shop at BooHoo without looking like mutton, and her instant understanding of TikTok, the gender spectrum, and which brand of oat milk was morally questionable that week. The phone clicked, and Stacy grabbed it back, zooming in on her own face before pocketing it.

'It's great to meet you too,' I gushed. 'I *loved* the book.'

This was the toll I'd found you must always pay in the publishing industry. You must first lie that you'd read the book the whole way through, and then you lie about having loved it.

Stacy accepted my payment, smiled, and offered up an equally inauthentic response. 'Oh, really? Thank you. That means so much coming from you, Fern.'

Me, a woman who needed formal identification less than two minutes ago.

We grinned inanely at one another, our cheeks aching.

'Do you have a few minutes to go through the event?' I asked. 'My questions?'

Her nose wrinkled. 'Do you mind if we didn't? I feel like I lose my flow if I know what's coming up. You know?'

'Oh . . . Of course.'

Hayley the publicist appeared at my side, while Stacy sat down again and disappeared through the portal of her phone screen. 'Stacy's just so comfortable in front of her followers that it all flows really easily,' she reassured me.

'Of course.'

'Honestly, just let Stacy be Stacy, and it will be amazing.'

'Of course.'

★

Of course, the event was the trainwreck I knew it was going to be from the moment I'd read her book. Not that anyone else a) noticed the trainwreck, or b) minded it. At least my reputation, and *Gah!*'s, didn't appear to be harmed by it. In fact, as Stacy had so kindly tagged me into her socials afterwards, I was privy to the hundreds of her fans *crying and shaking* at *the beautiful energy* of the *inspirational evening*. It was the easiest money I'd made in a long while. After we'd been mic'd up, we emerged in front of hundreds of cheering faces, and, as chair, I had to ask only one question to fill the forty minutes. 'So, tell me, Stacy, what led you to write this book?'

Stacy spurted into a manic monologue that was literally impossible to interrupt, even when she started sharing, in explicit detail, the exact methodologies by which she'd considered killing herself when she got 'cancelled' after a viral YouTube video, and discussing the success rates of each one. I winced and tried to interject as she broke every single Samaritans safeguarding guideline. As I watched this twenty-four-year-old talk about her gritty break-up, half of me wanted to hug her and the other half wanted to throw one mental health book at her that wasn't her ghost-written autobiography. Instead, I arranged my face into nothingness and reminded myself this was on *Gah!*, not me. Eventually, after calling her ex-boyfriend a *'carrot cock'* – which led to thunderous applause, and some eyebrow raises from stressed-looking parents sitting with their devoted eleven-year-olds – the show was over. Everyone stood and cheered, most of them in tears. I threw my arms in her direction. 'Ladies and gentlemen, Stacy Smith', and they all went crazy. As I mumbled the

Samaritans' helpline number into the microphone, they flung themselves out of their seats to join the queue to get their books signed.

Stacy turned to me, glowing with a dew of sweat and validation.

'Well done,' I said, trying not to lie. 'Everyone loved it.'

'Thank you. You were a *wonderful* chair. It was so great to meet you. We should *totally* grab a drink or something one time.'

'That would be *brilliant*.'

And we never spoke again.

Gwen vibrated over, giddy with how well it had gone. 'We're ready for you,' she said, and led Stacy towards her signing table, her fans swooning as she passed. I followed reluctantly, knowing it would only be an hour more, max, of work before I could go home to Ben.

While Stacy's queue snaked between aisles, my stand was essentially empty. Nobody seemingly in the market for a free corporate key ring. In fact, the queue contained only two people. I sat on my chair and smiled hello, nonetheless grateful to have them.

'Hello,' I said to a middle-aged woman wearing a damp navy anorak.

'Hello.' She picked up a key ring. 'These are free, aren't they?'

I'd been given literally no guidance from work, but nodded. 'Yep, totally free.'

'Great.' And she shamelessly picked up ten key rings, dropped them into her pocket and wandered off without another word.

Normal, totally normal, I thought, readying myself for

whoever was next. My next taker was younger, maybe twenty-one. Perfectly put together in the current cutting-edge fashions. She picked up a key ring and giggled.

'Hi, can I help you?' I asked.

'I'm Caroline,' she said, like I should know who she is.

'Hi Caroline . . .'

'I really loved your *Hold On For Tomorrow* project. I actually donated an entry.'

I sat up in my chair. 'No way!' I smiled. 'Really? What was your reason?'

She giggled again, turning the colour of her purple lipstick. 'I think it was number twelve thousand and eighty-three. *The first proper day of autumn.*'

'Oh, that was a brilliant one.'

'Thank you.'

'Do you want more than one key ring?' I asked, but she shook her head. There was nothing else to say, but Caroline lingered, apparently uninterested in joining Stacy's anaconda queue. We smiled at each other, and I was trying to figure out what, exactly, was going on, when . . .

'So, actually, I was wondering if you could help me. You see, I really want to become a journalist . . .' Caroline launched into a pre-prepared monologue about her career ambitions as if this was a job interview. I blinked and smiled as she talked me through all of her GCSE subjects, A levels, uni choices, and I tried to figure out a polite way of telling her that, no, I couldn't get her a job at *Gah!*. 'Yeah, so I sent *Vogue* the first page of my dissertation, but I never heard back. Do you have an email for them that works?'

More minutes passed as Caroline told me in detail about

her work experience placement at a local newspaper, until, mercifully, a person joined the queue behind her. 'So, at *Gah!* do you take on anyone . . .'

I held up my hand. 'I'm so sorry, Caroline, but there's someone waiting.'

'Oh, right.' She glanced behind her.

Now that I knew she would leave, I found space for generosity. I'd been where she'd been. Young, and hungry, and desperate to know the secret four-figure code that opens the door to your dream life. 'Honestly, you're doing all the right things,' I told her. 'Be patient. It will happen. And thanks so much for coming tonight.'

'Bye then.' Caroline left without a thank you, and I reminded myself this is what you can expect of people who fetishise the seasons, particularly autumn.

I closed my eyes to collect my remaining energy for my third and final key ring fan. I would be grateful. I would be warm. I would be patient. The evening was almost over.

'Sorry to keep you . . .' I said, looking up. 'Oh my God. Jessica!'

And, like that, the theatre wiped away, and I was a teenager again.

Fourteen

September 2000

I wiped a mascara blob off the mirror and took in the novelty of my reflection. Somehow my school uniform still fitted, which seemed impossible as I hadn't worn it for over six months. It wasn't even eight a.m., but the Indian summer raged on outside. No breeze fluttered through my window, but I still wouldn't be wearing my short-sleeved blouse to the first day back to school. I was calculating exactly how far I could push up my jumper cuffs before you got to the scars. Today, of all days, everyone would be looking for them.

Nausea squeezed my intestines together over my uneaten breakfast of Honey Nut Cheerios, while Mum's nerves crackled static around my freshly washed hair.

'Are you going to be all right?' she asked again over her cup of green tea. 'Are you sure you're up for this?'

'Christ, Mum, I'm going to be fine.' I picked up a spoon of soggying cereal and plopped it back into the bowl. 'Amy's meeting me at the corner.'

'Why don't I drive you both? Just in case you don't cope.'

'Mum!'

'Not every day. Just your first day back.'

'We're walking, it's fine.'

'Well, excuse me for trying to do what's best for you.'

It felt hugely surreal, reigniting the clockwork routine of getting ready to leave the house, like remembering the lines to an old play I'd once starred in. I re-trod my former footsteps, packing my JanSport rucksack, brushing my teeth, checking how much credit I had on my phone, digging out my old pencil tin filled with strawberry-scented gel Pentels, where the ink had hardened around the nibs. I'd missed the whole summer term of school. I hadn't done this since you could buy Easter eggs in the shops, and now it was September. Mum stalked me with wide eyes, asking inane questions to satisfy her anxiety rather than mine.

'Have you topped up your phone so you can call if you need to? You can always use the school phone. Do you want a chewy bar to take in? Take a chewy bar.' She shoved one into my bag as I was hoisting it onto my shoulders. 'Do you think you're going to need to call me or your father to come and pick you up? Because I do have a meeting, so I'd rather know now if you don't think you'll make it through the day.'

'Bye, Mum.'

'You can call me any time. Any time. Just not between ten and four.'

I had the distance between my house and the corner to feel my own anxiety rather than absorb my mother's. I paused at the end of my road and grasped my narrowing throat as the hugeness of this day engulfed me. I panicked about how people would stare at me. I panicked at how hot I was going to be in my uniform. I panicked at the sheer impossibility of getting through a school day without panicking, let alone managing to learn anything. I panicked Kim had got her desperate, pathetic hooks into Amy and taken away my best friend. I panicked my spots still showed through my thickly applied Rimmel concealer. Then I panicked all this panic would make me numb out again, and tip me back down into the mental hellhole that I'd been so carefully scaling my way out of. Already sweating into my synthetic jumper, it became abundantly clear that living my life was a complete impossibility. Dragging myself every day across a bed of shattered glass . . . for what? GCSEs? Uni? A job? A life? What kind of pitiful life? A life where every day was determinedly difficult, and unrelenting, with only minor pockets of happiness to break up the misery. Surely, I thought, that's not worth the effort? Surely I should just surrender? Tap out . . . ? Surely oblivion was better than surviving . . .

. . . And then I caught myself. I noticed my thoughts spiralling and my breath catching, and noticing was the most important step. They'd told me that in therapy. I patted my own chest to comfort myself.

I recognise I'm thinking about killing myself again, I told myself.

I notice that I'm assuming the worst.

I'm underestimating my ability to cope and overestimating how hard the world can be.

And, because I was, at that point, still highly medicated, I rubbed my heart through my jumper 'til my fingers were full of static, and it worked. I managed to short-circuit the path to oblivion.

Just in time, because, as I wandered around the corner, I found Kim waiting with Amy.

'Oh my God, Fern, aren't you boiling?' Kim grasped me in a friendly hug she definitely didn't mean. 'I can't believe you're wearing your *jumper*. It's, like, a *trillion* degrees today. It's so shit it's finally *boiling* on the first day back.'

'I'm fine. I'm not hot,' I lied.

Amy and I hugged while Kim watched on anxiously. As we started the familiar path to school, none of us mentioned Kim's presence. She lived twenty minutes in the opposite direction. I sneaked a sideways look at her, noting Kim's brand new fringe, and raised my eyebrows. They both were wearing their hair in scraped-back ponytails – cemented with gel to their scalps, with only their wispy fringes left out to oxygenate. 'Nice fringe,' I said.

Kim held it between her fingers. 'Aww, thank you. You think it's OK? It's not too short? I got it done yesterday.'

'It's lovely. Just like Amy's new one.'

They both erupted into giggles.

'We're basically twins,' Amy confirmed, apparently unbothered that her fringe needed patenting. 'We even bought the same purple shrug from Topshop the other day, without knowing the other had got it.'

'It's ridiculous,' Kim said. 'Someone in McDonald's the other day even asked if we were *sisters*.'

'Wow.'

'I know, right? Ever since Tenerife, we've basically become the same person.'

I grimaced and looked down at my shiny black Kickers. It had been less than two minutes before Kim brought up their holiday to Tenerife. You'd have thought the two had been to *WAR* together. I reminded myself Amy was *my* best friend and had been *my* best friend since Year Seven. She was just tolerating Kim out of sympathy because she was needy since her parents got divorced. Nonetheless, I watched Kim thread her arm through Amy's, so I pulled down my sleeve and threaded it through Amy's other arm – our chain taking up the whole pavement.

'So, oh my God, Amy, do you remember Chris from Tenerife?' Kim started. 'He was so fit. I can't believe he thought it was weird that I smelt him in the queue for the breakfast buffet. It was so embarrassing . . . and that night with the karaoke! I was so drunk from that Bacardi Breezer Mum got us.'

Amy shrieked with cliquey nostalgia, while Kim watched her every reaction. It occurred to me both of us had been counting down to this day. Me, to find out if I could manage school without suicide ideation. And Kim, wondering if she'd be demoted to 'spare wheel friend' once more. I was still reeling from the fact that I'd wanted to die only ten minutes previously. Now I was contemplating if it was worse to a) die, or b) not have Amy as my best friend any more.

I slowed a bit as we turned onto our school's road. 'How are you feeling?' Amy asked. 'Are you scared?'

'I'm OK. I just don't want everyone to stare at me.'

'They won't,' Kim barged in. 'I reckon everyone's forgotten about it over summer.'

I was unconvinced. 'Hmm.'

Amy patted my back. 'You have us by your side, remember? I will literally fight anyone who dares stare at you. Unless they're staring at how fit you got over summer, of course.'

I laughed. 'Unlikely.'

'Definitely. Your hair's grown so long. It looks gorgeous.' She pulled out a long strand of strawberry blonde, holding it up like a moustache, and I giggled.

That was how reassurance between girls worked, aged thirteen onwards – when a friend's troubles were too huge, you offered up a compliment about their appearance as a distraction.

Kim heaved a sigh. 'I hope Matt stares at me and thinks how fit I am this term. Did I tell you he said hello to me on MSN the other day?'

I caught Amy's eye for the tiniest moment and we shared a silent decision to entertain Kim's desperately fruitless crush. She'd been obsessed with Matt since he got overnight fit in Year Eight. Through osmosis, after many conversations, I knew Matt's star sign (Aries), his favourite colour (blue), his previous relationship history (he went out with Karly for two days in Year Seven, and kissed Gail at the Year Nine disco, but told her he wasn't ready for a relationship), and his GCSE options. Yet Matt remained totally oblivious to Kim's adoration, which was impressive naivety, considering last year she took to full-blown stalking him ('I just happened to be walking the same way as him and accidentally found out where he lived').

'What happened?' Amy asked. 'Did he write anything else?'

'Well, I asked him how he was, and he didn't reply. So I logged out and logged in again, but he didn't say hi again.'

As Kim spouted on about Matt's bone structure, I realised

I found it all quite relaxing. The banality of it – as if the last six months hadn't happened. I caught Amy's eye again and we shared a secret smile. The conspiracy of it glowed warm in my stomach.

'You OK?' Amy asked again when we reached the school gates.

'Remember, Fern,' Kim added, 'we are here for you. If anyone says *anything*, tell us, right? We are your guardians.'

That was two uses of the word *we* for her and Amy. Kim's battle lines really had been drawn. I stretched my arms up into a yawn, and the synthetic fabric pulled under my already sweaty armpit. I felt incredibly tired all of a sudden. I didn't have the energy to fight for my best friend. Not right now. I just wanted to survive the next two years of school. Staying alive came first, friendships second.

I was yet to discover how much the two were entwined.

School smelt exactly the same. That was the first thing I noticed. The acrid itch tickled the back of my throat as we merged into a homogenous blob of uniformed students, waiting to get through the main doors. It smelt of BO masked with Lynx Africa. As we pushed into the Year Ten corridor, too much school came at me way too fast. The dull banging of locker doors shutting. The colony of fellow teenagers buzzing with first-day-back energy. The frenzied catching-upness and showing-offness before the bell rang. Everyone figuring out who'd got hot over the summer, or lost their virginity, or both. Everyone stared as I passed, their eyes glancing towards my long sleeves.

'Everyone's looking.'

'You're going to be OK,' Amy whispered. 'Remember, it's school. They'll get bored by tomorrow.'

'I hope you're right.'

'She totally is,' Kim said loudly, clearly enjoying the corridor parting for us.

When the bell shrilled, I hugged them both goodbye. They had a welcome-back assembly, while I had an appointment with the school counsellor: Wendy, a woman who looked like she slept in her pearl necklace. In her office, she relayed to me the wide variety of 'measures' my school was taking to get me through my exams despite my mental illness. I could skip school assemblies. I could leave physics early on Thursday afternoons for my CBT appointments. They'd placed me into top sets based on predicted grades, and we could see how I got on. As she outlined all the logistical gymnastics required for me to function like a normal teenager, I felt myself detach from my balloon string and float off again. My body was nodding and my mouth was saying 'thank you', but I was watching myself from the ceiling.

This wasn't me. This wasn't my life. It couldn't be. Shouldn't be.

'So, what's your first lesson?' Wendy asked, and I snapped back into my body. 'Let's see? English? That's one of your favourites, isn't it?'

I nodded with a tight throat.

'What a great way to start.'

The bell rang, jolting me to my core. I'd forgotten the shrillness of it.

'And so it begins.' Wendy stood to usher me out, with a new firmness to her.

★

'Oh my God, Fern, how ARE YOU?' Abigail Goddarth sprang up to give me a hug as I shuffled into my English class, though we'd never really been friends. Her newly sprouted breasts squashed against my own flat chest as our jumpers crackled against each other.

'I'm good, thanks,' I mumbled. 'How are you?'

'Yeah. Good. Are you OK?'

'Fine, thanks. How was your summer?'

'Yeah, it was great. But how are you *really*?' Abigail tilted her head to one side in faux concern and her eyes drifted to my covered arms, scanning them for information she could use on the gossip black market that upcoming lunchtime.

'I'm fine. Like I said . . .' My lungs crunched in on themselves. This was just what I feared would happen. I strained my neck to the front, checking for Mr Dudley's presence to make it all go away. But he was late, leaving me the leading role in this play of curiosity disguised as fake sympathy.

But a distraction came from Richard – the biggest pervert in our year group. I yelped as my training bra strap pinged my back through my jumper.

'Fern! I heard you went nuts?' he said, before reaching over to ping Abi's too. 'Abi! These tits are new. You had a busy summer.'

'Fucking hell, Richard, you are so gross.' Abigail smacked him away and crossed her arms.

Richard laughed and followed me to the back. 'So, did they, like, lock you up?' he asked, perching on my desk. 'Were you in a straitjacket? Everyone said you overdosed. Or slit your wrists. Or both.'

'Oh my God, Richard, shut up,' I hissed.

A grin spread through his acne.

'Did you take pills so it didn't hurt when you cut yourself?'

'Honestly, you sad pervert, shut the fuck up,' I said. 'Maybe I'd rather kill myself than look at your fucking face every day.'

The class rippled with laughter, revealing they'd all been listening in.

Richard held both arms up. '*Oooerr*. Don't go all *psycho* on me.'

'Oh piss off, you giant VIRGIN.'

Hilarity descended as Richard called me a fucking bitch, then slunk into his desk chair, just as Mr Dudley blustered through the door in a cloud of teacherly obliviousness.

'Right, class, settle down.' He clapped for attention. 'Welcome to your English GCSEs. The good news is, you're about to read one of the best novels ever written.' Mr Dudley got us to hand out hardback copies of *We Have Always Lived in the Castle*, while he turned his back to write on the whiteboard.

I was initially so consumed in these normal activities – like getting out my notepad and writing the date at the top without crying – that I hadn't noticed her. The new girl sitting in the corner behind me.

Abi passed me the pile of books, and I plucked one out, before twisting to pass them on. And there she was. Hair dark and long, hanging over her stunning, pointed face. Her jumper sleeves drawn down over her hands, like mine. Looking as scared and out of place as I felt.

'Thanks,' the new girl said, taking the pile and passing it on. Her voice was husky and sexy, and sounded way too old for someone our age.

'Are you new?'

She nodded and smiled, holding a hand up over her mouth. 'First day today. I was so embarrassed when they introduced me in assembly just now.'

'You were great,' I lied, not wanting to admit I'd not been there. I wondered if she'd overheard Richard's comments about me. 'Do you like it here so far?'

'I don't know.' The new girl paused. 'It's weird . . .' She wrinkled her nose.

'What's weird?'

'This school . . . it smells exactly the same as my old school.'

I let out a cackle of recognition. The new girl joined in, revealing a set of small, pointed teeth. I felt the peculiar certainty of fate reach out and tug me towards her, and knew instantly we were going to become friends. That we didn't even have a say in the matter.

'Right, everyone. Chapter one, page one. Who wants to start reading?'

I leant over. 'I'm Fern,' I whispered.

She smiled, and, in her eyes, I could see she felt it too. 'Hi. I'm Jessica.'

Thirty-one

'Wow, *Jessica*.' My chair screeched as I pulled it back and side-stepped the table to hug my old friend. 'Oh my God,' I kept saying. 'Oh my God, oh my God. It's been years.'

I felt her thinness as we hugged, the gaps between her body and her coat that scrunched as our torsos collided.

She laughed into my shoulder. The exact same gravelly laugh she'd always had, plunging me down a hundred memory wormholes. 'Surprise!'

I laughed too, mostly in disbelief, as we released the hug and I perched on my table, taking her in. 'It's so crazy that you're here.'

'It's OK, isn't it?'

'Of course. It's just . . . I'm so shocked. It's been years, Jessica.'

What the hell was she doing here? It had been over a decade. She laughed again behind her hand, and the gesture located and unlocked another dormant memory. Jessica always laughed behind her hand as she thought her teeth were too pointy.

'Mad, isn't it? We're in our thirties. Thirties! And, oh my God, Fern,' she gestured to me with her dainty hands. 'Look at you. Look at all this. I'm so proud.'

She was here. In my life, saying she was proud, like nothing had happened. It was so jarring to see her, and yet her presence also felt like the most natural thing in the world. Like finding an old, forgotten pair of shoes that you hadn't worn in years. She'd aged a decade in a moment, and I drank in her new appearance, adding in her wrinkles as though I'd put her face through one of those ageing apps. She still had the perfect dewy skin I'd lusted after, but it was lined now, especially around the corners of her eyes. There was a slight puffiness to her jawline, a dryness to her dark hair from dye to cover the greys. But Jessica was still stunning. Stunning and perfectly put together. She wore a hot pink coat covering dark blue ripped jeans tucked into a gorgeous pair of boots. The outfit, as always, was simultaneously mature, sophisticated, individualistic, effortless, and stylish. And I was a teenager again. Feeling blobbish and frumpy – with my dank hair, potato-shaped head, and stodgy old jumpsuit.

But Jessica seemed oblivious to her win in the *who-has-aged-best* competition. *She must still be used to it,* I thought bitterly, amazed at how my adolescent jealousy could reignite so instantly. Instead she was staring around the packed theatre, spellbound by the scale of the event.

'It's nothing,' I said. 'I'm just chairing.'

'Fern, there's like, a thousand people here.'

'Yeah, but they're not here for me.'

'Well, I'm determined to be impressed, so there.' She grinned again, forgetting to cover it, and I caught the smile, grinned back. Forgetting myself for a second. That energy pull was still there, as potent as the first day I met her. Our bond plastering over this awkward and unexpected reunion. We hadn't spoken in years, we hadn't spoken about why we weren't speaking.

'I still can't believe you're here,' I said.

'You sure you don't mind? I couldn't tell if it was creepy or not. I got so excited by surprising you that it only occurred to me this could be totally intense and weird about ten minutes ago, when you were talking to that girl who wouldn't go away.'

'Oh my God. She really, really wouldn't go away!' I said. *Was it creepy?* It was certainly a shock.

'At one point, I thought she might superglue herself to your face.'

'I had my finger on the panic button.'

'So, it's not weird?'

I smiled, despite myself. 'Not at all.' And I was so lost in the crashing waves of nostalgia, that it took me a moment to remember where I was and what she'd done. All that mattered was Jessica's face, Jessica's pointed smile, Jessica's essence, Jessica's approval. A wild shriek from Stacy's table ripped me from it, and we both twisted in her direction. The influencer was squealing with delight at a present a fan had made her. A giant papier-mâché bust of Stacy's face.

'Oh my Lord, you made THIS for ME? I love it, LOVE it. OH MY GOD WE HAVE TO GET A VIDEO.'

The bust-maker sobbed with joy as Stacy beckoned her around to her side of the table for a hug. She proceeded to get multiple selfies of her, her sculptor, and her bust 'for the socials', and the young woman quivered in starstruck delight.

Jessica and I turned back to one another and shrugged. 'Umm, do you want to go somewhere?' I asked, unsure of her motives again.

Jessica glanced at an expensive wristwatch, and that was the first time I got a sense of her having money. 'I'm not sure I have enough time to go out for a proper drink.'

'Oh . . .'

'I mean, I'd love to. But I have to get a train back. My mum's babysitting, but I've been in the city all afternoon and I don't want to take the piss.'

'Babysitting?'

Jessica broke into another unhidden grin. 'Of course! God, it's been so long. Yes, I've got a daughter. She's almost seven.'

'Seven?'

'Bridget.'

'You have a *daughter*?'

'It's mad, isn't it? She's great. You'll love her.'

I shook my head. 'You're a mum? I can't believe I didn't know . . . That's amazing.' I blinked away a memory of Jessica chopping up a gram of cocaine with her battered Halifax debit card with the concentration of a Swiss clockmaker. 'Well, if you don't have time to go to a pub, do you just want to go to the green room?' I asked. 'There's booze there. I definitely need a drink.' The words fell from my mouth and then I couldn't take them back.

'Wow, the green room. Do I need a pass or something?'

I laughed. 'Not at all. Come on.'

'Don't you need to stay on the stand?' Jessica asked, glancing back as I weaved her around the endless snake of Stacy fans.

'I think people can pick up their own promotional key rings.' I pushed us through the stage door and led Jessica around the maze of darkened corners. 'Right, here it is. There's at least wine.'

'I can't believe I'm in an actual green room.'

I watched my old friend marvel at this ordinary table filled with ordinary things, as if they were made of gold. It was quiet and empty, staff busy attending to Stacy outside. It still didn't seem real she was there. After days, months, years of absolutely nothing. I poured myself a large glass of red, holding up the bottle.

'A million times yes.' Jessica said, nodding. 'Is it free?'

'It's free, yeah.'

'I still can't believe your life.' She took the fishbowl of merlot I handed her and perched on a chair, as if someone might ask her to leave at any moment.

'I still can't believe yours. You're a mother.'

She grinned again. 'Do you want to see pictures? I try really hard not to be that mum who bombards you with unwanted photos, but, well, do you want to see?'

'Of course. Gimme, gimme.' I beckoned her phone over, chucking some wine down my throat to prepare myself for the confirmation that Jessica had reproduced. Preparing myself for the inevitable deep conversation we needed to have, wondering why she was delaying it. She smiled again as she swiped through the candidates, then proudly held up an image of the most unusual and beautiful child I'd ever seen, jolting me out of my apprehension.

'Fucking hell. She's gorgeous.'

'I know, right? It's so weird. I can't decide if I should make her a child model, or an actress who plays haunted Victorian ghost kids.'

'Both. She'll make a fortune doing both. Those eyes!'

Two green orbs blazed at me from Jessica's iPhone, attached to a tiny, angular porcelain head framed by a long sheet of dark hair. 'Her eyes are her dad's,' she said, taking the phone away momentarily so she could pick another image. 'I suppose he's been good for some things.'

'Oh, you guys . . . ?'

'We're divorcing,' she confirmed, holding up another photo. 'Here, see this one? She wanted to dress up as *Frozen* for Halloween. Most generic thing ever, but look how cute she is as Elsa.'

'That is cute, but, Jessica. Divorced? A mum? I feel like we are very behind on each other's life stories.'

Jessica laughed and glugged down some wine. 'You're right. Sorry. Here I am, launching into all my dramas. You're going to be like, *Just like old times, why have you randomly showed up again?*'

I shook my head. 'Not at all,' I lied, when all I could think was *Why are you here?* and *What do you want?* 'But let's try and fill each other in on the last decade so I stop getting emotional whiplash.'

'Right, you are so right. As always. Jesus Christ, this wine is terrible. I take it back. Green rooms are not that impressive.'

It was not like Jessica to criticise any alcohol, especially free alcohol, but it had been a long time. We winced our way through our glasses, picked at the various fruit platters, and picked up where we left off. Colouring in the last twelve years of one another's personal development, like an entire series catch-up before the last ever episode of a television show. Jessica drained her glass and told me the whole story. She'd met Brendan when she was twenty-two, working at a hotel bar. Love at first sight, which, as I recalled, was the only way Jessica knew how to fall in love. Then, within six months of dating, he'd been offered a transfer to America, they thought 'what an adventure', got married in Gretna Green before they flew out to California, and along came Bridget a few years after.

'It's weird, you don't have an American accent at all.'

Jessica laughed, lubricated by the rancid wine. 'It's my proudest achievement – clinging onto my British accent. I swear it was the only reason I had any friends over there. The other US housewives didn't particularly like me, but they did love having a British friend. Wait 'til you hear Bridget's accent though. It's disgusting. The shrillness.' She shuddered while I let out a snort, remembering how I'd missed her piss-taking sense of humour.

Gwen jogged in, turbo-charged, muttering, 'Stacy needs fruit', hardly waving as she piled a plate with pineapple before running out again. Jessica's eyes followed her as she left, then turned back to me, impressed. 'I still can't believe this is your life, Fern. Hobnobbing in the green room. I've not asked you one thing about you yet. Like, what the hell? This is so amazing!'

My cheeks got hot and I kept trying to iron out the bump in my clothes, before realising it was my stomach. 'It looks more impressive than it is.'

'Don't put it down! You always used to do yourself down. I command you to grow out of it.'

I laughed with a sharp *ha*, and a warmth trickled into my

stomach, alighting a long-dormant fire. The fire of how it felt to have Jessica there, believing in me, and urging me to believe in myself.

Be careful, I reminded myself. *This is Jessica.*

'Honestly, your blog post about suicide, it was amazing.'

'You read it?' I took another deep sip of wine.

'Of course I read it. The whole world read it! It was going viral for days, with everyone adding in stuff. Actually,' Jessica put her glass down and glanced down at her winding hands, 'I tried getting in touch when I saw it.'

'What?'

'Yeah, I sent you an email, saying how proud I was, telling you all my news, wanting to catch up.' She looked up again. 'You never replied though.'

'I never got that email!'

'I was worried about coming tonight actually, after that. I thought maybe . . .' There it was. The unspoken, being danced around for the first time.

I shook my head, the awkwardness too much to bear. 'Oh my God, Jessica, if I'd seen the email, I definitely would've replied. I promise! That time with the blog post, it was so insane, it must've got lost in my inbox or something.'

I sounded like such a dick, saying that, despite it being the truth. It was such a whirlwind year of my life – my niche article about suicide going viral. I remember, when the blog post hit a million views, collapsing onto the rug of my shitty flat-share carpet and sobbing, praying for God to take all the attention away. The endless radio and TV appearances, the bombardment of emails from people sharing their own reasons to hold on for tomorrow, or their own suicide stories. Within a week, I'd gone from total obscurity as a not very successful journalist to being the face of suicide awareness. Each morning, getting picked up in a car and taken to a studio somewhere, then smothered in make-up, so I could then sit on a squashy sofa, and tell two TV presenters about the day I wanted to die. Each show created more emails, and more entries. Reflecting on it now, it seemed almost unsurvivable. And, yet, it's how I got my job at *Gah!* That job had led to so many good things, and now had led to Jessica being back in my life after all this time. Was that a good thing?

Jessica waved her hand with a piece of cake in it. 'Honestly, don't worry about it, Fern. It was years ago. I'm just relieved you don't think I'm a single white female for turning up tonight.' She stuck her pinkie in the icing and licked it off. 'I just saw online you were doing this, and I only moved home a few weeks ago . . . And, well, I've missed you.'

I met her gaze. 'I've missed you too.'

We were still a moment, drinking in its importance. It was all so long ago, wasn't it? 'So, tell me about you,' she said. 'What's the goss? No kids? Husband? Boyfriend?'

'No kids, no. No husband.' A smug grin involuntarily crossed my face. 'But, a boyfriend. A really lovely boyfriend.'

'Oh, Fern, that's great. What's he like? Picture, please.'

I pulled my phone out of my pocket. 'Yeah, Ben's great. He's really kind, and funny, and nice. He's a psychology teacher, which I think is so cool. I've started to train to be a counsellor too, so he's useful to have about the place to help me with my essays.'

'A counsellor? Wow. You'd be amazing at that. How cool.' I could feel her genuine joy for me as I pulled up my lock-screen of Ben's face. 'Oh my God, he's handsome.' Jessica took my phone and peered closer to inspect. 'I love the whole beard thing men are doing at the moment, it's super sexy.'

A shrill anxiety shot through me. A sudden burst of rage, and it took all I had not to hit my phone out of her hand. But Jessica was looking at the time. 'Shit, Fern, I've to go! There's still only one train an hour home, can you believe it? After all these years? I won't be back 'til eleven as it is.' She returned my Samsung and stood up. 'Sorry, I'd love to stay longer.'

'Oh.' I lurched out of my chair, and hovered while she applied scarf and gloves. 'That went quick.'

'Didn't it?' She pulled her hair out from under her scarf, and, with our time together ending, the surrealness of it all hit me full force. 'Well . . .' Jessica pulled a cute bobble hat over her perfect sheet of hair, 'if you don't find the idea totally off-putting, do you fancy grabbing a drink soon? So we can have more of a catch-up? I still haven't a clue what's going on in your life, or your job. Like, do you still see Amy and Kim?'

'Not much. Maybe once a year or so.'

'God, don't tell me. Kim finally married Matt?'

I couldn't help laughing, and, again, like a burst water main, memories of Kim's obsessive lovesickness roared in. 'No, but she has actually married someone called Matt.'

Jessica grabbed my hand. 'You're kidding?'

'No.'

'This is too much. Fucking hell.' She wiped under her eye with a leather-gloved finger. 'Anyway, a drink? Maybe next week? Mum is being very good on the babysitting front, what with all the sympathy she has for me being a pathetic divorcee.'

I knew there'd been a time where it was abundantly clear I needed to cut Jessica from my life. That the only healthy option was to take a scalpel and carefully trace around our friendship, lifting it out clean. The anguished tears, regret, grief, and missing her before I'd even undergone the surgery. And yet, standing there in the green room, being offered a drink with her, I felt weirdly excited by the prospect. 'Yeah, of course. Message me a date,' I said, reminding myself I could always blow her off if I needed to.

'That would be amazing. What's your number?'

She peeled off a glove so she could thumb it into her latest iPhone and drop-call me. My eyes travelled across her phone, to her leather gloves, to the Chanel handbag draped casually on her arm. It had been a day of shocks that kept coming. 'Right, there. I'll give you a date ASAP. Shit, the time. I literally have to run.' She squished me into another hug. 'Fern, this has been amazing. Tonight was amazing. All of it. I'm so happy to be back. Oh my God, my train's in less than twenty-five minutes.'

'Go go go.' I watched her run off like a gazelle in her knee-high boots. Even in her mad dash, she was perfectly put together. I pictured everyone noticing when she collapsed onto the Tube, glancing up from their phones and *Evening Standards*, and taking in this magnet of a woman.

I sighed into my chair and took in the green room around me, the excitable chatter from the theatre seeping around the stage doors. Stacy let out a shriek that pierced my ears and I winced. I didn't need to tell anyone I was leaving. Gwen was way too busy.

Jessica's missed call sat on the screen. I pulled up the unfamiliar digits and clicked 'save contact' – thumbing in her name. I hesitated and then added the 'warning' emoji next to her name. Just as I'd saved it, two messages came through.

Heather: Did it go OK? Sorry again I couldn't make it. Up to my eyeballs in coils. Don't worry about being a sell-out. Sometimes that's just work. I mean, I have to help literally EVERYONE who comes into the clinic, even if they voted Brexit xx
Ben: How did it go, my glorious sell-out? I bet you smashed it.

I reply quickly to Ben's.

Fern: It went OK. Stacy was exactly who I expected her to be. But hey ho, and yay for the money. Just getting on the Tube now.

It was only later that night, as I fell asleep, it occurred to me I hadn't mentioned Jessica to him. And I knew why.

Fourteen

October 2000

Eminem blasted from my CD player while we all got dolled up with Jessica, our friendship group's new addition. Our plan for that Saturday was simple and foolproof. We'd ascertained through Kim's stalking that Matt got a McDonald's milkshake every weekend afternoon. So we were all to dress up attractively, but not so attractively that we would 'outshine' Kim, head to town, primp up our faces even more with the testers in Boots, and then casually head to Maccy D's to casually also buy milkshakes and sit there casually, laughing, and looking casually attractive until Matt showed up. At which point, of course, he would see how casual and attractive Kim was, and fall in love with her – despite his failure to do this every day at school. The four of us in my bedroom rapped along happily to a song where you literally hear a woman's throat get slit. This was Kim's favourite song as it had her name in it.

'Don't you think Eminem looks a bit like Matt?' Kim asked, while outlining her thin lips with plum lip liner.

'No,' we all said in unison.

'They've both got blue eyes!'

I leant back against my headboard and fed myself another handful of crisps. 'That's crazy,' I said. 'What are the chances?'

Until that moment, Jessica had been sitting silently in the corner, flicking through my copy of *J17*. But she let out a quiet snort and we shared a fleeting moment of eye contact.

Kim, oblivious, smacked her lips together. 'If Matt and I ever had children, the baby would have a three in four chance of having my eyes, because I have brown eyes, and blue eyes are a recessive gene . . . Oh God,' she shrilled. 'Am I an intense person? I am, aren't I?'

We all burst out laughing, and then Jessica held up the magazine. 'You're just a SAGITTARIUS,' she reassured her. 'And look, it says here that today is your "red hot love" day, so I think Operation Casual is going to be a total success.' She flattened down the page to show Kim her horoscope.

'How did you know I was a Sagittarius?' Kim asked, her plum mouth stunned and open, as we all turned to Jessica as if she was psychic.

She shrugged. 'You can just tell.'

'What about me?' Amy settled down on the carpet next to her. 'Can you tell what I am?'

'Aries.'

'Oh my God!'

'You're a witch!' Kim declared with genuine excitement. 'Seriously, how did you know?'

Jessica shrugged again. 'I've just read a few books, that's all. I can't chart or anything, not yet.'

We all stared in amazement at this glittering new person

in our lives, tingling with the newness of her. Jessica had caused quite a stir in her first week – winning the unofficial Hottest Girl of the Year competition the boys always ran in September. But she seemed uninterested in her celebrity and had latched onto us after I invited her to have lunch on her first day. I felt a swell of pride she'd picked our group, alongside a deep jealousy that I hadn't made the Hot Girl shortlist.

'Is Sagittarius compatible with Aries?' Kim asked, without needing to tell us Matt was an Aries.

'Oh yes, they're very good together. Usually start as friends first.'

'You see!' Amy clapped Kim on the back. 'This is why Operation Casual is such a good idea. You two will become friends over our super casual milkshakes today and it will become something beautiful.'

'Do you really think so?'

'Of course. Though,' Amy picked up her phone, 'we need to get a move on if we want to shop beforehand. It's almost twelve.'

'But my fringe . . .'

'Is perfect. Come on.'

Once we stepped out into the autumnal sunshine, we fell into two pairs. Amy and Kim linked arms up front, while Jessica and I dawdled behind. She was quiet beside me, hiding behind her hair sheet, while I asked her more about being a Pisces. She paused for a second, her arms around her chest.

'Are you OK?'

'Hmm, yes.'

'Are you sure?'

She hesitated, and let out a small sigh, then granted me eye contact. 'It's just . . . is what I'm wearing OK?'

'What?'

In my fog of teen self-absorption, I hadn't noticed that Jessica hadn't yet taken off her denim jacket. 'Well, it's just . . . I didn't know what the "casual" dress code meant. I'm scared I look like a slut.' She sighed, flinging her jacket open to reveal her outfit.

'OK, you look amazing.' This was the first time I witnessed Jessica's ability to curate a look – any look, on demand, even with no money. She'd paired dark jeans with a red low-cut tunic top, hanging almost like a dress, the sexiness of the red balanced out by the casualness of the denim jacket. A pang of envy throbbed through me. I instantly hated my own outfit, with my stupid baggy jeans trying to be cool, and long sleeves to cover my scars. I wanted to shed my body and step into hers.

'You sure I don't look slutty?'

'*What?* No. Where'd you get that from?'

She shook her head. 'I . . . just. Back in Guildford, just as my dad fucked off with his new girlfriend, some of the girls weren't very nice. Not to me, anyway.' She shrugged. 'They called me a slut one week and then a geek the next when I turned up at a fancy dress party dressed as Hermione.'

I pulled a face. 'They sound like bitches.'

'They were.'

'You don't have to worry about stuff like that with us,' I reassured her. 'We're not like that. Well . . . unless you came to a party dressed as a slutty Hermione, but I'd only be angry because that isn't true to the books.'

Jessica laughed and we grinned at one another. Something glowing and growing between us. Then Kim yelled at us from outside the entrance to the shopping centre.

'Come on, guys, by the time we get there Matt won't even be an Aries any more!'

'OK, so do I look more casual if I slurp from the front of my mouth? Or the side?' Kim positioned her striped straw into her heavily lipsticked lips.

Only Amy took the question seriously. 'From the side of your mouth initially,' she said, nodding. 'But then, once you start talking to him, move it to the front of your mouth.'

'OK, so like this?'

Jessica and I shared another look while Kim trialled her sucking technique. To be honest, it was hard to taste my milkshake over the cloud of fumes congregating above our booth. We all wore at least four different kinds of perfume, spritzed from Boots testers up various parts of our inner arms, looking for our 'signature scent'. We all jumped whenever anyone pushed through into McDonald's, then giggled. The manager shot us dirty looks. It had not gone unnoticed that we'd made our four milkshakes last over an hour. Matt was late. 'By about twenty minutes,' Kim said, making me quite certain she really should be served a restraining order. The doors swung open and she let out a dog-like squeak. 'Oh my God oh my God oh my God, it's HIM. Be casual, eyes down.'

I was kind of deliriously excited by the whole plan. I had literally no skin in the game, as that particular gang of boys were about as sexually enticing to me as a bunch of rats wearing human clothes. Since I'd got sick, my sexual awakening had been more like waking up from a series of afternoon naps – where you sleep too long, and wake up confused about what time it is, and still feel really exhausted. Sometimes I felt no pull to any guys at all, and quietly wondered if I was a lesbian, or a potato, the only two options available on the current agreed spectrum. Other times, I was feverishly horny, yet the source of my crushes were unequivocally unreciprocated, maybe out of self-protection. I'd narrowed my two options down to Francesco, a very good-looking Italian boy in the lower sixth; and Leonardo DiCaprio. I was slightly worried Leo would be put off by my scars though.

The boys ordered their shakes and wandered away from the counter, so I waved at Eric from my chemistry class, and said, 'Hey, Eric.'

'What the fuck are you doing?' Kim whispered.

The boys took in the girl-shaped contents of our booth, silently nodded to one another, and made their way over.

'You all right?' Kim started manically giggling, and Amy elbowed her.

'Room for us?' Eric gestured with his head.

'Sure!'

We all budged up for them. They, too, had their own orbit of combined synthetic scent. As they crammed themselves in, their smell cloud and ours combined, and it was so overwhelming I'm surprised it didn't start its own weather system.

'Hey, do you guys know Jessica?' I asked.

The boys used this as an opportunity to look her up and down, pretending they didn't know she was the Hottest Girl of the Year.

'You're new, right?' Sean asked with faux naivety. He was

Eric's best mate. A very short boy, with chronic acne, who managed to dodge the inevitable bullying by being immensely good at football.

Jessica, who, as it happened, was sucking her straw effortlessly in a way that was both demure and sexual, smiled and lowered her cup. 'Yes. You're in my maths class, right?'

'Yeah, isn't Mr Ferris the absolute worst?'

'I can smell his breath from the back row.'

The three boys laughed together, with their heads thrown back, before realising a girl had made a joke, and then turning down the dial.

Matt – yet to speak – nodded his head. 'His breath's totally rancid. I'm not even taught by him, but he once walked past me in the corridor, and I almost puked.'

'This is really making me enjoy my milkshake,' I said. The boys reluctantly laughed again while Kim watched the exchange with bulging eyes, unsure how to interject.

'I LOVE milkshake,' she declared. 'I love the taste of milkshake so much.'

The table dissolved into hyena giggles, as Kim turned pinker.

'Sounds like you've drunk a lot of milkshake in your life,' Eric said, while all the boys hooted. Matt slapped his knee, as Kim reddened. Then, understanding the innuendo, she played along. 'Why are you all laughing?' she said. 'What's so funny about drinking milkshake?'

'Vanilla your favourite flavour?' Matt asked.

Jessica and I rolled our eyes at one another, while Kim delighted in the attention. This was the most interaction she'd ever had with Matt, and all she'd had to do was dangle the possibility she'd suck him off and say it tasted like a McFlurry.

'Why are you guys laughing so hard? I don't get it.' She moved her straw to the front of her mouth, but it didn't quite work. Her lips bunched up too much. 'I'm just saying I like milkshake, why's everyone being so weird?'

'Has anyone ever spilt milkshake on you?'

'Once . . .'

They all spluttered, while Amy mouthed to her, *'It's going really well!'* The innuendoes and jeering continued, as Kim played the part perfectly, glowing and glowing, before finally squealing, 'Eww, oh my God! You meant cum!' The boys high-fived while she acted outraged. 'Eww, you guys are disgusting. I've not drunk any milkshake like that, yet, no.'

Hats off to Kim, for putting the 'yet' in there. I wasn't sure I always gave her enough credit.

Eric's face was almost purple and he was laughing the loudest. He turned to Amy. 'What about you, Amy? Milkshake fan?'

'Eric,' she squealed. 'Stop being so disgusting.'

He reached out his arms. 'What? I'm just asking an innocent question.' It was an odd descent into macho posturing. This particular gang of boys weren't exactly known for their masculinity. Matt's new-found looks and Sean's keepy-uppy skills had them hovering in a slightly higher social tier than usual, but they were still all well-behaved, top-set boys. Not like Harry and Lloyd and the others from the popular gang, who couldn't breathe without letting everyone know how many girls they'd fingered and telling the year group whose vaginas smelt the most of fish.

'Well, of course I haven't,' Amy said. 'I'm not a total slut.'

'That's not what your dad says.'

The boys all whooped and high-fived again, ignoring Amy as she told them to shut up. I wondered briefly if perhaps my lack of sexual attraction was more an appropriate response to my current stimuli, rather than clinical depression.

A cloud moved outside and suddenly our booth was blasted with golden sunshine. My armpits poured with sweat into my long sleeves, and Jessica shrugged her way out of her denim jacket to reveal her red top. The boys forgot Kim instantly, their eyes roving to Jessica. Sheepishly aware of her allure, Jessica gave a nervous smile as she picked up her cup to block her cleavage.

'What about you, new girl?' Eric asked.

'What about what?'

I grinned at Jessica for making him spell it out.

'Are you a fan of milkshake then?'

We all watched her – this exotic stranger, who we knew nothing about. Growing up in a small town, we all basically knew one another's sexual progress, as the only real options for experimentation were each other. We all knew we were all virgins. But Jessica, Jessica could be anything.

If she felt the scrutiny, she didn't show it. She just slurped her milkshake again. 'Are you referring to actual milkshake, Eric, or to giving head?' she asked. 'Just for clarity?'

Eric was losing his nerve. Innuendo was his limit of masculinity – he couldn't quite handle an actual discussion about actual sex.

'I think you know,' he said, a blush appeared at his neck.

'I don't know, though, do I? That's why I'm asking.'

'I mean, *have* you ever given someone a blow job?' he asked, as his head dropped to the table.

Kim shrieked, which did nothing to dispel the awkwardness. I held my breath, marvelling at this girl next to me, who seemed so calm under such scrutiny. Nobody slurped. Everyone watched. And, Jessica, Jessica just looked up at him with big, innocent eyes.

'What's a blow job?'

I snorted. But everyone else stayed quiet. Eric was basically dying, his mates doing nothing to help. Matt's mouth was open, as mesmerised as we were.

'It's when you . . . er . . . come on . . . you know what it is . . .'

'Do I?' She shrugged. 'I don't think I do. I'd love for you to tell me.'

The boys started laughing, high on how well she was crucifying their mate with the simplest of questions.

'Go on then, tell me.'

'It's . . .' He coughed, and he suddenly seemed about ten, rather than fifteen. Blushing so hard he was luminous. 'It's when you, er . . . suck someone's penis.'

'Ohhhh . . . OK.' Jessica leant back and tilted her head to one side. 'And . . . what's a penis?'

It was too much. Sean exploded milkshake across the table, breaking the spell. Amy and Kim squealed as they were splattered. Matt and I burst out laughing. Eric looked like he wanted to kill her, but then Jessica broke, and gave him the widest, most mischievous smile. 'OK . . . sorry, sorry, but it was too easy!' she said. 'I know what a penis is, I promise.'

I patted him on the shoulder. 'It's that thing coming out

of your forehead,' I added, and the booth lost it completely. Eric just about laughed it off, and stared at Jessica with intense longing. All three of the boys did, but I think I was the only one who noticed it. Kim and Amy were both too busy dabbing at their splattered clothes. A spell had been cast. In one exchange, she'd managed to win their respect, dodge the question entirely, keep her sexual history a mystery, and yet dangle the possibility she knew a lot more than she was letting on. Plus she was funny, and looked like that in red.

Poor Kim, I remember thinking, as I glanced over at Matt, who had very definitely noticed this new girl from Guildford. She didn't stand a chance. Nobody did around Jessica.

Thirty-one

Jessica: Hey, how are you? Any chance you're free on Tuesday? My mum has agreed to babysit again.
Fern: Hi, I'm good thanks. Busy with work and my counselling course, but otherwise A-OK. Tues works for me. What time?
Jessica: It's so cool you're training to be a counsellor. God we have so much to catch up on!!!! How's seven at Charlotte Street Hotel? Shall we skip dinner and just head straight to cocktails? MUMMY'S FREE FOR THE NIGHT.

Why had I agreed to see her again?

This was the question I couldn't give myself an answer to. The question that kept distracting me from my tutor's slide show on Freud. I readjusted myself in my plastic chair, struggling to find a comfortable position. The adult education college only had those tiny chair/desk hybrids that left no space for limbs. Heat blasted from the vents, and my hand sweated around the biro as I jotted down notes I didn't understand because I hadn't been listening properly.

'So, psychodynamic counselling is NOT all about the past,' Linda, my tutor, said, jabbing at the screen. 'That's a common misconception. Psychodynamic is about bringing the past into the present. It's about making the subconscious *conscious.*'

I jotted her last sentence down and kept blinking away emerging memories of all my therapy – seeing the sessions in a different light now, as if a veil had been lifted. I'd spent three years in teen mental health services after my suicide attempt, and it was so strange to think of my therapist being trained, like I was being trained right now. Well, if I could concentrate enough to get trained. The air got hotter and stuffier as Linda talked us through Freud's list of defence mechanisms, and I planned my outfit for seeing Jessica. I ran through possible outfit combinations in my head, wondering if I should buy something new . . .

'So,' Linda clapped, 'are you ready to get into your listening pairs?'

I looked up to see my fellow students scrape their chairs back and funnel off to the different practice rooms. Hannah, my listening partner for the duration of the course, bounded over like an excitable puppy. She was the youngest in the class by miles – only twenty-six – and was determined to overcompensate with enthusiasm. 'Are you ready?' she said. 'I've booked us into the quieter room next door.'

'Thank you. Yep, let me just get my pen.'

For the second half of each class, we were put into our pairs to practise all the listening skills we'd learnt in theory. It was a pretty surreal thing to do with near-strangers. We had to take it in turns to role-play counsellor and client, and were urged to bring 'real problems' to rehearse our empathetic listening skills, rather than play-acting from a script. Hannah led me into the neighbouring classroom. There were only two other pairs in there, and we arranged our chairs at a forty-five-degree angle in the corner. Two older women had already started, and I could hear the murmur of one of them missing their son who was away at university. Hannah handed me a listening feedback sheet. 'Now, do you want to talk first, or do you want to listen?' She adjusted her chair so she had a better view of the clock, as we got marked on our timekeeping.

'I don't mind.'

I was still quite out of it, half wondering if I should cancel the cocktails, half planning my perfect outfit.

'I could listen first, if you'd like? Fifteen minutes then fifteen minutes?'

'Sounds great.'

'Right, OK . . . Let's begin. Hang on . . . let me get in the zone.' Hannah pushed her blonde hair behind her ears and closed her eyes for a second, grounding herself. It struck me as mad, how well I knew her already. The nature of our pairing meant social barriers that usually take years and lifetimes to fall down had collapsed early on, as we spilt our guts out to one another once a week. When Hannah opened her eyes, her face was relaxed, welcoming, her posture in the perfect open position.

'Hello, Fern, and welcome to today's session,' she said, her voice like melted chocolate. 'As you know, we have just under fifteen minutes to have a chat. Remember, anything you say in this space is confidential. Now,' she leant forward, 'is there anything in particular you'd like to talk about today?'

My mind initially went blank. I wiggled in my chair and

grasped at appropriate life issues to share. Linda had told us only to share minor problems until we had more experience.

'*Ergh,*' I said, laughing. 'I never know what to say.'

She smiled warmly, letting me fill the silence. I had to admit it, Hannah may have been the youngest in our class, but she was damn good.

'Well, something weird happened to me last week.'

'Weird?'

'Yeah, really weird. I was at a work event the other night, and this old friend from my childhood turned up. I'm meeting her for a drink tomorrow. It's all very . . . out of the blue.'

'An old childhood friend?' she asked, using a very good open question.

'Yes. Well, from when we were teenagers. Jessica . . .' Even saying her name out loud did something, unravelled a part of me that had been rolled up and stored at the back of some psychological cupboard. 'We were best friends from fourteen to about nineteen.' God, was it only a few years? It felt longer than that. 'We were, like, soulmate-close . . .'

'And you fell out of touch?'

I was quiet and looked down at the carpet. 'No. I kind of . . . cut her out. After . . . she did . . . something. It was such a long time ago now.'

Hannah's eyebrows went up for a second, breaking form, as we weren't supposed to show shock. 'How old are you now, if you don't mind me asking?' she recovered.

'Thirty-one.'

'Wow, OK, so it's been over a decade?'

'Yes. She moved abroad but she's back now. And, honestly? I have no idea why she wants to meet up. Things ended so badly between us, but she's acting like nothing happened. I'm not sure I trust her . . . but then again, it felt lovely to see her again.' Hannah nodded, and kept her hands clasped. 'And it's brought back other feelings of how I felt when we were friends. Not such good ones . . .' I zoned out for a second, and tuned in to the murmurs of conversation coming from the listening pairs around me.

I could see Hannah panic in my silence.

She glanced up at the clock. 'But you've still missed her?' she eventually managed, and I laughed.

'I have missed her, yes. I don't know. With Jessica and me, it's complicated. She's complicated.' I leant forward. 'Can I tell you something weird?'

Hannah nodded.

'I've not told anyone about it. Not my best friend, Heather, though she has been working all hours, to be fair. But I've not even told my *boyfriend* about *any* of it yet. And it's been almost a week. He knows I'm meeting an old friend tomorrow, but I've not told him anything about her. I've never mentioned our friendship to him before she turned up. When I said, "Jessica", he was like, "Who's she?"'

'And why do you think that is?'

I leant back and my eyes, too, went to the clock. We were almost out of time, and I was glad. I shouldn't have brought this up. Every sentence unravelled me further, shook dust off buried parts of myself and exposed them to light for the first time in years.

'I'm not sure. Jessica brings out these different sides of me. Some good, some not-so-good.'

'What do you mean by "not-so-good"?'

An instant headache. Standing alone at a party with my arms crossed, watching her throw her head back laughing before lowering her lips onto a boy's smile. The feeling of being spoken across whenever she was there. Invisible. Ugly. Looking at my reflection in the mirror and wanting to rip my face off and replace it with hers. The jealousy. The distrust. The *rage*.

I came back to the classroom. 'I don't know. God, aren't we all stupid when we're young? I mean, if we held everyone to account for the twats they were under the age of thirty, everyone would kill themselves with shame? Sorry, I'm sure you're not a twat!'

Hannah laughed, then her eyes went to the clock. 'Oh shit. Time! OK, hang on. Let me finish up.' Hannah took a breath and carefully curated her counselling voice. 'Now, we're just coming to the end of our time, Fern,' she said, silky smooth. 'Maybe reflect this week on what you've spoken about, and we can revisit in our next session. Yes?'

'What? Yeah, OK, of course.' My headache intensified; a sharp throbbing tapped itself against my left eye socket.

'Thank you for coming . . . There.' Hannah was back, the vibrant young thing, already jumping out of her chair to help me with my feedback sheet. 'OK, so, I think I did well with my questions today, but I KNOW you saw me check the time. Sorry. I just panicked when you went quiet. Don't you? God, it's so hard, isn't it? Your turn.' The pairs around us were also swapping places. I wiggled out of my chair and tried to shake the sticky mood off me so I'd be a good listener for Hannah. Last week she'd spoken about her housemate always eating her leftovers, making me grateful for Ben. Nobody tells you that the best thing about finding long-term love is not having to share a fridge and bathroom with four strangers any more.

'I must say,' Hannah said, adjusting her chair. 'It's quite intriguing, isn't it? Your friend turning up after all this time. I know I'm not supposed to comment, but I'd be a bit freaked out too.'

I laughed. Pleased that perfect Hannah had just broken the rules. 'It's the most dramatic thing that's happened in a while, that's for sure.'

'I wonder what she wants?' Hannah asked, before adding, 'Shall we start?' And, as I settled into my listening posture, I realised Hannah had, without meaning to, asked the most perfect question of all.

Fourteen

November 2000

My shoulders slumped as I took in my appearance in the mirror. I was disgusting. I also felt this huge disconnect between myself and my reflection, a strange detachment from my body. There wasn't enough black eyeliner in the world to truly portray how I felt inside. The pentagram necklace I'd found in the hippy shop helped things along a little bit, but I still had this painful knowledge that nobody really understood what I was going through.

'Fern,' my mother said, as I sloped into the kitchen before meeting Jessica to go shopping. 'I love you dearly, but you look like you've been punched in both eyes.'

'Well, you look like you've killed and skinned Laura Ashley herself, and are wearing her like a coat.'

'Fern!'

'What? I'm just saying, jogging bottoms exist. They are comfortable. You may want to relax sometimes.'

'It's hard to relax when your daughter is slouching around looking like a deranged panda.' She laughed, to try and make it a joke, then attempted to hug me, but I shrugged it off. We both bristled and stung from the incident.

'Can I have some money? For town? We're going shopping for Eric's party tonight.'

'Have you already spent what I gave you last week?'

'I needed a new notepad for school,' I said, peeling a banana for breakfast and taking a bite. An inch of that was true. I'd bought myself a posh notebook to write my potentially award-winning poetry in. I was just tweaking my favourite poem, 'Hi, Bloody High' – a two-pager about my self-harm – and was wondering how you got an entry form for the Pulitzer.

Mum's hand hesitated at the zipper to her handbag, and then she handed over a tenner. 'Just because I'm giving it to you, doesn't mean you have to spend it all.'

'I know.' I chucked my half-eaten banana in the bin and downed a glass of water on my way out. 'Are you still OK picking us up later?'

She smiled wryly. 'Yes, I rang Amy's mum to chat it through. They'll take you there, we'll come and get you at eleven thirty.'

'Midnight? Oh thanks, Mum.'

'Eleven thirty.'

'It's so great that I have a mum who lets me stay out 'til midnight.'

'Eleven. Thirty. And don't drink on your medicine, you know it's dangerous.'

'I won't.'

'Honestly, Fern. I've read the leaflets, and it's really not recommended. I still think you're too young to be on them at all, to be honest, but, still, if we're on this path, we have to do it properly.'

'Jesus, Mum. Can you not trust me?'

What Mum didn't know was I hadn't taken my medication for ten days now. I'd been flushing it down the toilet, feeling very dramatic whenever I did. The guilt overwhelmed me for a second and I randomly hugged her in a sharp burst of affection. 'I'll be back in a few hours,' I said. 'Jessica's coming over to get ready, is that OK?'

'I should start charging that girl rent.'

'Woah, your room is different,' Jessica said, as she entered my bedroom after our shopping trip and dropped her stuff to stare at my new wall.

'I've been making a collage this week,' I said, following her eyes and blushing to my insides. Maybe I was being a bit over the top? This was the first time anyone had seen it.

'I love it, it's cool.' Her eyes travelled around my project – taking it all in. I'd essentially painted the wall dark purple, then over that had created a collage of angst. Tacking up multiple sketches of a crying eye I'd done, or words cut from headlines that said things like 'PAIN'. My parents were worried about it – about me. Returning to school had been harder than I thought it would be, and I wasn't particularly coping. It was so busy and bright and chaotic, and my brain was fading things down to counterbalance the onslaught. I'd decided to stop taking my meds, hoping that may make me feel more alive again. I'd also started cutting the tops of my thighs again to try and draw out feeling in me, but it never worked for long. I lied to my counsellor about how well I was doing, then went home to attack my legs. I told literally nobody what I was up to. I didn't want to admit it was back. That I was failing again so quickly. The only moments I seemed to feel myself were the times I spent laughing with Jessica.

She walked right past my collage, as if it wasn't strange at all. 'Let's see what this Nirvana is like then,' she said, ripping my CD out of its cellophane. We'd picked up the CD after the Hot Guy in HMV had recommended it earlier. It had been yet another hilarious trip into town together. Even the everyday felt good with Jessica. We'd smothered ourselves with make-up testers and then taken multiple photos together in the booth in the shopping centre. On the walk back to mine, two cars had honked us as they passed, and one van driver had leant out to tell Jessica to 'suck his dick'. I felt vaguely put out he hadn't included me. 'Hot HMV Guy better have good taste in music. Let's try a few songs and see . . . oh my actual God, this music.'

'Smells Like Teen Spirit' blasted through my speakers, and both Jessica and I sat on my bed, stunned, as the drums started crashing into the angry chorus.

'This is really good,' she said, after the first song.

'Who is this man, and how come he has access to my soul?'

The party preening was temporarily forgotten as we sat, crossed-legged, on my purple duvet, and listened to the album in full. Both of us looked up occasionally to grin at each other, nodding our heads. When 'Lithium' came on, it felt so much like my own thoughts that I almost cried.

'You OK?' Jessica asked, her long lashes staring up at me in concern.

I wiped the back of my nose with my hand. 'Yeah, I'm probably getting my period or something.'

I hadn't yet told Jessica anything about my illness. I worried she must already know. It must've filtered down to her through school gossip lines. Even if it was old news, somebody would've loved the thrill of telling the new girl 'the truth' about her new friend. But, if she did know, Jessica had never once brought it up, nor asked why I wore long sleeves and left school early on Thursdays.

With only an hour and a half 'til we were going to walk to Amy's to get a lift, we started the laborious process of making ourselves up while eating the frozen pizza I'd cooked for us. With a slice of margarita hanging out of my mouth, I stroked more eyeliner onto my eyeliner. I smelt the armpits of my top for BO, and blasted it with Impulse body spray to cover the tang left from the shopping trip, while Jessica painted each one of her nails a different colour. We put the album on again and Jessica sat on my carpet with her knees up, while I braided her hair into tiny plaits. When I was done, we both looked at her in the mirror, burst into hysterics, and spent another twenty minutes unravelling each one.

'Do you fancy any of the boys in our school?' I asked her, while sorting her hair. She'd never spoken about any of them like that.

Her pretty face crinkled up. 'Eww. No.'

'Not even Francesco from the lower sixth?'

'When he's your future husband? I wouldn't dare.' We both smiled, and, though she was joking, my stomach relaxed a little. Jessica sighed. 'No, I'm just not in that zone, right now,' she said. 'To be honest, I'm still a little bit hung up on my ex.'

I dropped the tiny plait I'd been unravelling. 'You have an ex?' I asked, as if she'd just revealed she had a Fabergé egg.

In fact, I think that was the first time I'd used the word *'ex'* out loud. It felt weirdly grown-up, saying it, as if the act would suddenly make me like olives and want to read newspaper supplements.

She sighed again. 'I have more than one.'

HANG ON.

'. . . but the others weren't anything serious. Duncan, however . . . I mean, he's a dick. He dumped me when I moved here, but I still think about him a lot. He's a bit older. I'm worried he thought I was immature.'

'Duncan?' I still couldn't believe she had an ex. An older ex. *Multiple exes.* Oh my God, this totally meant she'd tongue-kissed a boy. She'd maybe even had her boobs touched. In a minute, Jessica had gone from being my equal to a faraway dot in the distance. I felt like a stupid child.

'Yeah. I saw him when I went over to my dad's to pick up some of my stuff. And we got together, but he's not called or anything since.' She shrugged. 'Boys, right?'

'Yeah, boys are stupid,' I replied, as if I had any expertise to offer on the subject at all.

What did 'get together' mean? How had I not known there was a Duncan? Let alone boys before Duncan . . . And that was the first time I sat in the uncomfortable knowledge gap Jessica would often leave, between what she did and what I knew she did.

My phone buzzed, interrupting the revelation.

Amy: GET HERE NOW AND BRING YOUR POWDER. OURS SMASHED AND IT'S A DISASTER x

We read the message together, laughed, and frantically put the finishing touches to our faces. While applying my eighth layer of mascara, I kept looking at Jessica in the mirror, seeing her through a totally different lens.

Thirty-one

I was too preoccupied with my reflection to notice the familiar sound of Ben scrabbling to open the front door.

'I'm back,' he called, in his air of perpetual jolliness. Usually, I'd rush to greet him like a needy puppy, but, in that particular moment, I was staring at my shoes in front of the mirror, frowning at my chunky calves. 'OK, so I broke the rule and brought some marking home, but I swear to God, it's not going to get done otherwise. Hello? Fern? You in?'

'Sorry, I'm in the bedroom.' I watched my lipsticked mouth sound out the words. 'Did you have a good day?'

His voice echoed down the hall as he took his coat off, something about UCAS personal statements, but I kept tuning him out. I was stepping in and out of two pairs of heels, trying to decide between them. I glanced at the time on my phone. Did I have enough time to release my perfectly done messy bun and wear it down instead?

Ben's voice got louder. 'Yes, so, I may have to work late most of next week, as they're all panicking about getting into uni. Usually I wouldn't bother, but . . . Oh my God, Fern, you look amazing.' He stopped in the doorway, his eyes registering the fruits of my efforts. I'd stopped working an hour early to get ready, and, by the look on his face, it had paid off.

'Do I look OK?' I was wearing a long green velvet dress, with a split up the front. I'd lost a few more hours of work the previous day, popping to Oxford Street after my counselling course, and trying to find something suitable. This dress was from Whistles and I'd found myself putting it on my credit card, like some kind of Carrie Bradshaw wannabe, alongside some expensive make-up from Liberty's.

'Fern, you look absolutely amazing. Where the hell are you going again, and can I come, please?'

'Just meeting an old friend from school near Covent Garden. I told you.'

'Yeah, but you didn't tell me the dress code was Bond Girl. Seriously, Fern, you look sensational.' He came up behind me, and I was enveloped in his scent. He wrapped his arms around my waist and I smiled at myself in the mirror as I watched him kiss my neck. 'I like this,' he murmured, his fingers skimming the velvet.

'Is it all right?'

'God, you look so sexy.' His voice was gruff, deepened, and he pawed at me with an urgency and fierceness I hadn't felt in ages. It was the Ben I knew from the start. Those frantic first six months, where we couldn't go anywhere, or accomplish anything, without having sex first. It had been over a year since he'd used that voice. Since we'd moved in, we'd gone from jokes about 'christening each room', high on the excitement of being able to shag in the kitchen without trau-matising our various housemates, to getting so comfortable with the fact we could have sex whenever we wanted, that we had it increasingly infrequently.

Ben tried to kiss my lips, but I ducked away. 'I've got lipstick on.'

His grin went up to his eyebrows. 'Well, just because you can't kiss me, doesn't mean I can't kiss you.' He rained kisses down my neck, my collarbones, before turning me to face him, and getting onto his knees, kissing the velvet of my stomach, smirking as he looked up at me.

'What are you doing?'

He'd tugged my dress slit open, and kissed my freshly shaved legs, up my thighs then through my knickers. 'Ben . . .' I closed my eyes, losing myself in the sensation, in the thrill of the novelty. I hadn't felt this wanted in ages. I stepped out of my heels so I didn't fall over, and Ben, his head buried under the folds of my dress, pulled my underwear to one side, pushing me into the wall with both hands. He cupped my arse while I groaned, and reached out to smack it hard, shocking me slightly. Then, he was un-burrowing himself from my dress, and unbuckling his belt. He went to kiss me again, the smell of me all over his breath.

'My lipstick, remember?'

He groaned, and went back to my neck, and I helped him pull his work trousers down, taking his boxers with them. Then he was in me, pinning me to the wall. I tried to get my dress out of the way so he didn't stain it, and revelled in the feeling of what having sex like this meant about us as a couple. It felt good. It mostly felt good with Ben, but

I still knew I wouldn't come. Not when I was worried about being late, and not with this little foreplay. But I knew I'd use the memory of this moment in times to come. The memory of being wanted this much would be the erotic kindling I would use to masturbate to for a good time afterwards. So, in that way, I was technically having multiple orgasms, spread out over a long period of time. Ben smacked my arse once more and I jolted with the shock of it. He yelled out as he emptied into me, holding me against the wall by his body. We were both still for a moment, his lips still on my neck, then the moment broke and we laughed as he took himself out of me.

'Hang on, otherwise I'll ruin the dress.' I ran down the corridor with it held artificially high and plonked onto the loo, breathless. A deep grin sewed itself onto my face as I lay my head on my knees, feeling smug and full. Ben followed me in, pulling his trousers up. He went to the sink to wash himself off.

'So, where are you off to again?' he asked, like nothing had happened. It was so unbelievably hot.

I smiled into my knees. 'Charlotte Street Hotel.'

'Oooo, very fancy.'

Was it weird, how much I still loved him, as I watched my boyfriend wash his penis in the sink? I wondered if my adoration would ever dampen down. If I'd ever stop feeling hit like a truck with the force of how much I loved him, wanted him, needed him . . . worried I didn't deserve him? Feeling ashamed, that I couldn't tell him in case it scared him off. Ben dried his penis off using the hand towel, and the love died a little.

'And who is this mysterious friend you've got all dressed up for?'

I paused, nervous to confirm her re-entry into my life. 'Jessica. We knew each other as teenagers.'

'Oh, cool. You've never really mentioned her before.'

My post sex high faded a little as I contemplated the night ahead of me. Were we going to talk about what happened? Or gloss it over? Which was worse? I asked myself again why I was going, what good I thought it would do. 'She emigrated to America with her husband,' I explained, skipping the part where I exorcised her from my life. 'She only just moved back.' I ran off some loo roll to wipe myself, noticing I hadn't told him she was divorced. 'She's a mum now too,' I added, wanting him to picture someone soft and frumpy, too exhausted to fuck like we'd just fucked, a child scratching at the door saying, *'Mummy, I can't sleep.'*

'Cool. Wow, sounds like you'll have a lot to catch up on.'

'I guess. I won't be back late. I know you're having a hard week.'

He batted the comment away. 'Don't be silly. Be as late as you like, you know I can sleep through anything. Just don't pass out on the last District Line train, like I did after my staff Christmas party.'

I smiled at him. 'I knew it was love when I drove and got you from Upminster, at one thirty in the morning, in the snow.'

'And I knew how lucky I was.' He leant over to peck me on the lips, and we were back. Me and him. Happy, loving, life partners – supportive, comfortable enough to pee in front of each other, with healthy boundaries, good communication, no secrets, etc, etc . . . and yet we could still fuck against a wall. What goals. I stood up and flushed, and we left the bathroom together, returning to the scene of the mirror, where his workbag lay discarded on the floor, burping up a pile of A level papers. He stood to collect them, and we didn't mention what had just happened. I picked up my phone and saw I had to be out of the door in ten minutes. Also a message from Heather:

Heather: I'm sorry I've been so AWOL. But the new nurse FINALLY started at the clinic today so I get my life back. Dinner next Fri at mine?

'Have you eaten?' Ben called as he padded into the living room. 'I'm going to treat myself to Deliveroo if you're out.'

'We're eating there,' I lied, stroking my hand over my stomach, as I punched out 'sure'. It used to be flat. Jessica's was flat and she'd had a baby. If I skipped a meal or two here and there, it could be flat again.

The hotel was such a bold contrast to the places Jessica and I used to hang out. There was no blotchy entry stamp on my hand, no sticky floor, no broken condom machine in the toilet. Instead I walked through a reception of mahogany wood, and told a uniformed woman at a desk that there was a table booked. She told me my friend was already here with what felt like genuine enthusiasm, and led me to Jessica.

'Fern, you look amazing, oh my God.'

Shame and self-loathing crashed over me as Jessica stood to hug me hello. I'd fucked it. I looked overdone and trying too hard, as if I'd dressed up to solve a murder on a nineteen-thirties train journey through fucking Russia or something. Jessica, in contrast, wore fiercely expensive dark blue skinny jeans, with an almost-naked cami and a black blazer, with lashings of gold earrings up her pierced lobes. Understated. Beautiful. Perfect.

'I feel a bit overdressed,' I said, crossing my arms. I didn't spend a huge amount of time in five-star hotels, but the bar was vibrant and non-imposing – not a chandelier in sight.

'No such thing. You look glorious.' Everything about her smelt expensive – her perfume, her shampoo, her hairspray. And, as she relaxed back into the poofy chair, she looked totally at ease, in a place where the cheapest drink was twelve pounds, and a room upstairs started at three hundred. Whereas I gingerly perched on my chair, awaiting a bouncer to come over and ask me for some kind of upper-class ID, before leading me through to the 'new money' section, even if I did produce one.

'Isn't this place fun?' she said. 'I saw Rizzo from *Grease* last time I stayed here.'

Hang on, stayed here? She had enough money for a room?

'. . . I've been in love with this hotel ever since. Such a gorgeous location too.'

I nodded, as if I had even an inch of a barometer to measure expensive hotels against one another. A waiter came over with a small bowl of almonds, and two crystal glasses with a water jug. 'Complimentary,' she said, before brandishing drinks menus at us.

'Do you know what you want?' Jessica asked, as I scanned the first page, seeing all the fifteen-pound-plus prices next to the cocktails. If I had three, that would be the same as going out for dinner, which we weren't doing, so, technically, I could afford four, if I pretended I hadn't just put this stupid dress on a credit card.

'Erm . . .'

'I'll have a whisky sour,' she told the waiter, before looking up at me. 'They're really good, you should get one.'

'Oh, yes, sure, OK.'

We were left alone, a table between us and our history to catch up on. It was impossible to know where to start.

'So you used to stay here?' I started, fiddling with the menu on my lap.

'Only twice. When Brendan had "business in the city" and it was a good time to combine it with seeing my mum, getting her to meet Bridget, etc.' She hadn't got in touch back then. I wondered what drove her to get in touch now. What had changed? I looked over at her perfect outfit, mistrustful . . . 'And, you live in London?' she asked.

I nodded and took a sip of water. 'In Hackney. It's OK. Rent's expensive. But, we're in this little village bit, near the park, which is nice.'

'And how long have you been living with Ben?'

'Not long. Just over a year. Did I tell you Mum and Dad moved to St Albans, randomly?' She shook her head.

'Dad's company had a shit time in the recession and they decided to downsize and move nearer my aunty. I lived with them for a bit in my twenties as I was so broke trying to get into journalism. Then the blog went viral and I got my job.'

Jessica grinned as she took a delicate sip of her water. 'Listen to you. *Going viral.* It's so amazing, what you've done.'

'Well . . .'

'Honestly, Fern. It's huge. Imagine what teenage Fern would've thought of it.'

I groaned. 'Teenage Fern would've probably thought I was a giant loser.'

'Not at all! She would be thrilled she'd become a badass mental health editor who's also doing extra badass training to be a counsellor.'

I leant back into the comfortable chair and thought about it. Teen Me. How would she view my life now? I smiled. Jessica was right – I would've been ecstatic and disbelieving. Not just at the journalism stuff, but at my whole life. Ben, holding down a job, managing as an adult. The fact that I was still alive, that I hadn't given into the urges to end it.

'You always knew what to say to make me feel good,' I said, laughing.

'It's true. I'm beaming with pride, Fern.'

I couldn't tell if she was overdoing the compliments to win my favour. Jessica had always been my cheerleader, but our estrangement, and the reasons for it, still hung in the air like her expensive perfume.

'Yes, well, you're not doing so badly yourself,' I said, gesturing to her put-togetherness, just as our hideously expensive drinks arrived.

Jessica rolled her eyes and laughed. 'I married a rich arsehole who has to pay me a lot in alimony.' She shrugged and laughed. 'Dream big.'

Her laugh drew the attention of a nearby group of well-groomed men, who turned to take us in. When I say 'us', I meant Jessica.

'But, you're a mum . . . And you're home now?'

'Yes, sleeping on my mum's floor, back in my home town.'

I leant forward to take a sip of my drink. It was so small, the sip took the water line down by about three centimetres, leaving only two thirds left.

'I'm trying not to leave the house much, in case I bump into anyone we used to know.'

'You haven't kept in touch with people?' I asked.

She shook her head and drained her drink, totally oblivious to the male gaze she was currently under. This was new. Me noticing men more than her. The fact she'd not tuned into the sexual frequency of everyone around her and cranked up her volume. 'No, I fell off the grid even before I went to America. You?'

As we finished our first drinks, and ordered our next round, using nostalgia's comfort blanket to get used to one another again, I temporarily forgot my suspicions, falling into the old habit of how well we got on. I told her about Amy's wedding and how strange it was to see Kim again. Kim who, incidentally, had been made bridesmaid – I hadn't made the cut. How Kim ended up 'accidentally' calling her child Jonah when Amy had always said that was her favourite baby name. The rest of the gossip I'd mostly picked up through Facebook before people stopped using it so much. Jessica gasped at the unexpected people making unexpected decisions, laughed at my bitchy hot takes on people we never liked in college, and said 'I knew it' about everyone who appeared to have voted for Brexit. As the third set of drinks arrived, we were dewy-eyed, reminiscing about all our old ways – trading memories like the scented glitter pens we collected at school.

'Do you remember when we held that vigil for Sirius Black on top of the common?'

'Do you remember when we drove all the way to Brighton in the middle of the night just to watch the sunrise?'

'And spent a tenner on pick 'n' mix from that shop in the Lanes for breakfast?'

'Remember our witchcraft phase?' Jessica said, her hands clasped together.

'*Phase?* I burnt sage when I moved in with Ben.'

'No way?'

'You've got to! If it doesn't work out with him, I need to know it's because of our incompatibility, not just because we got infected with a previous tenant's bad energy.'

Jessica wiped her eyes with laughter, and I remembered what a high it gave me, to make her laugh like that. 'Did you do it in front of him?'

'Hell no. I waited until he was out. When he got home, I had to blame the smell on the neighbour's cooking.'

I drained the last of my third delicious cocktail, feeling warmth bloom all over me. The bar was packed, everyone around us frothing with energy, glowing in the yellow of the giant lamps, waiters weaving expertly around the patrons, keeping everyone lubricated. The music wasn't too loud, the temperature was just right, everyone was behaving. I could sort of see the point of paying this much for drinks to spend time somewhere as nice as this. Not that I could afford to.

After we'd run out of laughter, her eyes intensified. She'd leant over conspiratorially.

'So Ben,' she said. 'Tell me all about Ben. How did you guys meet?'

The paranoia flooded in immediately, the hotel air getting colder. I picked up my glass to use as a barrier between us.

'The usual way,' I said, trying to keep it non-committal. 'On a dating app. I got lucky. I was super picky, and basically only went on about three dates in two years. Ben passed my very strict criteria.'

'So wise, as always. And what's he like? What does he do? You said he was a teacher?'

'He's . . .' I could never think of him without swooning. 'He's . . . basically the kindest man I've ever met. To the point where he's almost gloriously naive. And yeah, he teaches psychology at a sixth-form college. It's the perfect job considering everything a person has to take on with me.' I mimed a spiral next to my head.

Jessica nodded, and her eyes quickly glanced at my long sleeves. 'I mean, anyone who falls in love with *anyone* has to "take stuff on" – you know, right?' she said. 'I bet he has stuff for you to take on too.'

There she was. Jessica. My Jessica. Kicking in. On my side. Saying things I didn't realise needed to be said. My champion. My best friend. God, I'd missed her. But . . .

'Yeah, he's got his stuff. He was engaged, but she called it off last-minute. That messed him up a bit. But, well, I mean, you don't normally google your Hinge date and find their viral blog about suicide.'

She pulled a face. 'Yeah, well, you don't normally google your Hinge date and find they've started an international awareness campaign that made millions of people feel seen and probably saved thousands of lives.'

I went red with pride and drink, clashing with the green

of my dress, feeling guilty again that I had never read the email Jessica said she'd sent when the blog post went viral. I wondered if it was still in my inbox somewhere? 'That's what Ben said,' I admitted sheepishly. 'He's, like, proud of me rather than scared by it. Unlike all my other exes. God bless people with psychology degrees.'

'Well, I like him already. I'm so happy for you, Fern. He sounds wonderful! And he's fit too.'

'Hmm.' The whisky sour soured on my tongue, as she held out a finger to order a fourth round. 'So, is he the one then?'

'I think so . . . I hope so.'

'Do you think you'll get married?'

'I want to . . . He's not proposed yet though,' I admitted, then regretted admitting it.

I wasn't panicking about Ben's lack of proposal. Not just yet. Though it was starting to simmer. I'd decided it would take at least six months living together before I passed the *living-together test*. Then it would probably take him two months more to realise that it had been a test, and one I'd passed. Then I'd factored in an additional month for him to realise this meant a proposal was next. Then maybe another month for him to plan the proposal? So he was now only slightly overdue. The only problem was we'd never discussed it. Not since he'd told me about his jilting near the start of our relationship. We'd never spoken about marriage, and weddings, or how many children, and when, and what sort of age gap is least likely to give them psychological problems, and would we need to move to a better school area, and what if we were infertile? And didn't Ben realise that I was thirty-one, and really needed to know the answers to these questions? But I certainly wasn't going to fuck things up by bringing it up.

Jessica, sensing the sensitive spot, tilted her head. 'You said he was engaged before?'

My insides soured like my drink. I hated thinking about his previous fiancée. I hated admitting this weakness to Jessica – not when I still wasn't sure why she was here, what she wanted. 'Yeah. To this woman who broke it off a month before the wedding.'

'Shit. Well, maybe that's why he's taking his time?'

'But I'm not her. I'd never do that.' It stunned me whenever I thought about it, that anyone could throw Ben away. I still dreaded the day she came to her senses and tried to win him back. I could never imagine having the confidence to throw any man away who wanted me . . .

'But you guys are happy?'

I nodded so hard my earrings hurt, marking my territory. 'Yes. Really happy. I'm just being silly.'

Our new round appeared and Jessica swung her glass, and some sloshed over the rim. 'I mean, I'm a walking, talking example that marriage means fuck all.' She waggled her finger and I knew then she was as pissed as I was. 'Marriage does not equal happiness, I promise you. And divorce? Well! Divorce is even shittier than marriage.'

I leant forward, hoping we were finally getting somewhere. 'What happened with you guys? If you don't mind me asking?'

'Honestly, no. It's nice to have someone to talk to about it who isn't my mum.' She made a face. '*Well, what did you expect? All men are the same.* Yadder yadder. She's already unbearably smug. And, she's like, all extra bonded to me now we share some fucked-up *divorced-women* crap.'

'Woah, OK, so your mum is still your mum.'

'Even more so. She's my mum left low on the hob for twelve years to thicken. It's OK. I'll sort myself out and move out soon. I need the babysitting too much right now. What with all the trauma of my husband being such a fucking dick, and having to move countries, and no career, or anything. If I wasn't so desperate to come home, I would've determinedly stayed in California and forced him to stay too, so he couldn't set up home with that posh Chelsea bitch.'

'God, Jessica, it sounds awful. What happened?'

She drunkenly filled me in on it all. Meeting him when she worked at the bar of our local shit home town hotel, being swept off her feet, dazzled by his adoration and money and expensive dates. How he was the opposite of Ben, really. Constant talk of marriage, and babies, and commitment. He was all in. Of course he was; it was Jessica.

She sighed, and her sadness cut such a stark contrast against the bright joviality of the packed bar around us. 'I thought I'd played it right, you know? Finally. After all the shit I'd been through with boys, I'd finally learnt the secret.'

I leant forward. Jessica had never spoken this frankly to me about men before. 'What secret?'

Jessica ran a hand through her dark hair and looked me straight in the eye. 'There's no such thing as "good men" and "bad men". They are the same men,' she said. 'They just treat different women differently based on how they view you.'

My nose wrinkled. 'What do you mean?'

She stared at me defiantly. 'It's simple. Men see women in two separate categories.' She ticked them off on her fingers. 'There are the women they fuck, and the women they fall in love with. And it's not like the good men are the ones who want to fall in love with women, and the bad men are the ones who just want to fuck them. The men are neutral. They just treat you, a woman, differently, based on whether or not you fall into the "fuck" category, or the "love" category.' She sat back, all *voilà*! As if she'd delivered an expert TED Talk, with the confidence of a Flat Earther.

'I mean,' I said, 'I'm not sure if that's definitive . . .'

'Of course it is. A hundred per cent.'

I started to feel a bit sick. 'Do you really think so?'

'I know so!' She slumped forward conspiratorially, tracing the rim of her glass 'til it hummed. 'Look, Ben is lovely to you, right? But, I'm sorry, I bet you a *million pounds*, to some woman out there, he's some dickhead who fucked her and left her wondering what's wrong with her, because she didn't fall into the right funnel. Why was she left with a used condom in her bin and a polite phone call saying, "Just to be clear that was a one-off, right?", whereas you get to move in with him? Be the girlfriend? Same guy. Totally different to different women.'

'I don't think Ben . . .' I started, before trailing off, feeling completely sick now.

What did I think? *Would Ben* . . . ? I blinked a few times as her words unravelled me. We had spoken about our pasts. He had said he'd gone to a 'dark place' and 'slept around some' after the jilting, but he respected women, didn't he? I was so thrown, digesting her theory, that I initially didn't notice Jessica. She tipped back her narrow chin to finish the rest of her drink, and, when she placed the empty glass back, there was a film of tears in her eyes. Another shock.

'Are you OK?'

'Yeah, sorry, I'm fine.' She wiped her face with a red-manicured nail. 'It's just . . . with Brendan . . . I thought I'd figured it out. That I'd cracked the code, you know? I was so sick of being the girl everyone fucked, rather than the girl everyone loved. So I made myself different for him. I didn't sleep with him until, like, the tenth date. And, you know what? It worked. Brendan couldn't get enough of me. He was setting up dates three and four before we'd even finished date one. And we had dates. *Dates!* Not just flimsy fake plans to cover the fact we'd blow them off and fuck anyway. "Let's go to the cinema, actually, I'm not in the mood, are you? No? Let's fuck then. Oh, by the way, I have a girlfriend, I'm sorry I forgot to tell you. I love her very much. She's not a slut like you."' Jessica's voice slurred slightly. It was the first time she'd appeared less than Mary Poppins levels of put together since we'd reunited. As I slumped forward to hear her, I realised I was almost just as drunk.

'Hey, don't say that. You're not . . .' I couldn't say it.

'A slut? Maybe not any more.' A dangerous moment's silence that I almost couldn't break. The past crashing around me, the memories, the hurt. She drained the already empty glass, without noticing there was nothing left, and hadn't appeared to notice my pause. 'So, I played the part of long-term-relationship girl, and, easy as that, Brendan falls in love with me. I literally made him say "I love you" before we had sex for the first time, like fucking . . . Tara Reid in

American Pie. And, Fern? It was amazing. We were so in love. It was everything I've ever wanted. When the job came up in America I didn't even need to think about it. When he asked me to marry him, I cried my eyes out. We eloped to Gretna Green, just the two of us . . . Here . . .' She picked up her phone and her wedding photo arrived on her screen much too quickly for it to be anything other than something she regularly looked at. I took in twenty-two-year-old Jessica, on her wedding day. She looked like a film star – the photo taking on that vintage, classic quality you could imagine being used in a documentary about her life one day. She wore a white minidress with a veil longer than her hemline. She smiled with post-box-red lips. This was the first time I'd seen Brendan too, and he was so generically a 'handsome' man, I'm surprised he wasn't on Shutterstock. Strong jaw, designer stubble, piercing green eyes – and a look that just screamed 'money', from the cut of his suit, to the tasteful placement of his hand-kerchief, to the way he'd gelled his hair. I'd never seen Jessica with such a man before – let alone married to one.

'You looked stunning,' I said. 'And Brendan is handsome.'

She rolled her eyes as she took back the phone. 'Doesn't he fucking know it?' She sighed. 'Anyway, I thought I'd cracked it. I didn't tell him anything about my past, and, to be honest, he wasn't that interested. We moved over there. Then we were in this gorgeous love bubble of emigrating together, getting pregnant, Bridget being born, getting to know all the other ex-pats at his work. Honestly, Fern, I didn't drop the facade once. I was a perfect wife – demure, amen-able, tender, loveable.'

'So what happened?'

She threw her arms up to the ornate ceiling. 'Well, I was right. Men *do* have the women they love, and the women they fuck. And, so, like the biggest cliché ever, I found out Brendan was having an affair. Affairs, plural. With all the clichéd people. Like his bloody intern, like our neighbour. Then he found some stupid posho who was over there for a project. Dirty little rich girl from Chelsea. And there you have it. He'd left me. He's fucking her. I'm back here. Hilariously . . .' For the second time she tried to drink her empty drink, her mouth gasping like a fish, looking momentarily ugly, before she put it down and tried to catch the waiter's attention. 'Anyway, I'm divorced, and bitter, and exhausted. How are you?'

I couldn't believe it. This wasn't Jessica. She was never so open and honest and vulnerable. When I saw the pain on her face, my guard flew down and I pulled her into a hug over the table. Everything temporarily forgotten.

'You're brilliant and gorgeous and wonderful, and leaving you will be the worst thing he ever did,' I told her. Her arms stretched around my back, pulling me close, and we hugged 'til the bar around us went fuzzy. I could feel her breath on my neck, her heartbeat through her fragile chest. When we broke apart, she showed her pointed teeth, smiling shyly.

'Would it be absolute madness,' she asked, 'to get another round?'

Morning. Headache. The smell of a cup of tea.

'Fern?'

Ben's hand was on my forehead, as if I were a poorly child.

'Ouch!' I sat up, my brain roaring.

'What are you doing on the sofa, my darling?' There was laughter in his voice.

I blinked in the new day, found my body tangled in a blanket, my limbs crumpled up on the sofa. 'I . . . I don't know.'

'You must've been wasted.'

Everything after drink four was gone. I had no idea how I got home, when we left, what had happened next. I hadn't blacked out like this since I was a teenager – I forgot how truly disconcerting the feeling was.

'Sorry,' I said, holding my head. 'I drank too much . . .'

'This Jessica is obviously a fun girl.'

Hugging her. Squeezing her. Laughing with her. Being free with her. Loving her again. Swirls of memories filling the room like cigarette smoke.

'We just got carried away. It's been so long since we saw each other.'

'Well, take this.' He handed me a hot mug. 'It will help. I have to dash though, I've got form time at eight thirty.'

Ben had gone before I even thanked him for the tea. Left to stew in my confusion and dehydration – wondering why I woke up on the sofa, and not in his arms. I rummaged for my phone in my bag, which had spilt out its contents like an upended bottle of wine – thanking the Lord it was one of my working from home days so I didn't have to face a crushing Tube carriage. My phone screen was blank, and it took five minutes to get over the mental hurdles required to fetch my charger. I plugged it in and then ran a shower while it charged. I washed the night off me, my make-up dripping in black rivers down my face. A bruise was coming up on my leg.

When I was dripping in a towel, I perched on the end of the bed and loaded up my phone.

Jessica had left a voice note:

'God, sorry for just leaving like that. You home OK? I swear to God, I only caught my train by a frog's whisker. Is that the saying? Probably not. Fucking hell, I am drunnnnnnkkkkkkk. Anyway, I just want to say sorry for going so hard at you about how shit men are. Please ignore me. I am just a sad drunk divorced mother. Don't let me tarnish your life with my fucking consequences of my bad fucking life decisions. Anyway, GET HOME SAFE. Ignore everything I say, always. I've missed you so much, Fern.'

The last part of the night tumbled back to me. Fragments of memories making it through to my long-term. Of laughing so hard I spilt my fifth drink all down myself. Of reminiscing about our disastrous haircuts, fashions we couldn't believe we wore, music we couldn't believe we actually listened to, boys we couldn't believe we found sexually attractive. And then . . .

There's no such thing as "good men" and "bad men" . . . they are the same men . . . there are the women they fuck, and the women they fall in love with . . .

There it was. The reason I'd slept on the sofa. Dim recollections of stumbling into the flat shuffled through my mind. I'd stood in the bedroom swaying, watching Ben sleep, and the poison of Jessica's words seeped into my bloodstream. I hadn't trusted him. Had almost hated him, believing her mantra.

Was Ben a bad man to some other woman out there?

At one a.m. that morning, I'd certainly thought so. I'd been too freaked out to even share a bed with him. But now? With a headache, a cup of tea made with love, and the cold light of day. I shook my head, before holding my skull, as doing so hurt so much. No. Not Ben. I could trust Ben. Jessica, on the other hand, I still wasn't sure.

Fourteen

November 2000

Amy made her mum drop us off at the end of Eric's road. 'Thanks, Mrs Fisher,' I chirped, waiting for Kim to get out before me, watching her struggle to plant her heels on the pavement, tugging down her tiny skirt, goosebumps all over her body. Then Amy made us wait for her mum's car to be around the corner before we were allowed to knock. The door crashed open and a red-faced Eric appeared on the threshold, wearing a gold chain prominently over his jumper.

'Hey,' he grunted, clearly unsure how to greet girls. 'We're in the conservatory.' We could only follow, goggling at the weird exhibit of 'Eric's Family Home'. We were greeted by what appeared to be a resurgence of the Year Six disco in terms of gender segregation. Eric sat himself back on the sofa, joining all the other boys, who each nursed an alcopop and were in some sort of silent competition over who could open their legs the widest. The girls congregated together, all of them pretending they weren't highly aware of the boys watching from the corner, laughing all high-pitched and easy-going, and then checking to see if Matt had noticed them.

We opened and decanted our two bottles of wine stolen from Kim's mum's cupboard, sloshing it into the provided Pokémon cups. I felt the boys' gaze on us and my skin prickled. I covered my naked stomach with my arm, suddenly way too aware of myself. This awkward feeling of being eyed up and sized up like cattle in a farmers' market. I hugged the girls hello, including Abi from my English class, and we stepped away from the speakers to hear ourselves compare which alcohol we were drinking.

'I'm, like, soooooo drunk,' Kim announced, throwing her hair back and checking for the second time that Matt was there. 'I've had two Bacardi Breezers already.' The boy himself was in the corner sofa, his legs widest of all. I gulped my wine, pulling a face at its vinegary taste. With nothing much else to do, I took another sip, then a gulp, and then, quite quickly, finished it and panicked about how I was going to spend the time. Thankfully, two rounds of drinks were ice-breaking enough for the two sexes to congregate. We started making small talk about school and which teachers we thought were a) gay, b) sexual predators, c) virgins, and d) all three.

Sean sauntered over to us in a shiny blue shirt, and attempted to chat up Jessica. 'So,' he shouted, his face right near hers. 'I've been wondering about you.'

'Me?' she asked, while I looked on.

'Yeah.'

'What have you been wondering?'

'Have you done your maths coursework yet?'

'Oh, yeah, that.' Jessica shook her head with her straw still in her mouth. 'No. It's not due for ages yet, is it? Have you?'

Sean was already blushing, realising his smooth moves were maybe quite bumpy. 'Just some of it. No biggy. Do you like, er, maths?'

'I wake up every morning and think, *Thank God for maths.*'

'Huh. You're kidding, right?'

'Yes, I'm kidding.'

'Ha,' Sean said. *'Ha.'*

He hadn't even said hi to me despite being in my history class. I tried to believe it was because we hadn't been set history coursework yet, but understood it was because Sean had no interest in putting his hand in my bra. I stood there awkwardly, Sean blocking my exit to Kim and Amy – who were trying to get the boys to tell them their star signs. I clutched my empty Pokémon cup with one hand, and covered my midriff with the other, and looked around the conservatory with what I hoped was a cool, disdainful expression. Matt was watching us – his eyes flicking over to Jessica every three seconds or so between glugs of his Smirnoff Ice. Then I felt the warmth of Jessica's hand in mine.

'I'm really sorry, but I'm dying for a wee,' she told Sean. 'Fern? You coming?'

I compliantly let her tug me upstairs, while Sean watched us leave, looking slightly dejected. Jessica dashed into the loo, and when she reappeared, the alcohol she'd drunk visibly coloured her face. 'Do you want me to wait?' she asked.

'No, it's fine. I'll meet you down there.'

The noise of the party quietened when I closed the toilet

door. I sat on the loo seat and folded over, resting my head on my knees as my depression found me. Rushing in, numbing me out. *Pathetic. Disgusting. Weak. Invisible.* It started calling me names, as I replayed Sean blanking me to hit on Jessica. *Because you are nothing and no one and . . .* I pushed the voice down 'til I felt nothing, and spent many minutes sitting like that, blinking occasionally at the yellow shower curtain, the music vibrating through my toes. Time suspended, and I was totally lost in nothing until I was jolted out of it by a loud knock at the door, and a 'What the hell are you doing in there?'

Downstairs, I found everyone had got very drunk in the short time I'd been gone. Eric was cradling a bottle of something as if it was the Baby Jesus, a smug smile carved into his red face.

He brandished the bottle at the girls. 'Tequila?' he asked. 'It's the real deal.'

We all shared a nervous look.

'Where did you get that?' Jessica asked.

'My parents brought it back from Mexico this summer. It's the real deal,' he repeated. 'It's got the worm in and everything.' He held the bottle up for us to see the floating maggot and Kim shrieked. 'Gross!'

'It's not gross. Anyway, who is going to do a shot?' He produced four wet shot glasses from his armpit.

Another look passed, and the words 'peer pressure' floated through my brain. Kim checked Matt was watching and then implicated all of us. 'I'm totally in. Though I'm *so* drunk already.'

'And the rest of you?'

'I guess.' Amy looked suitably terrified. Jessica looked bored. 'I'll eat the worm,' she said, shrugging. 'It's not a big deal.'

The whole party turned to look at Jessica. I'm surprised the music didn't stop.

'You're going to eat the worm?' Eric couldn't quite believe it. 'You know it's like, super alcoholic, right?' he asked.

She raised an eyebrow. 'That's the point, right?'

Amy turned to whisper to me. 'She did four shots of vodka when you were upstairs.'

'*What?*' I looked over and saw her eyes were unfocused. 'Are you sure, Jessica?' I asked her.

'Why is everyone being *weird*?' Jessica laughed and threw up her hands. 'It's just a tequila worm.'

'LEGEND,' Matt called over.

Eric, flustered, started pouring out shots for us and we cradled them nervously.

'All in one?' Amy asked, sounding as if she really did not want to be doing a shot.

'Hang on,' Jessica said. 'Where's mine? I want a shot too.'

'On top of the worm?'

'I thought this was supposed to be a party?'

A group formed around us, as everyone pushed to see Jessica. Eric poured her a generous measure, and she winked at the rest of us. 'On the count of three, girls: one, two, three.' There was a slight lag between Jessica tossing her shot back, and us watching how to do it and copying her. The alcohol seared through my mouth and curdled in my stomach. I couldn't not make a face, wipe my mouth, and say *'bleurgh'*. Kim and Amy did exactly the same, whereas Jessica hardly flinched. She was already helping Eric scoop the tequila worm out using a spoon. I wasn't sure how I felt about Jessica being the centre of a chanting mob, shouting, *'Eat the worm, eat the worm.'* She was magnetic. Jessica tossed the worm down her slender throat while everyone cheered around her. She didn't grimace, only said, 'Gross – who has a beer?' Matt arrived at her side to hand her a Budweiser. She smiled as she thanked him, and downed half of it with feminine delicacy, and I think every single boy fell in love with her in that moment.

Eric kept making people do shots until his bottle of The Real Deal ran out, and Jessica had two more. The music got louder and awkward dancing started, with the boys circling closer. Abi, by that point, had out-drunk Kim, and flailed around dramatically, drawing as much attention to herself as possible. She flitted from boy to boy, stealing their baseball caps, squealing as they tried to snatch them back. Eric full-on chased her around the living room while she giggled. Then the two of them morphed seamlessly from play-fighting to dancing like they were having sex with their clothes on. Eric wrapped his arms around Abi from behind and started rubbing his crotch into her.

'What's happening?' I asked Amy over the music.

'I'm not sure,' she replied, equally stunned. 'But I feel a bit weird watching it.'

'Me too. Oh, shit, Dan and Lauren are doing it too.'

In fact, lots of boys were splitting off to find a girl's arse to rub against, as Amy and I took a step backward at the same time, plastering our behinds to the wallpaper.

'Oh, God, Matt,' Amy whispered, and I followed her subtly pointed finger heading towards Kim and Jessica. Kim waved her hands madly, laughing hysterically at nothing, while Jessica seemed to be quietly feeling the effects of the worm. Her eyes had reddened, her focus whirling around the top of Kim's head. Matt circled them like a shark, and, as my own tequila shot hit me, everything happened too quickly for me to do anything but watch. It was like watching a David Attenborough documentary: *'The male circles the two females, deciding which one's arse he would most like to rub against.'* Matt pounced – grabbing Jessica around the waist and yanking her to him. Jessica twisted her head as she tried to focus on who was touching her. Matt grinned and shrugged, while Kim's mouth fell open. Amy reached out and held my hand, as if we could see a comet about to crash into earth.

'What are you doing?' Jessica asked, her voice slurring.

'It's just a dance,' Matt replied.

Kim joined us against the wallpaper as we watched Jessica slump backwards into him. She closed her eyes, her head rolling back, as Matt greedily pawed down the sides of her body.

'It's just a dance,' I told Kim, while we stood with nothing to do but watch.

'But . . .' Kim said.

'I know.'

'It's just dancing,' Amy repeated. 'Look at Abi and Eric. They don't even like each other.' We glanced over, and Eric had fully bent Abi over now and was whacking her arse, while she giggled and helped him hit her.

'I'm going to get another drink from the kitchen,' Kim said. 'I don't need to see this.'

'I need the loo again,' I said. I really wanted to be out of that room. The tequila had hit me and the walls were warping, my feet not moving properly. Plus, emotions were getting on top of me – confusion at Jessica's behaviour, at *everyone's* behaviour – and numb sadness at my apparent invisibility.

I stumbled upstairs, and, when I found the bathroom locked, I opened a random door and found myself in Eric's bedroom. It smelt as though Lynx laced the blue wallpaper; the scent of his stale sheets pierced my nostrils upon entering. I closed the door and dropped to the carpet. The music thumped through my thighs and I lay my head against the wall, feeling it spin circles around my skull. I heard shrieks and laughter over the heavy bass, and felt the veil descend once more between me and my peers. The sudden sense of detachment. I briefly fantasised about killing myself, right there, on Eric's carpet. But, even with the tequila sloshing around me, my therapist's words echoed in my head and brought me back.

'*Remember death is a very permanent solution for a temporary feeling,*' she'd said, time and time again. '*Distract yourself. Wait the feeling out. Keep yourself busy because it will be temporary.*'

I got up and started rifling through Eric's bedroom. His walls were adorned with Man United and Eminem posters. I squatted down to take in the titles on his bookshelf – seeing the full set of Enid Blyton, I smiled, but then, as I pulled out a drawer under his bed, my expression collapsed. A stack of sticky porn magazines awaited me there – with dead-eyed women on the covers, touching their bare breasts and spreading their legs. They were the first really sexualised women I'd ever seen and I felt instantly sick. I flicked open the top magazine using my fingernail and found the inside pages even worse. Models sat with their legs spread, their neat labia wide open, pouting with giant lips, the accompanying text telling me that *Kelly loves it when people come on her tits.* I picked up the magazine and read it properly, learning about these additional sexual things I didn't know might be one day expected of me. Of the *extra*-extra-curricular acts boys like Eric were being groomed to expect. I didn't know men might want to ejaculate *onto* my body, rather than just into it. My breasts, my stomach, my *face* . . . Nausea roared up through my bones. I knew, from an intellectual perspective, that teen boys masturbated. I mean, they made jokes about it constantly at school. But there was something different about this evidence of what he jacked off to. Eric, the boy I sat next to in chemistry, who I often shared a Bunsen burner with. The boy who I considered a friend. The jokes we'd shared, the growing up we'd done together, that one time on my first day back when he asked me earnestly how I was . . . now I knew he came home, locked his door, and got off on these glazed Barbie slut dolls called Kelly. Did he ever think of me like that? Want to explode into *my* face? Expect my body to look like these bodies? I threw the magazine against Eminem's face, then the rest of them, and got up and left them on the carpet.

Downstairs, I found Amy and Kim sitting on the bottom step. Kim's head was hanging down as she sobbed. Amy's arm was around her as she made parental hushing sounds. 'There, there, hon, it's not worth it. I love you. You're amazing.'

'What's happened?' I asked, sitting two steps above them. 'Kim? Are you OK?'

Kim twisted her sodden red face around to me. 'She knew

how I felt about him, and now . . . now . . .' The crying returned and she reburied her face in her lap while Amy soothed her with increased urgency.

'She's not worth it,' Amy said, in a dulcet tone. 'She's just a fucking slut.'

'Hang on, are you guys talking about Jessica?'

Amy nodded at me grimly with the expectation I'd nod along.

'She's such a WHORE,' Kim cried, her knees still digging into her eye sockets. 'A disgusting, pathetic whore.'

'Come on, guys, she's just drunk . . .'

Kim's head whooshed up, revealing panda eyes. 'Are you honestly going to defend her?'

'I don't know what she's done yet, but she ate that worm . . .'

'And now she's eating Matt's face!'

'Oh, shit.' Our friendship group could've potentially worked through a sexy dance, especially as they were the current trend of the evening. But, if Jessica kissed Matt, that was a clear escalation. I'm not sure Kim and Amy would've even forgiven *me* for such a transgression. Let alone Jessica, who was still in her probation period. I was smacked with an instant, heavy wave of exhaustion, already seeing this play out.

'Anyway,' Amy said, patting Kim's back. 'My mum's coming to get us. Are you coming?'

'You're *leaving*?'

'I can't stay here with HER,' Kim yelled.

'My mum will be here any minute.' Amy hugged her and glanced up over her shoulder. 'You coming then?'

'You're . . . just going to leave Jessica here? We *can't*.'

They shared a look, already questioning my supposed allegiance. 'I mean, how else is she going to get home?'

Amy shrugged. 'It's not my problem. I just need to get Kim home, OK?'

'But, she's relying on a lift from my dad.'

'She can get a cab.' Amy's Nokia started bleeping with its Groovejet ringtone. 'Hey, Mum? Yep, we're coming out. Thanks, bye. So . . .' She levelled me with a stare, making it exceedingly obvious we were now in the desert of girl code and she'd drawn a line in the sand. 'Are you coming, Fern?'

'I . . . don't know.'

'Jessica will be fine. She's busy.'

'Busy being a SLUT.' Kim stood up. 'Come on, Fern.'

It was very clear what a huge mistake it was to leave Eric's porn-filled bedroom. I grasped for a solution.

'Look, Jessica has messed up,' I said. 'But I don't want to leave her to get home by herself. Not when she's so wasted.'

'. . . well, if that's how you feel,' Kim whipped her bag around her shoulder with such force it hit the back of her head, 'it's nice to know where your loyalties lie.'

'Kim, come on. I'm just trying to be sensible.' I widened my eyes at Amy, pleading for reason. 'I'm only staying to make sure she's safe.'

Amy gave me a grim smile – enough to show she understood the predicament. 'OK. Let me take Kim home. We can sort it all later, when everyone's less . . . you know.'

I gave her a quick hug. 'Thank you. I don't want to stay, I promise.'

'Hmm.'

Kim didn't hug me goodbye. I watched them walk away, leaving me alone in this glorified orgy.

I returned to the party and the music physically hurt my eardrums. The conservatory had descended into carnage. Abi and Eric sat on the table, plunging their tongues into each other's mouths. In fact, most people appeared to be kissing someone. Sean, who'd been left out of the fornication, was wandering around clutching the empty tequila bottle, asking the leftover girls if they wanted to play spin-the-bottle. They just screeched *'Eww! No way!'* and resumed their pre-rehearsed dance routines, while he scratched his ear and pretended the conveyor belt of rejection wasn't a) permanently traumatising him, and/or b) radicalising him to become an incel in twenty years' time. A group of girls I vaguely knew were dancing to 'Lady Marmalade', and I had no choice but to loiter on the side and do a steady step-tap. I located Jessica in the corner, though only her legs were visible. The rest of her was obscured by Matt's body. He had her pinned to the sofa, looking like a zombie harvesting her mouth for brains. He rolled to one side and I saw she was hardly responding to his kisses. Her mouth hung half open, making vague attempts to meet his but missing, with her purple lipstick wiped all around her mouth. Matt reached out and openly squeezed her breast through her top, while Jessica's head rolled forward before she pushed his hand away, and distracted him by finding his mouth again. It was so beyond the PG-13 scenes of courtship normally seen at parties. It was real, adult, sexy . . . a bit scary. As a result, the party had kind of turned their backs on them. The boys twisted their heads over occasionally, wistfully, but the girls mostly blotted it out. I had literally no idea how to handle the situation. I step-tapped and watched Jessica in a kind of disgusted awe. She was half pushing Matt off her, while simultaneously kissing him as if his mouth was an oxygen mask and she had pneumonia. The depression hit me again. I was at a party and no boys wanted to kiss me. Not even desperate Sean. Was this because I was disgusting? Or because they still thought I was mental? Would I ever kiss a boy? How come they all fancied Jessica so much? Why were all boys so obsessed with her? It wasn't fair.

A giant crash broke over the music and Abi and Eric fell to the ground, splayed under the collapsed dining table they'd been sitting on.

'Ouch!' Abi yelled. 'Ouch ouch OUCH.'

The music came off as we ran over to help them. Eric had fallen onto his wrist and clutched it to his chest while eyeballing the broken table in horror. I felt a hand on my arm, and found Jessica at my side, lipstick still all around her face. Matt went to help Eric up – though, just as he was almost standing, he let go, and Eric fell back onto the floor while everyone cheered. His face turned a deep red. 'FUCK YOU,' he yelled at Matt. 'And fuck you, Abi, you fat bitch. My parents are going to fucking kill me.'

Her mouth dropped open, and her friends were immediately at her side, stepping in front of her.

'Don't you call her that,' her friend, Jamelia, said.

'Yeah, Eric. You're such a dick.'

'Get out of my house!'

'Make us.'

Jessica tugged at my arm again. 'Fern?' She sounded as though she'd been shot with a thousand tranquiliser darts. 'Can we leave?' She strode towards the front door, bumping into the side of it twice before she made it through. I followed her out, leaving the chaos behind me, and I dashed after her while she ran around the corner so she wasn't in view of the house. I quickly rang my parents and told them we needed picking up early. 'No reason. Just the party got boring.'

'Your dad will be ten minutes,' Mum said. 'Are you sure everything is OK?'

'Oh yeah. Fine.'

But everything was far from fine. Jessica was the drunkest person the world had ever known. She slumped on the kerb. When I sat down next to her, she threw herself onto me, like she was pleading for her life. 'I'm sorry, Fern, I'm so so sorry.'

'It's OK. It's OK.'

'I've fucked up everything, haven't I? I knew I would.'

'It's going to be all right.'

'Do they hate me? They hate me, don't they? *I* hate me.'

'Look, my dad's here. Do you think you could try and act sober in the car?'

'You hate me too. I can see it in your eyes. You think I'm a slag.'

I hugged her. 'Please, Jessica, just act sober in the car.'

Dad appeared at the wheel of our Volvo wearing a coat over his pyjamas. I tried to act faux cheery to throw him off the scent.

'Thanks for getting us,' I chirped, folding Jessica into the back seat and putting her seat belt on. Her face smeared against the glass, and he noticed.

'Is she OK?'

'Oh yeah. We're just really tired.'

I got into the front seat next to him.

'How was the party?'

'Oh yeah. It was OK. Very . . . un-*antidisestablishmentarianism*.' I decided to throw in long words wherever I could. Surely a drunk person would never be able to pronounce such things.

Dad smirked. 'And that means?'

'You know. It was a . . . very interesting . . . er . . . *soirée*.'

'Soirée?'

'*Exceedingly.*'

'And was Eric's house OK when you left?'

'Oh, yes, it was left in an . . . *adequate* state.'

We heard Jessica moan behind us. Dad glanced into the rear-view mirror.

'Are you sure she's all right?'

'She's fine. She just might have . . . *gastroenteritis*?'

'Stop the car,' she yelled, sitting upright, making Dad swerve.

'Calm down, sit back down.'

'STOP THE CAR NOW I'M GOING TO BE SICK.'

'Shit.' Dad put his indicators on and drove up on the kerb. Before he'd even pulled the handbrake, Jessica had flung the door open, tumbled out onto the freezing pavement, and fell to her hands and knees, vomiting profusely onto the ground. Dad turned to me. 'Gastroenteritis?' he asked. 'Fern, honey, I'm not stupid.'

Jessica was paralytic. Dad had to crouch down and rub her back, while she kept saying, 'sorry, I'm so sorry' between retches. We carried her back into the car, thinking she would calm down. But, as we neared her estate, she started kicking the back of his seat.

'Stop now. I can walk from here.'

'Jessica. I need to make sure you get home safe.'

'No. NO! I don't want you to see where I live.'

'Jessica. Stop kicking my seat.'

'My house is so shit compared to yours. I don't want you to see it. Please. Let me walk. Please.'

My dad and I exchanged glances, and I was somewhat grateful to have a mature adult with me. I twisted in my seat, patting her knee. 'Jessica, hon, we don't care where you live, we just want you to get home safe.'

'I'm a mess. I'm such a mess.'

Dad indicated onto her road. 'Almost there, darling,' he said, braking outside a line of box houses.

'I'm sorry. I'm so so sorry.'

'Nothing to be sorry about.'

She tapped the window. 'It's this one.' We pulled up by a house at the end – where two dustbins and two doorbells revealed the house was two flats on top of each other. After her protests, I'd been expecting a crack den or something – but it was a perfectly legitimate-looking house. Small, yeah. But the driveway had a nice line of herbs growing up one side, the paint on the door was fresh.

'Fern? Do you want to make sure she gets to her door OK?'

I unbuckled my seat belt and opened the door for Jessica, where she stumbled out.

'Fern? I really am so sorry. Truly sorry.' She let me guide her to the front door. 'I know you don't want to be my friend any more. I've ruined everything.'

'It's going to be OK,' I kept repeating, though I wasn't sure if it was. It was going to take a lot to win Amy and Kim around. And I wasn't sure if I could be won around either. In twelve hours, Jessica had become a different person from the one I imagined. Sexually experienced, hedonistic, messy . . . It was a far cry from the girl I'd started to become friends with. The one who I chatted about Harry Potter with, or took silly photo booth pictures with.

'I can't believe what a mess I've made.' She tried and failed to get her key into the door.

'Shh, you just need to get some sleep.'

She grabbed both my hands, the door key clinking to the cold ground. 'No, but you don't get it,' she said urgently.

I looked down at our entwined palms. 'Get what?'

'I don't care about Matt. I don't care really even about Amy or Kim. I don't care about people in our stupid school. The only thing I care about, Fern . . . is you. And how I've fucked it up tonight, made things difficult for you. Made you not want to be my friend any more. . .' She was slurring, her words melting in together.

'Hang on . . . I'm not.'

'Look, I'm going to fix it. I'm not this person, I promise. Fern, you are so cool. You don't even know how cool you are. I want us to be best friends, don't you see? I'm so sorry. You're the only one here worth knowing. I'm sorry. So sorry.'

'Please stop saying sorry . . . I know . . .'

The door swung open and we turned towards the shadow in the entrance.

'Jessica?' her mum said. 'What's going on?'

It was the first time I'd met her mum, and, I can't lie, I was way more shocked by her mother than I was about her house. I'd assumed she'd be as glamorous as her daughter, but this woman was not that. Her hair was half badly dyed red and half grown-out grey, hanging limp around her face, which managed to be both haggard and plump at the same time.

Jessica sobered up fast. 'Sorry, Mum, I dropped my keys. This is my friend, Fern.'

'Nice to meet you,' I said. 'We're just dropping Jess home.'

'*We're?*' She craned around to see my dad, who waved from the car window. 'Oh, OK. Thank you. Honey, come inside, it's freezing.'

Jessica pulled me into one last hug, whispering, 'I promise I'm going to make it up to you,' before dashing inside.

I paused on her doorstep, trying to take it all in. I smiled. *She wanted me to be her best friend.*

'Fern?' Dad called. 'The engine's running.'

As he three-point turned out of the cul-de-sac, I waited for the lecture on the perils of alcohol. Or strict instructions never to see Jessica again. I shifted in the passenger seat, impatient for the axe to fall. But Dad started laughing.

'What's so funny?'

He shook his head. 'Sorry. It's just so . . . delightfully normal.'

'What is?'

'Picking up my drunk teenage daughter and her even drunker friend.' He laughed again.

'You're not angry?'

We pulled onto our road, slowed down when our house came into view. The big detached home, surrounded by garden, that I'd never really thought about until Jessica's shame about how it compared to her own. 'I'm not overjoyed,' he said. 'But, you rang me straight away, you made sure your friend was safe. It could've been worse. And, as I said, it's just . . . a bit of a novelty . . . you doing something most teenagers do that make parents worry, rather than . . .'

. . . *trying to kill myself.* We finished his sentence in silence in our own heads.

'Anything to make you proud, Dad.'

'Well, I mean, you're clearly grounded for the rest of the weekend!'

'Dad!'

'Let me talk to your mother.'

We parked up and I saw Mum peer at us from the sitting-room window. I wasn't sure what further verdict Dad was going to pass. 'Interesting friend you have there,' he said, as he found his keys for the front door.

Thirty-one

Jessica: Well that was an interesting evening. In other news, I'm dead.

Fern: Oh my God. My head. I hate you.

Jessica: Fern, I have a child to look after with this hangover.

Why are children so loud?

And demanding? And evil?

Please do not tell my former husband I refer to our child as evil.

The divorce hasn't gone through yet.

Fern: I love how you call him your 'former husband'. Got some Prince-esque vibes.

Jessica: My nemesis, formally known as hubby

Fern: I mean, if you were referring to him as 'hubby' I kind of see how it went wrong.

Jessica: Finally, I understand my divorce!

Seriously though, is your hangover really bad???

Fern: I woke up on the sofa with a bin next to me.

I didn't put the bin there

Jessica: Oh my God

This is hilarious but also terrible.

If you ever recover from your hangover, how do you feel about coming down someday soon? Meeting Bridget? Don't worry if it's too much of a mission

Fern: Oh, wow. It would be great to meet her. I'll look at my diary. I WFH on Fridays so may be able to bunk off one afternoon

Jessica: BRILLIANT. I am free basically every Friday. Can't wait for you to come down. Xxxx

And, once again, I found myself going to see Jessica, despite my misgivings. Not only that, I was skipping work to see her, answering her siren call. I promised myself I'd work on the train down, and honestly had the best intentions. I'd packed a bag with printouts of five articles that needed proofing, and I'd planned to go through my pitch inbox and figure out the next month of commissions. But, at London Bridge, I got way too distracted by all the things to do and buy, and when my train flickered up on the digital board, I cradled a coffee, a pastry, a vegan sausage roll, *Grazia* magazine, that day's *Times* newspaper, and a new posh notebook and pen. I collapsed onto the mostly empty train, setting out all my wares on the seats around me for the forty-five-minute journey. By the time I'd enjoyed my coffee, and wiped the croissant crumbs off my lap, there were only twenty minutes left. Not enough time to really concentrate, so I stared aimlessly out of the window. It was strange, doing this journey to my old home town after so many years, and I felt nostalgia crash over me as I stared out at this familiar moving view. My phone started ringing, jerking me out of my thoughts, and I saw it was my editor's number.

Shit.

'Derek? Hi, how are things going?' I said, praying we didn't go through a tunnel.

'Hi Fern, I'm good. It's Friday and all that. All well your end?'

I used my hand to cover the mouthpiece to drown out train noises. 'Yeah, just going through my pitch inbox. I'll send over anything good before end of play.'

'And ruin my weekend? Leave it 'til Monday morning, won't you?'

I relaxed a little. As editors went, I had won the absolute lottery working for Derek and *Gah!*. He was chill about however I worked, as long as I made my deadlines and unique users targets. I didn't want to be seen to be taking the piss, though.

'Monday it is. We've got a meeting at ten, don't we?'

'Yes. That's why I was calling actually.' I heard him shake some papers. 'Basically, it's good news, Fern. I read through your pitch and sample article for *The Other Side of the Tissue Box,* and it's fucking inspired. I want it to be a vertical, for sure. So we need to chat about how you can juggle this with your editing role.'

A smile melted through my face. 'Really? A vertical! You really think it's a good idea?'

'Stop fishing – if I say it's great, it's great.'

'OK, sorry.'

'Stop apologising too.'

'Sorry.'

He boom-laughed down the phone. 'Anyway, I'm ringing

to give you a heads-up that I'm letting publicity and marketing come to the meeting too, so we can really shape it. That all right?'

I nodded vigorously into the phone. 'That's brilliant. I need to double-check the college don't mind me writing it. It should be OK if I don't talk about any of the other students.'

'Yeah, yeah, we'll figure it out.'

'And . . .' I hesitated. 'Do you think maybe *Gah!* will be able to cover the expenses for my course fees?'

'Probably. How much is it? A few hundred . . . ?'

I swallowed. 'A few grand.'

'Jeez! OK, we definitely need a meeting. But I think we can make it worth the money. You'll be getting loads of copy – we'll save a fortune on freelancers. Maybe the college will give us a discount? As we're technically giving them free advertising . . . Hang on. I'm being dragged into a meeting. Congratulations, Fern, speak Monday.'

He hung up just as the train announcement boomed out, and I squealed like an excited mouse and hugged my phone to my chest. I'd pitched the idea for *The Other Side of the Tissue Box* a month or so ago: a series of articles exploring my journey from mental health patient to counsellor, and everything I learnt about therapy from 'the other side'.

Fern: Guess what? Derek loves the counselling course series idea, and *Gah!* may even PAY FOR THE COURSE?!!

Ben must've been between lessons because he replied right away.

Ben: Oh my God, Fern! Congratulations!!! Of course they loved it! It's a beyond brilliant idea. I'm so proud of you. Celebrate tonight?

Fern: I've got dinner at Heather's tonight, remember? I haven't seen her in bloody ages. Maybe we can go crazy at brunch tomorrow or something? Thank you! Couldn't have done it without you, as always. xxx

Ben: Brunch it is! Let's get hammered on mimosas, whatever they are.

I seeped back into my itchy train seat and profound bliss nestled into all my limbs again. I whispered, 'I love you, I love you so much,' to my phone. It had taken a few days to shake off my weird feelings towards Ben after seeing Jessica. A smell of suspicion lingered around him as her words tainted me, *'There's no such thing as "good men" and "bad men". They are the same men.'* But, his wonderful Ben-ness soon dislodged my paranoia. With every kiss, every hand squeeze, every lovely dinner chatting over our tiny table, just the two of us, the real Ben came into focus. He *was* a good man. Jessica was just in a bad place.

When the train spat me out on the familiar old platform of my home town, about two hundred memories smacked into me and I forgot my good news. It had been years since my parents moved away, but as the barriers gulped my ticket, I noticed nothing appeared to have changed. It was as if the town centre had been carefully preserved in Tupperware and pumped with suburban preservatives. The adult part of me was able to notice consciously how this town was in a time warp, and how different I was in comparison to it. But, already, a younger part of me was re-emerging, as if I'd stepped through a spell cloud on entry that returned me to my teen self. My posture hunched as I plodded through town. How I used to walk, back then, drawing myself in and then mourning nobody noticing me. My hand went to my face, tracing all its imperfections. My thin hair, slightly crooked front tooth, thighs slightly too big. What was going on? I started walking faster, trying not to see the shadows of past me loitering wherever I looked. Blinking away the memories.

'Oh my God, Fern? Is that you?'

It couldn't be. Liam's voice. Liam Gillingham, my crush from sixth form. It was just the same. I closed my eyes for a second, stunned this had happened within ten minutes of stepping off the train. Especially when I was here visiting Jessica, and Liam was so intrinsically linked to why I didn't trust her.

'Oh my God, Liam, hi. Wow, it's been ages.' Was this a sign? The memories that hit me as we went for an awkward hug–pat, both of us pretending we weren't taking in the other's ageing. It gave me a stab of joy, to see he was now mostly bald. His skin was grey, eyes crinkled, teeth yellowed. As I hugged him, I smelt cigarette smoke.

'What's it been? Almost fifteen years?' he asked.

'Yeah, I guess. My parents moved away ages ago. Oh my God, how are you?'

'Oh yeah. I'm good. Great.' Christ, I couldn't believe how bald he was. He used to have the most luscious head of hair, a curl that always fell over his green eyes – which, I noticed, were still just as striking, even with the red rims and wrinkles. I revelled quietly in his follicular misfortune, and didn't even feel guilty. This was all we had really, against men – male pattern baldness and small penises. They could slut-shame us, violate us, ruin our reputations, call us whores or frigid, bitches and mental, needy and desperate, boobs too small, too saggy, nipples too large. Too fat, or too skinny. The endless list of ways to degrade and destroy us, and our only weapon was to say they had a tiny dick and no hair. Sensing my judgement, maybe, his hand went to his head and I felt a small win at his insecurity. 'How are *you*? Are you still super famous?'

My eyes widened. Liam had kept tabs on my career? I never could've imagined he'd noticed, or cared. 'I wouldn't say that . . .'

'You're living in London now?' He smiled the smile I remembered so clearly, and the years plunged away.

Suddenly I wished I'd worn a better outfit, put more make-up on, done more lunges. 'Yes, in Hackney. With my *boyfriend*. So, you still live here?' I asked.

Boy, I needed this smugness hit. Especially from Liam. As he smiled again, a shock wave of memory surged through me. He'd smiled like that, just before leaning in to kiss me.

'Yeah, man. I'm still trundling along at Lloyds.'

'And, you're still in the band?'

'Trigger Warning?'

'Oh, no. The band you used to be in?'

'Scream Once for Yes?'

'No. I mean the one you were in at college?'

'Oooohhhh, Suicide Pact? Jeez.' He let out a whistle. 'You've been away a long time. We broke up years ago.' A woman pushing a double buggy said 'excuse me' loudly behind us, and I realised we were blocking the pavement. We stepped into a door alcove to continue chatting, and I felt a weird nostalgic thrill at standing so close to him, as if my teenage self had taken over my body, and was definitely going to write about this in her diary later.

'Oh . . . that's a shame,' I said. 'You guys were really . . . er . . . great.'

'Cheers. We had musical differences in the end, but I've lived to rock another day.' He said it without any irony whatsoever. 'Anyway,' his eyes glanced me up and down, and again, I wished I'd made even more of an effort, 'what are you doing down here?'

I paused for a beat. 'Visiting Jessica actually.'

'Jessica? She's back? Wow.'

'Hmm, yeah. She's moved back . . .'

'. . . from America, right?' I raised both eyebrows, unsure how he knew that.

'Yeah. Thought I'd come say hi. Old times' sake and all that.'

He smiled again, and my bloody knees turned to goo. 'You two were the closest two friends I've ever seen. It was like watching a cult. A very tiny cult.'

I grinned back. Our eyes locked. I wondered if he fancied me now. What would happen if I made a move, right then? A sudden fantasy of us gasping into each other's mouths and fucking in the alleyway around the corner, able to be discovered by anybody, as he whispered, *'I can't believe I let you go,'* into my neck.

'We were very close, yes.' I blinked away my strange vision and realised I needed to escape. 'Anyway, I better go,' I said finally.

'Of course. It was great to see you, Fern. Maybe I'll bump into Jessica next?' he said.

I knew bumping into her would be more of a big deal to him than bumping into me. And Teen Me still hurt knowing that.

We hugged awkwardly again and then I set off, imagining how I looked as I walked away. I ran through every single thing I'd said out loud and regretted it all. Wishing I was cooler, chiller, funnier . . . Feeling like I'd failed a test. A test that was beneath me, but I'd failed it anyway.

Just the once, I promised myself. *You are only returning here just this once.*

If I continued on this path, I would be undone.

'Fern, you made it! Come in.' Jessica smiled, welcoming me in to her mother's flat.

I felt weirdly angry at her after bumping into Liam, but strained a smile. I remembered it was a shoes-off house, and jumped about on the doormat, hobbling out of my ankle boots. The doormat still told me there was 'no place like home' and 'please remove your ruby slippers'. But there were new noises. The perky din of a Disney soundtrack.

'Bridget can't wait to meet you. Bridget, turn that down! Here, I'll take your coat. My mum's at Aldi, but she'll be back soon. She says hi.'

For a slobby Friday, Jessica still looked fantastic. She wore dark skinny jeans, with an oversized red jumper that fell off both slender shoulders, matched with a berry lip and messy bun. We stepped into the small living space, toys decorating the floor. The most stunning child I'd ever seen sat in the corner, playing with an Elsa doll.

'Bridget, say hello to my friend, Fern.'

The stunning child did not look up from her doll. 'Hello.'

'Bridget? Be polite, please, or no hot chocolate when we go to the . . .'

She jumped up and ran right over. 'Hi Fern,' she said, with immediate earnestness. 'It's very nice to meet you.'

'It's nice to meet you too.' I couldn't cope with how gorgeous she was. It was almost jarring – her dark lashes, angular face, long, luscious hair, and the confident way she held herself. Like Kate Moss was somehow trapped inside a seven-year-old's body.

'Can I go play with my dolls now?'

Jessica laughed at the rudeness. 'Yes. But not for long. We're going to the park soon, remember?'

Bridget was already walking away with her doll clutched in her hand.

'I do try.' Jessica pulled her jumper up over her shoulder. 'Cup of tea? Sorry again for not picking you up at the station. It's been one of those days.' She lowered her voice. 'Someone is missing their dad a bit.'

'Honestly, it's not a problem. Tea would be great.'

I leant against the wall as Jessica made the drinks, taking in the chaos. There were boxes everywhere – piled in Jenga stacks in the corners, cluttering the short walk to the bedroom. The door had been left open, and I saw an unmade double bed, and a child's mattress on the floor with a *Frozen* duvet cover on top. It had taken two years before Jessica let me into her flat. We'd always meet at mine, or in town – never at hers. Jessica was usually so defensive of her background, but she must've softened, because, as she handed me tea in a *Live*

Laugh Love mug, she said, 'Sorry about all the crap everywhere. As you can see, there is no space to put anything.'

She gestured to the sofa and we sank down into it, the battered leather letting out a hiss of air under us.

'It's fine. You're transitioning. Transitions are always messy.'

'True.' She laughed and held her pursed lips to the mug, managing to take a sip without damaging her perfect lipstick. I wondered what brand and colour it was, and what it would look like on me. Probably not as good. 'But, honestly?' she said. 'It's Mum's fault she still lives like this. Brendan and I offered to buy a bigger place, but she point-blank refused, and didn't speak to me for two months for even asking. Can you believe it?'

I could believe it. I knew where Jessica got her pride from.

'Anyway, it's not for too much longer. The final divorce stuff is still going through, then I can start house-hunting.'

'Do you know where you'll move to?'

'No idea yet. Anywhere but here.' She dropped her voice to another whisper. 'Although Brendan is putting the pressure on for me to be near him and the current replacement in London. I'm torn between moving there to make handover easier, or going as far away as possible to teach him a lesson about . . .' Bridget's beautiful head whipped up, tuning in with that amazing superpower children have at knowing a conversation is relevant to them. Jessica stopped talking, and got down on the floor. 'Now, honey, the all-important question is, are you going to let us play with you?'

Bridget raised an eyebrow, which I'd never seen a child do before. 'Only if you are Olaf,' she bargained. 'And your friend is Hans.'

Jessica and I shared a smile.

'I think we can work under those conditions,' she said.

Twenty minutes later, when Jessica's mum came back, we were all on the floor, hurtling our dolls through the air, following Bridget's dictatorship.

'No, Fern, he has to go over there. THERE! Behind the sofa.' I let the small child push me into the corner of the room. 'And Mum. Mum! Listen! Olaf is melting. You're not doing the melting properly.' Jessica had the snowman clutched to her stomach and was doing an overdramatic death scene on the cluttered floor. 'Wail, harder. That's better. Now. I am going to come rescue you. NOT YET. Keep melting!'

It was so surreal, watching Jessica flail on the floor, perfectly attuned to this little madam bossing her around. She was a totally different person to the one I remembered. This softness, this honesty, this openness. Maybe she really had changed? I marvelled at how the woman I knew – the one in a constant state of mess, with more mess poured on top of the mess – could be such a grounded parent. The door slammed shut, and her mum's familiar voice echoed, 'Hellooooooo?'

'Grandma's home.' Jessica got up mid-melt. 'Come on, we need to help her with the shopping.'

Her mum arrived on the threshold, cradling two packed Aldi bags, and looking about eighty years old. I almost gasped when I saw her. 'They'd run out of chocolate mousses so I had to get caramel yogurt. Oh, Fern, you're here. Hello!'

'Hi, Ms Payne.' I scrambled up to make myself useful. 'How have you been?'

'Oh, you know. The same.' She had the same battered voice

I remembered – where every sentence came out in a withered, defeated sadness.

Jessica took the bags – handing small items to Bridget, who, to my amazement, opened the appropriate cupboards and put things away without complaint.

'It must be lovely having Jessica back after all these years?' I tried.

Her mum huffed. 'Yes, well, obviously you'd want it under better circumstances. I did warn Jessica he appeared too good to be true.'

I swear it was a missed opportunity our mothers had never met and formed a 'my thoughts and feelings leave no room for yours' coalition.

Jessica rolled her eyes at me as she shoved tins into an already stuffed cupboard. 'And I'm sure you're just devastated to be proven right, Mum. And shh . . . Bridget, remember?'

Bridget didn't even acknowledge the dig at her father. She had found the caramel yogurts and was staring at them like Indiana Jones and that egg from the beginning of *The Temple of Doom*.

'Mummy? Can I have one of these?'

'No, honey, they're for after dinner.'

'But I want one now. I want one now, *and* I want one after dinner.'

Jessica bent over and prised the yogurts out of her daughter's vice grip, putting them at the back of the fridge. 'I know you do, sweetheart, but I'm afraid they're only for later.' Jessica smushed her into a hug. 'Now, how about we go to the park with your new friend, Aunty Fern?'

★

We stepped out into the cold, and were yanked through town by Bridget. I noticed every change in shopfront, every tree that wasn't there any more. I opened my mouth to tell Jessica I'd bumped into Liam, then found myself saying nothing. He was one of the many things we still hadn't talked about. I added it to our growing list. I noticed that people's heads turned as we passed them. People double-taking. At first I thought it was the usual Jessica effect, until I followed their eyeline and saw they were reacting to her daughter instead. Eyes flickered, gaze loitering longer than usual, trying to hide it while Bridget stomped past, telling me how high she could go on a swing.

When we reached the park, Bridget broke free, running in her light-up shoes towards the playground. 'Be careful,' Jessica called, but made no effort to catch up. We followed her in as she was swallowed by the colourful chaos of all the other children playing, while parents sank onto benches, exhausted, clutching cups of coffee. We found a spare bench and the cold from the wood bled through my jeans as we watched Bridget play. She soon appeared at the top of the giant wooden pirate ship and waved proudly at us. 'I don't know how to say this without sounding weird,' I said, waving back, '. . . but your child is unnervingly pretty. I can't quite cope with it.'

Jessica laughed. 'No, I get it. It's weirder when people pretend it's not the case! Everyone is freaked out by her. She gets model-scouted all the time, but I can't imagine it's a good thing for her to do. I don't want her to define herself by how pretty she is.'

I glanced at Jessica sideways. Wary. Was this coming from a place of personal development? Jessica had been defined by her attractiveness the whole time I'd known her, but we'd never spoken about that explicitly. We'd never acknowledged the huge win she had over me – the win she had over *every* woman. 'I don't know,' I said. 'I mean, she's going to have to figure out what it means at some point.'

Jessica twisted to me, her eyes dark. 'You know what I hate? She's so *young*. She's a child, and, please don't think I'm weird for saying this, but, men. When they see her, when they walk past her. I see it. Something. In their faces. So many of them look at her in this way that . . . OK . . . they're looking at my child. My actual child. And I know they're thinking about what she'll look like when she is older and what they'd do. Does that sound mad?'

I struggled to keep my face neutral. 'She's only, what, seven?'

'I know that. They know that. And you can see them be grossed out by themselves. It's so . . . I dunno. Maybe I'm too dark these days. Too distrusting.'

Distrusting of men? This was never something Jessica had suffered from. This new knowingness was one of the many new sides to her that made me feel safer, *more* trusting towards her, even after encountering Liam. I located Bridget, who was queuing at the top of the slide. Her face was easy to find as it was so distinctive compared to the chubby blobs of other children's faces. And she held herself already with Jessica's same odd knowingness. Poised, a bit guarded. As if she was aware people looked?

Jessica misread my silence. 'Hey, Fern? Look, I wanted to say so in person. I really am sorry for the other night. For going off on all those rants.'

'Huh?'

'I worried I went a bit too far. Infected you a bit with my mistrust.'

'You . . .' I smiled. 'Well, OK, so I came home and chose not to share a bed with Ben.'

Her face dropped. 'Oh my God – really? See, this is what I mean. I'm so sorry.'

'I mean, I was very, very drunk. I could've just as easily, in that state, accused him of looking at our kettle in the wrong way.'

She laughed, but her eyes were wide with sorrow. 'No, you wouldn't. He sounds great. I'm sure he is great. I mean, if he's with you, then he clearly has amazing taste. I'm so clearly going through something right now . . . not just the divorce. Everything . . .'

I turned towards her, the cold spreading on the new bits of my legs touching the bench. 'What do you mean, *everything*?'

'Just . . . my relationship with men. All men. This divorce. It's just made me re-evaluate everything. Who I am. What I've done. How I find worth . . . I don't want anything to do with men any more. I'm so done.'

Wow, she was saying it. She was finally going there and saying it. We were venturing together, hand in hand, to the Land of the Unspoken. My stomach could hardly take it. I wasn't sure if I wanted to join her there. If I was able to handle the pain of what had happened between us.

'When Brendan left, I realised I had no one to scoop me up, nobody to turn to. No real friends, not really. I've never found it . . . easy, getting on with women. They hate me. They always have. I'm only naming what's true.'

Oh God, it was almost too raw to hear. 'Come on. Nobody *hates* you . . .'

'They did. They really did. And that's the thing though.' Jessica looked at me, her dark lashes laden with tears. 'Fern, you're the only one who never did. You were . . . the best friend I ever had. And, I fucked it up. And then you hated me too. I know I fucked it up.'

There it was. The truth. Escaping in frozen vapour from her lips. We both knew why we'd lost touch. I couldn't believe I was finally getting my apology, was finally getting to see her self-realisation. I'd longed for this moment for so long, wanted to forgive her for so long, but she'd never apologised and given me a chance. And there was only one appropriate response to such vulnerable honesty – the same in return. I took a gasp, inhaling all the tears I'd cried over Jessica, all the grief I'd carried about losing her friendship. Not even losing it. Forcibly pushing it away, because she'd given me no other choice.

'You did fuck up,' I whispered, my own eyes now brimming with tears. 'You really did.'

Her head fell, her hair obscuring her face, and I felt an instant surge of guilt. This Jessica wasn't the Jessica I was mad at. Wasn't the one I needed an apology from. 'But, hey, come on. It was a very long time ago . . .'

She held up a hand to stop me, her face still obscured. 'No, Fern. Don't. You're right. I fucked it. And, for what it's worth, and over ten years too late, I really am sorry. Honestly, so fucking sorry.' My throat glued itself shut, the cold air caught in my mouth.

'It's OK,' I said eventually. And, on that cold bench, with

the playground dissolving around us, I realised it *was* OK. At least, I thought it was OK. I wanted it to be OK. I'd missed her too much for it not to be. 'And . . . cutting you out. I know it was cold, but . . . I . . .'

'No. I got it. I was devastated, of course. Angry, even. But I got it. I just didn't want to admit to myself what had happened.'

'Maybe it wasn't such a big deal . . .'

'It was. I knew it was. And I'm sorry, and I'm so happy you're here, and you're letting me apologise. I feel so lucky for that. For this second chance. Cos, Fern? I really want us to be friends again.'

I looked into her eyes and the strength of love I felt for her was almost romantic. She eyed me wearily, her heart held out in her hand. I took a breath and decided to take it.

'I really want us to be friends again too.'

Fourteen

January 2001

It turned out Jessica and I didn't need the others. We sat, cross-legged, on my bed facing one another, palm to palm, eyes locked, under my collage wall. I tuned in, staring into Jessica's eyes for answers, noticing how perfectly she'd blended two shades of green eyeshadow.

'OK, so I'm thinking of a number between one and five,' she said. 'Are you ready?'

I nodded.

'Go.'

She projected the number to me and I took deep breaths, letting the message come through. Two . . . no . . . three. It was definitely . . . 'Three,' I said.

She let out a squeak. 'Yes!'

'No way.'

'Yes. Oh my God! We did it, we're psychic.' We started laughing from our stomachs, feeling elated and a little bit freaked out.

'Let's not get too excited. It might've just been a fluke. My turn.'

Jessica redid her ponytail. 'You're right. Phew. Let's take a moment to cleanse ourselves.' We closed our eyes and waved our hands over our faces.

'I'm going to think of a colour this time,' I told her. 'Are you ready?'

She nodded and we lifted our palms so they kissed again. I took a deep breath and tuned into my psychic power, ready to broadcast to my best friend. 'OK, go,' I said, finding her gaze again.

'*Green,*' I whispered in my head 'til it itched. '*Green, green, green, green, gr—*'

'Green!'

I screamed and rolled off the bed onto the carpet, kicking my legs up into the air. 'We're psychic!' Jessica rolled off too, giggling. 'We have powers. Oh my God. Shit! What are we going to do with them?' I was practically hyperventilating. I'd kind of always suspected I was a psychic, but to have it proved, using such scientific methodology, was almost too much to bear.

'We should try one more time,' I said, twisting onto my stomach to get off the floor and back onto my duvet. 'Three out of three.'

'Right, do you want to project, or shall I?'

'You can.'

'What category shall we pick this time? Colours again?'

'Yeah, but not a too obscure one,' I said, already wishing I hadn't tempted fate by asking for a third go-around. 'Not, like, azure or something.'

Jessica chuckled, shaking the bed. '*Azure.* What a word.'

We lost ourselves into giddy hysterics for five whole minutes, which kept reigniting whenever we said the word 'azure' out loud. My stomach felt as if I'd done a hundred sit-ups. 'Oww,' I kept saying, clutching my stomach. 'Oww.'

'Azure.'

'Stop it. It hurts.'

'Mine hurts too.'

'Stop making me laugh.'

'You stop making me laugh.'

'. . . *azure* . . .' And we were gone again.

By the time we'd calmed down, Jessica had green eyeshadow rivers carved across her high cheekbones, and I was actually having to hold my stomach down to stop laughing.

'OK OK OK. I'm going to stop laughing on the count of three. One, two, three.' Jessica snapped her fingers and regained control again – sat up in a cross-legged position. I clambered to copy her. 'Are you ready for me to transmit?'

'One, two, three, go.' Jessica launched right into it, even though I'd been about to yell 'wait'. Too late. I met her face, tried to wipe my mind, and blusteringly attempted to tune into her frequency. I couldn't get the word 'azure' out of my head. The laughter threatened to spill once more. No no no, Fern, concentrate. I took another deep breath, listened for her whisper. *Pink? No . . . blue, maybe? An inky blue? No . . . pink. I think it is pink.*

'Pink,' I said hopefully, and Jessica's eyes fell with genuine disappointment.

'No,' she said, wilting. 'Black.'

'Oh, shit.'

'Maybe we don't have powers after all?'

We didn't speak for a moment, just bathing in the letdown of ourselves. 'I just couldn't stop thinking of the word "azure",' I told her.

When I looked up, Jessica was beaming. 'Me neither! I kept trying to think black, but I was really just thinking "azure azure azure".'

'So maybe we did it right after all?'

'We did! Three out of three!'

'Ahhh!' I stepped up onto my bed and started jumping. Jessica screamed and joined in, until Mum yelled up the stairs, asking what the hell was going on. We seat-dropped back down, and lay our heads on my pillow, our hair meshing together.

'Azure,' I said, out loud, reigniting the laughter once more. 'Azure.'

I felt relaxed and happy and myself for the first time in so long, connected to the world rather than lost in my darkness. I was so wondrously grateful Jessica had insisted on this sleepover.

The doorbell rang.

'The pizza's here,' Mum called up the stairs.

But there was no need. We were already hurtling down the stairs like a stampede of delirious elephants.

And so, it had become just the two of us. Well, more like the one point five of us, as, weirdly, after coming off my medication abruptly without telling anyone about it, I wasn't doing very well. The Monday after Eric's party, our little social orbit of school had been a festering mess of gossip. People were unsure of what part of the night to focus on. They didn't know whether to spread Abi breaking the table, and the quiet, inevitable fat-shaming, or the three-act structure of Jessica's downfall. The tequila worm, the getting with Matt, and the giant friendship spat that had followed. The boys remained oblivious and unimpeachable, as always.

'I'm really sorry about blanking you at school today,' Amy whispered down the phone. 'It's just, Kim is still so upset.'

'I'm quite upset too. I've not done anything wrong.'

'You didn't need to take Jessica's side.'

'I didn't. I just said, we shouldn't argue over boys. It's so dumb.'

'I just . . . don't trust her, Fern. I didn't want to say this before, but she's always made me feel uneasy. And look at what she did. First chance she got.'

I sighed. 'I think she made a mistake, yeah. But she said sorry.'

'Kim and I just aren't comfortable hanging out with her. We've talked, and we're happy to still hang out with you separately. But not if she's there.' She used this weird, grown-up voice and I knew she was secretly congratulating herself for acting 'maturely'. 'Sorry, Fern. We're happy to see you. Just not her.'

I could've chosen the other side. Could've heeded Amy's warning. But, despite all the drama, there was a magnetic pull to Jessica. I kept remembering her saying how cool I was outside her house, and not being able to stop grinning. Plus, it wasn't my love interest she'd got with. It was just stupid Matt, who Kim never had a chance with anyway. Part of me saw Jessica getting with him as retribution for how she'd stolen

Amy from me. And that twisted logic saw us merge into a unit. A twosome. Jessica and I. Fern and Jessica. Sewn at the hip. And yet the new friendship couldn't save me from my depression. I was slowly falling into a thick fog again. Losing my grasp on what was real and what wasn't. Attending school felt like walking through a fading photograph. In lessons, teachers' voices sounded like a low humming noise. I'd hurt myself just to feel something, anything. The darkness of the world felt too overwhelming and I detached from my body often, floating off. The only things able to pull me back into gravitational orbit were self-harm, or the healthier option of Jessica. A text. A joke. A lunchtime spent together laughing in the tucked-away table in the school library. But, sometimes even she couldn't tether me. I missed one day of school, telling my mother I didn't feel well. Then, the following week, I missed another, faking a really heavy period. A month later, I'd stopped with the charade entirely. I just plain didn't go in on the days I couldn't face it. Mum handled it brilliantly, of course. *'I can't believe you're doing this to us again,'* was a very supportive stance to take, alongside, *'What did I do wrong to make you like this?'* Whereas Dad quietly rang the school and explained, and I was sent work to do at home. But I hid the reality behind my absences from Jessica.

Fern: Wont b in 2day again. So soz. This fckin bug keeps coming bk

Jessica: Oh no! Poor u xxx

Fern: Did I miss much 2day? Sorry I couldn't come in again.

Jessica: Not much. Just spent lunchtime with the boys. Matt still being weird.

Fern: He LOVES u
Jessica: He's such a child
Fern: Still sick. Mb bk on Fri? Sorry Im so crap
Jessica: Stop being sorry! I just want you WELL

I had no idea what she knew, or what she'd no doubt been told. She still hadn't asked. I knew there was only a limited time left when I could hide the truth from her. Or at least dispel the horrid rumours that had probably been whispered during my absences. But, on the days I was in school, we were in such a honeymoon-period glow, I didn't dare ruin it. I was too scared she might realise how dark I could be.

The pizza delivery stank out the whole house. Mum and Dad met us in the kitchen, claiming their own box, fighting us for half the bottle of Pepsi that went with it.

'We're psychic,' I told them, as if I'd been accepted into Oxford. 'We just did a test now, and we are totally psychic.'

'That's right,' Jessica said, her eyes still glowing. 'They're going to hire us to solve mysteries soon.'

Mum sighed, while Dad broke into a big smile. If my parents had any reservations about Jessica after the party, they'd been displaced by how much she cheered up their troubled daughter. I watched Dad glance at Jessica as she went to our fridge and took out the array of dips we'd bought from Sainsbury's earlier that day. She was always treating our house as if she lived here, which she practically did – coming over after school to watch CITV with me on the days I hadn't gone in, bringing me my sheets of homework diligently, and never making me feel bad about not being at school.

'Is that right?' he said. 'You can read minds, huh?'

'Yes, and we're going to do magic later. That reminds me, do you guys have a fire hydrant?'

'No fire,' Mum said, while Dad laughed. 'Seriously, Fern. It's nice to see you happy, but no fire inside.'

'Fine, fine, no fire.'

We took our laden trays back up to my bedroom and ate with gleeful abandon – dangling drooping pizza slices over our mouths like a Roman emperor eating grapes. We dunked the crusts into creamy pots of dip, discussing how best to mix the various options into the best 'mega dip'. Before our bodies could even acknowledge what we'd done to them, we moved onto the crisps, sweets, and the chocolate. Then we lay on my carpet, backs against the bottom of my bed, listening to the The Smiths CD I'd bought. We spent some time chatting to people online in a music chat room, getting into a private chat with a boy called *Fisher* who claimed to be sixteen, until he sent us a photograph of him masturbating and was clearly forty years old. We screamed and clicked off the screen and ran away from the family computer, laughing. Eventually it was time for magic, and I glanced down at the relevant page of the *Teen Witch Handbook* I'd bought from WHSmith, and instructed Jessica on how to make a magic circle.

'We need to say *"as I will it, it will be"* over and over,' I explained.

Jessica saluted. 'Perfect. As I will it, it will be.'

As I watched her set up the candles, I wondered what on earth someone as pretty as her could possibly wish for. We poured table salt around us, lit candles, and, with one eye half open on my hot pink spell book, we put our 'manifestations' out into the universe. I prayed that I would get better. I prayed that I wouldn't totally fuck up my exams with my relapse. I prayed that boys may finally start to fancy me. And, finally, I prayed that Jessica and I would be best friends for ever, and that, maybe, she'd still accept me when she found out the truth about me. I prayed until a candle fell over onto my bedroom carpet and the smoke alarm went off.

We were still laughing at 2 a.m. My windows were wide open to let out the remaining smell, and a late-night furniture rearrangement covered the scorch mark.

'I still can't believe your parents didn't ground you.' Jessica was zipped up in her sleeping bag, with the hood over her head, so she looked like a fuzzy glow-worm. We'd braided our hair before bed, so we'd have matching kinks the next morning.

'They're such soft touches at the moment,' I admitted, staring up at the ceiling.

'Why's that?'

I hesitated, dancing on the cusp of the truth. If I told her who I really was, there would be no coming back. Did I trust her? I'd trusted Amy . . . and now I hadn't spoken to her properly in over a month.

'I . . . Well, they're just so relieved I'm mostly back at school,' I started. The moment I'd said it, I was frantically trying to think of a different story instead. I turned over in bed and looked down at my Jessica glow-worm on the air mattress. Her eyes were patient, kind.

'Back at school?'

'Yeah. I, umm, I stopped going to school, for a while last year.'

'How come?'

'I . . . Well, I bet everyone at school's already told you.'

'I don't want to hear about this from them. I want to hear about it from you.'

That was the moment I fully trusted her. When she quietly confirmed my worst fears that, yes, people at school still whispered about me. She didn't deny something painful to placate me, but she also didn't revel in telling, to get off on the drama of being the one who got to tell. It was so . . . *not secondary school*, and I loved her for it.

'So, I've always been a bit . . . dark, I guess? Like, in my head a lot,' I started, sitting up against my headboard and huddling my knees up to my chest. 'I just have all these awful whirring thoughts and then they get too much, and, I suddenly go from feeling everything, to feeling nothing at all. If that makes sense? I sort of . . . numb out. Sometimes for just a minute or two, sometimes hours, sometimes . . . well . . . weeks.'

She pushed herself up in the sleeping bag, but I couldn't look at her face.

'Last year, I disconnected for a really long time. Like I'd stumbled through this door into another realm, where everything was dialled down to a whisper, and I couldn't find the exit anywhere. I couldn't feel anything for ages, apart from this kind of dull, melancholic ache, this certainty that everything was pointless. That I was worthless. Unloveable . . . I'd keep making myself sleep, hoping, when I woke up, I'd be back in the real world again, but every time I woke up, I was still stuck. Nothing to look forward to. Nothing to care about. Nothing to live for . . .'

'That sounds really scary.'

I nodded and coughed, as the agony of the memory raged up my throat. 'It was really scary. And nobody seemed to understand it. My mum kept telling me to stop being selfish, like I was doing it deliberately to stress her out, and then she'd argue with Dad when he defended me, so I stopped trying to explain it, and I was really pissing Amy off, as I was so shit to hang out with, and I wasn't doing my homework, and getting really bad marks, and I didn't even care really, I was just passing the time until I was allowed to go to sleep again. And then . . . then . . .'

I sniffed and wiped my nose with the back of my hand. There was a rustling noise and glow-worm Jessica climbed onto my bed, hood still tied around her face. She reached out of her sleeping bag and her hand found my hand. 'And then?'

'Well, I'd been . . . er . . . deliberately hurting myself for a while. As that kind of, er . . . helped me feel again.' Her hand squeezed hard. The webs of our fingers squishing together. 'And, one day, it was so bad and I felt so lost and saw no point in anything any more. I wanted an exit route, a way of getting out of this numbness I was trapped in, and I thought the only way to get out was to rip myself out, so I . . .'

I started weeping. Head on my knees. Back jerking. The memories of that day regurgitating through my head. The desperation. The cold decision. The calmness that descended as I went to the mirrored bathroom cabinet to find a razor, staring at myself, imagining my reflection not existing any more. The way the world fell quiet. The nick. The blood.

The sound of my heart racing. The blood, the blood, the blood. Doing what it was supposed to do – ripping me a portal back into the realm of the real, but then the blood wouldn't stop, and I was back, but it was too late, I was going, going, gone . . .

'I don't remember screaming,' I said, as tears sloshed down my face, the words gasping out. 'But I must've done, because Mum came running up the stairs and couldn't get in because I'd locked the bathroom door. She looked under the gap and saw . . . blood, and had to ring 999. I don't remember any of that. I mean, like, I didn't pass out or anything, but, honestly, I don't remember anything until, like, two days later, when I was still in hospital. I'm not sure I want to really. I'm kind of glad it's gone.'

My head fell against the wall in exhaustion, my knees slumped to one side. Reliving it always plugged my body back into it again. I expected Jessica to recoil at this point. To find an excuse to flee in the middle of the night. Or to change the subject, and then freeze me out at school the following week. I prepared myself for the pain and rejection. But instead she wiggled up so her head was level on my pillow. The wide whites of her eyes glowed in the dim light.

'You must've been so scared,' she whispered.

'I was . . . I still am.'

She stayed there throughout the whole sorrowful monologue as I explained the long dull recovery story to her. Of what it was like in the hospital, of all the CBT exercises I've been given, the side effects of my medication. I told her about Amy replacing me with Kim. Of how my parents treated me like I was made of bone china on one hand, and slightly resentfully on the other. 'The whole time, in family therapy sessions, Mum kept saying, *'I don't get it, we've given her everything, I don't get it'*, like I'm just this ungrateful brat or something. She was so upset about her . . . I dunno . . . *failure* of a daughter, there was no space for me to feel how I needed to feel.'

'That's horrid,' Jessica said. 'It's not like you've chosen this, have you?'

I shook my head so furiously that the tears flew off my face like paratroopers. 'Of course not. My therapist says maybe that's why I'm like this. That my mum, as she's so . . . "my-mum-like", I've learnt maybe that there isn't space for my emotions, so that's why I numb out. But then I feel guilty, because she does really love me and tries her best with her mad daughter. It's hell. Like, everyone at school thinks I'm crazy. I haven't even kissed a boy yet, and nobody will come near me cos they think I'm a psycho. I've lost my best friend. I'm fucking up my GCSEs. I've ruined my skin for ever.'

'Can I see?' Jessica asked. Not out of curiosity, but something else. I pulled up the sleeve of my pyjama top, though it would've been less intimate if I'd stripped naked. 'My body is a mess,' I said, as I saw her take in the cross-hatching of old white scars and new red ones across the light hair on my forearms. The hair sparser where the scar tissue was too solid to push through. 'It's all on my legs too . . .' I wiggled out of my pyjama bottoms and Jessica gasped a little. I thought it was disgust at first, and was about to pull them back up in shame, when she said, 'Oh Fern, it looks so painful. You poor thing.'

Revealing my scars would be a barrier to intimacy for the rest of my life. An additional concern to revealing my naked body. Something always running through my mind as kisses got more urgent and hands pawed under my bra – tugging me away from any desire and into worry about whether to tell, would they notice, what would they think, how terribly un-erotic the whole thing was. But, the one thing I held onto, was the first experience I had of showing them to someone – Jessica. How my new friend saw the depths of my pain, and it only cemented the bond between us. Anyone who recoiled or scorned didn't deserve entry to my inner life. How do you ever repay someone for a gift like that?

I wiggled back into my pyjamas and we were both silent, not sure what to do with all the intimacy floating between us. Jessica pushed her hood down, revealing her stunning head. 'Thanks for telling me all that,' she said. 'I'm a bit . . . scared about what to say next, in case I get it wrong, but, firstly, don't worry about not kissing a boy yet. Or anything like that.'

'I don't want to die a virgin though.'

'You won't! And you need to get better first, before worrying about stuff like that.'

'What do you mean?'

'Well, Fern, you've stopped coming to school. And some of those cuts look fresh. What's going on? Are you . . . thinking of . . . you know, again?'

'I . . . I don't know.' The question made me start to cry. 'You're going to think I'm so stupid and weird and . . .'

'I won't. Just tell me.'

The entirety of it came out. About secretly coming off my medication. How the sadness and the numbness was creeping back. Of feeling ashamed and disgusted and angry at myself, up to the point where I felt nothing, only too exhausted to get out of bed. She listened into the small hours, hand on my knee, judgement never once creeping into her head-nods and her hand-holds. Then she clutched me so hard it hurt.

'You've got to promise me, Fern,' she said, her voice laced with urgency. 'That you're going to start taking your pills again. And that, if you ever feel like doing anything to yourself, you've got to tell me. Promise? You've got to talk about it.'

'I can't put that on you.'

'Promise me? Or I'm leaving. I will get out of this sleeping bag and I will walk home in the middle of the night.'

'OK, Jesus Christ, I promise you.'

'Even if it's the tiniest thought, you reach out.'

'OK, OK.'

'Because, if you don't, I will kill you. I will fucking kill you, I swear to God. Even if you're already dead . . .'

In the midst of this melodrama, I let out a giggle. She laughed too. The mattress shook beneath us as laughter rocked our bodies – the release valve for this moment we were too young to fully comprehend.

'I promise you,' I said, through new tears, these ones of joy.

Thirty-one

I could tell Heather was worked up from the second she opened her flat door.

'Fern! You're here. I fear the risotto is ruined. It's OK, there's Deliveroo.'

I handed over my garish bunch of train-station tulips. 'I'm sorry I'm late. I swear Victoria Station was like the last train out of Saigon.'

'Don't worry. The risotto was ruined before you were late.' She strode down the communal hallway, forgetting to keep the fire doors open for me as I ran after her. 'What were you doing at Victoria, anyway?'

We pushed into her delightful flat, greeted by the warmth of Farrow & Ball on the walls and the aroma of mushrooms in garlic sauce. Her wife, Katie, nodded hello from where she was making cocktails in a rose-gold shaker.

'I actually came from my home town,' I said, putting my bag on the floor by the sofa. 'I was meeting an old friend there today. It was very fucking surreal and I'm most glad for any alcohol being provided.'

Heather brandished the tulips to her wife and they swapped roles efficiently and silently – Heather shaking the margaritas, while Katie located a vase. I stepped into the kitchen area and spotted a congealed grey mush in a saucepan on their stove.

'Oh my God, your home town was hilarious.' Heather started pouring the cocktail into frosted glasses that Katie had rimmed with salt. 'Do you remember when I came to stay in the summer after first year? Before we flew to Thailand? You took me to that awful club.'

'I mean, Selfridges is an institution.'

Heather spluttered with laughter. 'They played "My Hips Don't Lie" three times in one night,' she told Katie, who smiled but didn't laugh. 'Three.'

'As I said, an institution.'

'And, there was literally not one shop or restaurant or cafe that wasn't a chain. Not one.'

'OK, Heather, we weren't all lucky enough to grow up in fucking Primrose Hill.'

'My parents bought their house back when it—'

'—only cost ten pee and a handjob to the estate agent. I know, I know. And now it's worth twelve billion pounds.'

She grinned and carried the drinks over to their circle of velvet chairs. 'Fucking boomers, right? It's not fair.'

'Hmm.'

I reached out and took a Kettle Chip from the hand-thrown bowl Katie brought over. I tried not to feel bitter, but it had all come as quite a shock to me, aged twenty-seven, when most of my friends who I'd thought were also broke, suddenly, quietly, started moving out of gross houseshares and buying new-build flats in gentrifying areas of London. All of them going red and muttering phrases like *'well, Mum and Dad said it made sense to give me this money now to save on inheritance tax'*. Heather was one of them. Maybe I would've been too if my dad's company hadn't fallen apart.

'So, who were you meeting?' Heather leant back in her chair and ran her hand through her mad curl of hair.

'Umm, this girl, Jessica. You may remember her? She came up to visit me in first year.'

I waited to see recognition cross my friend's face. Heather was there the night everything fell apart.

'Jessica . . . Jessica.' She took a slurp of her drink and found inspiration. 'Oh yeah. I think I remember. Is that the girl who got totally obliterated?'

I nodded as the memory flooded in like iced water. 'That's her.'

'I didn't know you were still in touch.'

'She moved to America, but she's back now.'

'God, it's all coming back to me now. She was, like, insane pretty, wasn't she? She was hell-bent on getting trashed, from what I can remember.' She barked out a laugh of nostalgia. 'God. Uni. And Jessica. What a hot mess.'

I nodded. As usual, Heather's words were exactly the right ones. I took a deep slug of my drink. 'That's one way of putting it.'

After the first round, we traipsed over to the stove to see if the risotto could be resuscitated, before Heather ordered artisan pizzas to rescue us. Katie stared at the pan and bit her lip, muttering her first utterance of the evening.

'Honestly, Heather, your only job was the risotto.'

She laughed and pulled Katie in for a big hug and kiss, while she squirmed. 'I know. I'm sorry. I got distracted. I'll pay for the pizzas myself.'

'We're married. Your money is my money.'

'But it's a gesture. A gesture.'

I started rummaging in my bag for my purse. 'I'm happy to pay for my pizza?'

Heather batted me away. 'Don't be ridiculous. We invited you over for dinner. It's our fault I cannot concentrate for forty minutes. Shall we have some red wine?' She didn't wait for our reply and uncorked a bottle of merlot, swilling it into three globe glasses, before we all returned to our plush velvet chairs.

'Was work bad today?' I asked. Heather worked for a drastically underfunded NHS sexual health clinic, so the answer was almost always 'yes'.

She rolled her eyes. 'Oh, you know. The usual. Two women with STIs who didn't understand how they could have caught them as they're in long-term relationships. It's always such a blast telling them their boyfriends are cheating and not using condoms.'

It hurt every time she reminded me of this daily occurrence. 'So a quiet day then?'

'Yeah. But at least the new nurse means I'm not working back-to-back shifts any more, so that's something. How's your coil? Strings where they need to be?'

I smiled and nodded. It had taken most of our friendship

to let Heather see my vagina, and I was mad at myself for not making full use of this gynaecological resource.

'It's all tucked in comfortably,' I said. 'Ready for its bedtime story.'

We all sniggered and caught up on each other's lives as we waited for the delivery. They were both wonderful about my *Other Side of the Tissue Box* news. Heather even pulled me in for a hug, saying, 'You've come so far, I am legit so proud.' I absolutely loved coming to theirs. Their flat was exactly how I would decorate my own dream house – from their paint colour choices (one of which was honestly called *Elephant's Breath*), metallic lamps with giant light bulbs, and a gallery wall of prints I would've picked out myself. 'We only need three more houseplants, and a framed sketch of a naked woman, and then we get gold platinum millennial cards,' Heather said. I asked Katie what artsy books her indie company were publishing, and then pretended, as always, I understood what the hell she was talking about. I nodded a lot as she explained her recent acquisition from an up-and-coming conceptual artist who made all her work out of dried spaghetti. Heather filled me in on her current list of furies – which ranged from erasure of the word 'lesbian' to 'inadequate pain relief for gynaecological procedures' – her mouth a Gothic lipstick stained from the wine. The pizza took for ever to arrive, and the red wine painted me mellow. I curled up on my dusty pink chair, and let Heather rant on about the bizarre male domination of gynae surgery, smiling at her with love. I worried often about alternative-reality Fern, who didn't meet Heather at university. From the second she strode into my room, took me down to the Students' Union for the 'Freshers'

Mingle' before promptly tugging me back out again and calling it 'a Rape Myth Masterclass', my life fell into a *before* and *after*. Heather was my very own Morpheus, exposing basically every problematic thing at university to me, of which there was a lot. It was a surprise when she met Katie in third year, and brought her back to ours for lasagne. Katie was shy and had basically no political opinions whatsoever. Whenever you asked her view on anything other than conceptual art, she'd just shrug and say 'I don't really know enough about that to say'. It infuriated Heather but also made her a calming influence.

Their buzzer finally went, and we stuffed ourselves on lukewarm sourdough crusts, battling over the one tiny dipping sauce that came with it. Heather shouted, 'Broccoli, I made broccoli,' and dumped some cold, purple tenderstems onto our plates. We each had a second glass of red, and made appropriate *oooh* noises when Katie delivered her homemade chocolate cheesecake to the table.

'Some of us kept up our side of the cooking bargain,' she said, looking pointedly at Heather as she cut three generous slices.

'Oh my God, this is gorgeous. Thank you. How did you make it?'

'Found the recipe on the BBC.'

'That's where the mushroom risotto recipe came from too.' Heather loaded her spoon with gooey chocolate and put the whole thing in her mouth. 'And yet mine went wrong.'

Katie raised both eyebrows. 'And I'm sure the recipe said to stir continuously, rather than constantly refreshing the *Guardian* website, getting into a rage about something, and then wandering off – leaving the pot on the stove – to tell Twitter why you were so angry?'

Heather gave her a giant grin as she removed the spoon. 'What can I say? Those two hundred and seven followers need me.'

I pointed a bite of cheesecake at her. 'You should totally write your book, and then you'd have more.'

'I love your optimism, Fern, but nobody wants to read *The Diary of a Vag Nurse.*'

'But there's so much to say about what you do, and the patriarchy, and the NHS and hormones and bodies and . . . and . . . herpes.' My arm felt pretty heavy from waving it about, and it was then I realised I was tipsy from drinking on an empty stomach.

'So, what's with your hot mess friend, anyway?' Heather asked through another mouthful. She always changed the subject when I talked to her about writing a book. I thought maybe she was worried how she'd cope having her opinions contested. Heather liked to be righteously right about everything. I feel like she truly believed, one day, a historian would sit the whole world down and say, *'Right, let's judge every single human living between the years 2010–2022 and work out who was on the right side, and give their surviving family member a medal.'*

'Her name is Jessica,' I said, feeling protective rather than suspicious of her for the first time since our reunion. 'Not a hot mess.'

Katie laughed as she carved a tiny slice of cake with a teaspoon. 'Don't say that, you'll ruin her new working theory.' I raised my eyes over my glass of wine. 'It's my fault. I made her rewatch *Fleabag*, and she reignited.'

Heather rolled her eyes in good humour. 'I'm just saying, I strongly believe millennial women have been brainwashed into this weird "hot mess" version of supposed empowerment that, as fucking always, benefits men.' She pointed at me. 'Woke bros just lurve feminism if it comes from a sexually available, skinny, pretty, white mouthpiece, who they think might let them do anal given half the chance.'

Katie laughed and waved her arms. 'Honey, thanks for all your sweeping statements. They've cleaned all the cake crumbs off the floor.'

'Oh you, who never cares about anything,' Heather countered.

'I just want to watch television without it having to mean something all the time. I'm sorry.'

They grinned at one another to reassure the other the joke was safe. And I felt a stab of longing for this. The ease with which they argued. The long-term love that thudded through them, the experiences shared, fights healed, shadow parts of themselves exposed to light over time and still loved anyway. Something only time could give them. Things were mostly great with Ben, but I still felt slightly on a trial period, waiting for his verdict. It was so hard not to see moving in together as an audition I could fail, and I longed for a relationship where I'd already got the part.

'I'm really tempted to indulge her,' I told Katie. 'I might ask her to elaborate.'

'Don't, please.'

Heather didn't need prompting before launching in again, her face tinged from the wine. 'I'm just saying, men our age were raised while consuming giant amounts of free porn which normalises brutal and often violent sex in this hook-up culture clusterfuck, and women have been groomed to be *chill* with it. Hell, they're even watching porn WITH these guys to show just how chill and cool girl and *not-vanilla* they are. And then we're claiming women are *choosing* to have this sex that hurts them? Actually physically leaves marks on their bodies? With men they don't even fucking know half the time? And we're not allowed to question that? Not even once?'

Heather's rant had the desired effect of being a total brain-fuck, and I had a sudden rush of memory of the sex Ben and I had the other night. Angry, thrusty, minimal foreplay, against the wall, not even looking at each other. There was no way of dodging it. It had been porn sex. Ben loved and respected me . . . and yet that was the hardest he'd ever been, fucking me like that, like I wasn't really a person. Whereas I didn't even orgasm . . . I got off only on how much he'd wanted me, on the playing of the part, even though I wasn't technically getting off at all . . .

'Maybe these women are just horny?' Katie suggested, her hands a steeple under her delicate chin. 'Maybe they're just horny, and maybe they just like sex like that?'

Heather threw her head back. 'Then riddle me this,' she said. 'If that's the case, how come only *seven* per cent of straight women orgasm during a first-time hook-up?'

'Is that true?' I asked, sitting up in my chair. The statistic made me feel instantly better about myself.

'Yes! If straight women aren't even coming through these porn-show one-night stands, why the hell are they even having them?'

I was very still for a second. 'Validation?'

'No, Fern, *empowerment,* remember?'

And we all laughed at how ludicrous Heather had made that seem now.

She put her feet up onto the side table, moving a book about Annie Leibovitz. She was in her element, off on a rant like this. 'In my opinion, any man who has fucked a very drunk woman, who he hardly knows, in a borderline violent way, and thinks that's not slightly problematic, needs to check himself. Yeah, she's consenting. Well done, here are your fucking woke points. But, also, aren't you questioning her reasoning? Oh, hang on. You don't care. You're just happy the drunk hot girl has let you spunk in her face, and it's OK because she has a feminist badge on her tote bag.'

Katie put her bowl down next to the art book. 'Are you enjoying your pudding, Fern?'

I laughed and put my empty bowl next to hers. 'Seriously though, what's any of this got to do with Jessica?' I asked. 'I mean, she's the last person to have a feminist badge. And I haven't seen her for years, but back then, she did seem to be having fun. I doubt she'd call herself a hot mess. She's too busy—'

'—being a hot mess?'

'Being a single mum. Being let down by men. And making bad life choices.'

'And she's stunning?' Heather checked.

'Well . . . yeah.'

'So, she's a hot mess.'

'But Jessica . . . her life now . . . it's not empowering. I feel . . . sort of sorry for her. She seems to love being a mum, but, I mean, everything that's happened to her around that, it's all just very . . . sad.'

Heather's eyes widened. Despite her spiky quips, she genu-inely seemed to care about every woman she'd ever met, heard about, or came across at work. 'But that's why it's bad we're fetishising the whole concept,' she said. 'Because the reality is . . . it *is* really sad. Women have learnt the only acceptable way to deal with trauma is to be really pretty, drunk, and to process it through casual sex. God forbid they're chubby, and plain, and just want to scream into men's faces twenty-four hours a day while sobbing with rage.'

I thought back to earlier that day. How different and deter-mined Jessica seemed, sat in the playground. Heather was right . . . The Jessica I used to know really could be defined by two syllables, 'hot' and 'mess', but now . . . 'I really don't think she's like that any more. She said today that she's given up on men.'

Heather levered herself up and padded over to the kitchen to put the kettle on – knowing without asking that all of us needed tea. 'That's interesting,' she said, as she was running the tap.

'What is?'

'That Jessica has told you she's given up men, and now this is the first time in years you've been able to be friends again.'

We laughed until late. After our peppermint tea, we arranged blankets around our feet that Katie had crocheted herself, streaming our phones onto their television and taking it in turns to pick our favourite songs. We got up and danced around the room to 'Power' by Little Mix, tuning out Heather's changing the lyrics to 'You're the Man, and I'm wearing, wearing a tiny leotard'. We fell down a *songs-that-always-came-on-at-uni* spiral – swinging our limbs around the living room to 'Crazy Chick', 'Love Machine', and *The OC* soundtrack. I usually hated dancing – could never quite shake off the insecurity that makes you too stiff and aware to look good. But, as it was just the three of us, it didn't matter. I screamed along to the songs, I threw my body around like a maniac. We giggled, pretended to hump their walls, cackled, and spun until we were dizzy, giddy as children rolling down a hill – all three of us almost entirely sober. Freedom loosened my muscles; I smiled 'til my face hurt. And then I had a thought of Ben. I thought how much he'd love to see me like this – so free, so loose, so unobtainable in that moment, so not needing of him. He loved it when I was able to let go, which rarely happened in a man's presence. He'd want me so much like this. And, the moment I had this thought, I became aware of my body. Of how I looked. *Was I dancing well? Did my face look pretty?* I laughed at Heather as she slut-dropped, but the laughter was forced because I was imagining what I'd look like to Ben if he saw me laughing. I used the window to check my reflection, and noticed my stomach bulging over my jeans – full of pizza and cheesecake – and turned away. I continued dancing with my stomach sucked in, so the imaginary voyeur of Ben wouldn't be put off by my imperfect body. Within five minutes, our impromptu party died. My self-consciousness seeping into the vibrant air, poisoning even the two lesbians.

I thanked them again and said my goodbyes.

'Good luck with your hot mess friend.' Heather hugged me one more time before leaving.

When I got in the taxi, my Uber driver just wanted to listen to Classic FM in total silence. I laid my head against the window, watching the city swish by, and, again, I viewed myself as if there was a camera, live-beaming me to Ben. I tilted my chin so it was a better angle. I pictured him noticing the change in me when I walked in. Pulling me into a kiss, wanting access to my independent woman energy field.

'Just here,' I told the driver, as he turned onto my road. 'This block of flats here, on the left . . . Yeah yeah yeah, by the street light.'

'Hello?' I called quietly, stepping into the flat, my imaginary camera still trained on my face. 'Ben? I'm home.'

A groan drifted from the living room.

'Ben?'

I found him passed out on the sofa, still in his teaching clothes, tie loosened, odd socks protruding from under his trousers. 'Hey Fern,' he mumbled into the leather. 'Very tired. Not drunk, I promise. Very tired. Few drinks after work but not drunk.' He stank of sweet stale beer. 'Good day?' he asked with his eyes still closed.

'Yeah. Amazing day.' I tried to keep hold of the perky free spirit from earlier. I wanted him to see me like that – to see the shine of my good day radiating off me. 'Jessica was great. And we all went a bit berserk at Heather's. We were dancing around her living room. You should've seen it.'

A light snore was my reply.

My fantasy popped. Ben's snore the prick in my bubble. The record button switched off on my imaginary camera. The only person who could see me right now was me. I stood in the conflicting feeling of love and disappointment, then got a blanket out of the cupboard and tucked it around his body.

'I love you,' I told him, stroking back a piece of his hair, trying to turn the record button back on. Wanting him to watch this scene of me being so caring and thoughtful and feminine, putting that blanket around him.

'Yeah, you too.' He turned away from my touch, and dozed off again into a scatter cushion.

Sixteen

July 2002

My body lay sprawled out in the sun, my face carefully positioned under the hotel umbrella. Sweat collected generously in my belly button, and my skin tightened as it baked under the heat.

'How long until we turn over?' I twisted my head to Jessica, who lay on the lounger next to me, reading a *Cosmo* article called 'Bad-girl sex – moves to show him your naughty side'. She picked up her wristwatch from the ground.

'Five more minutes, then we rotate.'

'It's so damn hot.'

'Our tans are going to be brilliant. We will be literal golden goddesses. Julio and Julio won't be able to contain themselves.'

I smiled as I closed my eyes, letting the sounds of the pool bar's aggressive music wash over me, combined with the excitable splashing of kids in the pool. This whole holiday was about finding and betrothing ourselves to the two imaginary Julio twins. When we'd shopped for our bikinis in

Topshop, we asked ourselves what the Julios would like. As we bought SunIn for our hair, it was to impress the Julios. And, after arriving at the hotel in Greece with my parents, with the stupendous independence of our very own hotel room, we dressed for the Julios – despite the fact there was not one teenage boy at this complex. Just families with kids, and couples who seemed really annoyed that kids were there, and old people, who were annoyed *anyone* was there.

'What do you think they're doing in Newquay now?' I asked, shuffling down to get the sun on my face. Jessica's had turned a glorious gold within a day of arriving, whereas I'd turned into a giant freckle.

'Probably hiding in their shit caravans from the rain, and listening to the boys drone on about surfing after one whole lesson.'

I let the uncomfortable mixture of superiority and jealousy join the prickles on my burning skin. 'You reckon?'

'Yeah. Also, it's such a cliché. To go to Newquay after exams. Like, literally, the most obvious thing to do in the whole world. I bet they've all got matching T-shirts.'

'And no Julios.'

'Julio and Julio would rather die than go to Newquay.'

What I would never tell Jessica is that I'd been invited to go on the caravan holiday by Kim and Amy. They'd asked me over MSN in March, while we were having one of our secret chats that I also didn't tell Jessica about. It went without saying she wasn't welcome, and so, here was the alternative. My parents, utterly delighted that I was now well enough to do normal things like go on holiday, booked ten days at an all-inclusive resort, and I was allowed to bring a friend. Jessica '*only*' had to pay for the flights, which, when I told her, turned her mouth into a grim line. But she'd turned up at mine a week later, clasping a ball of twenty-pound notes, a grin splitting her face open, screaming, 'WE ARE GOING TO GREECE, BABY.' I never asked how she got it – assuming, perhaps, she'd extricated the money from her father, cashing in on his sporadic feelings of guilt.

We'd counted down towards the holiday as eagerly as we had the end of school. We made packing lists as early as April, when we were supposed to be revising, passed each other cartoons of us on the beach surrounded by Julios; we fantasied about our tans, our freedom, what to save '*for holiday*', and what to have now. Of course, the reality of the holiday was quite different. Jessica quaked with fear the whole flight there as she'd never been on an aeroplane before. My parents' constant presence made the freedom quite restrictive. They expected us to eat breakfast and dinner with them, knocked on our door regularly to '*see what you are up to*', and complained about how messily we were keeping the room. But we evaded them in the daytime by refusing to partake in any of their planned boat trips to boring old towns and historical ruins. Four days in and we were still more than happy to baste ourselves like turkeys, pretending we didn't mind we weren't in Newquay, getting fingered and puked on.

I flickered my eyes open and tortured myself by glancing at Jessica's body while she read. Her curves filled her bikini so well it looked as if it'd been drawn around her. I'd spent a lot of my Saturday job money on a pricey striped one, but it bunched where my chest should be, and the metal hoop detail on the bottoms left an imprint in my thighs. Those weren't the only unfavourable comparisons. Jessica's hair morphed into long effortless beach waves, whereas mine frizzed into an impenetrable tangle. Jessica waltzed around with hardly a scrap of make-up on, wearing a kaftan she got off a market stall, clashing it perfectly with the free sunnies and flip-flops that came with our magazines. Me? Despite blowing my savings on an assortment of beach dresses, expensive sunglasses and sandals, I still looked frumpy, awkward, and like I was trying way too hard.

It was no matter, however, as there was not a boy to be found on the complex. Julio and Julio had failed to materialise, and we were all the happier because of it. I'd never laughed as hard. Daily sunstroke had turned us slightly bonkers, and, if we weren't shoving dollops of damp sand onto our bodies and pretending they were spa treatments, we were watching bizarre Greek television on our stiff-sheeted beds, during the heat of the day, speaking over it in a variety of crazy accents. We'd survived school, exams, the clichéd predictability of the Leavers' Ball, and, during our siestas, we turned our holiday masterplan into a sixth-form college masterplan, plotting our reinventions as if they were diamond heists.

'I may just turn up on the first day, wearing all black and never speaking,' I'd told Jessica, the day before, my sunburnt legs up against the white wall, as I smothered them with aloe vera. 'Everyone will whisper and wonder about me. I'll be so mysterious that everyone will fall violently in love with me.'

'I'm just really excited about not being known as *That-Slut-Jessica.*'

I winced. 'College is going to be so much better than school.'

'It's going to have to be.'

Jessica picked up her watch again from her sunlounger and turned to me seriously. 'It's time to turn,' she said. 'Fifteen minutes on our fronts, and then we can get into the pool.'

'Yes, captain.'

I fumbled about with my towel, getting it in the right position, and lowered my stomach onto the bendy rubber bands. The sun slowly baked my back while I twisted my head to one side and watched children screaming as they splashed around the babies' pool. Then an actual teenage boy appeared. Holding the hand of a much younger sister, walking her towards the paddling pool.

'Jessica,' I hissed urgently. 'There's a boy.'

'A what?' she asked from under her straw hat.

'A boy. Our age. Over by the kiddy pool.'

'So?' said the hat.

'So . . . well, a boy.'

'I'm not interested in anyone but Julio, to be honest.'

She yawned and continued her siesta, while I put on my sunglasses so I could spy on him.

By the time our backs were done, I'd confirmed, quite decidedly, that I was in love with him. I'd decided he was kind, because he was playing with his little sister. I'd decided he was attractive, because he was the only teenage boy I'd seen in five days, and scarcity mindsets are dangerous things. And, I'd decided he was going to fall violently in love with me, and I'd have a *'holiday romance'* and be able to put to good use all the relevant advice I'd read about them in the damp teen magazine under my lounger. I scrambled up to arrange my body as best as I could in case he noticed me – tucking my sarong around me to hide my scars, throwing my shoulders back so my AA cup buds protruded to maximum effect. I smiled to show just how naturally happy I was.

'Why are you sitting all funny?' Jessica asked, pushing herself up off her front. Her back was now a delicious shade of brown.

'Am I?'

'Yes. Like you need a wee. Do you need a wee?'

'Shall we get in the pool?'

'Why? Are you going to pee in it?'

'Jessica!'

'We all do it, Fern. It's OK.'

'I'm not . . .' I glanced over at The Boy, and lowered my voice into a whisper, 'going to piss in the pool. I just want to get closer to this boy.'

'OK, OK, let me take a look at him.' She lowered her sunglasses and stared directly at the rare adolescent male. 'He's no Julio,' she said, 'and he's got spots.'

'Yes, but look, look at his sunlounger.'

'Which one is his sunlounger? How do you know?'

'I've been watching him,' I whispered. 'And it's that one with the Arsenal towel on it.'

She examined the vacant plastic sunbeds. 'So . . . ?'

'So, he's reading a book!'

'So?'

'Well, I read books.'

'What are the chances?'

'I think I fancy him.'

Jessica shot him another unimpressed look over the top of her sunglasses. 'You do that, then.'

But, as the week and our tans progressed, Jessica began to share my interest in The Boy. That's what we called him, and we started monitoring him in ways Kim would be proud of.

'The Boy is eating pancakes in the corner,' I'd whisper as we loaded our plates with melon slices from the breakfast bar. Jessica had taken one look at all the pastries on offer on the first morning and not picked any up, so I'd duly copied her. I stared wistfully at the miniature chocolate croissants each day, but even more wistfully at her figure in its bikini.

'The Boy is reading a new book,' she told me, when she'd returned from using our hotel room toilet. 'I saw him reading by the tennis courts.'

'The Boy is wearing a different set of swimming trunks.' I stared at him from under my sun hat. Sunbathing was pretty difficult when you held your stomach in the whole time, had a full face of make-up on, had an open shirt and little skirt on to cover your scars, and were using your arms to push your flat boobs into a cleavage.

Jessica, head lolling back, legs slightly spread, totally relaxed and still looking better than me, smiled under her hat. 'He's such a maverick. What will he do next? Wear a different T-shirt to dinner?'

On reflection, The Boy was totally unremarkable, but he was everything to someone as romantically starved as I was. Since getting better from my depression, with a medication and therapy formula that appeared to be working, I now had time to worry about all the rites of passage it had robbed from me. If I could just have someone fall in love with me, put their tongue in my mouth, grasp my non-boob over my jumper, and, maybe, prod a finger into my vagina, I could catch up. All of this could easily be achieved that week, if only The Boy noticed me.

Two nights later, my parents were on a full-day excursion with seemingly the rest of the hotel, and Jessica and I were celebrating our evening of freedom by getting righteously drunk. I held up my head with my hand as we played poker with matchsticks, slumped forward on the hotel bar table, blearily looking at my cards.

'Hit me,' I mumbled to Jessica.

'We're playing poker, not Black Jack.'

'Hit me.'

'No, we need to bet before we see the next card.'

'Hit me.'

Jessica cracked up so hard that she slumped forward onto the table, banging her head. 'Oww,' she said. 'Oww.'

'Hit me.'

'Stop it. I'm going to die I'm laughing so hard.'

'Hit me.'

'Stop it.'

Jessica sneezed and blew away the cards, which only added to our drunken hysterics. A nearby family cast disapproving looks, the mother's lips pursed as she sucked on the straw of her Sex on the Beach.

We were making full use of my parents' absence. We'd been worried we wouldn't get served, but Fabio, the barman, took one leering look at Jessica and happily poured us generous Malibu and Cokes. 'You English girls know how to have fun, don't you?' he'd told us, with multiple eyebrow raises, and we simpered and giggled so he'd keep pouring us drinks on our all-inclusive tab.

While Jessica picked the cards off the floor, I found I could hardly focus. I leant on my elbow, but it slid across the marble table.

'They're going to ask us to leave,' she said.

'Nah. Fabio loves us, don't you, Fabio?' I called over at the cocktail waiter. Luckily he didn't hear me – too busy making a giant goldfish bowl for two older women dressed entirely in Per Una.

'Do you think he knows the Julios?' Jessica asked, shuffling everything back into the deck.

'He's hiding them from us. He's too jealous, and he's blocking us from our true loves . . . God, I'm going to piss myself.'

Jessica's laughter followed me out of the bar into the marble corridor. The hotel had that annoying habit of placing all toilets miles away from anywhere useful. I plodded up a flight of stairs, stumbling and losing a flip-flop, swearing, and finishing the journey barefoot. I collapsed onto the loo and felt my head dizzying as I lay it on my knees. At the sink, I saw my reflection had gone somewhat downhill. My hair had wilted, mascara melted under one eye, and the top of my dress was exposing some bra. I sighed and tried to correct myself, before flip-flopping my way back, preparing an apology for taking so long. But, when I reached the bottom step, I heard Jessica's laugh echo down the hall. Not just her laugh. Her flirty laugh. A more discreet husky laugh she used with the boys. I turned the corner and found The Boy was sitting at our table, hair gelled back, nice crisp shirt on, laughing back at Jessica in the usual lovelorn way.

'She's back!' Jessica launched her arms in the air. 'Fern! Meet George. His name is George.'

Suck stomach in. Push out non-existent breasts. Smile sweetly. Act coy. Don't be drunk.

'Oh, hi,' I managed.

Jessica threw him a smile. 'We've been calling you *The Boy* all week.'

'Jessica!'

'What? Only because you're the only other person here our age.'

George's blush meshed with his sunburn. 'The Boy, eh?' he said, revealing a Midlands accent. 'I mean, I'd rather be known as *The Guy* or *The Man.*'

Jessica laughed her hot laugh again. 'Well, you're The Boy, sorry.'

I had a light-bulb moment. 'Boy George,' I said, delighted at myself.

But Boy George looked confused. 'I don't get it.'

'You know, like the singer? From the eighties.'

'Oh. Yeah, right. I get it now.' He didn't laugh or look slightly impressed. 'So, Jessica said I can join your game of poker?'

'Is that OK?' Jessica asked. She gave me a wink, all *'Look what I've done for you'.* 'We can redistribute the matches?'

'Oh, of course. That's, er, fine. Yeah. Cool. Really cool. Poker, huh? Shall I get us another round?'

'Amazing idea,' Jessica said.

When I returned with more Malibu and Cokes – upping my order to a double – they'd rearranged the table so George could fit in. He sat with his legs out, making it so Jessica and I had to tilt ours to one side.

'Shall I deal?' he asked, picking up the stack before we could say no.

I slurped down half my drink in one. My mouth was swimming with the taste of synthetic coconut. 'Oh, yes, please,' I said. 'I'm terrible at shuffling.' That wasn't actually true. In fact, in the darker moments of my school refusal, I'd spent a week teaching myself how to shuffle. George dealt, and I picked up my hand, looking at my two cards, forgetting what they were the second I put them down, focusing solely on how to get this boy to fall in love with me.

'I'm big blind.' Jessica shoved two matchsticks forward, looking like a cool poker shark. As usual, the presence of a male hadn't derailed her at all. In fact, she was almost even more comfortable than before. I finished my drink with a second giant slurp. 'I'm small.'

George matched our bets, and then proceeded to reveal the flop.

'Flop it out,' I said, then burst into giant hysterics. Jessica snorted and joined in, whereas George raised a confused eyebrow.

'I need another drink.' I leapt away. 'Another double Malibu and Coke, please,' I told Fabio, who scowled now he'd clocked a boy at our table. I shoved the straw in my mouth right away. I just needed to relax. Be more myself.

Put less pressure on this. Show how naturally wonderful I was. Be casual . . .

'So, yeah, like, what's your favourite type of vermin?' I asked George, trying to rest my head casually on my fist.

'*Vermin?*'

'Yeah. I mean, if you could be any type of vermin, what vermin would you be?' In my intoxicated mind, I was being manic-pixie cute. George would return to Birmingham and think of my sexy quirkiness whenever he saw a squirrel.

'Umm . . . I'm not sure I've . . .' He was looking at me with mild worry, probably wondering what the sectioning regulations were in Greece, until Jessica interrupted.

'I'd totally be a pigeon,' she said. 'They are very misunderstood birds. I'd reinvent them. Make them as sought-after as the robin.' She winked at both of us, and it was as if she became the projection of everything I was trying to be. A cutesy answer, a cheeky wink. She'd suddenly made a conversation about *vermin* totally whimsical.

'OK, OK.' George was happy to play along now. 'I'll be a . . . fox?'

'You better not eat me . . .' Jessica winked again, and I lowered my mouth onto my straw. Did she really have to do that second wink?

Another blur of time passed.

'So, George, the Midlands . . .' I was asking. 'What's that all about?'

'You're showing me your cards.'

'Oh shit.'

'We need to reshuffle now.'

Another double Malibu and Coke. I went to the toilet again, and felt as if I was in a fun house trying to get back to the table. When I returned, Jessica was doing her hot laugh again, sitting next to George, who was happily protesting as she put his hair into a ponytail. Jessica jumped backwards, a guilty look on her face as I plonked myself down.

'Isn't the weather just glorious here?' I announced.

'Err . . . yeah . . .' George's hair stuck up like an antennae. 'It's very . . . sunny . . .'

'I'm going all in.' I pushed my matchsticks dramatically into the centre to show George how wild and brave I was.

'Those are my matchsticks.'

'Whoops, sorry.' I tried to scrape them back to him, but they got muddled with the existing bets.

'Don't worry about it. I think we've played enough poker now.'

'You're right.' I nodded furiously. 'Let's do something *CRAZY*. Let's . . . go *skinny-dipping*.'

I didn't wait for their reply. I knew, from watching films, that if a sexy girl mentions skinny-dipping, all she had to do next was run towards water, leaving a trail of clothes behind her, then dive under the surface, giggling at her wild freeness, not even noticing the boy following her.

I started running off towards the pool, which was incredibly difficult in flip-flops, and let out what I hoped was a gleeful, sprite-like giggle.

'Fern! Wait!' Jessica called, and I could hear them follow me. My plan was working. 'She's really drunk,' I heard her tell George.

'I'm not drunk,' I called back. I reached the edge of the empty pool, and started scrambling out of my dress. But my dress got caught over my head, and I felt my balance go, going, the long, suspenseful feeling of falling, and I plunged into the pool, dress still around my head, not sure which direction anything was, swallowing loads of water. The alcohol made me feel heavy and sleepy, and I didn't fight very hard to get to the surface. I heard the sloshing noise of another body arriving. *George.* A sharp tug under my armpits. His skin slippery against mine. The tingles it gave me. I'd never been touched by a boy before. I felt momentarily happy that he was touching me in water and therefore I'd be weightless. But, when he dragged me up onto the stylish concrete, my water-soaked maxidress meant I was a dead weight. Jessica had to come over to help fully drag me out of the water on my stomach.

'I need to get her to bed.'

'Do you need help?'

'No. I'll be fine. Her parents will be back soon. I don't want them to see her like this. They'll blame me.'

I sat up, and tried to shake myself out like a dog. 'You never asked me what sort of vermin I would like to be,' I pointed out.

He ignored me. 'So, what day are you leaving?'

'In two days. Help me get her up.'

My memory failed me after that point. A smudge of time, and I was in our hotel room, Jessica putting me in the shower to warm me up. Another smudge, and she was putting me into pyjamas. 'I don't think he likes me,' I started wailing. 'Why do boys never fancy me?'

'*Shh. Shh.*'

'I really like him.'

'*Shh.* Go to sleep.'

Lights out.

Lurched up in the dark. 'I'm going to be sick.'

The acidic burn of coconut liquid projecting from the back of my throat. Crying like you always cry when you're sick.

'Sorry. Sorry,' I repeated, grasping the edges of the loo.

Jessica's hand rubbed my back. '*Shh. Shh.* It's OK. You're going to be OK.'

More sick. More sick. I had a little sleep on the floor next to the toilet on the bathmat, Jessica spooning me from behind. I smiled. Fell unconscious again.

I woke up when she put me back to bed. 'Who won the poker?'

'Don't worry about that now. Come on, go to sleep.'

When I woke, I initially thought it was morning. I sat upright, expecting to see a thin line of light escaping the hotel's blackout blinds. I was mostly sober now. Though my throat burnt and my mouth was bone dry. I tumbled through the darkness and shoved my mouth under the tap, gulping as much water as I could. I peed, wiped, and flashes of the evening revealed themselves. I folded forward on the toilet, my stomach hurting at the half memories. Maybe I'd start going on my parents' excursions? I could avoid George that way. I put the loo seat down, not flushing in case it woke Jessica, and padded back to my pretzel of white sheets, listening to the dim hum of the air conditioner and the sound of Jessica's heavy breathing.

Except, I noticed, there was no sound of Jessica's heavy breathing.

'Jessica?' I whispered.

No stirring. No sound coming from the bed beside me.

'Jessica?' I asked a little louder.

I reached out and gently prodded her bed, expecting to find the warm lump of her body, but my hand found only air. I sat up and turned the light on.

Her bed was empty.

I stared at it in total shock for a moment – taking in the unmade sheets, the dent in the pillow her face had left, the complete lack of Jessica where she was supposed to be, at 1 a.m. in a foreign country. Then I closed my eyes and sighed as the truth whispered itself to me.

She was with George. I knew it right away. A rendezvous arranged in the gasps of time they had between my antics. My grand seduction completely destined to fail from the start – even without all my self-sabotage. My knees found their way to my chest. I couldn't stop staring at the empty bed. Imagining what she was doing. Knowing George wouldn't forget her, whereas I'd become a tiny side joke in his wet dream come true.

I didn't cry. I wanted to, but I felt too weirdly empty to let tears fall.

Eventually, I leant over and turned the light off, waiting for her to come back. I listened in the dark to the click of the lock, the careful closing of the fire door, the sticky sound of her bare feet against the tiles, the delicate rummaging of her body back under the sheet. I could hear her breathing in the blackness. I could tell she wasn't asleep yet. I could sense she knew I was awake.

We lay in the dark, listening to one another's ribcages expand and contract. But we never spoke of it. Not once.

Thirty-two

I watched Ben sleep in the morning murk of our bedroom. It still felt like such an unfathomable privilege, to be able to see his vulnerable face surrendering to unconsciousness. His mouth was slightly open, his hair fell over one closed eye, and he'd tugged the duvet up into his fist, clutching at it like a small child napping. I propped myself onto my elbow and drank in every detail of his face, thinking, *I'm the only one who gets to see you like this. Me.* I reached out and traced the skin of his cheek, watching the tiny hairs prickle to meet my fingertip. *Me, just me.* Ben let out a small groan and rolled away, stirring himself awake.

I wondered if he ever watched me sleep?

I wanted him to. I wished he looked at me like I looked at him. I played out the fantasy of him watching me unconscious, of how I'd look serene and naturally beautiful, my hair splayed over my pillow. He'd watch me breathe and think how lucky he was. Another grunt. Ben turned again. Maybe this was my chance? The mattress squeaked as he turned for a third time and I flattened myself to the bed and fluttered my lashes closed.

Ben threw his legs over the side of the bed and sat up. I let out a small, sleepy sigh, wishing I could peek to check whether he was watching me. I waited, waited. Hoping I'd positioned myself so I looked at my most blissful and beautiful. But Ben just let out a deep hack of a morning cough and padded away to the bathroom. My eyes opened as I heard him take a piss, coughing again, the coughs audibly interrupting his urine flow. I had a choice. To get up and say good morning, or to feign sleep when he came back. While he took a shower, I reached for my phone and scrolled through social media. A few nice messages had come in overnight from my first *Other Side of the Tissue Box* series, and I screen-grabbed them and saved them to my gallery. Then the shower turned off and I jumped back under the covers. I kept my eyes closed as Ben took for ever brushing his teeth, gargling with mouthwash. Then I heard him coming towards me. A pause in the doorway. *This was it.* He was looking at me! He was watching me sleep! I'd pulled it off . . . hang on . . .

Within less than a second, he'd gone into the living room. That was not watching me sleep. That was a *glance*, tops. I lay there and silently seethed as *The Andrew Marr* show came on, wondering if he'd watched his ex-fiancée *Tiffany* sleep, and making myself feel sick.

'Morning, sleepyhead,' Ben said, beaming at me when I stumbled in five minutes later. 'I hope I didn't wake you.'

'Oh, no. It's fine,' I lied. Wondering what would happen if I said, *'I was awake before you, actually, but I thought you might want to watch me sleep, so I pretended.'* 'Have you been up long?'

'Just long enough for a shower.' He beckoned to me. 'Morning kiss, please.'

I grinned and bent over to oblige, forgiving him for the slight he didn't even know he'd committed.

'*Mwah.* Sorry. Do you want the telly off?'

'No, no, leave it on.' I curled up next to him on the sofa, and he pulled me closer, kissing the top of my head. I closed my eyes, savouring it. Wondering if his love would ever be something I took for granted, rather than treating it like a finite resource I was scared of squandering too quickly.

'I shouldn't watch politics in the morning. It puts me in a bad mood.'

'I'm sure you'll cheer up when you're sticking a fifty-pound note up a stripper's vagina at the stag do later,' I half joked. 'Or whatever the hell Simon's got planned.'

Ben's nose wrinkled, passing the test I hadn't even realised I'd set until he passed it. 'Eww, no. I don't have mates like that.'

I pretended I was much, much cooler about this than I was, and reached out and stroked his leg, enjoying the feeling of his strong calf through his pyjama bottoms. 'Well, you know, some men say it's just what men do.'

'Well, not men like me, jeez.' He laughed. 'If I asked Joel if he fancied going to Spearmint Rhino, I think he'd ask if I was OK, and suggest we go watch the football in the pub instead. Woah, good morning!'

I'd launched myself on him. His body sank under mine as I lay on top of him, nestling my nose into his neck.

'Thank you,' I whispered.

He patted my back hesitantly. 'I mean, it's weird you're even rewarding me for this.'

He carefully rolled me off him so we were lying horizontally. Every inch of the fronts of our bodies touching, breathing in one another's out breath. He reached out and tucked my hair behind my ear, making my stomach rumble with longing. I kissed him. Still wanting to compensate him with some kind of bare-minimum medal. The front fabric of his jogging bottoms twitched.

'So, when's the mysterious Jessica arriving?' he asked, when we broke apart for air, his hand skimming over the curve of my arse.

'After lunch. I've got to finish that article first and clean the place up a bit.'

Ben's hand now paused on my breast, and I felt my body harden under my pyjama top. Our conversation was pointless now. A facade in exchanging sentences when we both knew we'd be having sex within the next five minutes.

'It's so great your college has given you the all-clear for the series.' His hand now gently cupped my boob and I sighed.

'Yeah. The class has been great too. A few of them were a bit worried I'd break confidentiality. But when I explained I would literally only talk about my own experiences, and the content of the course, they . . . *oh* . . .'

I closed my eyes as Ben's tongue pushed into my mouth, sighing with relief again, with longing, with love. He was such a good man, and he wanted me. *Me.* That would never stop turning me on. Our clothes melted away, hands everywhere, mouths everywhere. He tried to go down on me, but I was too worried I'd smell, as it was the morning, so I tugged him back up, pulled his mouth to mine, and used my hands on his arse to pull his body into mine.

'I love you, Fern,' he muttered into my shoulder.

He'd said it first. It always meant so much more when he said it first. Lust poured through me and I tried to pull him in even further – the deepest still not deep enough. Not for how strongly I felt. Not for how much I wanted him. Loved him. Needed him. Could never lose him.

'I love you too,' I whispered back. He twisted his head towards mine, so we were nose to nose, and it felt so perfect, so complete, so totally filled with love, that I worried he needed me to take the edge off it. I didn't want him going off on a stag do with just a *loving fuck*. I wanted to give him a fucking fuck too. Just in case . . . I'm not sure what. 'I also love you fucking me.'

The words had the desired effect and he let out a grunt and took things harder and faster. And, though it felt less nice, it also felt more nice, because I knew he was enjoying it so much. I wrapped my legs around his back and let him impale me. With every thrust, I said in my head, *'Choose me. Pick me. Decide on me. Please. Please. Soon. Please. I cannot bear the waiting to be chosen. Look what I'm giving you, so please, please, pick me.'*

I picked up Jessica at Mile End Tube station, as she, like most people unaccustomed to London, felt like you needed a special Masters to understand the bus system. We shrieked as we flung ourselves at each other.

'I'm here,' she said. 'I know I sound like such a fucking country bumpkin right now, but I honestly, truly think I should get a medal for figuring out the difference between the Circle, District, and Metropolitan lines.'

'You got it right first time?'

'Yes.'

'You're a natural Londoner.'

Her face cracked open at that, and she hugged me again. I guided her to the bus stop, and her neck twisted in every direction as she took in the chaotic bustle of Mile End. She looked incredible, of course. Even for a lazy spring-like Saturday. She'd teamed a long-sleeved maxidress with biker boots, an expensive-looking leather jacket, and a perfect red lip. I smoothed my white T-shirt down over my high-waisted jeans – feeling a tiny bit silly for the printed headscarf I'd tied around my ponytail. I shouldn't have bothered trying 'effort-less chic' when I knew I'd be competing with Jessica.

'God, it's so busy,' she shrilled, as we tapped onto the bus, holding onto the pole tightly as it lurched us towards Victoria Park Village.

'It's cos of the weather,' I said, slightly defensively. 'First warm day and all.'

'No, no. It's great. I feel so ALIVE.'

I pointed out inane landmarks along the way. *'Here is where I sometimes get coffee. Here is another place I get coffee if I'm not at the other place. Here is the park, here are all the ways why it's better than other parks.'* But, my urge to impress was unwarranted. Jessica practically spun when we got off at the bus stop. 'Oh my God, it's actually like a village! In the middle of a city? That's so cute. I LOVE it.'

I pointed out all the unremarkable things and places that are somehow more remarkable because they're in London.

How a simple pub or cafe can be lifted with the presence of thirty-year-olds in see-through glasses frames, with an undercut and a podcast side-hustle. Jessica bought totally into it, making me swell with pride at the life I'd built.

'This is me,' I said, outside our block of flats, helping her with her bag as we staggered up the communal stairs. She dropped it inside the front door.

'Oh, I love your place, it's so YOU,' she said, tugging her boots off and padding down the small hall to the living room. I followed her in, feeling further pride at everything I'd managed, when, for so many years, I'd felt certain I'd never manage anything even close to this. Jessica went to my bookshelf. 'God, you have so many books,' she marvelled. 'I forgot how much you read.' Her hands found a framed photo of Ben and me, and she plucked it from the shelf. It was one of my favourites, taken at Joel's wedding the previous summer. I'd loved that day – it was the first time I'd felt properly integrated into Ben's life. Attending a close friend's wedding made a relationship a new version of official. Every time the wedding photographer encouraged me into the frame of a photo, I felt a further pulse of security. If we broke up, this photo would be ruined. Ben wouldn't have invited me unless he was quite certain my presence wouldn't contaminate his best mate's wedding photos. I joined her side.

'He *is* handsome, isn't he?' Jessica said. 'You guys make a beautiful couple.'

I was glad she'd said the second half of the sentence, because the first half made me want to snatch the photograph away. My trust was getting there, but not yet. Not when she said things like that. It made me never want to introduce her to Ben . . .

I showed her around the rest of the place, which took, in total, less than a minute, despite how expensive the rent was. But Jessica still acted impressed. 'God, it's gorgeous outside,' she said, looking out of the window. 'Shall we go explore?'

East London was putting on the most spectacular display, getting out its very best groovy hipster china it just *happened* to find in a charity shop, and laying it out on a table made of recycled railway sleepers. I took Jessica to the park, which was bathed in a low golden light, and she gasped at all the right moments. The reveal of the Chinese pagoda, the water fountain in the lake, the vast assortment of people bundled up against the cold, wearing their carefully collated winter–spring transition outfits while walking their pedigree puppies.

'I've never seen so many people roller skating in real life,' she marvelled, as two young girls glided past. 'Or so many un-ironic hats.'

I laughed as we sat down to drink our expensive thimbles of flat white, watching the promenade glide past us.

'Did I tell you I saw Liam the other day?' she said.

There he was again. *Liam.* Our sixth-form albatross. I fought to keep my voice neutral.

'What? No way?'

'Yes,' she said, laughing. 'In Boots. While holding a packet of tampons, of course.'

'Wow, Liam . . .' I hadn't told her I'd also seen him, and I panicked briefly that he would've told her. 'What happened?'

'We just bumped into each other in town. He's gone totally bald, Fern. Can you believe it?'

I could. I'd seen it for myself. '*Liam?* Oh no, but he always had such good hair. Did you talk long?' The sun drifted behind a dense patch of cloud, turning the park's colour palette into a depressing array of greys. I had a million questions, but asked none of them, and Jessica, too, shut down the conversation as quickly as she started it.

'No. Not really. He suggested going for a coffee but, as you know, I am over men. The coffee would just be a giant headfuck, anyway.'

We finished our drinks in a grey, uncomfortable silence, and I suddenly wished she wasn't there, that I hadn't invited her. I wished I could point a wand and vanish her away. I wanted to get up and stomp off, leave her stranded in a place she didn't know . . .

'Are you sure you want to stay in tonight?' I asked, forcing myself to be breezy. 'You don't want to go out in the city or anything?'

She shook her head. 'Nah. We'll just get bothered by men. And I want to catch up. As I said, I'm over all that.'

'Are you sure you're sure? There's this place up the road that only serves alcohol made from Seville oranges?'

She laughed. 'No.'

'Or there's this club night in Hackney, where they only play the Fugees' first album over and over?'

She laughed harder. 'No.'

'Or there'll be some gig going on at The Dolphin? This dive pub? There's a mariachi band that plays sometimes, and they've agreed not to wear sombreros any more after someone started a petition?'

Jessica's cackle pierced the air and dissolved the tension. I laughed with her, the bench wobbling beneath us.

'Honestly. I just want to make the world's best indoor picnic and catch up,' she said. 'I really don't want to go out.'

That evening, as the sky got dark, we changed into our pyjamas, started a never-ending game of poker, and stuffed ourselves senseless on the junk food we'd picked up on the way back from the park. I slathered my crisps in creamy dip, crunching on them with abandon, while Jessica experimented with dipping Quorn cocktail sausages into different pots. We sloshed wine into cups, swinging our heads back to throw it down our throats, as we traded bets and reminisced about all the munchie food we enjoyed back in our stoner days.

'Kettle Chips?'

'Oh my God. They were the best! Although you were terrible at sharing them,' I said.

Jessica shrugged, laughing. 'Do you remember that time we got stoned in the woods, but you didn't want to get fat so you brought loads of tubs of couscous?'

'And then puked it all up?'

Jessica wobbled the whole table with her hyena laughter. 'Puked up? It was more like coughing up! Clouds of couscous just kept exploding from your mouth, like some sand dragon.'

'My mouth has never been dryer.' I wiped away tears at the edge of my eyes.

We were pretty damn drunk by the time Jessica had to call Bridget to say goodnight. As she went into my bedroom, sweet coos of 'I love you, honey' drifting below the closed door, I got out my own phone, and smiled blearily at the message waiting for me.

Ben: So the 'surprise' part of the stag today was fucking PAINTBALLING. It was awful. We were the oldest guys there for miles. Pretty cringe. I now have loads of bruises. Can I make some gross joke about us playing Doctors and Nurses when I get home, or has this one day around porn-addled 27-year-olds desensitised me from what's appropriate?
Fern: I didn't know they even still did paintballing! Watch out, next you'll be doing a military assault course so you can all get new social media profile shots of you covered in mud.

My smile widened as I saw the 'typing' symbol right away.

Ben: Well done for dodging the Doctors and Nurses question. I am horribly drunk and will hate myself tomorrow when I read this back.
Fern: Ha! I'm happy to play as long as I can also be a doctor. It being the Modern Times and all.
Ben: Done. How's your night going? Having a good time with Jessica?
Fern: Lovely thanks! We've eaten out the whole of the Sainsbury's Local. What you guys up to tonight?
Ben: Eaten out, eh? OH GOD, I HATE MYSELF. SORRY, THE STAG DO HAS BITTEN ME AND THE POISON IS SPREADING . . . Luckily tonight we are NOT going out. We are playing midnight football in the cottage. I like being old sometimes. Don't think I could face a club.

Fern: Have a good time. Love you xxx

Ben: Love you too my darling. Keep thinking of this morning xxx

'Well, that's the biggest smile I've ever seen,' Jessica said, plopping herself down onto our sofa so vigorously that she fell backwards. I caught her contagious laughter and went over to pull her up, joining her on the couch. We tangled our limbs together, leaving our card game unfinished on the table, and started slurping our pink G&Ts.

'Ahh, just Ben being nice,' I said. 'He's very drunk though, so I'm not sure it counts. How was Bridget?'

Jessica reached down and found a discarded furry blanket that had fallen onto the floor. She picked it up and draped it over us. 'A bit homesick for Mummy, bless her. Is it pathetic that I miss her?'

I rubbed her leg under the blanket. 'Not pathetic at all.'

'But, it's also so nice to have a night off being a mum. Like, I can sleep in tomorrow! Drink as much as I like tonight.' She drained her glass and plopped it down on my coffee table, away from its coaster. 'God, I'll tell you what I fancy?' she said.

I smiled. 'What?'

'Some *coke*. Can you get us any?'

'Oh, what? Umm . . . no, I don't think so.'

Her face fell momentarily. 'There must be someone. I mean, it's *London*?'

'Er . . . yeah, but I don't . . . really do that any more.'

Jessica laughed. 'Me neither! But one night won't hurt, will it? Is there anyone you could call?'

There probably was, if I thought hard enough. 'Umm. No, I don't think so,' I lied.

'Really? No one? Surely there's an app?'

My fingers twitched under the blanket, one hand curling itself into a fist. *Please stop*, I thought. *Please. We're having such a good time. Why can you never leave it alone? Go the fuck home.*

'I'm wasted enough already.'

Jessica was quiet, taking in my body language, noting it all, though I was trying very hard to stay loose and relaxed. Something passed over her face, something she wanted to say, and I watched her, waiting, but she threw me by grinning.

'You're right. Me too. Jeez, one night without my child and I'm like that clichéd *"Mummy's got the night off"* nonsense. Gin is more than enough. Sorry.'

My fist unfurled, though my stomach still felt slightly uncomfortable. She'd tainted the evening a bit, reminding me of Past Jessica. The one who always pushed that bit too far, who was never happy with the current set-up, no matter how much fun we were having. I plucked a stack of Pringles from a bowl, twisting them so they could fit into my mouth. The salt stung the corners of my lips as I crunched.

'It's OK,' I said, not making eye contact. 'I'm just a bit . . . old for all that now.'

'Yeah, me too, me too.'

I could sense her panic that she'd lost me. As I stuffed more crisps into my mouth, I danced briefly on the small feeling of power I currently held. Of knowing she wanted forgiveness. Then I smiled up at her, and she relaxed, her eyes going to my phone.

'So, how's Ben's stag do going?' she asked, leaning over to take her own stack of crisps, setting off a new cycle of us stuffing ourselves beyond full.

'Yeah, OK. He's pretty annoyed they had to go paintballing today.'

Jessica pulled a face, as if she'd just hit the vinegar flavouring of her crisp. 'Men are so weird. Why would anyone find that fun?'

'I know, right. But then, we can't really talk, can we? I've lost count of how many knicker-fucking-making classes I've been on, on bloody hen dos. I once had to spend sixty quid learning to cross-stitch my own sash that said "Girl Boss" on it. I actually vomited at that hen do, and I'm still not sure, to this day, if it was the Jägerbombs or the cross-stitching that did it.'

I expected Jessica to laugh, but, instead, she pulled her knees to herself. 'I've never been to a hen do before. No one's ever invited me to one.'

'Oh . . . well, you're not missing much, I promise.'

'Have you been on loads?'

The last five summers of my life whizzed through my consciousness – a montage of novelty sashes, penis straws, sharing bedrooms with strangers in country cottages, applauding pixilated husbands on pre-recorded videos because they knew how their fiancée liked their tea, screeches on arrival, the noise of twenty wheelie suitcases being pulled along the pavements of some new city, small talk with women about how great the woman in common was, women I'd never see again, and yet had to get blind drunk with, and was expected to dance to bad music alongside . . . 'A few. As I said, you're not missing much.'

'Hmm.' Jessica stared into her knees.

'Hey? If Ben ever proposes, you'll get to come to mine.'

Jessica's bright eyes met mine. 'Really?' she asked, as if she was an orphan child I'd promised to adopt in time for Christmas.

'Of course! And I'll try very hard not to force you to pay sixty quid to make your own floral head garland.'

She sniggered. 'That does sound quite fun, to be fair.'

'Stop it. Or I'll un-invite you from my imaginary hen do after my imaginary proposal.'

She rubbed my calf over the top of the blanket. 'Hey, if Ben's on a stag do right now, I'm sure he's thinking about marriage this weekend. It would be hard not to.'

I'd had the same hope myself, but pretended I hadn't. I'd watched him pack his bag, badgering him with questions about who was going, and felt great when I realised most of them were married. We'd still not had the marriage conversation but I was hoping he'd hear from his mates about how nice it was, and maybe, finally, he'd discuss the future with me. 'Really?' I asked, innocently, feeling that weird feeling again, that a camera was on me, sending my reaction to Ben.

'Yeah, you know what men are like. Pack-like. They want to be doing what all the others are doing. Anyway.' Jessica leant over and made a move on the remaining chocolate buttons. 'What's he doing tonight, anyway? Knee-deep in strippers, I'm taking it?'

I shook my head. 'No. Of course not.'

'What? Why not? What's wrong with strip clubs?'

The repaired good mood slipped out of our clutches once more, and my heart started thudding urgently in my throat. I reached out a toe and delicately tried to ballet-hop around the landmines. 'Umm, I'm just . . . well . . . I don't think they're a particularly . . . umm . . . great thing. And neither does Ben.'

Jessica's nostrils flattened. 'I don't see the problem with them. Strippers make a fortune!'

'Umm, they're actually not very safe places for sex workers. Some make OK money. Most really don't. In fact, due to house fees, on a quiet night, they can take off all their clothes multiple times and actually come home at a loss. Plus, you know, rape culture and all that, and the links to stripper use and domestic violence. Lots of them are verbally and sexually assaulted, even with bouncers and protection, because, you know, men who want to pay money to objectify women usually aren't the nicest . . .' I was parroting a lot of what Heather had said. Her voice in my head like an echo.

'What if it's a stripper mum who needs to feed her kid?' she shot at me. 'Don't you want her to make money?'

I shrugged. 'Of course I do. But if single mothers are struggling to feed their kids, shouldn't we fight for a society which helps them do that without them having to wax off all their body hair, and rub their labia in the face of a stranger who has literally paid for the privilege of dehumanising someone?'

Jessica was scowling. 'OK, so I didn't understand half of what you just said.'

My lips strained into a tight smile. 'Look, we don't have to go into it. I want sex workers to be safe, but I'm also glad Ben isn't the type of guy to use them. Shall we leave it at that?'

Jessica pushed herself up and raised her chin slightly. 'I took Brendan to a strip club once. I paid for him to have a private dance, and I watched. It was fun. It was hot.'

I sucked in breath, wondering why I was surprised. 'OK.'

'We had amazing sex when we got home,' she said, defiantly.

'WELL GOOD FOR FUCKING YOU!' I wanted to scream. But I didn't. Instead I said, 'I see.' I was having weird jealous flashing visions of Jessica and her ex-husband at the club. How easy-going Jessica was. How free. How *proud* Brendan must've been to have such a sexy, relaxed wife . . . *But he still left her*, I told myself. *She played the part and he still left her.*

'Look, if a woman is hot and she wants to make a lot of money out of it, I say "good for her",' Jessica said.

'Objects don't object,' I reminded myself silently to try to keep my temper. Of course Jessica was going to defend the hot women capitalising on their hotness.

'And what about burlesque then?' she pushed. 'Is that any better? Are you against that too?'

Heather's voice bleated through my brain again and I copied her word for word. 'That's just middle-class stripping.'

I hadn't been joking, but Jessica burst out laughing and the tension broke. She threw her hair back and roared, wiping her eyes, and I caught her laughter. 'Oh my, *middle-class stripping*,' she said. 'I love it.'

'My friend Heather say it's stripping for girls who went to private school. You'd never see *Tabitha* from Exeter Uni waving a pint glass around for tips in a seedy strip club. But, you will see her wave around a pair of two-hundred-quid designer nipple tassels, while other middle-class men get huge "ethical boners" because *"the gaze has been reclaimed"*.'

Jessica wiped her eyes again. 'Tabitha,' she repeated. *'Tabitha.'*

The air softened, and I did too. We finished off a bottle of wine and started reminiscing about some of the private school girls we'd encountered at sixth-form college. The ones who turned up at the same parties as us, groomed like King Charles spaniels and telling us how working class they actually were because their grandma had been an air stewardess in the fifties. 'Sorry,' I said, as I ate the last Quorn cocktail sausage. 'About the stripping thing. I didn't mean to get so high-horsey.'

Jessica waved her hand up in the air. 'No, I'm sorry. You're always smarter than me about these things. And, look where taking Brendan to one got me. Maybe you're right. Anyway, music, I need music. I want to dance like Tabitha is watching.' She found our vinyl collection, pulled out *Tapestry*, and demanded I put it on. We started dancing around to 'I Feel the Earth Move', the sort of dancing where you openly try to out-do the other in how bananas you look. We screamed along, grabbing one another's hands and twirling and twirling.

'SHE JUST GETS WOMEN,' Jessica said. 'SHE GETS THEM SO WELL.'

By the time, 'Will You Love Me Tomorrow?' came on, we were floppy and practically non-responsive on my sofa, our arms reaching down to our empty glasses, eyes fluttering shut. My flat was a tip. It stank of cocktail sausages, houmous with an orange glaze, the sweet stench of alcohol drying onto the sides of glasses. I drifted off, my head on a cushion, my limbs entwined with my old friend's. I thought she was asleep, but . . .

'This song is the most true song that's ever been written,' Jessica half whispered.

I hmmed and took in the lyrics again – about a night of love-making. The sort of vulnerable, soulful sex men were occasionally able to give you. The urgency in their eyes. The worship. How much they needed you. How moments like that were everything we anticipated, everything we worked towards, everything we strived for, and the sweet bliss of what it felt like when it had finally been reached. The ecstasy . . .

'I feel like that every time I've ever slept with a man,' Jessica told the dark.

Just as she said it, Carole King asked if he would still love her tomorrow.

The question. The question you're never allowed to ask. Even though it plagues your head so rampantly that it's hard to stay in moments where things are good.

'Really?' I asked. Shocked, but too sleepy to sit up. 'I wouldn't have known.'

'Does that make me, like, a pathetic person?' There was a wisp of tears in her voice – a childlike question, wanting a reassuring answer.

'No,' I said, in total honesty. 'It makes you a woman.'

She reached out and squeezed my hand, and I squeezed it back.

Sixteen

October 2002

So, it was great to know I was still pathetic and unfanciable at college too. I was at my first party, hosted by this girl Georgina, and couldn't believe my bucket hat wasn't having the desired effect of total sexual magnetism. I sat with my back to the wall, nursing a bottle of beer I didn't like the taste of, watching a collection of my peers lie on top of each other in various corners of the party, tongue kissing. Yet, not me. *Never* me. Not even with my new hat. This was not how college was supposed to start. A groan echoed out to my right over the thrash metal, and I wasn't sure where to look. All around me were displays of public sexual experimentation, just not involving me. I wore a long-sleeved fishnet top to blend my scars, over a clingy vest top, with poker-straight hair and loads of eye make-up. And I didn't look half bad, you know. But try telling that to all the boys determinedly sexually rejecting me.

'Shall we go to the kitchen?' Jade, my new friend, whispered. 'It's starting to get weird in here.'

'Yes!'

We tiptoed around the moving lumps into the empty kitchen where the music level made conversation possible. The place was littered with empties from earlier. One can was on its side, dripping beer onto Georgina's parents' laminate floor. Jade ignored the mess and opened another bottle of beer, handing me one too.

'Thank God you came with me,' she said, wiping her mouth.

'I don't get it,' I replied. 'Like, one minute it was a normal party and then everyone decided just to . . . *rub* on each other.'

Jade laughed. 'Rub on each other. I love it.'

I smiled at her, letting a new bond form. Jade had been a surprisingly welcome addition to my college experiment. Coincidently, we'd gone to the same Brownies as kids and been super close. This September, after eagerly counting down to the start of college, Jessica and I were pretty overwhelmed when we'd rocked up on orientation day. There were just so many people we didn't know. We stood around, wondering who the hell to talk to, and how, and contemplating, briefly, if instead we should've stayed in the sanctuary of our old school's sixth form. Then Jade's familiar-but-older face had found us, and she broke into a smile, pushing through the strange crowd to get to me.

'Oh my, Fern. It's been for ever! How are you? Someone I know. Amazing.'

We hugged and exclaimed at the time passed, before introducing our best friends to each other – hers a girl, Sally, from her school. A tall girl with long black hair. We stood together and took each other in. Jade had hennaed her hair red and wore giant baggy jeans, while Sally wore a Courtney Love

T-shirt, and I felt instantly relaxed now we'd found people like us.

'Isn't it amazing not to be in a school any more?' Jade had said. 'I feel so *FREE*. We're allowed to call the teachers by their real names and everything.'

Sally raised both her dark eyebrows. 'Jade doesn't need much to get excited.'

We'd clicked pretty instantly, glad to have an anchor to our pasts. As the first week continued, our friendship group grew. Sally met this quiet, ethereal girl in her art class called Georgina, who seemed cool. She talked a lot about her upcoming parent-free house, and how she collected different pairs of fairy wings. Jade then bumped into a boy from her primary school called Mike. He was a very exciting acquisition, with his blue spiked hair teamed with a dog collar necklace. He was in a band, which seemed way too cool to comprehend, and introduced us all to his bandmates. *Wow*, I remember thinking, speaking to Mike and seeing black nail polish on one thumb. *This boy is so cool, and he is speaking to me. So maybe I am so cool?* The boys talked constantly about bands like Metallica and Pantera, assuming we had the vaguest idea who they were referring to, never asking us what music we liked. And, us girls, we merely nodded and said, *'oh yes, love them'*, then later quietly went to HMV, bought as many CDs as we could afford, sat ourselves down in our bedrooms, and taught ourselves to like them too.

And, so, I was at my first house party since my new life began. A life where nobody but Jessica knew me as the girl who tried to kill herself. *Fern* for the first time in a long time. I was in my third year of CBT, and my medication was at the perfect level. I'd dropped all the lessons I hated, and was geeking out by taking both English Literature and English Language at A level. It was All-new Fern, apart from the age-old problem . . . Boys still did not appear to fancy me. I couldn't believe my bucket hat hadn't done the trick. Jessica had promised me it was cool.

'Where's Jessica?' Jade asked, combing her red hair through with her fingers. 'I've not seen her for about an hour.'

'I think she's in the downstairs bathroom.'

'Woah, she's been some time.'

'She's in there with Mike.'

'Oh . . .' Jade held her bottle to her lips and chugged half of it down. 'Oh . . .'

'Are you OK?'

She sighed and laughed. 'Yeah. I'm fine. I've just . . . always had a crush on Mike. I thought he might have gone to buy cigarettes or something.'

I didn't know what to say. My loyalty to Jessica was paramount. I couldn't exactly break ranks, take Jade's hand, and say, *'Look, if you're going to be friends with her, it's probably better not to fancy anyone at all.'*

She sighed. 'Speaking of cigarettes? Do you want one?' She reached into the low waistband of her baggy jeans and pulled out a packet of Marlborough Menthols. It took a mere second to decide that taking up smoking was a brilliant idea.

'Yeah, that would be great, thanks.'

We stepped out into the frigid air of the garden, and trampled our way through some flowerbeds to reach a bench next to a water feature. Georgina, our ethereal host, was currently half passed out in the living room, while this guy from Mike's band, Dave, lay on her and kissed her. Maybe they were doing more by now. I was incredibly jealous, even though I didn't even fancy Dave. He was pretty stocky, with long hair that he never washed, and one eye that didn't focus properly. But I'd sort of thought I was prettier than Georgina, and significantly less strange. When we'd arrived at her free house, she'd greeted us wearing a pair of her fairy wings.

The cold bloomed across my butt cheek as we sat on the bench. I watched Jade light her cigarette, concentrating on how she did it, then I copied her. The second I had the cigarette in my fingertips, it felt completely at home. We inhaled and released, our combined smoke drifting off into the black freezing air.

'So, you like Mike, huh?' I asked. It was understandable. He'd very quickly established himself as the alpha of our emerging friendship group. He was hilarious, and wry, confident, and a very talented musician, in a band with an actual gig coming up.

'Yeah, maybe.' Jade let out a long stream of smoke. 'It's just, I've known him since I was a kid. It's been nice hanging out with him again.'

'I'm sure Jessica didn't know . . .'

'Honestly, it's nothing. Please don't tell anyone.'

'I promise.'

We sat and watched more smoke drift away. 'Sort of sucks, doesn't it?' I ventured. 'Going to a party and just watching people get off with each other.' If I was with Jessica, I never would've felt able to name this rejection, but something about Jade felt comfortable, and she laughed, immediately dispelling my nerves.

'And here I was, thinking college would be different.'

'Me too.'

'So, you never got off with anyone at school?'

'Nah,' I said. 'I must be too ugly.'

'Don't be stupid, you're gorgeous.'

'Aww, *you're* stupid, but thank you,' I said. 'And, you too. Boys are blind not to fancy you.'

We smiled warmly at one another as our cigarettes burnt themselves down to white stubs.

Jade withdrew another one and handed me the box. 'It's hard to feel pretty with a friend like Sally . . . she's like boy catnip.'

'I'll take Sally and raise you a Jessica.'

Jade laughed out her smoke, and there we sat, hidden from view from the party. But the party was better, with this new friend to share it with. Throughout my life this was a skill I realised I naturally had . . . collecting girls as friends and turning them into deep relationships with minimal effort. If there was a pretty privilege, maybe there was a plain privilege too?

We finished our second cigarettes listening to the thrashing music from the house. The thought of returning indoors seemed unbearable, and Jade must've shared my opinion, as we stayed out in the cold, sipping our beers, until Jessica came tumbling out of the back door.

'Oh my God, Fern, there you are,' she said, her teeth catching the moonlight. Her hair was dishevelled, and a strap from her top hung around her shoulder. 'I've been looking for you for AGES.' She made her way over, squealing as the wet grass soaked her socks. 'Hi Jade.'

'Hi,' she replied, her eyes also travelling to Jessica's dropped strap.

Jessica held something up in the air. 'Look what I've got!' We squinted at the wedge-shaped cigarette between her fingers. 'It's a spliff,' she added. 'Mike has been teaching me how to roll up.' Jade's shoulders relaxed at the possible explanation. 'Sorry for vanishing. But he said everyone would be nagging him if they knew he had weed on him. But looky here! I've made one just for us.'

I didn't know how long it took to roll a spliff, but Jessica and Mike had been in the bathroom for at least forty-five minutes. 'Do you have a light?' she asked Jade. 'Do you want some?'

We shuffled ourselves down to make space for her on the bench.

'Umm, I don't know,' she said. 'I . . . haven't smoked it before.'

'Me neither. But it will be fun. Fern? You up for it?'

I stared at the blunt held delicately between her fingers as if it was a bullet. We'd had an assembly on drugs in Year Eleven, where a fusty man wearing a novelty tie had passed around LSD tabs encased in glass, and told us that everyone who took any drugs ended up in prison or dead.

'Are you sure it's . . . safe?'

She laughed. 'Oh my God, yes. Mike said it's safer than drinking. Come on . . .'

'OK, I guess . . .'

'Wicked. Right, lighter?' Jade handed it over and we both watched as Jessica held the packed joint expertly between her lips, using her hands to shield the wind as she lit it, before taking a delicate puff. I waited for her heart attack, or spontaneous combustion, or epileptic fit . . . But she just coughed and said, 'Woah, it tastes funny.' She took another small sip on the end. The sweet smell filled the air and landed on our clothes. She handed it to me, and I almost dropped it into my lap. 'Careful,' she said, laughing, while I blushed. I took in the orange embers glowing at the end and, not wanting to show hesitation, I raised the roach to my lips. I sucked in and the embers glowed brighter, then I erupted the smoke in a series of hacking coughs.

Jessica and Jade giggled as I hacked my lungs up, then Jessica started coughing too. Determined to look cool, I sucked in more smoke and held in the next cough. Three drags later, I passed it onto Jade, who also coughed within seconds. The blunt made its way back and forth, getting moist and floppy from our combined spit.

'I don't feel any different yet,' I said, when it had burnt down. The relief I wasn't dead replaced with disappointment that drugs weren't such a big deal.

'Me neither,' Jessica added. 'Maybe Mike's stuff was a rip-off or something?'

I snorted. 'We should tell Anne Robinson, get *Watchdog* on it.'

Jade snort-laughed at my snort. 'Did you just snort?'

I snorted back. 'So did you.'

Jessica involuntarily snorted, and then the three of us found ourselves in hysterics, seeing who could snort the longest or loudest, laughing 'til we were all crying.

'It hurts, my nose, it hurts,' Jessica kept saying, but snorting regardless.

I bent over, cradling my stomach to try to stop it from aching. My smile a Chelsea grin, my whole face aching. Away from the glare of boys, tucked away in our little safe coven in the garden, our bodies gave in to the hysteria, and it was only when Mike came out and said, 'What the hell are you girls doing over there?' that we were able to stop.

An hour later, we were in Georgina's little sister's bedroom, watching a VHS of *Aladdin*, screaming whenever he came on screen because he didn't have any nipples. The boys had popped their heads around the door a few times to check what the noise was, but quickly wandered off when they realised there wasn't any weed left, and we were too stoned to find any of them attractive any more.

'WHERE DID THE NIPPLES GO?' Jade asked, grasping my hand and tugging at it like a scared child.

'Why didn't he use up at least one genie wish on getting nipples?' Jessica asked, through a mouthful of cereal she'd stolen from the kitchen, spraying some over her lap with laughter. 'Surely that's the obvious first wish?'

Aladdin came onto the screen again and we all screamed. Mike's blue spikes appeared around the door, and he grinned. 'I keep thinking you're watching a horror movie and then, every time I check in on you, it's still just Disney.'

Jessica reached up and took his hand, pulling him down onto the duvet. 'Don't pretend Disney films didn't scare the shit out of you when you were young,' she said. In the blurred edges of my consciousness, I noticed a knowing smile on both their lips, and knew, with certainty, that they'd done more than roll a joint in that bathroom. Jade didn't seem to pick up on it though. 'I've got a bong going next door if you're interested?' he asked, just Jessica.

She tilted her chin down as she smiled. 'We're all good with our movie night. Thanks.'

'Are you sure?'

'Will you turn the music down?' she asked, flirt lacing every syllable. 'I don't want Pantera drowning out "A Whole New World".' Her megawatt charm meant she could say anything and it was cool and sexy, and Jade and I hid in it, knowing we were protected from their judgement. When Mike closed the door, Jade asked, 'What the hell is a bong?'

'I have no idea,' Jessica replied, and we all burst out laughing again, before screaming once more at Aladdin's no-nipples.

This time, Sally's head peered around the door.

'What the hell is going on in here?'

We pointed at the screen. 'Aladdin. He. Has. No. Nipples.'

She smiled in her smudged lipstick. 'No way! You guys notice it too? It really freaked me out when I was a kid.' She clambered onto the bed with us, as Jade put a pillow on her shoulder and let Sally rest her head there.

'The boys are all being really boring,' Sally informed us. 'They're taking it in turns to do bongs. And now most of them are just basically lying against a wall, half dead.'

'Drugs are bad,' Jade said, then laughed again.

'We definitely haven't had any,' I added.

Sally took in our trio of red eyes, and the in-jokes we'd created, and I could see her jealousy at the bond Jade and I had formed. She eyed me slightly nervously, and I smiled to silently reassure her I would not poach her friend. She relaxed and started laughing when we did. And our giddiness must've sent out some kind of bat signal, as more girls peeled away from the pushy boys, pawing their bodies through their clothes, and began poking their heads around the door, squealing 'I love this movie' and joining us. Soon, seven of us filled every space in the garish child's bedroom, and boys were forgotten. We all just sang 'A Whole New World' at the top of our lungs. The cannabis started to mellow me and make the world around me take on deep and meaningful qualities. I turned towards Jessica, her eyes almost entirely red, but her face relaxed and happy, and I felt profound love pulse through me. She sensed me looking and smiled back. She was so different when boys weren't around – so relaxed and funny and open and warm. I loved her like this so much. We rewound the song to karaoke along again. The door was closed. The boys were too busy sucking bongs to notice us missing, and, freed from their gaze, the girls became their best selves, found themselves actually enjoying a party. We gathered like a pack of wolves, shrieking along, becoming quickly hugely tactile with one another – picking up random sections of someone's hair and plaiting it, or stroking someone else's legs through their jeans. The door flew open and we all stiffened, twisting to the threshold with our stomachs sucked in. But it was just Georgina, wearing her now-bent fairy wings, looking as if she might've been crying.

'What are you guys doing?' she asked, her voice still sodden from drink.

Jessica held out her arms. 'We're watching *Aladdin*. Want to join?'

She paused, then folded herself down into a hunched ball on the carpet next to us, not quite looking at the screen.

'My house is so trashed,' she said so quietly, we almost didn't hear.

Jessica and I looked down at her. 'I can come back tomorrow and help you clean?' I said.

She ignored us, and stared at the ceiling. 'Dave's body was too heavy,' she murmured. 'What happened?'

'Georgina? Are you OK?' Jessica glanced over at me. We both slid off the bed and joined her on the floor. She sat with her dress splayed out around her like a fancy toadstool. It took a moment for her eyes to focus on us.

'He was so heavy. I'm so drunk,' she told us. 'Really . . . drunk . . . thirsty.'

'I'll go get you a glass of water.'

She half nodded, then twisted her head to the television, smiling a little. 'I love this movie. I want a pet tiger.'

I pushed myself up to standing, my mouth furry and dry, to get her a drink. It didn't occur to me that something more serious was wrong with Georgina. She just needed some water, to get put to bed, and help cleaning up her house the next day. In fact, I was still vaguely jealous she'd been chosen by Dave. I wondered, briefly even, if I should drink more at the next party to appear looser? Maybe then I'd be chosen? Maybe I was too uptight and sent off the wrong vibes, and, if I got wasted, boys would fancy me more? In the hallway I was engulfed in thick smoke, and I was temporarily distracted from my mission when I discovered Georgina's hallway had slightly embossed wallpaper. Totally baked still, I ran my finger over the ridged bits and it felt so nice that ten minutes passed, with me, alone, just stroking a wall. I eventually pulled myself away to go to the desecrated family bathroom. There was no loo roll left, urine stained the floor around the toilet, and someone had stubbed out a cigarette in the enamel of the bath. I turned the tap on and leant my head into the sink, guzzling down water, getting it down my chin, my neck, making my top wet. When I was finally sated, I stood up and caught my reflection in the mirror. A wave of disgust rolled through me – my ugly face, my stupid hair, my puffy gross body. I opened the mirrored cabinet to escape myself and found a toothbrush mug inside. I threw the brushes to one side, filled the mug with water, and carried it back to Georgina. Just as I came up to her bedroom, there was a roar of macho laughter where the bong smog hung even heavier around the door. And I leant against the wall and listened to their deep voices over the music.

'Hey hey hey,' a voice I couldn't place said. 'Have you heard this one . . . *it's not rape, it's SURPRISE SEX.*'

A tsunami of macho cheers blasted around the room, pulsing out of the door. I frowned, took a sip of Georgina's water, and kept listening.

'How about *no means yes, and yes means anal?*' That was Mike's voice, so it got a louder laugh, naturally.

'*What do nine out of ten people enjoy? Gang rape.*'

'*What do you call a fat girl with a rape whistle? Optimistic.*'

These jokes weren't something they saved for just themselves, I would soon learn. They were regularly rolled out over the next two years at college, and the girls would all laugh along – sometimes even coming up with 'better ones' of their own. The boys loved it when we joined in. You could joke about rape in a place as safe as Surrey. Nothing like that happened around here. Eventually, I took the water in to

Georgina, and Jessica and I held her up so she could drink it properly. She begged us to get everyone to leave, weeping into her knees, using her skirt as a tissue. We turned off the music, and, with quite a lot of protest, eventually managed to get everyone out. I saw Dave high-five a friend as they walked up Georgina's drive. Mike stayed a bit, loitering around Jessica, as Jade, Sally, and I tried to tidy up the worst of the mess. There was a significant burn in the carpet. A broken chair. A smell that her parents would definitely still notice when they returned home to their husk of a much-loved daughter. From what I could tell, all the mess had been caused by the boys, almost like they'd revelled in creating it. Jade watched Mike and Jessica closely, and I watched her watch him.

'Do you think Dave and Georgina will become a couple after tonight?' Sally asked us, as we chucked away plastic cups with cigarettes floating at the bottom.

'I'm not sure,' Mike said. 'Dave's quite a sensitive guy. And Georgina . . . I dunno, with her fairy wings and stuff? She might be a bit much for him.'

I checked on her one more time before we left. She was curled up, foetal, on her sister's bed, her beloved wings crushed under her. I put a bucket and a glass of water next to the bed, and a note with my phone number, telling her to ring me when she wanted me around the next morning to help clean up properly.

But Georgina never called.

In fact, Georgina never hung out with us ever again.

After that night she found a group of Christian students and sat with them in the cafeteria. She started carrying a

Bible with her everywhere, under her arm, like a designer bag. She wore aggressively unsexy clothes – a giant rainbow hoodie with pompoms hanging off the sleeves, teamed with baggy jeans covered in pink glitter-pen initials of *WWJD?* Weight started clinging to her hips and thighs as she stuffed plates of chips down herself each lunchtime, straining the fabric. She hardly acknowledged me when I said 'hi' in the corridor.

It became a joke. Georgina joining *God Squad.* Dave was teased for ever having got with her. *What happens in Bible Camp stays in Bible Camp . . . Did she whisper the Lord's Prayer as you fingered her?*

'Oh, shut up, it was only one fucking time,' Dave would say, red and angry.

Georgina became an easy joke. A footnote in a story about an epic party. Georgina became someone he had to live down.

Thirty-two

Here was how it was supposed to go: Ben and I host our first-ever dinner party. It is an astounding success, with us basically becoming the epitome of a Richard Curtis couple, laughing with our diverse group of friends around our dining table. Ben would look over at me as I served coffee towards the end of the night, dewy and smiling, and realise I was The One. That this life we'd built was beyond special. That I was beyond special. That he needed to lock this down immediately or risk losing the best thing that had ever happened to him. However, instead, the night before, as we sat on our sofa, discussing what to cook for everyone, he mentioned that the HR lady from college had got engaged.

'That's nice,' I said, curling my feet up and glancing down at our hand-written menu so my face wouldn't reveal anything.

'Yeah, for her, I guess.' Ben stretched his arms over his head, and then shrugged, before muttering the words that would undo me. 'I dunno. I'm so over the whole marriage thing, but she seemed happy, at least.' He leant over and looked at our shared scrap of paper that was now shaking in my hands. 'Do you think charcuterie meats AND bread and dips is too much for a starter?'

The walls of our flat squeezed me in. My breathing quickened in my throat. I tried to suck air into my ribcage to keep my voice steady as I said, 'OK. I didn't know you felt like that.'

'About the bread? Just, aren't we having bread with the lasagne?'

'No. Not the bread . . . the whole marriage thing.'

'Oh, that.' Ben looked up at me, shocked, as if he would've been more surprised if I'd objected to the lasagne. 'I mean, it's not such a big deal, is it? It's certainly not something I've thought about with us. Don't you agree?'

The menu fluttered to the floor. My whole world caved in. I wanted to burst into tears, scream, and smack him in the face, all at the same time. I was such an idiot. *Such* an idiot for thinking he was on the verge of choosing me. I knew what his words meant. I wasn't stupid. He may as well have said, *'It's not marriage I'm unsure about, it's you. And I'm wasting all your last fertile years by dithering, until you get too old to conceive, and then, suddenly, I will believe in marriage again, just not with you, but with this hot twenty-eight-year-old.'*

'Umm,' I managed, while Ben put a hand on my knee I wanted to smack off. 'Umm.'

How could this be happening? How could I have got it so wrong? I knew his former engagement had slowed him down, but it hadn't occurred to me it had put him off altogether. I felt so internally humiliated . . . especially as I'd thought it could've happened any day now. After this fucking dinner party. But, of course I couldn't say any of this to him. Not out loud. That would make him want to marry me even less.

'Oh,' I got out, on top of the *umm*.

'I mean, do you really not agree?' Ben asked, taking my hand now, as if he was asking a mild political opinion about fucking fair trade oat milk, not our future together. 'Like, what does it mean, anyway?'

'Marriage?'

'Yeah.'

'I think it means wanting to spend the rest of your life together.'

He grinned, almost smugly. 'But you don't have to be married to do that, do you?'

'Hmm.' I bit my lip to withhold the scream. *No. Not you. Not you, good one. Not the one I am counting on. Not the one I finally thought it would be easy with.*

'Well, do you?'

'I . . . guess not.'

He relaxed back into the sofa, sighing happily at my lack of disapproval, pleased I was playing the part, while chaos reigned behind my ribcage. I leant over and picked up the menu, just to give myself something to do.

'I guess I'm just surprised is all,' I said, twisting towards him. I said it so neutrally I wanted an independent body to watch this back and award me some kind of medal. 'You know? Because you were engaged before?'

Ben shrugged with his whole body. 'If anything, *Tiffany* made me realise how stupid the whole thing is. How it means nothing. Not really. I mean, yeah, we were that committed that we'd promised, literally *promised*, to spend the rest of our lives together. And look, it clearly didn't mean anything. Being engaged is not the same as showing up every day. Not like you and me do.'

He smiled – knowing, maybe, that the compliment would placate me. Which, frustratingly, it did, but only for a milli-second. Then he turned his glorious face to mine, his eyes wide, glinting, and aggressively changed the subject. 'So, do you think it's too dangerous to try the lasagne tomorrow? I've had one triumph and one disaster, but I think, if I don't rush it this time . . .'

He'd determinedly kept us off the topic for the rest of the evening, which was almost as unforgivable as what he'd said in the first place. I hated him as he brushed his teeth, humming, like nothing had happened. I hated him even more when he kissed me goodnight, dared to tell me he loved me, and then turned off the light and fell asleep with no effort whatsoever. I sat up, watching him in the gloom of the city night, wondering if all men are actually sociopaths. I hardy slept, as anxiety pulsed through my body, making me physically nauseous. Ben, however, leapt up when the alarm went at six thirty. Bright-eyed, bushy-tailed, and commitment phobic. 'I'm so excited about tonight,' he said, kissing me on the lips, before dashing out of the door with a grin on his face, leaving me alone in my spiral. I managed one whole hour of going totally mad in the flat, before I decided to go into the office and escape myself there, despite it being my working from home day.

The office initially provided some distraction, but too much to get any work done.

'Oh my God, she's here on a Friday,' Derek said, when I got

in, flustered and with no make-up on. 'You missed QUITE the office goss fest last night,' he added, grinning, before delightedly filling me in. The previous evening, some 'after work drinks' had led to an almost all-nighter, and the open-plan floor was buzzing with hungover gossip. Apparently Ally from the Sports desk had got hammered and kissed the weird IT guy, and nobody was going to let her live it down. After a morning of non-stop whispers, I'd taken myself to an isolation cubicle with my laptop in an attempt to focus and meet my deadline. I sighed and stared at the blank wall above the tiny desk, looking every-where but at the dense *Counsellors' Ethical Framework* I was supposed to be reading. But I was distracted. Since Jessica had come back, I'd been recalling lost memories from the past, and they were combining with insecurities of the present. I pulled out my phone and found temporary distraction with Jade.

Fern: Guess who I'm having around for a dinner party tonight?
Jade: Well not me, obviously. Thanks so much for the invite, NOT
Fern: You live in Scotland!
Jade: No excuse.
Anyway, who is it?
Sigmund Freud?
Ooo! I know . . . the Obamas
Fern: Negative
Brilliant guesses though
My dinner party guest is . . .
drums rolling . . .
JESSICA!!!!
Well, her and some of Ben's colleagues etc
Jade: Woah.

Bloody hell.
Headfuck.
Fern: ???

I stared through the glass wall at my colleagues chatting enthusiastically about the socio-political developments. I forced myself to look down at the document again. That week's counselling homework was to read it and circle all the 'grey areas' where the breaches of boundaries would be less clear-cut. I also needed to read it for my latest vertical article I'd pitched called 'What If Your Counsellor Knows Your Ex? And other ethical dilemmas they're quietly working through.' But my brain wouldn't cooperate.

I sighed again, picked up my red pen, coloured in a few 'os', and put it down again. Jade hadn't replied to my message, so there went that distraction. And Ben was very adamant he wanted to cook tonight's big dinner party, so I couldn't even faff about buying last-minute ingredients in Sainsbury's Local. I was sort of dreading that evening and the fake I'm-fine-ness I'd be forced to perform. The inevitability of my next action hung heavy in the air around me. My finger twitched over my laptop mouse in anticipation, waiting for the signal. I knew what I was going to do, and I knew it was wrong, and unhealthy, and fucked up, and pathetic, and yet I also knew I was going to do it anyway. Bile prepared itself in my body and I actually gave myself credit for how long I was holding out. *Nobody will know,* I reminded myself. *Nobody will ever know. Especially Ben, because I would never, ever, tell him.*

I put the Ethical Framework down and clicked my mouse to reactivate the screen. I pulled up a fresh incognito tab and twisted my screen so nobody walking past the cubicle would see what I was doing. *Who first? Who first?* I pondered how to order my act of self-harm. I decided to start on the *less-bad*, and build up from there – as if I was building a cheeseboard with stronger and stronger flavours. I pulled up Instagram and typed in the name of Ben's university girlfriend. *Claire Upton*, and there was her familiar avatar, with its familiar *'this account is private'*. The same on her Facebook page. Claire hadn't changed her profile picture in over a year. Didn't she know that was the only thing to stalk her by? Apart from her fucking perfect 'psychology blog', where she only said appropriate things about clients and revealed nothing about herself whatsoever, like a perfectly reasonable psychologist would do. The pre-produced bile started rising up my throat as I clicked through her latest posts about 'Anxiety in the Time of Social Media' and 'The Mother Wound'. There was still only one promo shot on her *About Me* page, which I knew by heart, but clicked on anyway. My breathing fell short even though Claire was not an ex who worried me that much. She and Ben had dated for two years, after meeting on their psychology degree course, and had inevitably but amicably split up after graduation, like so many do. Plus, she was a qualified psychologist and had behaved reasonably and healthily since their split. They never really spoke. According to Ben, mentioned in passing, she was married now, with one kid, which he only knew about through mutual uni mates. Of course, it hurt deeply that Claire was so clever and successful, but I still had a good enough career for it not to trigger me *too much*. Her blog post on the Mother Wound was actually really good, and I felt a stab of self-congratulations that I was mature enough to praise her, even while stalking her like a crazy person. I shook my head and clicked off, laying my face down on my desk, thudding it once against the wood.

That's enough now. Do your work. You have a deadline. You have a dinner party tonight. Don't feed the monster. The only person you're hurting is you . . . and . . .

OK, so Delta Riley was such a total Pick Me girl. I couldn't quite believe she and Ben had been together. When I'd first found her on Instagram, I'd almost vomited. She did pole-dancing fitness classes, and most of her snaps were her hanging upside-down with her legs wide open. Yet all her pole-dancing clothes had slogans like 'HOT FEMINIST' and 'GIRL BOSS' on them. Last year she'd posted a picture of her licking a vibrator, with the caption 'Night In With My Boo'. As her page came up, I saw she'd posted a new black-and-white photo of herself totally naked, splayed in a sexual pose, head thrown back like she was mid-orgasm, her nipples and vagina only just hidden, while she mimed touching herself. Under the photo was an earnest caption about her 'being the fat kid in high school' and 'swipe to see my puppy-fat days, it took a lot for me to post this photo'. I clicked along and burst into a sharp sarcastic laugh as she revealed a photo of a pretty girl, who couldn't have been more than a size ten. I checked to see if Ben had liked it, and felt sick until I saw he hadn't.

'We were never serious,' he had said, when we were stupid enough to have a conversation about our relationship histories, thinking it wouldn't cause any issues. 'I met her in a hostel, and she was just someone to go travelling with, really.'

'How long did you travel for?'

'Only like two years.'

'Oh, so you were together for two years?'

'I guess. It was more like a fling though, you know? We always knew it couldn't be serious as we were from different countries.'

Everyone knew 'fling' meant 'good fucking', so I was already freaking out inwardly, while quietly saying 'hmm' and smiling serenely to show him how mature I was.

'She's got a bit weird since,' he admitted. 'We're still mates online, and she's one of those people who behaves like a celebrity, even though she only has, like, five hundred followers. I mean, whatever she wants to do, but she wasn't like that with me. Well, actually, she took a lot of photos for Facebook, I guess, when we were travelling. . .'

I know, I thought. I've clicked through every single tagged one of you on your account and wondered who the hell the hot American girl is. I'm so glad I did it. It makes life so much better that I have the mental image of you kissing in front of the Grand Canyon burnt on the backs of my retinas whenever I close my eyes. Also, why the hell did you 'like' her comment on your post last year where she said she missed you, you fucking dick?

Still lost in the rabbit hole, I went into Ben's Facebook and put myself through hell, looking at him and Delta's travelling snaps again. Each click turned my stomach to cottage cheese. Ben looked so young, tanned, free, happy. What must their relationship have been like? No work stress, no exhaustion from the drudgery of life, waking up and going on an adventure every day, free time for sex in the afternoons rather than cramming it in on the weekends?

'STOP,' I said out loud. 'For God's sake, Fern, just fucking STOP.'

I clicked off all the tabs and leant back in my chair, holding my heart through my jumper. The theatrics were half for myself, half for my invisible voyeur, watching me or judging me – maybe Ben himself? Because I knew I wasn't going to stop. Not after last night's conversation about marriage. Since the second it had ended, I'd tortured myself with her fucking name. And, even though every atom of my body was now curdled, I wouldn't finish until I got to . . .

. . . *Tiffany Quinn.*

God, she looked so fucking smug in her fucking profile picture. On a boat, with sunglasses on, her long chestnut hair blowing in the wind. The shared photos of her and Ben came up, the ones she'd tagged him in over four years ago. My fingers shook as I clicked on, wanting to die, wanting to stop, wishing their relationship had never happened. There it was. The engagement photo. His mouth kissing her cheek, her beaming like a smug slug into the camera, holding up her fourth finger for everyone to see the ultimate display of being chosen.

'He liked it so . . . he didn't put a ring on it, because he knows me too well to DARE try and pick a ring for himself, so he put a Haribo ring on it and then took me to a jewellery store to pick out the ring for myself. THAT'S why I said yes.'

I pushed my wheelie chair back, until I was grabbing the edge of the desk at arm's length, forgetting anyone walking past could see me. Why had they both kept this photo on their profiles? Wasn't it too humiliating? She broke off the engagement. She broke his heart. She, according to my intense stalking, had a new boyfriend, the one with the boat from her profile picture. The only time I'd ever sort of questioned Ben about it, saying 'Wow, remember Facebook?', he'd laughed and said, 'Yeah, Christ, who still goes on there?' so it was likely he'd forgotten this photo was still up. This historical document of him believing a woman who wasn't me was The One. The woman he would be married to now if she hadn't told him, *no, I don't choose you back*. Christ, the power in that! To be a woman and to not choose someone back. I hated her so much. I'd never met her, but I despised her. The power she held over me. The knowledge that my happiness with Ben only existed because she had ended things. That I was the consolation prize, even though he'd never admit that to me . . . I was stumbling into crazy town, I knew this. I knew my thoughts were poison, lies, bad feminism. I knew Ben loved me, cherished me, and probably would not choose Tiffany now. The man I knew and loved would never in a thousand years pose for a *'he liked it so . . .'* engagement announcement. Time had passed. People grow and change. The past is in the past. I knew this, I knew this, and yet . . . for fuck's sake! Why did he propose to her and not me? What was wrong with me? What was so much better about Tiffany fucking Quinn? God, I felt sick. I needed to stop. God, if he ever knew that I did this. WHY did I do this? Did anyone else do this? Was I a crazy troll nutcase, or did everyone else do this too? My hand hovered over the mouse button, deciding whether to click off her profile, or click through to torture myself with the photos from when they went to Kefalonia together when . . . my phone buzzed on the desk, saving me from myself.

Jade: Holy fuck, Jessica.
Woah.
What? Why? How? Wasn't she in America?

Then, after a pause of her typing, not typing, and typing again.

Jade: I've not thought about that time for so long.
I have to say, Fern, it fucks me up a bit, thinking about those lot from college.

I inhaled sharply at the last two messages, the sheer brutal honesty of them. I'd always been grateful Jade and I had stayed in touch. She was the sole surviving link between me and sixth form, and I was hers. Sally had married young, similar to Jessica, and had four children and moved to Cornwall. She now mostly posted lots of mad conspiracy shit on her profiles. Whereas Jade had gone to uni like me, and also like me, her parents had left the area. She currently lived in Edinburgh with her long-term girlfriend, Maggy, after coming out to me as bi over the about-twice-yearly catch-up drinks we tried to fit in whenever one of us was nearby.

Fern: Sorry
Didn't mean to upset you
I'm still quite surprised by it all really

I tapped my hands on the desk as I waited for her reply, drumming a beat on my unread Ethical Framework. Trying to slot Jade into the memories I'd been dancing through since

Jessica returned. Though we met at college, we never really talked much about college, which didn't seem strange until now. Jade worked for a homelessness charity, so we spent lots of time chatting about our work, sharing ideas, occasionally attending the same conferences.

Jade: Sorry too.
Don't mean to be weird.
It's just . . . do you ever think back on those days and just feel really . . . angry?

'I . . .' I said out loud, as if she'd asked me in person. 'I guess . . .'

I'd mostly been reliving why I'd been so angry at Jessica for so long, and what she'd done, and hadn't thought much about the rest of it. But, with Jade's prompt, a thousand more memories arrived, pre-packaged in my mind, discarding their bows as if they were in *Fantasia*, and started dancing behind my eyes.

Georgina's party . . .

Jade: Like, I've never told you this but, I actually had to go to therapy about it all.
I was telling Maggy about it, and she was the one who pointed out how . . . fucked it all was.
Fern: Oh my God, you never said. I'm so sorry!
Jade: It's fine.
Like, I'm fine. I just . . .
Woah, Jessica. Headfuck.
Fern: Are you mad at her or something?

Jade: No.

The girls I'm fine with.

But the boys?

Don't you remember, Fern?

It was fucked.

Old names and old faces started to blur into view. Mike's blue spikes and charming smile. Liam smiling as he wore a pair of fairy wings at Reading Festival . . . *Fairy wings* . . . Dave with the long Jesus-like hair he'd flick around at gigs, grinning as we sat around him afterwards, plaiting it, almost like a willing uncle. Those boys had been our friends and boyfriends. We'd grown up together. They'd been nice, middle-class guys. They walked you home to make sure you were safe. But then . . . the rape jokes. *Georgina's party.* Games of spin-the-bottle when everyone was too wasted and it was always their idea. The comments they made about us. The song lyrics they wrote about women in the gigs we went to, and cheered on . . .

My hand went back to my mouse. Tiffany's profile was cancelled without me giving it much notice. The hours I'd spent poring over all these women, and yet I had never thought to check up on the boys from my own past.

Boys who were men now.

It was almost a shock when Mike's name came up on the drop-down menu. This mysterious alpha from my adolescence on something as basic as Facebook. He looked way older than thirty-two, crinkles all around his eyes. In his profile picture he held up a baby, presumably his, and . . .

'*No fucking way,*' I said out loud, but this time not because

I imagined I was being watched through a portal. But it was ludicrous. The baby was wearing a Babygro that said 'My Daddy's a Feminist' on it. I clicked through and met Mike's wife, going backwards through their love affair, laughing with a sharp *ha* as I saw pictures of them together on the Women's March. Jessica's words drifted poison through my brain again.

'*They have the women they fuck, and the women they fall in love with.*'

Did *Gillian* know about the jokes he used to tell? Girls he used to use and shame? Did he even remember himself? How easy it was for these boys. When they needed a groupie to screw and discard, there we were. Throwing ourselves around to their shit music, worshipping their mediocrity, and feeling lucky if they chose us that night to touch up and then tell everyone we were a slut afterwards. And, now, when they needed girls to love them, and still want to fuck them even though they're fat and bald and their shit band never made it, girls who will grow their child inside their body, and make them look like good guys with their pointless slogans – they'd managed to find those girls exactly when they needed them too.

Fern: OK, so you are so right.
I'm sitting here alone and remembering everything and feeling fucked up too
Jade: RIGHT?
Sorry to unleash this on you. We should chat about it properly. Over drinks. I've got a conference next month, maybe we can meet?

Jessica can come too!

Bloody hell.

Jessica.

Is she still ridiculously pretty?

Fern: Yep.

Jade: Fuck it. She's not invited :)

I laughed, feeling soothed by Jade's joke, even though she was the one who'd ruffled me. I took a giant breath and vowed to turn my computer off and actually do my reading. But, as I went to close the tab, a name in Mike's *Friends* caught my attention and my hand guided the mouse to click on it.

Dave.

He still had his long hair, though it was more straggly now, and frizzy from age. He'd padded out, his stomach straining against his KISS t-shirt, his arms decorated with crap tattoos. All of his photos were of him playing the guitar, and I clicked through his *Work and Education* and found the name of his current band.

Angry Girl Collective™.

It couldn't have been more ridiculous. There he was, part of a female-fronted band. The only guy there. The singer had long pink hair, and the drummer had long blue hair, and there was Dave, arms around both women, beaming at the camera. I clicked through onto the band's website, and muttered 'fuck' as their angry guitar music blasted out of my laptop. I turned it down, but not off, as it was sort of catchy. I clicked on the *About Us* page and read about the band's ethos. *'Female empowerment'*, and *'putting women at the front of the metal scene'*. Dave smiled to the tips of his ears in each photo. Of course he did. From what I could tell, this was the first and only band he'd ever been in that had actually achieved anything. I zoomed in on his smile. I'd seen it before. At Georgina's party. When a friend had high-fived him while she lay comatose with crumpled wings beneath her.

I'm not sure how much time passed until I came to again. Blinking myself out of the uncomfortable disassociation I'd fallen into. I hadn't lost time like that in years, and a shiver tingled through me. A quiet rage is what yanked me back. A pulsing urge to do something.

I pulled up the band's website, clicking on their *Contact Us* page.

Name: A friend
Email address: DontTrustHim@AFriend.com
Message: Dave is a rapist. I thought it was important you should know. Be careful.

I stared at what I'd written – knowing it was true, but also too filled with doubt to send it. My finger hovered over the Send button, picturing the mess it would make. Confusion it would cause. The denial, maybe even genuine, from Dave. Who knew how he viewed that night at Georgina's party where he got with the Christian girl who was too drunk to push him off? Did he ever think about it when he saw women marching on the news, or his band members sharing their own #MeToo moments? Or did he truly believe he was one of the good guys? This message was a clusterbomb, and one that was nothing to do with me. I slowly deleted each character until the screen was blank again. Annoyed at myself for not sending it, furious at Dave for his shamelessness. I could see my reflection in my laptop screen, my face scrunched up in rage. I took a deep breath into my stomach and clicked off the website, forcing myself to focus on my Ethical Framework. I needed to drag myself together. To get home in time for the dinner party tonight and pretend I was fine.

Getting lost in the past was a pointless endeavour.

Seventeen

February 2003

It took at least a term and a half before I realised Liam Gillingham was staring at me in our English Literature lessons. I was quite certain he just found the wall display behind my head inherently interesting. I mean, this was *Liam Gillingham*. Possibly the best-looking boy I'd seen in real life, with his green eyes and good hair. When he finally noticed me noticing, he cracked a huge smile across the classroom, nodding, all like *'yes, I've been looking at you'*. And, of course, I fell in love with him instantly. It just kept getting better. He was in a band. He didn't know Jessica existed, and therefore found me attractive. And, finally, after two weeks of intense eye contact across the classroom, he came over and asked me out on a date. A date. Me. My very first date!

'I'm not sure what's wrong with him,' I told the girls, who squealed when I told them. We sat in a car park with kebabs on our laps, passing around a spliff. 'Do you think he's had a significant head trauma?'

Jessica rolled her eyes kindly as she took the blunt from

me. 'Have you considered there's nothing wrong with him and he just legitimately finds you fit?'

I took a mouthful of shredded cabbage drowned in burger sauce. 'Well, it won't be that.'

'Don't be ridiculous. You're gorgeous and smart and mysterious.'

Jade and Sally nodded along with red-rimmed eyes. Sally stabbed a forkful of lettuce in her plastic container. She'd not had her kebab in pitta bread, as she was currently on the Atkins diet. Last week she'd been on a diet where she could only eat branded cereal for two out of three meals.

'You're all wrong. He definitely has a head trauma,' I insisted.

'How did he ask you out again?' Jade asked.

'Well, as we know, he's been staring at me all term in English,' I said, 'but then, this morning, he came and actually sat next to me, and we got partnered to talk about *Doctor Faustus* together. Then he kept deliberately brushing his arm against mine . . .'

The girls squealed again. Jade started coughing from the excitement.

'. . . and then, when the bell rang, he told me he had a gig coming up and I should come along and, I quote, *hang out after.*'

The squealing cranked up multiple notches. It was so strange, being the centre of attention in this telling-about-boys dynamic. It was often only Sally who got this treatment, who fell in love once a month. Jessica kept her dalliances quiet. Despite Jessica's constant silence about her sex life, since that first party of Georgina's, she'd created quite a reputation for herself. Jade's worst fears were proven correct when Mike and Jessica indeed had 'a thing' for a month or two before deciding to be 'just friends'. Murmurs on the wind were that she'd let him do 'kinky shit' with her. Though, whenever questioned about it, both of them just smiled – Jessica raising her eyebrows, Mike shrugging. They broke it off for no obvious reason, unclear who had ended it first, but seemed to remain friendly. Then Jessica had got with this guy from the year above called Karl. When they broke things off, further murmurs went around that she was 'filthy'. The boys would make jokes when she wasn't there, calling her 'nymph' or 'Slutty Jessica', while the girls laughed along, me included. Especially as Jessica didn't seem to mind. In fact, she even started wearing a belly top with 'nymph' on it – calling everyone's bluff – and Mike had declared her a legend once more. Of course, the subtle slut-shaming eased the second Jessica was there, and the boys would instead bombard her with adoration – hoping they'd be next to be picked, showing the rest of us no attention at all. And Jessica's smile never waned, her confidence never faltered. She never addressed the rumours and mostly played up to them. Her current favourite trick was putting a lighter down her cleavage and then brandishing her breasts at any boy who asked for a light. 'There you go,' she'd say, smiling innocently, and they'd pluck it from her body, grinning, using the opportunity to let their fingers drift over her skin.

So, until now, it was never me getting any attention, and it felt bloody amazing.

'So, what do you know about him?' Jade asked, being very gracious considering we were now on slightly unequal footing.

I'm not sure how I would've felt if she'd suddenly been plucked out from our 'ugly friend' obscurity.

'Well, he hates capitalism,' I said, feeling very grown-up for using the word capitalism. 'He keeps wearing this T-shirt that says "The proletarians have nothing to lose but their chains". And, last lesson, when he was telling me about the gig, he said they have a song about capitalism called "Burn the Bin".'

They all nodded like that made perfect sense. Did *they* understand what the bin was? Because I hadn't figured it out yet.

'What else?' Sally said. 'He's got such good hair.'

I blushed. It was incredible really, how much I fancied Liam Gillingham, even though we'd only had about two conversations.

'Mike says their band are really good. They're called Suicide Pact.'

My three friends nodded again, like that made perfect sense.

'And that's about it so far. He seems quiet and mysterious and deep mostly, and, yeah, weirdly into me because of his head injury.'

Jade and Sally chuckled, while Jessica threw a chip at me. 'Stop being INSANE,' she said. 'Just enjoy it. I can't believe I'm missing this band night and can't watch this whole date unfold. Stupid divorced-parents weekend away. Jade? Sally? Will you take detailed observations the whole night?'

Liam's 'gig' coincidentally was at some open band night in Croydon, and Mike's band was playing too, making my first-ever date something our entire peer group would be watching. I couldn't decide if that made it better or worse.

'That would be voyeuristic and weird and of course I will,' Jade said.

We all cracked up and got back to our kebabs, moving onto planning my perfect outfit. While Jessica asked for his star sign to figure out our compatibility, I watched her with a funny feeling. What I could never admit to her was that I was *relieved* she couldn't come. It was my chance to shine. And the only way I could do that was for her not to be there.

Thirty-two

Ben returned home after me in a mad rush, just as I was plumping the cushions in the living room.

'I know, I'm late. I'm so sorry. Sorry.' He dumped his coat and bag onto my freshly washed floor, slid in for a quick kiss, then ran into the bathroom for a shower.

'Did your phone die?' I called. I'd spent a good five minutes convinced he might be having an affair, before reminding myself that was crazy, and his phone regularly lost battery.

'Yes, sorry. Fucking iPhone,' he called over the running water. 'It's all in hand, I promise. The dinner WILL be ready in time.'

'Can I help?' I asked, not adding all the pass-agg extras I wanted to add, like *'Everyone will be here soon'*, and *'I knew this would happen'*, and *'I can't believe you're making me go through with this dinner party after last night'*.

'No, no. You've done enough by cleaning the place. Thank you. Just chill and relax.'

Of course, I didn't chill or relax, and ended up helping

because we didn't have enough time. We squeezed together in the kitchen and I plopped deli olives into bowls, arranged crudités into circles, and decanted shop-bought dips into their own bowls to make them look posher. Still only in his boxers, Ben assembled a lasagne at startling speed.

'OK, we've got loads of time. Loads,' he lied. 'Sorry again. Friday staff drinks spiralled. I kept trying to leave, but kept getting cornered by Matthew, droning on about the UCAS process. And I couldn't tell him I needed to get home to a dinner party because that would highlight the fact we'd invited the rest of the department and not him.' He chucked some grilled courgettes onto the rectangle of tomato sauce and clicked some pasta sheets over it. Ben was at his best in chaos, thriving in it like it was an unruly classroom.

'Talk me through who's coming again,' I asked, gently prodding his back to get access to the drawer I needed.

'So Douglas, my head of department, and his wife, Sophia. You'll like her. She's a clinical psychologist. She's read your articles and says they're really good.'

I smiled. He was right. 1 liked her already.

'And then Joanie, who works in the English department. She's really nice. And her boyfriend, Frederick. I've not met him before. I get the feeling he's a bit posh, but we'll see.'

'I hope they don't mind the ramshackle table situation.'

'Relax. People are just happy to be fed. It's going to be great.' He planted a wet kiss on my lips. 'Our first proper dinner party, Fern. It's going to be great.'

I kissed him back, feeling a huge rush of love, despite everything. This felt so nice . . . feeding others, nesting, publicly declaring our relationship to important people that he worked with. 'And, hey, tonight I get to finally meet Jessica,' he said, eyes wide. 'It's about time.'

I widened my eyes to match his. 'It is indeed.'

'Is she going to tell me all the awful things you did as a teenager?'

I laughed. 'With Jessica and me, that's usually the other way around. She was always the *crazy* one, in that way. Whereas I was too busy being crazy in a different, mental-health way.'

He grinned and planted another kiss, this one on my forehead. 'Poor Mini-Fern,' he said. 'If only she knew she was going to grow up and meet such a hot, wonderful man.'

'Which everyone knows cures you of all mental health issues.'

'Oh yeah. That's what I was teaching the kids today. Freud was very clear on this – *get laid, hysteria vanishes*.'

We'd not mentioned the previous night, but, with his arms around me, and him laughing gently into my hair, I felt maybe it didn't matter. That having him, like this, was enough. Maybe . . .

When I was convinced Ben could just about pull everything together, I went and got ready. Jessica's imminent arrival made me up my game, and, after showering and spritzing my naked body with perfume as if I was a Bond girl, I stepped into a black, backless halterneck dress, adorning it only with a red lip stain and piling my hair on top of my head.

'*Hubba hubba,*' Ben said as I stepped out into the living room, now complete, with a laid table and the scent of bubbling cheese. He practically ran over, claiming my body with his hands. 'You look amazing, Fern.'

'Did you just say *hubba hubba*?'

'Please still sleep with me.' He pawed at my naked back and kissed my neck. I closed my eyes, savouring this feeling of temporary power over him. For all the times Ben said how much he wanted me to 'feel comfortable and look natural', he didn't half give me the most attention when I'd made the most effort. He ran his hands down my arms and I pulled away. 'Be careful, you'll get make-up on your fingers.'

'You've put make-up on your scars?'

I tugged my arms behind my back. 'Just a little. Don't want to scare your colleagues.'

'They're from the psychology department, Fern.'

'Yeah, still.' I smiled brightly, just as the bell went. 'That will be Jessica.'

'Let me quickly get dressed. See you in a sec.'

I buzzed Jessica in, and checked my reflection as I waited for her to knock. I smacked my stained lips together and smiled at myself. The door went and my heart temporarily flew into my throat. This was it. The introduction of old world to new. A twinge of paranoia ached through me and I hoped I'd made the right decision. But Jessica seemed so different from the girl I'd known, wiser, more self-aware, less of a threat, and . . . still stunning as I opened the door.

'Hi,' she said nervously, waving with a bottle of expensive-looking red wine in her hand. 'I'm not too early, am I?'

I took the wine and hugged her thin frame. 'Not at all! Come in. You can leave your bag in our room when Ben's finished changing.'

She took tiny steps in, looking all around even though she'd been here before. She was wearing a deep red jumpsuit that looked effortlessly sexy and effortlessly casual at the same time. 'Am I the first here?'

'Yes, but Heather and her wife will be here soon. She's always aggressively early. You remember her, right?'

'Yes, sort of.'

'Don't worry. I don't know half the people coming either. They're from Ben's college. Do you want a drink? Wine?'

'Yes, please.' She had her arms crossed, almost distracting from how good she looked. As my eyes glanced over her flat stomach, I still felt shock that a baby had once been in there.

I sloshed out two generous glasses of wine and we stood, eating the olives, while I kept checking the progress of the lasagne through the glass of the oven door.

'Is Bridget OK with you being away?'

'Worryingly fine. I was hoping she'd at least say she missed me, but all she said was "Grandma lets me have two choco-late mousses when you're not here".'

I laughed while her eyes darted around as if she was about to be attacked. At that moment, Ben bowled in, looking ridic-ulously sexy in a smart, baby-blue shirt, his hair still slightly damp from the shower. He broke into a grin and walked with an outstretched hand. 'You must be Jessica,' he said. 'So nice to finally meet you. Thanks for coming all this way to be let down by my shit cooking.'

My eyes were on his, taking in him taking her in. I saw his gaze flutter up her perfect body, quickly reaching her stunning face. He betrayed no hint of attraction, but would be blind not to have at least a stirring.

Jessica gave a small smile. 'So nice to meet you too. I've heard so much about you from Fern.'

'All good I hope. Ahh, great, you've got wine. I need one.' He unscrewed the bottle and poured himself some. 'So, you guys have been friends since . . .'

'. . . we were fourteen,' I said.

'Yes.' Jessica was gulping her wine down. I'd never seen her so nervous before, especially with a man in the room. I'd been expecting her to dazzle and charm and flirt and bowl him over with her Jessica-ness, but she still had her arms clasped around her. 'I was new in school, and she was the only one who was nice to me.'

Ben put an arm around my waist. 'Sounds like Fern.' I beamed, relieved he'd never know all my dark jealous thoughts. 'It's great that you're back in touch now,' he said. 'Fern's loved seeing you again.'

I saw the compliment plant a seed in Jessica's face, one that bloomed into a quick, full smile. 'Really?'

'Yeah. Of course. You'll have to tell us all about America over dinner. I'm fascinated to know what it's like to live there.' The buzzer went. 'Hang on, I'll get it.' Ben dashed out to let the other guests in. Jessica had already drained her wine.

'Are you OK?' I asked.

She nodded. 'Yeah, sorry. It's just . . . it's been so long since I've been to anything like this. Especially on my own. I was only ever *Brendan's wife*, you know?'

I put my glass down and gave her a hug. 'Just be yourself and it will be great.'

As guests poured through the door, clutching wine and flowers, hugs and introductions, the Jessica I remembered reappeared. She shook hands with everyone, smiling, bowling them over with her beauty. 'Hello, lovely to meet you, I'm Jessica. How do you know these guys? What do you do? Psychology? That's so cool.' When Heather and Katie let themselves in with their spare key, Jessica stiffened for a second, then went over to say hello.

'Hi there, do you remember? We met in your first year of university?'

Heather glanced over at me and raised an eyebrow. 'Of course. How could I forget?'

'Thanks for that,' I muttered as I filled her wine glass.

'Oh come on. It was all years ago.'

I couldn't look after Jessica properly, as I was too busy performing the perfect host. I flitted from wine glass to wine glass, making sure everyone was topped up, popping my head around the kitchen door to check Ben was coping with the mammoth task of arranging charcuterie onto a plate. I'd met Douglas before, but not his wife or Ben's other colleagues. I managed to extricate from Joanie that she'd done a year abroad in America, and pulled Jessica over and said, 'Oh that's funny, Jessica used to live there,' and let her take over.

'I still miss In-N-Out Burger every day,' Jessica said, finishing her second glass.

Joanie nodded. 'Oh, yes, I agree. Their animal-style fries were like my religion over there. Nothing here compares. So, when did you and your husband move back? Is he here tonight?'

Jessica shook her head. 'Ex-husband,' she said, not dropping her smile. 'But I moved back a few months ago.'

'Oh, of course, I'm sorry.'

Maybe I was imagining it, but the second Jessica said the

word *ex-husband,* Joanie stood slightly in front of Frederick, blocking him from Jessica's view.

Ben appeared in the kitchen doorway, wilting with a sheen of sweat and brandishing two giant sharing plates. *'Ta da!'* he said, as I ushered everyone to sit down. 'Starters!' He squeezed my sides through the thin fabric of my dress. Everyone dug into the olives and breads and hams, helping themselves, passing plates, draining their wine. We'd deliberated for ages about who would work well as a group, and it seemed to be paying off.

'Yeah, I'm a gynaecological nurse at an STI clinic,' Heather told Douglas, looking meaningfully at the slab of wafer-thin meats he had on his plate. 'You can ask me more about it when we've finished eating, I guess.'

He laughed but didn't finish his meat. 'I don't even want to know how many of our students you've probably seen.'

'Hey, if they're seeing me it means they're being responsible.'

'True, true.'

Jessica leant over, her face luminous in the candlelight. 'Do you still give out free condoms? I remember feeling like it was the most exciting thing ever, getting a bag of free condoms.'

Heather reached into the pocket of her baggy jeans and handed a condom to Jessica and we all cackled with laughter.

'Heather, you carry these around with you?'

She laughed. 'You never know!'

Katie smiled and took her hand. 'Don't get me started,' she said, speaking quietly. 'Honestly, sometimes when we're coming back from the cinema, she'll see a couple kissing outside a pub or something and offer them a condom.'

The table erupted into roars while Heather shrugged. 'What? Super gonorrhoea is becoming resistant to antibiotics.'

'Can we save the super gonorrhoea chat for after my lasagne?' Ben asked, and we all laughed again.

We got through our first three bottles of wine, then another three. Rarely, nobody was pregnant, and everyone seemed in the mood to drink heavily, the air growing thicker with companionship as we all got collectively more inebriated. While we waited for the lasagne to settle before serving, the men grouped together at one end of the table and started inevitably talking about football. Speaking so loudly and with such arrogant authority that everyone else sort of had to listen.

'Yeah, so Everton's chances tomorrow aren't looking great,' Douglas said. 'We just keep choking it.'

'Same with Arsenal,' Frederick added, nodding seriously, his mouth a ripe blackberry from the stain of wine. 'Arsenal are so unpredictable. It's bloody frustrating.'

'*You're* frustrated?' Ben added. I always fancied him, on average, forty per cent less when he talked about football. 'Try being a *Derby* supporter. I swear, there's only so long you can psychologically handle being an underdog.'

I saw Heather sigh and she leant over the table to the women, almost setting her red hair alight on a candle. 'Is it just me, or is it crazy that football chat is taken seriously when it's basically *astrology* for men? Having these weird identity markers you're effectively born into, and then constantly discussing what that means for your fate?'

Jessica's eyes were on Heather, a huge smile tugging the corners of her mouth. 'Oh my God, that is so true,' she whispered back.

'Right? Yet they never have mercury going into retrograde as a news segment, do they?'

And all the women cracked up laughing, just as the oven timer went off. 'I think it's time for lasagne,' I said. 'I'll go serve up.'

'I'll help you.' Jessica stood with me just as Ben was faux pretending that he wanted to help. I got out a stack of warmed plates from the oven, thanking Jessica as she started expertly scooping cubes of food onto them and adding string beans.

'OK, so I'm actually obsessed with Heather,' she said. 'I want to *be* her.'

I laughed. 'We all want to be her . . . Well, maybe we don't. She rubs a lot of people up the wrong way. But she doesn't give a shit.'

'Exactly. Not giving a shit. It's . . . I love it. I'm going to channel her for now and always,' Jessica said, and she was even more confident once we left the kitchen. I marvelled at what a pinch of Heather does to a person.

With football chat over, the table settled into murmurs of laughter and arguments about over the scandal of a current reality TV show. Forks squeaked on our IKEA plates, mopped empty with garlic and rosemary bread. More wine was opened. Joanie and Sophia realised they'd grown up in the same area and we were all united in the coincidence of this. By the time conversation got around to mine and Jessica's teen years, we were all righteously drunk, and Jessica was centre stage, red-faced, and being her most charming self, with me basking in her glow as if it was a brilliant contagion.

'OK, so we used to go to these dreadful gigs,' she told the table, brandishing an almost empty glass.

'Literally the worst gigs ever,' I added.

'But the boys made us believe they were the next Metallica or something.'

'Metallica?' Frederick asked, looking at the two of us dubiously. Me in my black halter dress, Jessica in her fashionable jumpsuit. No piercings or tattoos between us.

'Look, I'm going to break something to you,' Jessica said, 'but, sometimes, just sometimes, girls lie about liking music so boys will fancy them.'

Ben let out a burst of laughter. 'Oh God, really? You do realise that a teenage boy does not need any encouragement in fancying someone? Agree to sleep with him and he won't even care if you're an ABBA fan.'

Everyone started laughing.

'ANYWAY,' Jessica said, bringing us back to her story again, 'they played metal.'

'Misogynistic thrash metal,' I added.

'Hell, yes. Their single was called "Bleed Her Out".'

The table gasped so hard that the candle flames flickered. 'Oh, two thousand and three, how I don't miss you,' Heather said, finishing her glass of wine.

I put my hand on her hand. 'Oh, sweetie, you don't understand how clever this song actually was. You see, initially you think the guy in the song is slitting his wrists in response to a break-up and is "bleeding her out" as he dies.'

'But the twist was,' Jessica chipped in, 'is that *actually* he was getting the knife ready to kill HER, not himself. He then stabs her and watches her bleed out in her childhood bedroom, but it's OK because she did cheat on him.'

The whole table rocked with shocked laughter again.

'I mean, you couldn't make the lyrics out,' I added. 'What with all the guttural scream-singing. I only realised that was what the song was about when I bought a copy of their LP and read the accompanying lyric sheet written in Comic Sans.'

'Nothing says "damn the man" like Comic Sans,' Ben said. He leant over and squeezed my hand, eyes red, telling me he loved me, enjoying me performing like this. He'd never seen me glow in the Jessica glow. This was his first experience of the magic of the two of us.

Douglas clapped his hands. 'Oh God! I remember local bands and their LPs. They got an erection whenever they said those two initials.'

Everyone laughed and I felt warm to my core. As empty plates were stacked, and fresh bowls set out ready for pudding, everyone bonded over sharing their teenage angst.

'I was such an emo,' Joanie admitted. 'Do you know one student actually recommended *The Bell Jar* to me the other day, like I hadn't considered getting sections tattooed on me?'

Ben and I sniggered, listening in, as we huddled in our tiny kitchen, plating up slices of the chocolate torte. He kept leaning over and kissing the bare skin around my neck, his eyes doing that dewy misting that men's eyes do sometimes when you know they're really, really into you. The success of the evening was gluing us together as a couple. I felt us evolve just from this one night. Maybe he could change his mind about marriage? Surely tonight proved how great we were?

'Jessica is hilarious,' he whispered as we sprinkled icing sugar onto the last plate.

'Isn't she?'

'I love you,' he told me, before I had time to get insecure about the 'Jessica is hilarious' comment.

'I know,' I said, winking, and he slapped my arse as we headed for the table with chocolate-laden arms.

By the time the torte was demolished, everyone was beyond drunk. Slurring. Leaning over the table and uttering nonsense about who we used to be.

'I miss being young.'

'The skin!'

'The lack of hangovers.'

'The energy.'

'No tax on your Saturday job cos of the student exemption.'

'The drugs,' Douglas said, wistfully. 'So many drugs.'

'Oh my God, it's been a very long time since I've . . . dabbled,' Ben admitted, and I must've really loved the man if I still loved him after he used the word *dabbled*.

'I was such a stoner at uni,' Joanie admitted. 'Gained a stone. Best stone of my life.'

And, before anyone knew what to do, Jessica had reached into her handbag, her trademark grin on her face, and held up a stuffed white baggie. 'Did someone say drugs?' she asked.

The chatter hit a full stop, everyone staring at Jessica and the bag of cocaine in her manicured hands. She laughed lightly. 'What? It's only some coke.'

'Where the hell did you get drugs from?' I asked.

Jessica shrugged. 'A drug dealer?'

Ben and I shared many things in one look. Panic. Ben's *colleagues* were here . . .

'Amazing.' Douglas clapped his hands. 'I can't believe you

just produced drugs like that. If I say how much I want a red Ferrari, will one appear outside?'

Jessica laughed her tinkly laugh. 'I'll see what I can do. Anyway,' she tapped the bag with her finger, 'who's in?'

I found myself in the weirdly nostalgic position of looking around my peers to see who said what first. Heather, never one to care about peer pressure, shook her head. 'It's a no from me. But you go ahead.'

Joanie strained her neck over her empty bowl, eyeing the bag. 'Is it ethically sourced?' she asked. 'I only do cocaine if it's woke.'

Heather stifled a giggle next to me while Jessica nodded. 'Oh yeah. My dealer said so anyway.'

'Brilliant.' Joanie did two thumbs-up. 'All right then. A line would be great. Thank you.'

Time flickered as I watched my friend rack up a line. We could've been in the dank toilet of a shit gig venue, snorting up off a tampon bin, not in my flat in Victoria Park Village.

'I'll have one too,' Frederick said. 'And let us know the number of your dealer. We had to stop using ours when we found out his woke coke was still quite . . . asleep.'

Heather really did laugh then. I sort of couldn't blame her. 'Really? Was the cocaine from a Colombian drug cartel not fair trade after all? Shocking!'

'I have to say,' Ben added. 'I've never heard of woke coke before.'

I desperately tried to make eye contact with him, to figure out what the hell he thought of this pharmaceutical detour, but he just seemed genuinely interested by the ethical storyline of Jessica's gram.

Douglas took it upon himself to explain. 'It's just a joke term for a serious issue actually,' he said, pushing his glasses up his nose, using the sort of voice I could imagine he used to his class. 'I mean, if they're not going to stop this pointless war on drugs and ensure ethical supply lines, some dealers have started posting it, for example, to stop local turf wars, etcetera. It makes it less problematic.' He turned to Jessica. 'I'd love a line actually, if that's OK? Thank you.'

'Coming right up.'

I could sense Heather's bullshit radar scanning the room, taking no prisoners. Her wife could too, as I saw Katie take Heather's hand under the table.

'This is fascinating, *fascinating*,' Heather said, leaning over and crossing her arms. '*Wow*, so, like, all the female drug mules, who get threatened and coerced into stuffing the coke up their vaginas and risk horrific jail sentences to get it here, they're like, *empowered* and stuff?'

Jessica, busy making a fourth and fifth line, didn't notice the sarcasm and nodded. 'Yeah. They get paid more, you see?'

'Wow.' Heather leant back. 'So if they get paid a bit more, we know they're *choosing* to do this?'

'Well, it might be better than other options,' Jessica said, glancing up to smile before returning to her job.

'Douglas? If that's the case, you should totally get a drugs mule into your college to motivate your female students. It might be a line of work they've not considered.'

Ben, sensing the danger, reached out and laced his fingers with mine. '*Ha*, line of work,' he said, with a boom of faux laughter. 'What a pun.'

The distraction had the desired effect and everyone giggled, derailing the conversation. Even Heather looked suitably impressed. I mouthed, 'Are you OK?' and she gave a thumbs-up. As suspected, the group were too inebriated to take her digs in, all of them focusing on the almost finished rows of rocky powder. I was still pissed at Jessica. This was the sort of behaviour that had made me wary about having her back in my life. But my outrage was dwarfed by a stronger feeling – a pull to the powder. Cocaine. Shit. I hadn't taken it in for ever. Not since I started university. Not since I was friends with Jessica . . .

Frederick started asking people if they'd watched the latest David Attenborough about deforestation, and the conversation moved away from the coke to them all agreeing how important the rainforest is. Heather started urgently whispering to Katie. I heard, *'Oh, because cocaine production has nothing to do with ruining the rainforest either.'* I tuned her out and leant into Ben, our hands still interlaced. 'Are you all right?' I asked. 'Jessica . . . I didn't know.'

'It's fine. It's quite funny really.'

'I mean, it's your colleagues.'

'I know they take drugs. They're often slipping off to the loos on a Friday night. It's London,' he told me. 'They find it more surprising that I don't.'

'Do you want to tonight?'

He tilted his head and grinned. 'I dunno. Do you?'

His eyes were bright, betraying his excitement. We'd spoken about our pasts before, on lazy Friday nights when we were both too exhausted to do anything but get into bed at nine p.m. and share stories about what we used to be like. He knew that I'd been in with a druggy lot at college, but then pulled my shit together at uni. Whereas he said uni was when he got into drugs. Pills, mainly. Took them about a dozen times a year – at clubs and music festivals. It was hard to imagine one another like that. We'd met as grown adults. Our wilder sides tucked away in bits of history I thought were unknowable, until . . .

I turned back to Heather, whose nose was wrinkled, preparing myself for her judgement when I next saw her. She would rinse me later relentlessly. When I was around Heather, I felt strong, stable, knowledgeable, and right . . . but tonight, laughing with Jessica, remembering the careless fun we used to have, I felt . . . fun, young, engaging.

I leant over and kissed Ben's neck.

'Jessica?' I said, in a voice I hadn't used for quite some time. 'Yep?'

'Rack us up a line too, won't you?'

Her grin. 'I already have.'

Gums were numb. The last line trickled down the back of my throat. Woah, I'd forgotten.

Laughter. Anecdotes. More laughter. Ben couldn't stop stroking my arm, turning my limbs to sherbet. Each touch sent electricity through my body. I felt this intense, singular pulse between my legs. I picked up his hand and entwined our fingers. I felt so sexy. So proud. What an incredible dinner party. He will want to marry me. He will . . .

One a.m. A complaint from our neighbours about the music.

'Sorry, so sorry,' I kept saying to an angry mother whose children could not sleep. 'We will keep it down.' She stared at my wide black pupils and her lip curled slightly. 'Sorry, so sorry.' By two a.m., another complaint about all the talking, and the party had to end. Blearily everyone ordered Ubers. Thanked us. Thanked Jessica for the cocaine. Said what a lovely evening. Ben and I saw them out. Another neighbour came to tell us off for the noise in the communal hall. Once we'd waved off their cabs, Ben turned to me, a hungry look in his wide eyes, and pushed me against the wall of our building, kissing me deeply, kissing like how we used to kiss when we first met. The drugs made his touch exquisite.

'Jessica's still upstairs,' I said, savouring the kisses on my cheek, my neck, my shoulders, my chest.

'I want you so much.'

'She'll wonder where we've gone.'

'I like Jessica, she's hilarious.'

'I like her too.'

I was too high to be insecure. I led Ben back to our flat like a dog on a lead, smiling seductively in a way I never usually felt capable of pulling off. He kept pulling me back to kiss my neck, sending fireflies through my skin.

'Come on. We have to be good hosts.'

I was so horny that I was pretty annoyed Jessica was in our flat, and would no doubt want to stay up until the buzz wore off. But, when we stumbled through the door, she'd cleared all the dirty dishes into the kitchen sink, pulled out the sofa bed, and was wearing a pair of baggy pyjamas with sheep all over them.

'You didn't have to clear up,' I said, taking in this make-up-free, ordinary woman on my sofa. She was still stunning, of course, with her dark hair tumbling down her back.

'I've left things to soak, that's all.'

'That's amazing. Thank you. Do you want a cup of tea or something?'

'Honestly? Would you think I was the saddest person ever if I just crashed? Bridget is going to torment me tomorrow, and it's already past two.'

'No, of course,' I said, surprised. 'I'm tired too.'

Ben squeezed my hand, all *don't-you-even-think-that-you're-going-to-sleep*, and I squeezed back, the secret of our impending coitus sending another deep throb through me. 'I'm going to brush my teeth,' he said. 'Though I can't really feel my mouth.'

We laughed, and I watched the way his arse moved in his trousers as he walked down the hall.

'Fern?'

I turned back to Jessica, distracted. 'Yep?'

'You're not mad at me, are you? For bringing the coke? I don't know why I did it, why I got it . . . It was your dinner party . . .'

'It's fine,' I said. And, in that moment, it was. In days to come, I would reflect on it and get angry about it. But, right then, I was glad. 'I mean, Heather will be pissed off, but she's always pissed off. I was surprised, I guess. I didn't know you still . . . did stuff like that.'

'I don't. I'm not sure why I bought it. I think I'm just . . . so bored of being just a frumpy divorced mum, you know? I miss feeling like how I used to feel, I guess.'

Jessica who held everyone's attention. Jessica the lighthouse beam.

'. . . so, you're not mad?'

I leant over to give her a hug. Her body so thin in my arms, like a fragile baby bird. 'You got everything you need? Blankets? Pillow?'

'Yep. Sorry I'm being so pathetic and going to bed.'

'Are you kidding? It's almost three. I swear it's going to take two weeks for my biorhythms to recover.'

We laughed quietly, before I turned off the living-room light, hearing her roll onto her side under our guest duvet. I clicked the bathroom light on, brushed my teeth, coated mint around my mouth. I wet my hands and quickly washed my vulva, enjoying the feeling of cold water on my skin, of imagining Ben waiting for me in our dark bedroom. I looked at my wide eyes in the mirror, my hair dishevelled, all my skin showing in my halter top. I was wrecked but I'd never looked better. The way I held myself . . . I smiled and went to find my boyfriend.

'You're so gorgeous,' he whispered in my ear, undoing my straps. His words stronger than the white powder coursing through me.

'Shh. Jessica might hear us.'

Every touch of his fingers. Every compliment on his lips. Every look from his eyes. The urgency. The desire. I leant backwards, exposing my body to him, letting him take me, high on how he was seeing me, how I was seeing myself. Forgetting the tension of the previous night. I'd been at a party, and the hottest guy there had wanted me. *Me.* I was the one gasping into the bare shoulders of a man, not the one sleeping alone in the next room. I had been chosen. Me.

Seventeen

February 2003

'I'm going to be sick,' I told Jade as we got off at the bus stop and walked to the gig.

Jade squeezed my hand. 'You won't be sick. And, even if you are, you've basically not eaten all day, so the sick will be nice and see-through.'

I sighed. 'You're right, you're right.'

'It's going to be great.' Sally looked up from her phone where she'd been texting this guy, Ryan, she'd met online. 'We will laugh at all your jokes and make you look awesome, and it's going to be amazing. Here . . .' She handed over a small bottle of vodka. 'Have some of this.'

'Thank you.' I pushed the bottle to my lips and wiped my mouth. 'Is vodka not a carb?'

'What? Why would it be?'

'Because, you know? It comes from potatoes?'

'IT DOES?' Sally grabbed the bottle off me and frantically scanned the label while Jade and I laughed.

We turned the corner, the club coming into sight, and I

tripped slightly on my super baggy jeans. This was it. My first-ever date with Liam Gillingham. I took the bottle from Jade and swigged again before we bumped into Mike outside.

'You're such bus losers,' Mike said, hugging Jade and the rest of us hello. I watched Jade hold him tightly, not wanting to let go. But he broke off and turned to me, and his eyes flickered over my appearance. I'd made a big effort to look good, with my hair in four quirky buns planted around my head, leaving two wispy bits framing my face, and four layers of Maybelline mascara. Mike grinned. 'Hey, Fern, I met your (*boyfriend* during the soundcheck.'

'Mike!'

'He seems into you,' he said, laughing. 'He told us you have great legs.'

I simpered at the compliment, like Liam has just compared me to a summer's day, while Jade and Sally let out shrill shrieks. Mike winced, as boys always do when girls make a noise of genuine happiness.

'I'm too nervous,' I declared. 'I'm going to mess this up.'

Mike put his arm around me in a fatherly way and guided me towards the club. 'Come on, calm down. I'll get you guys stamped for free. Follow me.' He'd never given me so much attention before, and I marvelled at the focus I got when Jessica wasn't there, stuffing a lighter between her boobs.

Hot air painted our bodies with sweat the moment we walked down the stairs into The Illustration – the dive bar gig venue, where nobody ID'ed you if you didn't complain about the superglue floors and the toilets with no seats. It was jam-packed already; seemingly every angry teenager who wanted to reject their upbringing had followed a bat signal there. I crossed my arms as we stepped inside, but Mike reached over and uncrossed them. *'Confidence,'* he told me. 'Fern, you're hot, OK. You just don't know you're hot, and that makes you less hot.'

'Wow, Mike, thank you,' I said, with full sincerity, like he'd just taught me an incredible life lesson, rather than implied that, given the chance, he might consider fucking me. My phone buzzed in the butt of my baggy jeans, and my insides turned to butter as I pulled up a message.

Liam: Broke guitar string! Restringing now. C u after our set instead? I'll find you in the crowd after.
Fern: OK. C u later. Good luck for the gig

My body was a firework factory. I could hardly concentrate on what was happening around me. The jostling around the bar, the ocean of teenagers wearing black, congregating at the front of the small stage to get the best view. The sound guys walked around the stage setting up, tweaking amps, saying *one-two-one-two* into mikes. We joined our cluster of college friends, and I clutched my plastic cup and listened to the boys take the piss out of Scott for drinking an Archers and lemonade, the girls all laughing at the boys' jokes and making none of their own. Then the lights went down and everyone started cheering. I could make out Liam's silhouette in the blackness. This boy onstage had just texted me. This boy onstage had stared at me in my English lessons. This boy onstage wanted me to be watching him. The lights went up and the crowd pushed forward, taking me with it. The lead singer, Declan, clutched the microphone off its stand, his unwashed hair hanging in long clumps around his face. 'This one's called "Burn the Bin",' he said, before screaming indecipherable noises while the guitars and drums started up. The crowd quickly became a mosh pit, and the girls and I squealed as we got jostled and elbowed by young men flinging their bodies into each other. We were edged away from the stage, genuinely scared we'd get accidentally punched. It was far too exciting, watching Liam play. He had one leg up on an amp, thrashing his head, looking so confident and sexy, and *wow*, even though I had no idea what was happening musically. Mike and his friends seemed to approve. They were reigniting the pit, smacking their chests into one another. Some of the cooler girls from our college tried to join in. They launched their skinny bodies in with the blokes, but only lasted ten seconds before running out again. Jade turned to me, rubbing her shoulder from where a boy had smashed into her, and, with too much nervous energy and nowhere for it to go, I smiled and started randomly doing a mad dance routine. She laughed and joined in, and Sally started too. I was laughing so hard I almost forgot about Liam. I looked up to find him staring at me from the stage. He smirked and shook his head, before returning to his thrashing, and it was possibly the sexiest moment of my life to date. When their set finished, a mist of sweat hung over us. I cheered and clapped and jumped, feeling this sense of pride that I was connected in some way with the band that was being cheered for. The lights came back on and everyone looked at each other blearily, like we'd been in a collective fever dream, then ran over to the bar before the line got too long.

'I'm pinching your guitarist for our own band,' Mike told me as we queued for snakebites.

'Hey,' complained Pete, their guitarist, behind him.

'He's amazing,' Mike said. 'His shredding is totally insane. Right, dude, we're on next. See you later, girls.'

I waved Mike off as attractively as I could, wondering where Liam had got to, and wanting to look pretty if he was looking at me. As Jade and Sally chatted, I could hardly listen, I was so hyper-attuned to every movement of my face. We sipped our purple drinks and retook our places, my heart going berserk in anticipation for the next hour of my life. The lights went out again, the crowd cheered again, gearing themselves up for another orgy of musical violence. My heart slid into my stomach with disappointment. Where was Liam? Had he found another girl on his way to me? Jessica wasn't here to take the shine off me, but somebody else might've done. Jade squeezed my hand, silently asking if I was OK. I gave a fake grin back, still aware of how my face might look if he was searching for me. Mike's band started, with no semblance of difference from Liam's, and the pit got even more dangerous now everyone was pissed. One guy was bleeding from the head, and even the cool girls didn't go into it. It was all just loud noise and disappointment, until suddenly there was a soft whisper in my ear, and the fireworks of two hands around my bare waist. Liam was behind me, pressing his body against my back.

'I liked your dancing,' he said into my ear, with no hello, nothing, before placing his chin on my shoulder. It was such an escalation after only a few conversations in our English lessons, but God, it felt good. He pulled me in closer, tugging me backwards away from the crowd, into the dark. It was so upfront, so sexy. 'I'm glad you came.'

'Me too.'

Then, without fanfare, Liam spun me around, cupped my face and kissed me. My first-ever kiss, with one of the most gorgeous boys I'd ever seen, who'd just been onstage. I panicked for about two seconds that I wouldn't know how to kiss, but then got lost in it and how great it felt. He pulled me backwards until we were up against a dark corner, and Mike's set passed in seconds as our lips merged. At points, Liam would stop kissing me and gaze at my face instead. It was my first hit of feeling truly desired by a man, and I'd be addicted from that moment forth. No matter how well my life was going, my career was going, or my friendships, there would always be a hunger in me to be recreating moments like this first one. The heady feeling of being admired, adored, touched, *picked*.

Liam pulled away for a final time. 'Shall we go outside? It's too hot in here.'

I let him lead me out, twisting around to wave to Jade and Sally, who were screaming and clapping this development. Liam tugged me past the bouncer and around the side to a dank car park, and the cool air hit my skin.

'That's better,' he said. His arms were around my waist, this time his mouth on my neck. 'Shall we sit?' He took me to a romantic lump of concrete and we perched next to each other.

'You guys were really good,' I told him. 'In fact, my mate Mike wants to poach you for his own band.'

'Really? I mean, those guys rock . . . maybe I should?'

I was dredging up advice from all the teen mags I'd read – deliberately copying his body language and asking him lots of questions. 'Have you always played guitar?'

'Yeah. Since I was twelve. Writing songs is how I make sense of the world, you know?'

I nodded earnestly. I couldn't stop looking at his hair. It was so perfect. Dark curls tumbling over his eyes.

'How do *you* make sense of the world?' he asked, cupping my face.

'I mean, often, I don't,' I said, and we both laughed. 'But, er . . . I like reading and writing, I guess. I write about things I'm angry about in all these notebooks.'

'Oh yeah?' He tucked a lock of my hair back behind my ear. 'And what makes you angry?'

I searched my mind for the answers I'd been practising for such questions – answers that I hoped would make him fall for me. 'Umm . . . like our obsession with capitalism?'

He nodded profusely, proving I'd got it right.

'Yeah, like, we just buy and buy stuff to fill the void, you know?' I said. 'And I hate shallow things too.'

'Yeah, me too. Shallowness is just the worst.'

'Yeah. *Deepness* is so much better.'

'God, you're so smart.' He pulled me to him and rewarded me with a kiss, and I couldn't believe we'd made such a spiritual connection. We eventually broke away, staring at one another. His eyes were so green, so pretty, I sort of wanted to poke one with my finger.

'Do you want to come back to mine?' he asked, as casually as you'd ask someone if they wanted one of your fruit pastilles. 'My parents aren't home. And I'll walk you home after.'

After WHAT? I panicked, but said, 'Oh, yeah, sure.'

'There's space for you in the van.'

'Wow. Great.'

When we kissed again there was a new edge to it. A hunger from him that scared me, and I was tugged from the romance, worrying instead about what might be expected from me. His hands crept down to cup my arse through the baggy material of my jeans, and I wasn't quite sure what I was supposed to do in return. I didn't get a chance for a pep talk with Jade and Sally before I had to wave goodbye – bundled into the van with Liam's band. My friends could only wave and squeal as I feigned total delight at the evening's development. When we drew up outside Liam's house, the drummer let out a loud sex groan and I blushed as the rest of the band cracked up. But Liam flipped them his middle finger, and said, 'Fuck off,' which made me feel marginally relieved.

'Where are we?' I asked, looking around the dark street while he rummaged for his keys.

'Oh God, yeah, sorry. Didn't mean to drive you to a strange place in the back of the van.' His acknowledgement of my predicament further reassured me. 'I live on Oak End Road, near the church, you know it?'

I nodded as he let us in, and felt oddly relieved I could run home if I wanted to. 'Ahh, OK.'

'I'll walk you home whenever you like.'

'Thank you . . . oh . . .'

His lips were on mine the second we were inside, and his guitar dropped to the plush carpet in its case. We staggered backwards, him guiding me by the lips throughout the strangeness of his empty house, until the backs of my knees found the edge of a sofa, and we collapsed into the cushions, Liam's body pinning me down. We kissed until my lips were swollen, my back hurting from his weight on me. It was delicious, but also . . . a lot. When were we going to have a conversation about capitalism or philosophy or something? I had been rehearsing clever things all week in preparation. When he eventually pulled away, I took the opportunity to slow things down. I wiggled backwards with my knees up to act as a barrier.

'What's your favourite book?' I asked, which did seem a bit out of the blue in that context.

Liam tilted his head, slightly puzzled. 'Umm, I'm not sure. I mean, in school, we did *Of Mice and Men.* That was OK.'

I nodded. I hadn't done that book in my school because it was for lower sets. I felt this strange feeling of intellectual superiority creep in, combined with a pull to hide that from him. That he wouldn't like how smart I was. 'Oh, I've not read that,' I said, waiting for him to ask me my favourite book.

Instead he asked, 'Do you want to go up to my bedroom?' He wiggled his eyebrows. 'It has, you know, a bed and stuff.'

The mood shifted. The evening soured. Every fibre of my body knew I didn't want to do anything further, and yet surely a bedroom's sole purpose was further? Kissing was so great. I'd had such a great time kissing him. Wasn't a first kiss enough of a milestone for one day? I decided to dodge the question. 'My favourite book is *1984,* by the way,' I told him, which wasn't true (it was *Are You There, God? It's Me, Margaret*) but I thought *1984* might impress him more. 'Have you ever read it?' He only half nodded. 'Don't you find it, like, super weird that it's already happening? With CCTV and stuff?'

'Hmm.' Liam scratched his ear and started biting his nail,

clearly bored. Panicked, I lurched over and started kissing him, both of us falling backwards from the velocity of my lurch. His lips parted and he was with me again. We crumpled onto the carpet, our legs beginning to entwine like vines, his hands travelling up my side. He pressed his whole body against me and I felt a strange stiffness prod my thigh, and it took a moment to realise this was his erection. *Oh my God*, I'd given a boy an erection and it was on my leg. I really wished I could pause the moment, run into a cupboard and freak out a bit at how grown-up this all seemed. It all felt too fast, too aggressive, and also too . . . unromantic. Didn't Liam want to know anything about me? I was kind of pissed off at him for not caring about my favourite book. I wiggled my lower half away, so he switched to pulling up my top. His cold hands crept up my stomach, bringing the fabric with him, exposing my breasts, in their shit New Look bra. It hadn't occurred to me this bra would be unveiled that evening. I didn't want him to see my bra if he wasn't interested in my opinions on George Orwell. A spike of anger ran through me. *No.* Also, if he took my top off, he'd see my scars, and I didn't feel safe showing them yet. I stiffened and he paused, a hand one millimetre over my breast.

He raised his eyebrows as a question.

'It's late,' I said. 'I should probably get home.'

I swear, there was a flare of his nostrils, a reddening of his eyes because I hadn't given him what he wanted. For a second, he clearly hated me, and my chest tightened, before he nodded and wiped his anger away. 'Yeah, of course,' he said, smiling and making me doubt my reaction. 'I'm shattered from the gig anyway. Come on, I'll walk you.'

I was relieved and disappointed as we scrabbled up from his living-room carpet, rearranging our clothes. I wanted him to want me to stay. I would've stayed all night, happily, if only he'd asked me one question about myself and listened to the answer. I put my coat on and hobbled into my shoes, and he laughed and provided his shoulder to lean on, while I hopped into them, our faces close. 'You're funny,' he said, briefly kissing me again, making me luminous with simper. 'Come on, let's go.'

The cold air calmed everything down, and Liam became Liam again. The boy who'd smiled at me all term in English. I asked him how he felt about Mike wanting him to join the band, and he spoke at length, with his arm around me, guiding me through the dark, about how he wasn't sure he could do that to his existing band, but also how great Mike's *'work'* was. I listened intensely, making encouraging noises.

We reached the end of my road, the houses still and sleeping in the cold night. I slowed my pace. 'This is me.' I looked at my feet. 'Hey, have you done the reading for English on Monday?'

He tilted his head, smiling. 'Not yet. No.'

'Me neither.' We had so much in common, it was insane. 'I should probably go in.' I waited for him to say, *'No, stay, wait, I want to know everything about you,'* but he didn't.

'Yeah, man, I'm tired.' He stretched up, revealing a bare line of skin under his T-shirt and my body throbbed with desire at the sight of it. He was so much sexier when I couldn't touch him, couldn't be touched in return. 'Thanks for coming to the gig.' He moved his face towards me and I stared into his eyes. He looked at my lips, before bringing his head down to kiss me, and I kissed him back feverishly, our hands all over each other's backs, bodies pushed together. Then he pulled away and winked one beautiful green orb. 'See you at college on Monday.'

I watched him walk through the smudges of orange street light, his figure turning dark navy, to orange, and back to navy again. I touched my lips, which still fizzed with desire. I waited until he'd turned the corner before I squealed and hugged myself, jumping with joy on the pavement. I pulled my mobile phone out from my jeans pocket and sent a message to Liam right away.

Fern: Thanks for walking me. Great gig! Great night! C u on Mon x

Liam didn't reply until the next morning, when I was about to ring Jessica to give her a giant debrief:

Liam: Hey. Just worried i gave u wrong idea. Im not looking 4 a relationship right now. We can still b mates tho, yeah?

And my phone dropped to my bedroom carpet with a thud.

Thirty-two

I stepped out into blinding lights, trying not to trip in my power heels. Applause billowed around the rafters. A packed out Southbank Centre, my biggest chairing gig yet. I think it was fair to say my *Other Side of the Tissue Box* series was going well.

'Welcome, everyone,' I said into the mic that dangled Madonna-style under my chin, trying not to drop my cue cards as I sat on the sofa. 'Thank you so much for coming. I'm Fern, mental health editor of *Gah!*, and I'm delighted to introduce the amazing Dr Petra.' The crowd cheered at the sheer mention of her name. All I could see were the blinding white lights in my eyes and the collective blur of a thousand faces. Ben, my parents, and Jessica were out there in the blur somewhere, supporting me. 'She's got four million Instagram followers, and her bestselling book, *Your Diagnosis Is Trauma*, has challenged the world's perspective on mental illness. Here in London, for one night only, she's going to talk to us about trauma, healing, and everything in-between. Here she is,' I threw out my arm, 'Dr Petra.'

The crowd went wild, drowning the stage with a giant roar as Dr Petra strode on, waving and grinning, polished and perfect. Dr Petra was the real deal, and her book was the best thing I'd read about mental health in years. When I got the call from Dr Petra's publicist, asking me to chair her London event, my knees practically buckled into dust.

'She's seen your blogs about the counselling process, and she thinks they're great,' the publicist had emailed. 'She'd love you to host this part of her UK tour.' I'd danced on the sofa as Ben read the email aloud, giving me a giant thumbs-up, but still not marrying me . . .

But, yeah, as I took my seat onstage and started asking her my questions, I couldn't deny work was going well. I was getting daily emails from counsellors and psychologists, saying how helpful it was. How they were even posting links to my articles on their websites about the different types of therapy and what they meant. And the other students in my counselling class were quite enjoying their anonymous fame. 'Put this in the blog,' they said in every lesson, whenever we learnt something important. 'Write an article about this.'

Chairing Dr Petra was easy work. Glossy and rehearsed, she was a pro, and I could totally relax, despite the thousand pairs of eyes on me.

'The biggest misconception about trauma is that it has to be this earth-shattering event,' she told the enraptured crowd, painting the air with her hands. 'Society itself can be traumatic, especially if you are a woman. Especially if you are a further marginalised group within womanhood.' She let out a *woooo* sound to break the tension, and there was a ripple of laughter. 'As I keep saying in this book, over and over, and on my

Instagram page, until I'm blue in the face . . . There's nothing *WRONG* with you; if you struggle in life, it's about what's *HAPPENED* to you.'

The final applause was thunderous. I actually almost panicked the balcony would collapse in on itself from the women in the audience stamping their feet. Before we left the stage, Dr Petra, very kindly, held her arm out to me, and I got my own smattering of cheers. We hugged and posed for photos with official photographers, and I was pleased I'd shelled out on professional hair and make-up, as Dr Petra could've easily wandered onto *Oprah* in how put together she looked.

'That was so great,' I told her, trying to keep the gush from my voice as we handed back our microphones to the technicians. 'Honestly, your book. It's so good.'

'You're too cute,' she drawled in her Californian accent. 'Keep up the amazing work with your articles.'

We hugged one final time, before she was escorted to her giant signing queue, while I wilted back to the dressing room to collect my stuff, pumping with adrenaline.

Ben held out a bouquet of roses when I stumbled out of the stage door into the foyer. 'You. Were. Amazing,' he said, flinging his arms around me, the flowers thwacking my back. 'Best chair I've ever seen.'

I sighed relief into his shoulders, my body glowing with love. 'Really? I was OK? I'm still shaking.'

'You were brilliant.' Jessica appeared at our side and I let go of Ben, taking the flowers before greeting my friend and parents.

'Thanks so much for coming, guys,' I said, hugging them

hello. Jessica was wearing the perfect white shirt, tucked into her jeans with the perfect amount of French tuck.

'You were wonderful, Fern,' Mum managed, holding herself stiffly. 'That was . . . very illuminating.' My heart ripped a bit when I saw a copy of *Your Diagnosis Is Trauma* clasped in her arm. I didn't know if she'd perfunctorily bought it, or actually planned to read it.

'Really well done,' Dad said, standing mildly uncomfortably, highly aware he was one of the few men there. 'You were spot on. And it's been so lovely to catch up with Jessica again. I still can't believe you're a mother. That makes me feel very old.'

She grinned in her red lipstick. 'I had a child young, if that helps?'

'So you were a mum at eleven, eh? That's the only age that won't make me feel ancient.'

We all laughed. Ben's arm wrapped around my waist, pulling me into him. Having him there, with Jessica, with my parents, this merging of my past and present felt so . . . right, so long overdue. Thank God I'd taken this second chance with her.

'Do you want to see a picture of Bridget?' Jessica reached into her clutch bag, and brought out the latest model of iPhone, only been out two weeks. 'Or will that send you over the edge?'

Dad laughed. 'Oh, go on then.'

Both my parents peered at the screen, Dad applying his glasses, as they took in a snap of Jessica's extraordinary daughter.

'Oh my,' my dad said, awkwardly. 'She's, umm . . . very striking-looking.'

Jessica caught my eye and I rolled mine back, getting it.

'She's ridiculous,' Jessica said. 'We came up to London to the Natural History Museum during half-term, and I got approached by three model scouts.'

'She's a looker, that's for sure,' Mum said. 'But then, that's no surprise. You were quite the knockout as a young girl, I remember. Fern was always so jealous.'

'Mum!'

'What? It was years ago.'

My arms crossed into my teenage hunch, but Ben laughed, smoothing everything over. 'You should've seen my acne when I was a teenager,' he said. 'I was jealous of my little sister, even though she was only seven.' He pulled me further into him, while Jessica attempted to hide a small smile, one I tried not to let annoy me.

I felt someone tapping my shoulder, and jumped around, stunned to see a group of earnest young millennials staring at me.

'Excuse me, Fern?' one at the front said, wearing a giant pair of hipster owl glasses.

'Umm, yes?'

'Yeah. Sorry to bother you, but can you . . . sign this piece of paper for me?'

My mouth fell open and I twisted back to my guests, asking their permission, and they all beamed and fluttered me away with their hands. Jessica showed my parents more photos while I shepherded my crowd over to a table clogged with empty plastic wine glasses. The air buzzed with post-show positive feedback, a collective sense of belonging and being seen, as groomed women around us queued for glasses of white wine and their chance to meet Dr Petra.

'OK, wow. I wasn't expecting to do a signing,' I told the owl glasses girl, still taken aback. 'Umm, do you have a pen?'

She plucked one out of her bag. 'Thanks so much. Tonight was great.'

'Well, I was just the chair,' I said. 'What's your name, by the way?' I nudged some empty wine glasses out of the way to make space.

'Jessica.'

'Oh my God. That's the same name as my best friend over there.' I pointed over, but my Jessica didn't notice me pointing. She was deep in conversation with Ben, while Mum and Dad milled around, looking old and out of place. She was leaning into him, mouth close to his ear, smiling. He leant in closer to hear her, and smiled at whatever she was saying. The intimacy of it unleashed a vile monster that raced through my body, unleashing hell. Ben's hand was almost touching the small of her back, and it took everything I had not to peg it over there, and smack him away from my friend as if he was a toddler trying to grab a cooling cupcake.

'Oh, cool. So, yeah, thanks again for tonight,' she said, while two of her friends gathered around her, scraps of paper also in their hands, blocking my view of my boyfriend.

'We love your new *Gah!* series,' one of them said, before giggling at having spoken.

'Yeah, it's so cool,' another girl thrust her paper into my hand. 'Make it out to Mabel,' she instructed. 'Yeah, so, I read one of your articles and realised why my CBT wasn't working. So, I transferred to a "person-centred" counsellor and it's made such a difference.'

'Wow . . . wow,' I said, while I scrawled my signature. 'I

mean, that's so great. Genuinely.' I craned over her head to grab another glimpse of Ben and Jessica. They were still enraptured with one another. Jessica was speaking a lot with her hands, while he nodded enthusiastically. Then, sensing me, they both looked up, and I felt relief surge through me as no guilt passed their faces. Instead they gestured to my swarm of young millennials and gave me a giant thumbs-up.

God, I was such a terrible, insecure person. Thank fucking fuck nobody could ever hear my crazy thoughts. And, here I was, with actual readers coming up to me in actual real life, and I was ruining the moment with paranoid jealousy.

I refocused my attention. 'And your name?' I asked the next young woman, taking her paper, and nodding and listening intently as she told me about her own therapy journey. I was transported back into what mattered, what was important. My eyes glazed with tears. I hugged these fragile, excitable girls, and told them what it meant to me. We chatted for a bit about my counselling training, me laughing when they asked if they could book a session with me, then I sent them on their way to queue for Dr Petra.

I was walking practically two feet in the air when I returned to my family, noticing how heads twisted towards me as I passed. The swell of importance worn like a crown.

'Oh my God, sorry about that,' I said breathlessly. 'That was very unexpected.'

Ben hugged me again. 'My rockstar girlfriend.'

I could be your rockstar wife, I thought bitterly. Still stinging that Ben hadn't brought up our tricky conversation in weeks now. Jessica was looking at us with somewhat dewy-eyed admiration.

'This is so cool, I feel like a groupie,' she said when Ben and I broke apart. 'My friend is proper famous.'

'I'm not sure about that.'

Mum still had her pinched face on, and kept glancing at her silver wristwatch, twitchy about the trains back to St Albans. Dad put his hand on her shoulder. 'No Heather tonight?' he asked. She was his favourite of all my friends, and he asked after her constantly. She came to visit the first summer after uni, and spent the whole evening telling us what a *'female chauvinist pig'* was with drunken gusto. Dad was totally charmed and could never mention her without saying what a good influence she was.

'She's got dragged into another late shift.' I put my hands above my head to stretch. 'Plus she's not a fan of mental health books. She says Dr Petra should use her million-pound book advance to invest in pre-emptive mental health care, or something like that.'

Mum's finger pointed to the air. 'I must say,' she said, her words tumbling out quickly, as if she'd been desperate to get this out. 'Some of the stuff she was saying was a bit . . . unfair on parents. I wasn't impressed.'

I kept my face blank. Unsurprised.

'I mean, it was all a bit Philip Larkin. Interesting she's not a mother herself, isn't it?'

'How do you know she isn't a mother?'

'I just googled it on my phone.'

Ben reached over and squeezed my shoulder, all, *I know, I know.* We'd spoken so often about my mother. Me gradually telling him some of my darker memories of her. Of being left to cry alone because she couldn't handle it, how she'd put in earplugs and keep working through it.

'. . . I'm just saying, all of these things about "what parents should do" *are* great in theory, but, unless you've actually been a parent yourself, it's not the wisest plan to cast stones. Anyway, there, I've said it, I've said my piece.'

Jessica had her head tilted, nodding at my mother. 'You're totally right,' she said. 'That's what I kept thinking. Oh my God, the amount of unsolicited advice I get from people who aren't parents themselves. It drives me nuts!'

They glowed at one another with a shared conspiracy, and that's when I noticed Jessica hadn't bought a copy of Dr Petra's book from the stand. I'd wondered sometimes if it had ever occurred to Jessica to go to therapy, but she appeared to share my mother's defensive mechanisms.

'Fern, honey, we're sorry, but we really do need to get the train.' Mum glanced at her wristwatch again. 'They go from being four an hour to two an hour soon.'

'Of course.' I took a calming breath. 'Thanks so much for coming.' I kissed each of them on the cheek. 'It meant a lot.'

'We're always very proud,' Dad said, nodding. 'You did great.' I pulled him in for a tight hug. Then waved at my mum, who was already tugging his hand away, scouring for the fastest exit point through the sea of wine-drinkers.

'Right, another glass of wine each?' Ben said. 'You don't have to rush off, do you, Jessica?'

'Are you kidding? I will never stop exploiting my mum babysitting.'

'Red? Red?' He pointed at us, and we nodded eagerly. 'Right, I'll be back in twelve hours by the looks of the queue.'

I watched my boyfriend expertly navigate his way through the ocean of women, wondering if I would ever stop feeling such overpowering love for this man. Jessica watched me watch him.

'He really is great,' she said. 'I'm so happy for you.'

'Thank you. He'll do.'

She laughed.

'He still hasn't mentioned proposing or anything since our big talk,' I said. 'Which makes me a little on edge, but then he's so nice I remind myself to stop being stupid.'

'You definitely should. He's lovely.' She noticed another small group of grinning women spying on us from afar. 'Shall we go find a quiet table somewhere?'

'Yes, please! I've not asked you about your day yet at all. Did you only come up for this?'

We spotted a tucked-away table, littered with discarded plastic pint glasses, and stacked them to one side, sitting down. I fired off a message to Ben to let him know where to find us, then faced my friend.

'I've been up all day actually,' she said, suddenly twisting her hands into each other.

'Oh yeah? How come? Did you need to meet Brendan or something?'

'God, no. I've literally not seen him since I've been in England. Isn't that mental? He sends a fucking . . . car to collect Bridget, like she's a royal or something.'

I scrunched my nose. 'That's not normal. At all. My God. Sorry.'

'It's OK. I think he's got some kind of magic circle cast around him. All women over the age of thirty who go near him turn to dust.' She started playing with the necklace I'd been admiring. 'Actually, I was hoping to chat to you about why I was up here today.'

'Oh, yeah?'

She nodded. 'I was actually house-hunting. Looking at places around East London.' She held up her hands. 'But, I swear, if that's too weird for you, let me know! It's just, I really like the area when I visit. And I don't want to stay in Surrey cos I will kill myself. Being in London makes Bridget's car pick-up less weird, and it will be easier to maybe train for something, get a job, become a proper person, you know? But I'll totally understand if you feel like I'm single white female-ing you.'

My voice came out shrill, giving my shock away. 'Oh my God, you're moving to East London?'

'Only maybe. As I said, I don't want to freak you out. I just love the park, and the canals, and the village vibe. And all your mates were so lovely at that dinner party.'

'Wow, that's . . . great.' My eyebrows jumped into my hairline and I had to concentrate on lowering them again.

'Really?' Jessica could read me better than anyone. 'I chatted to Ben about it just now, and he said you'd be fine with it, but I thought it was worth checking.'

Oh God. Jessica, within walking distance of Ben. Why did that make me want to projectile vomit? What was wrong with me? My head started screaming, *'No, get away, my life, my life!'*

'. . . I mean, we had so much fun living around the corner from each other when we were younger.' I could tell her mind was made up, and asking my permission was perfunctory. Not that she needed my permission anyway. As my shock settled, I let her words bed in. I mean, she was right. Our teen years had been quite something. We were like roommates who didn't share a house. Upon waking, the first thing I'd do was message Jessica so we could meet instantly. We'd walk to college together, home together. We'd stay out late during school holidays, high on drugs and the thrill of being young and seeing the sunrise, hugging as we said goodbye as if we were about to be separated for years, rather than hours. Weaning myself off her had been like coming off heroin. Life seemed dull and meaningless, an emptiness gnawing at my stomach. Everyone else was boring. A limb had been amputated. I'd practically shake under my university duvet with cold-turkey convulsions as I resisted the urge to text her, to forgive her, to have her back. A beautiful addiction I'd managed to quench, who now wanted to live around the corner again. *But remember why you needed to cut her out,* I thought. *Can you trust her to be so close again? To be so close to Ben? Especially when Ben may be losing interest in you . . .*

'We did have fun . . .'

'I mean, I promise, now we're grown adults, I won't have breakfast at yours every single morning.'

I smiled. 'Mum and Dad even bought you your own cereal bowl, remember?'

'I loved that bowl.'

I wondered where it had ended up. If they'd lost it in the move, or whether it was still stored away in a cupboard, somewhere in St Albans, a lost relic to a lost friendship.

'This new chapter is all about Jessica being Jessica. A cool hipster independent mum, living in a place where she doesn't have to bump into twats she slept with when she was young. Where nobody knows me . . . well, apart from you.'

I kept forgetting she wasn't who she used to be. How we'd both changed, grown up, become adults. How, apart from a few blips, she seemed different. Trustworthy.

'So,' I asked. 'Whereabouts were you looking?'

Her whole face relaxed into the warmest smile, as she sensed I'd given my permission.

'Well,' she said, 'there's this great two-bed, right across from the park . . .'

When Ben eventually returned, brandishing a tray of red wines with a war-worn expression, he found us huddled over her phone, swiping through floor plans.

'Ahh, so you've told her then,' he said to Jessica, handing over her wine and greeting me with another proud kiss as he sat by my side. His palm found my knee and I leant my head into him.

'Hell yeah, neighbour,' Jessica said. 'See you at the local council meetings.'

'Cheers to this.'

Ben held out his arm, brandishing a crimson globe of wine into the centre of our circle, and Jessica and I joined him, clanking so hard we wet our hands with overspill.

'Cheers,' I said, telling myself to let go of the past. Embrace the future. Enjoy having her back. 'Cheers cheers cheers.'

Seventeen

April 2003

I knew something was wrong from the moment we landed. My phone lit up like a Christmas tree the instant I'd turned it on – a floodgate of messages arriving in my inbox before I'd even disembarked the plane.

Jessica: Hey it's really important u call me when u land. I want to speak 2 u first.
I love you btw. I hope you had a lovely holiday xxx

'What the hell?' I muttered, clogging up the aeroplane aisle as I reread the messages. Then another one came in.

Jade: Hey hon. Umm, so, I hope u r ok. Jessica n Liam r together. Long story. Call me when u hav landed. I love u, Im here. I know u said u didn't like him any more but still. hope u are ok xxx

And, just like that, all the relaxation from my holiday vanished. Blood hardened in my veins and my phone shook in my hand while my parents gently tapped my shoulder, and said, 'Fern, honey, you're holding up the people behind you.'

What was so stupid is that I'd spent the whole week fantasising about Liam realising he was drastically in love with me when I got home. My parents had taken me to Tuscany for a week to celebrate my dad's company having a stellar year. I'd spent seven days lying beside a villa pool, doing nothing other than rereading the entire backlist of Louise Rennison. It had been seven days without smoking, without drinking, without weed, without smothering myself with eyeliner and going out to get wasted on a park bench with my friends. I'd just been allowed to be . . . Fern again. No make-up, a comfy swimming suit nobody could see, reading books I loved and listening to music I loved, rather than forcing myself to understand Hunter S Thompson and Megadeth so the boys would think I was cool. And, there'd been no internet, no mobile phones. I'd just relaxed into the sun, let it tan my arms and turn my scars even whiter. I was returning home a new Fern. I imagined turning up at The Ram's Head – the underage pub in town – freckled and chilled, tanned and mysterious. And how Liam would notice the change. Would look up from rolling his cigarette, his green eyes finding mine, and thinking, *Woah, Fern got hot in Tuscany. Maybe I shouldn't have ignored her in all my English lessons after we kissed?* And saying, '*I know you've told everyone you don't fancy me anyway, but I fancy you. Please give me another chance.*'

But of course not, because of Jessica.

She tried ringing me twice while I was in baggage reclaim,

and three times on the taxi ride home. I switched my phone to silent, so as not to arouse the suspicion of my parents, and stared out of the window, blinking madly as I digested the news.

Jessica and Liam together.

My best friend and the boy I had a major crush on.

How could she? How could she? But, then again, why not? In my desperate attempt to preserve my pride, I'd sworn to literally everyone that I was 'fine' and 'unbothered' when Liam sent me that text message after the gig. But I'd assumed Jessica knew I was lying . . . that she'd show some fucking loyalty and decency, but . . . oh God. It stung. Of course Liam got with Jessica. Of course. The only reason he had fancied me was because he hadn't met her.

Ugly, disgusting, invisible, anxious, frigid me, compared to my fun, sexy, confident, alluring friend who always put a lighter between her massive tits.

'Oh my God, Fern, why haven't you been picking up? I've been going out of my mind.' Jessica's voice was breathless on the phone when I eventually returned her call, lying on my bed, staring at the ceiling, scratching the old scars on the tops of my legs over and over.

'I'm sorry,' I said, almost robotically. 'I've . . . er . . . I got really bad food poisoning on the last day of holiday and the flight home has been a vomity chaos.'

'What? That's awful. Are you OK?'

'Hmm, yeah. Just going to have to lay low for a few days.' I turned over on my side. 'How are you?'

'Well, I've been freaking out, to be honest. Scared you'll be mad at me. Did you get my texts?' She paused. 'Have you heard about me and Liam?'

'Oh, those? Yeah. And yes, Jade told me.'

'And . . . you're OK? We're OK?'

One tear slid down my face and landed in my hair. 'What? Of course.'

Another long pause, as Jessica tried to decide if I was being genuine or not. I think we both knew I wasn't – that what she'd done was a problem. But I had too much pride to go there, and she obviously had none by going there. Yet I also knew I had no claim on him, and she knew it. She could claim innocence. Which, after a big breath, she did. 'Oh, I'm so relieved. I knew you'd be OK with it, but still, I wanted to check. Honestly, Fern, it just happened. We were all just having some drinks before the Easter weekend, and we got talking. I've never really met him before, and it's just . . . well . . . honestly, Fern, I think it's love. I know that sounds mad, but we clicked instantly. I went back to his, and because his parents are away, I've all but moved in . . .'

My throat sewed itself shut as the details poured out. To make it worse, I knew what the inside of Liam's house looked like. I knew they had green wallpaper with green sofas. I could imagine Jessica behaving the exact opposite to how I behaved there – confident, alluring, knowing, unafraid. I scratched my leg again, and felt a nick, a warm streak of blood.

'. . . but I just couldn't relax until I knew things were OK with me and you. I mean, you did kiss that one time. Your friendship means the world to me, Fern. I would never have gone there if I thought you had feelings for him. You know that for sure, don't you?'

Did I?

No.

'Of course,' I said, trying to unhollow my voice. 'Jessica, I'm happy for you, I really am, but, I think I'm going to throw up again. I have to go. I'll let you know when I feel better. My parents think it may be a good week.'

'Yes, of course. Go vom. I can't wait to see you.'

'Hmm, yes, bye.'

I hung up and chucked my phone across the bed, not knowing what to do. The peculiar detachment that had haunted me in my earlier teen years soaked through me like rain, and zipped me up so tight I felt I almost floated to the ceiling. I huddled my legs to my chest and stared at the wall for a good two hours.

Amy was surprised to hear from me. 'Oh my God, Fern, it's been a while! How the hell are you?'

'Can I come over?'

She recognised it in my voice right away, and despite our drifting, she reactivated. 'Of course. Kim's here. We're just messing around doing our make-up. Come right away. Is everything OK?'

'Not really,' I said robotically.

Amy sighed. 'It's Jessica, isn't it?'

My phone shook by my ear. 'How do you know?'

'Just an educated guess. Come over.'

Two hours later, my hair had been straightened within an inch of its life with this new contraption called a 'GHD'. My heavy eyeliner was replaced with frosted pink eyeshadow, and my lips were a matching glossy pink. I sat awkwardly on Amy's bed in a borrowed miniskirt, drinking a Malibu and Diet Coke they'd made me.

'I still can't get over what a fucking slut she is,' Kim said, as she lowered her lips onto her neon straw. She was having the best day of her life. All her resentment about Jessica finally able to unleash like a burst fire hydrant. 'But I'm so sorry she did that to you, Fern. Like, I didn't know her very well when she took Matt away from me. But you guys have been best friends for years, and she stole your boyfriend.'

'That's the thing though, he wasn't my boyfriend. I only ever kissed him once.'

Kim's eyes were glassy with the early signs of drunk. 'But you were in love with him,' she said, dramatically.

'I'm not sure . . .'

'IN LOVE with him.'

Amy gave me her *Kim-is-a-bit-mental-yes* look, and reached out to take my hand. 'I know you guys were super close,' she said. 'That must really sting. I'm really glad you've come over though. We've missed you at school.'

Feeling her fingers in mine, I realised I'd missed her too. It was nice to be doing all the things my college friends ridiculed people for doing. Watching *The OC* boxset on her TV, dancing around the bedroom to 'Crazy In Love', planning to try and get into the local nightclub, Selfridges, which my lot always scorned and called 'Sell Fridges' because they said it was full of chavs.

'Thanks, guys. You've been amazing. Who else is coming tonight?'

Kim's eyes went even wider. 'The whole gang. It will be like a reunion with you there. Matt's coming!'

'Oh, is he now?'

'Yeah. We're trying to go out every night this week. As a challenge.'

'They'll be pleased to see you,' Amy said. 'We chat about you sometimes in the sixth-form common room. Eric says he misses having you as his chemistry buddy.'

These were good people, I realised. I'd seen the worst of them because Jessica had brought out the worst in them. But, before her, they'd been good people. They'd stayed my friends when I'd been sick, protected me from the judgement of the school. I slurped down the rest of my drink and held out my glass for a refill.

'Tonight's going to be great,' I said.

After five Malibu and Cokes, I was more numb than ever. I couldn't feel the cold Easter breeze as we all stood in line, waiting to get into Selfridges. It was a wonderful distraction, catching up with all my old friends, who greeted me with open arms, giant hugs, and genuine questions about how I'd been.

'Fern, dude, it's been so long.' Eric clapped me on the back. 'You look so different.'

'Can't believe I'm seeing you in a skirt,' Matt said, his eyes all over my body. 'First time for everything.'

'It's Amy's.'

It was so strange having my legs on show. I felt this different feeling of attractiveness, dressed up like this. Girly, soft . . . a clear signifier that I was dressed to receive a certain type of attention, from a certain type of guy who had certainly come out that night to give it. Though, I didn't realise just how bad it would be until we nervously passed the bouncers, cheering when we weren't ID'd, and emerged into the throbbing pulse of the nightclub. A swarming mass of bodies was lit by strobe lights, while others watched on, holding drinks, queuing at the bar. My old friends walked straight onto the dance floor, their fingers pointed in the air, joining in with a song I didn't know. I followed the back of Kim's straightened hair as we pushed into the centre of the dance floor. Then I jerked hard as I felt a sharp pinch on my arse. I jolted around to see a guy about my age, grinning at me all the way up to his pierced ear. He winked, while I was too shocked to do anything other than keep following Kim. I leant forward, covering her ear with my hand. 'Some random guy just pinched my arse,' I told her, expecting outrage. Instead she beamed, like I'd just learnt to ride a bike.

'Oh my God, you've pulled within a minute. Who?'

I reached out a finger and she found my assailant in the crowd, dancing with his head thrown back, not even looking at me after he'd left a pinch mark on my skin. 'Oh, he's quite cute,' Kim said. 'A bit of a chav, but I quite fancy that shaved-eyebrow thing. Are you going to go over?'

'Why?'

'To talk! You could totally pull him if he pinched your arse.'

'Er . . . I just want to dance with you guys.'

Within three songs, two more boys had touched my body. Another arse-pinch from a random hand striking out under the cover of the crowd, alongside some balding guy, who came up behind me and started rubbing his crotch on my back. I could feel the bulge of his genitalia through his jeans and froze, feeling totally sick. Eric, thankfully, noticed my facial expression and plucked me away from him.

'Put your arms around me so you look like my girlfriend,' he said, and, still shocked, I complied. Eric made some gesture, and the old man gyrated off, planting his genitalia onto the back of another unsuspecting teenager to the right of us, as though he was a tired butterfly who just needed a leaf to land on.

'Thanks,' I told Eric's ear, about to remove my hands, but he pulled me into him, pressing our bodies together.

'I've always liked you, Fern,' he shouted, his hand moving up my back. 'I'm only saying this because I'm pissed, but I've always liked you.'

'What?'

No time for an answer. My old friend simply plunged his tongue into my mouth, tugging me so we were squeezed together. My eyes bulged, and all I could hear was Amy and Kim's excited shrieks as they applauded this development behind Eric's back. And, something switched in me that would stay switched for quite some time. I pushed aside the disgust that my body was being pawed at without permission, and instead told myself that I felt . . . desired, and that it felt good. I had never particularly wanted Eric. I'd certainly never fancied a boy with a shaved eyebrow, and definitely not some seedy older man bordering on paedophile, and yet, as I wrapped my arms around Eric's neck, the group whooping their approval at our union, I felt some strange validation. I'd been chosen. Out of all the girls in this place, with all their skin on show, and faces painted to be the best they could be, I'd been chosen for grappling, above them. And though the pervy old man had moved onto someone else, he'd picked me first. After the years of constant rejection being Jessica's friend, and still reeling from her getting with Liam, it was a giddy thrill being chosen right now. I felt powerful and attractive. Two things I needed to feel that night. So I kissed Eric back, letting his hand prod my butt cheek as if it was dough he was checking had proved. And that was how I spent the last few nights of my Easter holidays. Telling Jessica I was still sick, and then heading over to Amy's, getting 'tarted up' and wasted on sweet-tasting spirits mixed into low-fat carbonated drinks. Then we'd head to Selfridges, letting boys paw at our bodies, grind into our buttocks, offer to buy us drinks in exchange for rubbing on us for a while, and kissing back anyone who kissed us first. I got so drunk I didn't really know what they looked like before I kissed them. I was attractive. Boys did fancy me. In fact, they fancied me so much they couldn't contain themselves around me. Not waiting to see my face before they reached out and pinched my body. What a body I must have. And the little voice in my ear ruining it wasn't the shrill voice of feminism, but one that whispered, *'You're only being picked right now because Jessica isn't with you.'* I started not being able to enjoy my night out until I got groped. If no strange boy pressed his groin against my back, or stuck his tongue down my throat, then I'd feel totally empty. Wondering what was wrong with my body if boys weren't willing to take it, even when I was offering it up? I was laughing, smiling, drinking, and catching up with people I'd known for years, but, on the inside, I felt practically nothing. Whenever my thoughts drifted to Jessica, I'd hover out of my body and stay stuck outside my skin until the thoughts passed.

Two days before term started again, I returned home from a shopping trip with Kim and Amy, to find Jessica sitting on my garden wall.

'So,' she said, taking in my shopping bags. 'You're feeling better then?'

'Finally over the worst of it.' I took her in. She was dressed differently. No 'nymph' mini-top and low-cut jeans. Instead she wore a long floral dress, her hair tied with a scarf. Softer, feminine, more girlfriendy . . .

'I've missed you this holidays.'

I gulped. 'I've missed you too.'

And, with her, there, in person, I realised I had missed her. Terribly. In fact, I needed to get closer to her right away. I put my bags down and opened my arms. 'Hug?'

Jessica's eyes moistened and she threw herself off the wall and into my arms. I held her to me, taking in the sweet smell of her strawberry shampoo, letting forgiveness flood through my body.

'I've got you a present,' she said into my shoulder, before drawing back, and taking out a small velvet bag from her pocket. I dipped inside and withdrew two delicate bracelets, each encasing a small blue gemstone.

'Oh wow.'

'They're azure,' she explained, grinning. 'Azure friendship bracelets.' I laughed as she slipped mine over my wrist and then put its twin on her own thin arm.

'I love them,' I said genuinely, holding it up to the sun.

'To remind you how much I care,' she explained, holding her own bracelet up so it was next to mine.

There was so much to say. So much to unpack and to talk through and to understand and forgive. I knew I was supposed to shower her with questions about Liam, and squeal at all the right parts, and say *I'm so happy for you*. And she knew she was supposed to beg for forgiveness, and say she knew I still liked him but she did it anyway, but she couldn't help herself and promised we'd work through this.

But we never said any of it. Instead, we hugged once more, our matching jewellery dancing in the sun, and went inside, arms around each other.

Thirty-two

I absentmindedly scratched at one of the scars on my arm to distract myself from my nerves. Spring sunshine beat through the classroom window, as Hannah and I eyeballed one another from our perfect forty-five-degree-angled chairs. Our counselling tutor, Linda, lifted her glasses from their chain around her neck and applied them to the bridge of her nose. It was the first time we'd been assessed on our listening skills – taken to a quiet room so Linda could give us intense feedback.

'Now, who wants to listen first?' she asked, getting the sheet on her clipboard ready. I gave Hannah a *go-ahead* look, as I knew she was even more nervous than I was.

'I'll listen first, if that's all right?' Hannah raised her hand.

I nodded, feeling my head roll around heavy on my neck from the heat.

'Now, Fern,' Linda instructed, as she jotted Hannah's name on the top of her assessment sheet. 'As I'm present, and you guys have been paired for a while, make sure you give Hannah a problem meaty enough for her to practise some of the more complicated listening skills.' She pointed at me. 'Obviously still keep it safe and appropriate, but do feel free to bite off something a bit bigger. I'm here to make sure everything is contained.'

I nodded again.

'Have you got something to talk about?'

I wasn't sure. I was never sure what I was going to bring to listening practice until it started tumbling out of my mouth. And now I had the added pressure of Linda observing. 'Oh, yep, I think so.'

Linda leant back in her chair and picked up her clipboard. 'OK, right, good. Well, start now . . . Hannah, don't be discouraged if I jump in here and there to demonstrate a particular skill.'

Hannah nodded and smiled, and readjusted herself into the listening body language position we'd been taught – straight back, uncrossed legs and arms, leaning forward slightly. Nobody tells you that counsellors need a core of steel. We'd all basically got abs since starting the course.

'Hi, Fern. Welcome,' Hannah started, in her soothing counsellor voice. 'As always, we have a short bit of time to talk about anything that may be on your mind today.' Linda was already scribbling on her assessment sheet, and we both glanced over, momentarily distracted. 'Yeah . . . er . . . so, umm, what's on your mind today?'

'I . . . umm . . . I don't know, I guess . . .' I shifted around uncomfortably in the plastic chair, wondering what my mouth was going to say. 'I guess I'm a little worried as I'm feeling a bit . . . anxious at the moment,' is what came out. 'I'm feeling quite preoccupied with stuff.'

Hannah leant further forward, her blonde hair spilling over her shoulder. 'Stuff?' she repeated.

I nodded. 'Yeah. I'm just getting a bit jealous and paranoid, which, to be fair, I've always been like, but it's worse enough to feel a bit worried, I guess.'

Linda's biro scratched around the paper, ticking off criteria from Hannah's response – jarring me out of it all slightly.

'And you're worried?' Hannah asked.

'Well, yeah. I don't want it to get worse.'

She shifted in her chair. I could sense her struggling under Linda's gaze. 'So, you're worried about it getting worse?'

'Yeah . . . oh . . .'

Linda put her hand up, interrupting us, and we both turned to face her, blushing. 'Right, Hannah, your posture is great, and your empathetic response is great,' she said. 'But you're focusing too much on repetition right now. I sense you're a bit nervous to ask any questions, is that right?'

Hannah turned redder and laughed. 'A bit. I never know what questions to ask. I think I'm nervous because you're here.' She gestured at me. 'And I didn't know whether to go for the empathy or to ask her why she's feeling like this, and I just sort of panicked, I guess.'

Linda smiled, her eyes wrinkling. She pushed the table in front of her to one side and scooched her chair closer. 'It's to be expected. Don't worry. Let me demonstrate a few open questions as an example. Fern, is it OK if I jump in here for a while?'

I nodded, whirling my hands around in my lap. 'Yeah, of course.'

'Right, Hannah, watch this,' she said, before turning to me, a totally transformed woman. No longer our quirky teacher who made jokes about Freud, but this calm, authoritative container.

'So, Fern, you say this jealousy is something you've always had,' she enquired, voice like silk. 'Do you mind telling me a bit more about that? It sounds like it's left quite the impact on you.'

I shuffled in my seat, feeling my back sweat against the plastic chair. 'Yeah, of course. I just. Well, I said in my application form and stuff that, when I was younger, I had some mental health problems. I mean, I'm fine.' I held up my hand. 'I'm sane, don't worry!' I laughed, but Linda didn't. She just nodded, like she totally understood it. Hannah watched, equally blown away by a master in action.

'This sounds almost too hard to talk about,' she said. 'Is that why you made a joke?'

Emotion coursed up into my throat and I croaked as I spoke. 'No. It's fine. Honestly. I'm just a bit thrown that I'm feeling like this again. I'm not sure what's causing it. Like, everything in life is fine right now. Fine.'

Linda nodded slowly, as if she understood but didn't believe. 'You don't have any inkling about what has caused it?' she pressed.

And I collapsed under the scrutiny, let out a sigh, and felt more emotion bubble in my stomach. 'Well, an old friend from that time in my life has got back in touch. She's just moved around the corner actually. She put an offer in on a flat last month and it got accepted.' I looked everywhere but into Linda's penetrating eyes. I knew, if I looked back, her gaze would be there to greet me, but I couldn't. 'And my boyfriend and I have had another argument about him not wanting to get married, which freaks me out. And, I guess that, combined with being around this old friend, has brought back a lot of memories and insecurities.'

'Of course, that makes sense. Memories about anything in particular?'

I wiped my palms on my trousers. 'Well, when I was younger, I always compared myself to her. She was a lot prettier . . . sexier than me, and it always made me really insecure.' I shook my head, smiled. 'Just stupid kid stuff.'

'It doesn't sound like stupid kid stuff to me. It sounds quite painful.'

'Yeah, well, there were a few times she really let me down. Like, when I was seventeen, I really liked this boy and he chose her over me.'

Linda kept nodding, like she totally got it. Even though I felt like a fifteen-year-old sharing it. Such pathetic teenage stuff. 'You said the word *"chose"*,' she prompted. 'What does that word mean to you?'

Hannah was goggle-eyed behind her, scribbling notes, while I felt pinned against my chair by Linda's question. 'Well, it means being picked, doesn't it?'

'And you felt this friend was picked more? And you're feeling the repercussions of that now she's back in your life?'

I laughed and rolled my eyes. 'Well, she WAS picked more. And I've never had that with guys. Mainly because she was always around. And, when she wasn't in my life, I got chosen. Because she wasn't there as a better alternative. But now she's back . . .'

'You're worried you won't be chosen any more? That she'll be picked instead?'

'I guess . . . fuck . . .'

Linda gave me one more blast of therapy smile, and then she turned back to Hannah and the spell around us turned to vapour. 'You see there? How I used questions to draw out more about what she's said?' she asked her student. 'Now, you think you can try that?'

She reshuffled the chairs, told us 'good work', and that we had five minutes to debrief before she'd come back to observe me.

'Wow,' Hannah said. 'Fucking hell. I'm never going to be that good. She's like a fucking . . . Jedi counsellor.' Then she noticed me sweating and holding my hand to my chest. 'Shit, Fern, are you OK?'

I nodded but couldn't speak. For the first time in weeks, I was fully in my body again, and my body was a choked-up, jittering mess. I almost couldn't hold myself up on the chair, Linda's questions whirring through my head.

'I'm fine,' I said. But I wasn't.

Holy shit. Could it really be that I hadn't matured one inch since I was young?

I got home late, after calling Heather, begging her to meet for an emergency post-counselling-lesson debrief. I pushed against our front door that always sticks and half fell into our hallway. 'I'm home,' I called out, kicking off a sandal and examining the red marks left on my foot. The first day in them always required a week's recovery time, and I hoped there were plasters in the bathroom cabinet.

'Please don't ask me what I've done all day,' Ben called back. 'I'm too ashamed.'

I smiled as I kicked off the other sandal. 'You're in your pants, aren't you?'

'Stop it. No! Well . . . maybe.'

As I turned into our living room, I found my boyfriend sitting topless, wearing only a pair of old orange boxers, with his legs apart, playing his games console. He paused the football game and looked up at me, grinning.

'I'm a teacher on half-term,' he pleaded. 'You cannot judge.'

I looked around the mess of our flat, that Ben had promised he'd tidy properly once it was the holidays. It had got worse today, his first day off. An assortment of dirty plates and half-drunk mugs of tea littered the flat surfaces. He was also pretending we hadn't had another run-in the previous day about the marriage thing. He'd gotten all quiet and weird after I admitted 'it is kind of important to me'. But, as I'd just spent two hours complaining about him to Heather, I felt too guilty to be annoyed now. She'd patiently listened while I'd totally spiralled on her about his lack of proposal, and feeling insecure, and weird that Jessica had moved nearby. I followed his lead and didn't bring it up again, climbing onto the sofa to give him a kiss.

'Did you leave the house at all?' I teased.

'I love you. Please never leave me for being so gross.'

'I promise.' I pushed myself up to get a glass of water and wash my hands after holding the sweaty pole of the Overground.

'Did you have a good day?' he called, turning the football game back on. 'How was your course? How was Heather? She wasn't on the rampage, was she?'

I glugged down some water and refilled my glass. 'She was on surprisingly good form. She's very excited by this new gonorrhoea vaccine that's on the horizon.'

I saw the back of Ben's head shudder and laughed, then I waddled into the bathroom and ransacked the cabinet for the remaining plasters, choosing which two blisters to prioritise. Heather and I had circled Clissold Park several times while she relentlessly told me off for being an idiot. In typical Heather fashion, her main response was, 'Why would you yearn to join an institution that is scientifically proven to make women unhappier?'

'Not all women.'

'I feel like you're complaining about failing the physical of a military draft.'

I'd bumped her with my hip. 'May I point out to you that YOU are MARRIED too.'

'I'm not fucking married, yeesh. We have a civil partnership. And we only did that so Katie can get my state pension.'

'Well, maybe I want a piece of Ben's state pension.'

'Now you're talking. Those are reasons to get married . . . not fucking weird patriarchal Disney princess hangover shit.'

When my feet had been salvaged from their leather thong wreckage, I came back to sit with Ben again. We'd planned a night in, watching the one film on Netflix we currently both wanted to watch, and had been saving for this rare event when he wasn't totally shattered. I felt we both needed this night to clear the weird between us.

'Any preferences on Deliveroo?' I asked, having to push him to make space on the sofa.

'The noodle place.' He didn't look up from his screen, and, as I watched him play, I realised he'd spent a lot of time making his football avatar look exactly like himself. 'Oh, Jessica was around earlier,' he said, face still on the screen, his hand jabbing buttons.

'What?'

'Yeah, she popped around. I think she was upset. Said she couldn't get through to you?'

'I left my charger at home all day. Did she stay?' I was more upright on the sofa, trying to push down the odd sensation I felt that the two of them were alone in my house without me. She'd only been moved in for two weeks and I was still acclimatising.

'Maybe an hour?'

An hour?!

'Did you have pants on?'

Ben laughed. 'Of course. No top on though. I hope I didn't scare her.' I looked down at Ben's chest. His gorgeous bare chest, with the line of chest hair that split him in two like a banana pudding. The chest hair only I got to see, and touch. Jessica had seen it. *My* Ben's chest . . . God, why was I being so crazy?

'I'll go plug my phone in now.'

Ben had already picked up his console again. 'Yeah, cool. She kept saying she was fine, but she wasn't. She seemed a bit better after we'd had a cup of tea and a chat.'

I resisted the urge to ask what they'd chatted about and went to charge the phone in our bedroom, making the bed while I waited for it to turn on.

Jessica: Hey, are you around? Mind if I drop by?

Hey, Bridget's at an after-school club and I'm around the corner, going to come say hi, hope that's OK

Ben was very nice! Sorry for just gatecrashing like that. Ring me when you see this? I think your phone must be dead.

She answered on the first ring. A croak of a voice.

'Jessica?'

'Fern.' She said my name and then the sobs hurtled down the phone, and she couldn't speak any more. Jessica crying. Jessica never cried.

'I'm coming straight over.'

Seventeen

August 2003

Mike's face glowed orange from the festival campfire, lighting up his numerous facial piercings. He held the bottle of whisky up with a smug smile on his face. 'Sideshow Bob,' he said, knowing we'd all laugh, and we did. I blinked away the tears caused by the fire, while he passed the bottle to Phil, whose smile was equally smug. 'Troy McClure.'

'EPIC CHOICE,' someone yelled. Phil stumbled onto his feet to bow. A wider circle of onlookers had formed around our fireside huddle, random passers-by interested in our *Name a Simpsons Character* drinking game.

'Mr Burns.'

It was Jade's turn coming up, and she wasn't faring well. 'I told you guys, I've never watched *The Simpsons*,' she complained as the bottle edged nearer, in a tone that was more drawl than voice. She took it with unfocused eyes and Mike leant over with a full shot glass in preparation. 'Err . . .' Jade said. 'Umm . . . Principal Simpson?'

'DRRRRIIIIIINK!' everyone yelled.

Mike shook his head, smiling, as he held the shot glass to his old friend's mouth. 'Honestly, Jade, *Principal Simpson?*'

'SHOT SHOT SHOT SHOT SHOT,' chanted the mob, and Jade obligingly threw the whisky back. Everyone cheered their approval. 'I'm so fucking drunk,' she complained. 'I hate this game. Shouldn't we be watching a band or something?'

'It's one a.m.,' Mike said.

'Well, shouldn't we be doing something in a tent or something?'

Mike raised both eyebrows. 'We can do whatever you want to do in a tent, sweetheart.' Everyone cheered again. It was our third night at Reading music festival, and things had become progressively messy. I was relieved we only had one day left before I could go home to wash off the grime and sweat and hazy memories. It hadn't helped that the festival had come only days after our AS results day, with many of the group getting abysmal grades. The boys had done much worse than the girls. We quietly kept our papers covered with As and Bs held to our chests as Mike, Liam and the others got completely trashed in the park, complaining that the system was rigged, and exams didn't mean anything in rock and roll anyway, and also, Miss Wood from Music Tech was such an uptight little bitch for failing their coursework, and they wouldn't even rape her if they got the chance.

Reading Festival was going to be epic, the boys assured us. It would fix everything. Live music was everything that mattered in life. But, apart from the fact we were sleeping in tents, in an endless field of fields, and trying to hold in our poos whenever we dared use the gross Portaloos, I couldn't help but wonder what the difference really was between our life at home and this music festival. Everyone was too wasted most of the time to see many bands, only managing to stagger into the arena once a day, around evening time, to see the headliners. And everyone there appeared exactly the same as us, as if we'd all been cloned from the same guitar-plectrum necklace. Whenever I flip-flopped towards the arena, I passed group after group of seventeen-year-olds – girls with hair dyed a rainbow of colours, mooning over a group of boys wearing black, strumming their guitars and getting everyone around them to sing 'Tribute' by Tenacious D. At least once an hour, somebody, somewhere far away, would shout the word 'bollocks' long and loud, and it would start a giant Mexican wave of people shouting 'bollocks' too, and it wasn't appearing to get tiresome any time soon. And, at that moment, in the distance, someone yelled the word, 'booooooolllllllll-loooooocccccckkkkkss', and we heard the wave of it come crashing towards us. We all grinned through the flames, waiting in anticipation 'til it hit us, and then we threw our heads back to the moon like wolves and screamed 'bollocks' 'til our lungs hurt. Dave, who'd been lying quietly up against his tent in a k-hole, lifted his heavy head for a second, and whispered, 'Bollocks,' before crashing his head back down. Mike got up and checked on him. 'You OK, dude?' he said, casually taking his pulse.

'Where am I? Can't talk . . .'

'Shh, dude. It's OK. You're safe. You're just in the hole. It will pass. We're right over here. We won't leave you. You're going to see Metallica tomorrow, remember?'

His head lifted briefly again. 'Metallica,' he whispered, before his neck released his head to his chest.

There had been a significant change in our group over the Easter holidays. Mainly that all the boys had moved onto much harder drugs, with ketamine and cocaine and indiscriminate 'pills' now being the source of hedonism at gigs and parties. I'd been shocked when I'd returned to college for our summer term, hearing them all talk about 'lines' and 'gurning gummies to chew on', and even more shocked to learn Jessica apparently was taking everything the boys were. Anything Liam took, she did. They were very much modelling themselves on Kurt Cobain and Courtney Love.

The drinking game continued.

'Reverend Lovejoy,' I said, relieved not to have to do a shot, as I was a bit worried about the state of Jade.

'Smithers.'

'I told you,' Jade said. 'I don't know any of the Simpsons!'

'SHOT SHOT SHOT SHOT SHOT SHOT SHOT SHOT SHOT!'

Jade fell into my shoulder, her body flopping, and I wrapped my arm around her. 'You OK?' I whispered.

'I really like Mike,' she whispered back, her voice slurring. 'Why doesn't he like me?'

'He does.' I glanced up at the object of her constant unrequited affection. He was playing his acoustic guitar, his fingers moving deftly as he plucked out 'Stairway to Heaven'. I watched him look over at Jade and his face go warm. A smile. She smiled back, before collapsing onto me again.

'I hope so,' she told my shoulder. 'I've fancied him for so long.'

She kept drinking, and I decided to stop doing anything so I could keep an eye on her. We held onto one another's denim shorts and let the atmosphere of the night take over – the only two girls left standing that evening. Sally had fallen in love with a roadie called Trigby on the first night, and hadn't been back to our campsite since. Jessica and Liam were still love's young dream, four months on, and she'd followed him into their tent a good hour ago. They hadn't resurfaced yet. Mike started playing 'Nothing Else Matters' and we all sang in choirlike voices, and I let a calm settle on me. I was doing it. I was at a festival. I was being a normal teenager. I was pulling it off. I was boiling hot, as it had been thirty degrees every day since we'd arrived, and I couldn't let my arms out, but I was doing it.

Our singing was interrupted by a loud grunt from Liam's tent, and everyone applauded and cheered.

'SOMEONE'S HAVING SEX,' Phil shouted, and some of the guys went over and banged on the canvas of their tent.

'FUCK OFF.' Liam's head popped out from the top of his zip, clearly naked from the neck down. I heard Jessica's laughter behind him. The boys cheered again. 'Seriously, fuck the fuck off.' He disappeared and the air was a bit different when the zip went back up. Charged. All of us outside not having sex hugely aware of the people who were, only a few feet away. I imagined they were all picturing Jessica and wishing they were Liam. The perfect girlfriend. That's what all the boys called her now. Since Easter, she'd been upgraded from Slutty Jessica to the Perfect Girlfriend. Whenever she turned up with crisps, or coke from her dealer, or looking particularly sexy and stunning in one of her new floral crop-top ensembles, 'Liam, your perfect girlfriend is here,' they'd say.

Inspired, perhaps, by the events of the nearby tent, Mike stood up with his guitar, staring straight at Jade.

'Any requests, old friend?' he asked, before sitting next to her.

She tried to straighten up, tossed her long hair down her back. '"Colors of the Wind".'

I expected him to wince or tell her to fuck off, but Mike broke into a grin, sat at her side, and started playing the Disney song. Jade started waving her arms in the air – oozing that sort of carefree charm that only totally wasted girls can exude. They started harmonising in the chorus, and all of us turned to watch them, enchanted, our faces orange, our eyes red. When it came to how high the sycamore can grow, Jade stood up, reaching into the dark sky, screeching the lyrics 'til her throat closed, and everyone cheered, Mike laughing so hard he almost stopped playing guitar. He stared at her in wonder, as if he was seeing her for the first time, and I felt this thumping jealousy. Him and Jade finished in a harmony, their heads falling together, and were greeted with applause.

'You guys are too cute,' Phil said, and Mike raised his eyebrows, enjoying the kudos.

He moved closer to Jade. His arm crept around the back of her bare midriff and he pulled her into him. She carried on chatting to everyone, pretending she wasn't hugely aware of the development, reaching out and demanding more whisky. 'Play "I Won't Say I'm In Love" from *Hercules*,' she demanded.

'I don't know it.'

'Well, I know it.' She stumbled up, waved her arms as if she was conducting an orchestra, and launched into a solo, cementing herself as legend of the night. Everyone joined in.

Laughing when they couldn't reach the high notes, just about droning out another strange sound coming from Liam and Jessica's tent, that only I noticed. I craned my head, worried. It had sounded like someone crying. But then Jade fell backwards off her camping chair, laughing with her legs in the air like a bug. Mike was on her, claiming to help her up, but, instead, lay on top of her and kissed her while pinning her to the ground. I tilted my head, checking she was OK. But she'd wrapped her legs around him and seemed delighted.

'Get a room, guys,' Phil called, and Mike reached backwards and flipped them off. There was an awkward silence as I became very aware I was the only girl left. Not that anyone was making moves on me. I stared determinedly into the fire and tried to ignore the groans coming from Mike's mouth and the sound of a hushed argument from Liam's tent. I wasn't the only one feeling the awkwardness, as Phil got up and retrieved Mike's guitar. He strummed and got everyone to sing 'Tribute' for the twentieth time that day. I looked around me, at the city of tents, the circles of friends around campfires, the hundreds of thousands of boys – none of whom had thought to find me attractive. Yes, I was alive, sane, and at a music festival, but that was the limit of my achievements. I faked a yawn and started thinking wistfully of the giant bag of Kettle Chips I'd hidden at the bottom of my sleeping bag. I could pretend to go to bed, eat them, and wait for Jade to come and debrief me.

'I'm gonna go sleep,' I announced to nobody in particular.

'Guys,' Dave said, from against the tent. 'I'm starting to feel my legs again.' Everyone applauded him, while I crouched down and tried to get through to Jade.

'Jade?' I asked the writhing mass of her and Mike. 'I'm going to our tent now? You OK?'

She broke free for a moment. Her eyes were out of focus, rolling widely into the night. She gave a thumbs-up. I hesitated. Unsure. 'I can stay out here if you like?' I added, which drew an angry look from Mike.

She sat up and pulled her top down, and I waited, not even sure I trusted her to give an answer I could believe. 'I'll come in soon,' she promised, her eyes managing to meet mine.

'Are you really sure?'

She nodded with a grin on her face.

'OK, I'm literally six feet away.'

Mike shot me a look. 'You're being a bit weird, Fern.'

I stepped back with my arms up. 'I was just checking; have fun, guys.'

I waved goodbye to nobody and unzipped my tent. The noises quietened slightly once I was ensconced in my canvas. I sighed and rummaged around for a bottle of water and Kettle Chips. I stuffed the salty crisps into my mouth, staring at nothing, listening to Dave's updates outside.

'Guys, I can finally move my fingers.'

'Guys, I can turn my head.'

After I'd demolished the crisps, I spread some toothpaste onto my teeth straight from the tube, and cleaned off my eyeliner with a baby wipe. I vaguely needed the toilet, but Jade and I agreed to never go alone at night-time to stay safe from sexual predators, so I got into my sleeping bag and waited for Jade to finish making out. My eyes grew heavy in the heat of my tent and I told myself I'd close them only for a moment. A distant chorus of 'bollocks' throbbed towards me, then away from me, and I smiled as I fell into an uneasy sleep.

The crusty heat in the tent woke me, my body sweating in its sleeping-bag cocoon. I fluttered my eyes awake, disorientated. Shit, I'd fallen asleep . . . Then I saw the body on Jade's air mattress and let out a sigh of relief.

Except that wasn't the colour of Jade's hair . . .

'Jessica?'

She yawned and wiggled over to face me, the previous day's make-up smudged around her eyes, her hair all crazy. It was the most un-groomed I'd ever seen her. 'Sorry for scaring you,' she said, trying to sit up. 'I hope you don't mind me sleeping in here.'

I reached about for my water bottle and downed the warm leftover liquid at the bottom. It barely made a dent in my thirst. From the heat, I guessed it was mid-morning, but you wouldn't know from the dead quiet of the campsite around us. The festival slept, wanting to preserve its collective energy for the last day ahead. And, here was Jessica, acting as if it was totally normal to sneak into my tent in the middle of the night.

'Is everything OK?' I asked, sitting up too. I could already smell myself, so leant over to find my pack of baby wipes for my armpits.

'Yeah, fine. All good.' She held out her hand for her own wipe and I could tell from the tone of her voice she was lying. 'I just figured, we've not spent any quality time together in so long, and I hate it.' I bit my lip. That was very much her fault. Things were OK between us again, but she had been very preoccupied with being the perfect girlfriend for Liam. 'So I thought we should sack everyone off and enjoy the festival, just us two. Make a girls' day of it, you know? I'm fed up of being outnumbered.' It was obvious something had happened, but I knew it was pointless to ask. 'So?' she asked, biting on her bottom lip. 'What do you think?'

And the thought of escaping this gang, this circle of chairs, this year-long history of labels, was intoxicating. Jessica and me, alone, at a music festival. Jessica and me, best friends reunited. My smile erupted through my freckles.

'That sounds pretty awesome.'

'I know, right?'

'What about Jade? She . . . must've gone to Mike's tent.'

Jessica shook her head. 'She's fine. She had a giant grin on her face when I saw her last night. She's been obsessed with him for ages.'

'She was quite wasted.'

'So was everyone.' Jessica dismissed my concerns and got to her feet, crouching so her head didn't hit the fabric roof. 'We'll leave her a note and keep our phones on so she can find us. Come on, let's get breakfast somewhere while it's still quiet.'

We flip-flopped to the toilet block together, squealing when we found only one cubicle that was vaguely respectable.

'Who would leave a turd on the seat? What the fuck is wrong with people?' she said, waiting her turn while I hovered over the drop inside. We washed as best we could under the tap, filled up our water bottles, and brushed our teeth. Then, after decorating the greasy parts of our hair with headscarves, and drawing flowers over our sunburnt cheekbones, we left a scribbled note for Jade on her bed, and giggled the whole walk to the arena. Just as we were about to go through, Jessica pulled me over to a cluster of dormant tents. 'Hang on, I just need to put the coke in my knickers.' She withdrew a giant bag of white powder from her bag, and balanced on one tanned leg as she stuffed the baggie into God knows where.

'It's Liam's,' she said, smoothing herself down again. 'But he's pissed me off today. And he was so obliterated yesterday he'll just think he did it all.' She winked and linked arms with me, as though we were two teenagers on our first shopping trip alone. 'Come on, shall we get pancakes?'

What followed was one of our most special days together. We found a pancake van, ordered a giant stack each, and sat at this little table, laughing about everything that had happened so far, watching people trickle in as the sun rose higher in the sky.

'Mike's tattoo is so bad,' she said.

On our first day there, Mike had panicked about his lack of originality, and got a terrible tribal tattoo on his arm.

'So bad.'

'I mean, who gets a tattoo in the back of a van?'

'He doesn't even know what it means.'

'He'll go travelling one day, and end up getting murdered by some tribe because he actually has "cunt" or something written on his arm in their native language.'

We laughed so hard a piece of pancake came out of Jessica's nose, and that was it, we were done. We were on the cusp of hysteria for the rest of the day, everything a brilliant, sunstroked joke. The arena slowly packed out, the ground like dust under our feet. The air was sweet with the smell of marijuana, the sun beating heavily, stewards handing out free water wherever we went. I paid an extortionate amount for two pints of beer, wanting its coolness even though we didn't like the taste. We wandered around before the bands started, shopping at all the little market stalls the boys had never let us stop at. Jessica made us get matching henna tattoos on our hands, and we held them up towards the sky as they dried, our heads rolling into each other's shoulders. Heavy strums of guitar riffs signalled that the music was starting, and we looked at the line-up on the lanyard around my neck.

'Literally all the bands here are fucking boys,' Jessica complained, as we sat on the grass reapplying sun lotion. 'Radio One tent looks the most fun.'

'Let's go there then.'

'Do you want some coke first?'

A nervous drop blodged into my stomach. 'I don't know, Jessica.'

'It's not a big deal.'

'It's a Class A,' I whispered. 'A! Like . . . heroin.'

She burst out laughing. 'Oh my God, it's nothing LIKE heroin. Honestly, I think you'll love it. You feel so much more with it than when you're stoned, I promise.'

I chewed on my lip. 'I don't want to die . . .' I'd seen photos on the news. Teenagers stuffed with tubes in comas, warning headlines telling me to just say no.

But Jessica just laughed again. 'You won't die! Oh my God, I promise. We'll be sensible with it. I honestly think you'll really like it. It just makes you more confident. And if anyone needs more confidence . . .'

'I mean, I actually have the highest self-esteem of anyone I've ever met.'

'Yeah, you're up there with Eeyore. Come on. The tiniest bit. Cover me . . .' She bent down on herself and started arranging a little set-up on her lap, while I looked around, terrified. 'Look, here, barely anything, see? It's not even a line, it's a sprinkle.' She held up the groove of her hand. 'Just a sniff.'

I still wasn't sure, but I looked at her hand, and it was such a tiny amount. Surely nothing that tiny could hurt me? 'If I die,' I warned her, 'I'm haunting you for ever.'

'You're not going to die. You're going to love me for stealing you shitloads of free coke off my awful boyfriend.'

I sighed, apologised silently to my parents, lowered my head, and sniffed.

I sniffed and sniffed. I couldn't stop sniffing. God, this band was great. Music great. Festival great. I was great. Jessica was great. Weather was great. My whole throat was numb. Eyes wide. Arms in the air. Dancing, literally for the first time, like I didn't care. Maybe I was quite pretty, really? I imagined how I looked to everyone looking at me, lost in the crowd, lost in the music, moving my body, being that fun girl. I bet I looked fucking hot. Jessica looked fucking hot.

'I fucking love today,' she shouted over the music.

'I fucking love today too.'

We hugged and jumped in the air together, lost in the crowd, no idea where any of our friends were and what they were doing. We didn't care.

'Jade has texted,' I said, as we took a break, sipping water on the ground, as the sun started sprawling its descent across the sky with pink ink. Jessica had been sensible, as promised. Making us take breaks, drink water, not get too dehydrated.

Jessica was dabbing a bit of powder into her gums. 'She OK?'

I looked at my phone. 'She said her and Mike are getting a spot to watch Metallica together.'

'Sounds promising . . . Though, it's Mike. He'll be bored of her within a week.'

I reached over and dabbed up the rest of the coke from her hand, already a fan. 'He fucking better not.'

'Do you want to go meet them?' she asked. 'I guess we could?'

She hadn't mentioned Liam all day, and I'd followed her lead. 'Do you want to?'

She stretched up. 'You know what I want? I want to stay right here, at the back, with just you. Is that so bad? You and me, like the old days. I don't want to get my feet trampled, or piss thrown over me, or punched in the tit by some moshing child. I just want to watch the sunset with you.'

I almost cried. 'That sounds pretty good to me.'

And so, as the crowd surged forward, becoming a giant mass, awaiting their royalty for the evening, we stayed put. Watching it all as if it were on television, our arms around each other to keep one another warm. While everyone waited, the cameras started beaming the crowd to the giant screens, making everyone in shot scream and wave as if they were famous. At first it was funny, seeing bunches of teenagers go ballistic when they saw themselves. But, pretty quickly, the cameras started honing in on girls sitting atop their boyfriends' shoulders.

'*Get your tits out, get your tits out,*' the mass started chanting, whenever this happened. Most girls, swept up in the shock of the moment, obliged, and threw their top above their heads, rewarded with the cheers of twenty thousand people. Then the camera fell on one girl and the chanting started, but she refused. Crossing her arms over her chest, looking as if she might cry, the camera zoomed right in on her and the mass turned on her. Everyone booing this spoilsport for not getting her tits out.

Even Jessica wrinkled her nose. 'Gross,' she said. 'Everyone is always so fucking gross.'

I was about to ask if she was OK. Like, really OK, but that's the moment Metallica came on. The music thrummed our eardrums, and the crowd instantly morphed into a chaotic, violent stampede where punching a stranger appeared to be the best way to appreciate it. We forgot the girl, giggled, and poked fun.

'I don't know this song,' I admitted, while the crowd went wild.

'Me neither.'

'Don't know this one either,' I said, about the next.

'Ditto.'

We were giggling ourselves stupid – my stomach aching from our constant laughter. Whenever a song came on that we knew, we screamed, '*WE KNOW THIS ONE*,' and fell into hysteria. It only happened about five times. With credit to Metallica, as the sky turned black, they got out 'Nothing Else Matters', and all the teenagers struck flames on the Zippo lighters they'd purchased mostly for moments just like this. They waved them in the air, and it really did look quite beautiful. Jessica lay her head on my shoulder, and I found myself wiping a tear away. The weight of Jessica's head, the glorious symphony of the chorus, the sea of flames, it made me get all sentimental. I reflected on how far the two of us had come. How long we'd been friends now. The things we'd supported one another through. How proud I was of that. And then I thought of how only a year remained. How this time, next August, we'd be on the cusp of a giant change.

'Are you really not going to go to uni?' I asked, the music dimming at the importance of our conversation. I'd heard on the grapevine that she wasn't applying to UCAS that upcoming autumn.

Jessica stiffened slightly on my shoulder. 'Liam and I are going to get a place in London together. See what happens with his band.' It was the first time she'd mentioned him all day.

'But you got all As and Bs,' I reminded her. 'Even though you never revise. I watched you with jealous disgust.'

Jessica laughed with her head to the sky. 'Exams are easy. It's just a system and you have to learn the hacks.'

'Teach me the hacks, please.'

'Can I point out that you also got all As and Bs?'

'Yeah, but I tried really hard for them.'

She laughed again. Picked up a section of my hair and started plaiting it.

'We'll see. I just . . . couples who go to uni never end up staying together. And Liam's band has a real chance, you know. I'm going to be the next Courtney Love! I'm going to sit on the side of the stage, wearing amazing outfits . . . like Penny Lane in *Almost Famous*.'

'I mean, she does try to kill herself in that movie.'

'But her outfits, Fern. Her outfits.'

After the band's encore, there was endless cheering and whooping. Reading Festival was over. A vast stampede of shivering people started filtering back to their tents, ready for 'riot night' as we'd been told it was called. Mike had promised to look after us, as apparently loads of girls got raped on the final night. Jessica and I stayed put for a while, watching it all pass, still detached and in our own little bubble. Eventually, when the arena was almost empty, she stood up, held out her hand to get me out of the dust.

'Come on, let's go find the others . . . go back to the stage,' she said, and I was buzzing so much I missed the subtext of what she'd just said.

When we got back to our camp, everyone cheered as if we were returning vets.

'Here come the defectors,' Mike said, with a sleepy Jade on his shoulder, smiling like a cat who'd snorted condensed milk.

Out of the side of my eye, I saw Jessica physically push her face into her Jessica glaze. Flirty grin, relaxed attitude, ready for quips and cool-girlness.

'Weren't Metallica TERRIBLE?' she said, raising her arms. 'Worst band I've ever fucking SEEN.'

The circle went mad, laughing, collecting her in with their arms, putting her crown back on. I watched as she found Liam, sunk in a camping chair with a drunken smile across his face, hardly able to hold himself up.

'What are these?' Jessica asked, taking in her boyfriend's unexpected fancy dress. The boys collapsed in on themselves and let out shrieks of laughter, while Jessica, frowning, held out a giant pair of novelty fairy wings Liam had on his back. Liam shrugged, playing innocent, as Jessica bent closer to read what had been scribbled all over them in black marker pen. The words *'Brown Wings'* over and over across the pink netting.

Mike's face was leery and red, Jade practically forgotten at his side. 'A little bird told me that Liamsy here learnt how to FLY last night,' he said, getting a giant cheer. I wrinkled my nose in naivety. *What were brown wings?* It was only later that night, after Jade explained, that I understood the connotations, before she asked me if I'd go get the morning-after pill with her before we got the train home. Everyone chanted *'Brown Wings'* and made aeroplane noises, while Jessica laughed at the joke, and leant over to kiss Liam, before giving the rest of the group a knowing wink. They kept chanting *'Brown wings, brown wings, brown wings'*, until she held up her hand to stop them. The circle fell silent, bewitched, waiting for the drop. Then my friend smiled her biggest smile, cupped her hands over her mouth, flung her hair past her shoulders and shouted 'BOLLLLLLLLLLLLOOOOOOOOOCCCCCKK KKKKKKSSSSSS' into the night.

Thirty-two

It was the first time I'd seen Jessica properly cry since that very first house party. I almost stepped backwards off the front step, twisting my ankle slightly in shock.

'Sorry . . . thank you for coming . . . sorry . . . Bollocks, I'm a mess.'

I tried to hug her, but she was already walking into her flat barefoot, snuffling into a twisted tissue. Bridget sat in her pyjamas, watching *The Little Mermaid*, a straw leading from her mouth to her milk. She glanced up, her beautiful eyes wide and concerned.

'Mum's allergic,' she explained. 'Her eyes are hurting.'

Jessica let out another small sob and kissed her daughter's head. 'That's right, honey. Mummy's got hay fever today. Are you ready to go to bed soon?'

Bridget nodded. 'Can I watch the rest tomorrow?'

'Of course, poppet. But Aunty Fern is here now. So bedtime.'

Shock was still making me stiff and useless. 'How about I put you to bed?' I managed to get out.

I was expecting the humiliating jolt of a child's rejection, but Bridget registered me and nodded. 'Will you read me a story?'

'Of course. Go get me your favourite ready.'

'Brush your teeth!' Jessica called after her in a tight throat, as Bridget ran down the hallway of their tasteful flat. She shook her head at me, tears streaming down her face. 'I'm so sorry, I don't know what's wrong with me. Sorry to disturb . . .'

'Shh.' I hugged her and initially she resisted, staying frigid in my arms, before she collapsed onto my shoulder.

'I don't know why I'm so upset . . . I can't . . . Bridget is . . .'

'She's fine! Let me put her to bed, then we can chat. Mums are allowed to get upset sometimes. Christ. My mum cried once a week at least. And look at me. Only one suicide attempt.' Jessica laughed into my back. 'Thank you. For being great.'

'You're great too.' I got my bag out and gave her the bottle of wine I was supposed to be sharing with Ben. 'Right, open this. Get glasses. I'll be back.'

Bridget, remarkably, went to bed with no resistance. She laughed at the voices I put on, then, sleepy, she asked me to turn on her night light. I stood in the doorway and watched her fall asleep instantly.

Jessica was staring into space when I crept back to her living room, marvelling at how nice she'd made the place already. It was my dream flat. Victorian, two-bed with a garden, on a quiet road literally on the park. An impossible place to own, or even rent, unless you fell into a pot of gold, or divorced

a very rich man. But, as she wiped away tears at the sight of
me, I felt maybe it wasn't worth it.

'Did she go down OK?'

'She is an angel child. Do you put drugs in her squash?'

'I can't believe she's seen me like this. That you have . . .
I hate people seeing me like this.' Jessica broke down again,
hiding her face, while I crouched down, and told her it was
fine. My toes tingled by the time her sobs subsided, her face
a blotchy blur. Every defence down.

'Sorry,' she said for the millionth time.

'Don't apologise,' I replied for the millionth time. 'Are you
ready to talk about it?'

'I'm being stupid.' She pushed herself upright in her squashy
sofa and leant over to pluck the wine glass from her stained-
glass coffee table. I took the cue to take my own, and sat
cross-legged next to her.

'What is it?'

'It's just, Brendan rang, and, well, Isobel is pregnant.' Her
voice cracked again. 'They're getting married too, of course.'

'Ahh.'

'He asked if Bridget could be a flower girl.'

'What a dick.'

'And even said, *"You're welcome to come if you want"*.'

'Double dick no returns.'

'I just . . . can't believe she's pregnant. I thought . . . I knew
it was over with us. But she . . . she's only twenty fucking six.
She was his rebound plaything. A girl to fuck, remember?
But no. She's a complete replacement.'

I reached over and took her hand. 'Honey, you're irreplaceable.'

She laughed harshly. 'Not to men, I'm not. No woman is.'

She shook her head. 'It's just . . . poor Bridget. She's going to be the awkward sidelined child from a first marriage. I hate that. I hate that he's going to make her that.'

'Jessica, it would be impossible to sideline Bridget. She's like a siren trapped in a child. It's fucking weird, but it's true.'

She laughed properly, having to put down her glass so she didn't spill. 'God, don't. I worry about that with her, every day. Argh! I'm so angry. How dare he replace me with some fucking . . . teenager! And, you know what I hate most? He won't leave her like he left me. Nope. Not even when she gets saggy and tired like I dared to. *Respectable* men like him only remarry once, to the younger one. They know if they do it again then people will whisper. God, it's so clichéd, I hate him so fucking much! I hate them all so much!' She picked up her cushion and slammed it down onto her lap, while I could only look on. Not sure what words would make it better. Nothing she'd said was a lie. It was a tale as old as time, what Brendan was doing to her. And no girl grows up wanting to be Spurned First Wife, Catherine of Aragon vibes. But, though my heart was breaking for Jessica, there was a tiny part of me, that I wasn't proud of at all, that was vaguely marvelling at this moment. This unravelling. This true Jessica. And how painful it was for her to be replaced by a better model . . . when Jessica had always been the better model for so many other women . . . *No, Fern, shut up, she's your friend. Don't even think it.*

I kept pouring the wine, dashing to the Londis on the corner to buy another bottle. I messaged Ben to tell him I'd be home late, and I was sorry our evening was missed.

Ben: No worries. Poor Jessica. I hope she's OK. Send her all my
love xxx

I winced slightly at his use of the word 'all', then had to have
another stiff word with myself. The night drew itself around
us. We put on *Tapestry* and sang along. Jessica lit all her Jo
Malone candles, bathing us in a sweet rich scent. My head
turned to velvet, tongue to velvet. By the end of the second
bottle, she was laughing again.

'You know what?' Jessica's head lolled against her sofa
cushion as she pointed at me.

'What?'

'I feel sorry for her. This . . . Isobel.'

'I feel sorry for her too.'

'But no, you don't get it. The thing is . . .' She sat up
slightly, raised her finger to her mouth and whispered the
rest. 'Brendan was shit in bed. Totally shit.'

I raised both eyebrows. *'Really?'*

'Oh my God, YES. Literally he was, like, how do I put it?
Half repressed Victorian, half porn star?'

I giggled. 'That's quite a combo.'

'Isn't it? I swear. It would be like . . . these weird chaste
kisses, pressing his lips to mine, no tongue. Touching me
weirdly, awkwardly, like he was scared of my skin. Then,
BAM, he'd just switch and suddenly he'd be like a fucking . . .
teenager from *The Inbetweeners* or something. Basically
wanking into me, calling me a whore. Never touching me. He
gave me whiplash once. *Whiplash.* Total switch. Mr Darcy
into Hugh Hefner. No!' She pointed her finger to the air. 'Not
Mr Darcy. Too hot. Mr Collins!'

I shook my head. I couldn't imagine a world in which Jessica ever had bad sex. 'You mean, you married someone you've just compared to *Mr Collins*?'

'I know, I know. But come on. All men are crap in bed, if we really admit it to ourselves.'

I shook my head again, feeling my brain swill from side to side. 'I am in total shock right now. I can't speak.'

'Why are you in shock?'

I gestured towards her. 'It's you. Jessica. Sexual Goddess. You don't have bad sex!'

'Fucking hell, Fern, I've only ever had bad sex.' She tried to drink from her empty glass, complained, then refilled it. 'Even with good sex I wasn't getting off . . . Like, it was good because there was such insane chemistry with a guy, not because my body actually felt good.'

'Wait wait wait wait wait.' My speech slurred. I, too, reached for the wine. I couldn't believe I was going to be this drunk during an epiphany. I held up my heavy arm. 'You're saying you don't . . . come?'

'Basically never.'

'What?!'

'I know.'

'But . . .'

'I mean, do you . . . ?'

'Well . . . not often.'

'See!'

'But you . . .'

'What?'

'You . . . you . . .' Oh God, how did I phrase this? 'You . . . always seemed to really like having sex.'

Her head fell to one side. I saw I'd stung her, and sat in silence, feeling a bit guilty, waiting to see if she was OK. Finally she looked up at me with total honesty. 'I liked boys wanting to have sex with me. That's different from liking having the actual sex. Well, that's not true. Hang on . . .' She drained her glass again. 'I love everything about sex right up until the actual moment they're inside me, you know what I mean? The chase of it. *Is it going to happen?* The look men give you when they want you so much. The power of it. The will we/won't we of it. And, I always think, right before that moment, maybe this will be the time it feels really good . . . it's the best feeling, the anticipation . . . and then . . .' she slammed the wine glass down, 'the moment they're inside you, nope. It just feels . . . like a dick inside you. And the guy always sort of goes away in that moment, don't you think? And the power has gone, cos, all of a sudden, it's switched, and they're just . . . poking your body and getting so much more out of it than you. It didn't always feel bad . . . but it rarely felt . . . amazing. Especially with all the shit men want to do with you once they've got access, and you're constantly having to make a million micro-decisions in real-time about whether it's OK they're slapping your arse, or flipping you over, or trying to finish on your face, or slip it into your arse, or fucking . . . spitting on you. Brendan spat on me once. Spat! On his wife! And I didn't make the decision in time that I didn't want to be spat on, because, well, it wasn't something I'd given any thought to until the moment my husband, who I really fucking loved, said, *"Can I fucking spit on you, you whore?"* I was in such shock that I just half nodded, and then I'm lying there, with gob in my fucking FACE, Fern. In my eye! Horrified that it's just happened, and wondering if I'm going to get conjunctivitis. And yet, I did sort of agree. And that sort of thing is always going on, them always wanting to take it to some . . . dark, weird, painful, fucking *YouPorn* place, and you don't want to deny them anything, but also, a lot of it hurts. Actually physically hurts. And you're wondering if it hurts for just you, if there's something wrong with you, and other girls are . . . I dunno . . . and, so all of this is going around your head, always trying to get the reigns back from the horse that bolted, the horse that, until moments ago, you were totally in charge of . . . and then you're supposed to come somehow? HOW? I don't fucking get it. I don't get why I've done any of it. Fuck them. Fuck them fucking all. If Isobel wants to get spat on for the rest of her life, well, be my fucking guest.' She leant over and poured the rest of the bottle into her glass, not offering me a top-up. All I could do was stare, my mouth unhinged, brain cluttered with the total cabinet reshuffle of everything I thought I knew about Jessica.

'I can't believe it,' I managed to get out. 'I always thought . . .'

'What?' Her head snapped around, she was suddenly sober. 'You always thought what?'

I inhaled sharply. Chose my words carefully. 'That . . . well . . . that you were having good sex, I guess. At the very least, not bad sex.'

I waited for her verdict, my stomach swimming, but she, thankfully, smiled, and was drunk again. Shook her head. 'Certainly not with Brendan, no. So she can have him. Take him,' she yelled, putting her hands around her mouth. 'You can fucking have him, my love!' I laughed and tried to *shh* her. 'Honestly, she's welcome. I've got my flat. I've got Bridget. I'm all good. Whereas she's going to be stuck with Mr *I-Love-It-When-You're-Tight* for the rest of her pathetic life. I mean, what does that mean, Brendan? You love it when I'm tight? Being tight means I'm fucking UNAROUSED. It means you've not done your foreplay job properly. Being tight means it fucking hurts! You get off on hurting me, you cunt?' She pointed at me once more. 'Do you know, after I had Bridget, he complained about how loose I was?'

'He didn't!'

'He fucking did. I'd given him his child. I'd grown it inside my body for nine months. Ripped myself apart pushing her out. Fed her with my own body. For the rest of his life, there is a child in this world with his DNA, his chin, his nose, his legacy – at the expense of my body, my pelvic floor, my tits, my opportunity to have a career. And rather than thanking me, every single moment he's conscious, for this ridiculous gift I gave him, he complains my vagina is too loose. Well, twenty-six-year-old bitch, yours is going to be loose soon, so you're bloody welcome to him. I am done. I. Am. *Done*.'

'I can't believe it,' I kept saying. 'I honestly can't believe it.'

'Yeah, you can.' She shrugged, before her face closed down, the curtains shutting. Then, she looked up at me and I felt suddenly on edge, and I wasn't sure why, until: 'You're so lucky to have a man like Ben,' she said.

'I know.'

'Honestly, I need someone like that.'

I tried to put my immediate nausea down to the wine. My stomach swimming, hands shaking, head buzzing like a disco had just started inside it. 'Hmm,' I managed, wanting to run, wanting to slap her, wanting her to stop, go away . . . my friend was crying. What was wrong with me?

Jessica, oblivious, sighed and smiled. 'Hey, Fern? Would it be mad to go get another bottle from Londis?'

Eighteen

September 2004

The pub was rammed. Full to the brim with eighteen-year-olds flinging their arms around one another, promising to stay in touch. It was as if the whole college had crammed into The Ram's Head, a three-person-deep queue at the bar.

'Got to get up at five a.m.,' someone boasted behind me, swilling a pint. 'We're driving all the way to Edinburgh.'

'I'm not going to Sheffield until Sunday.'

I watched Jessica weave her way towards me with her face set, cradling a bottle of wine for herself, and a lime and soda for me. 'Christ, I cannot wait for you to all fucking go to uni. Then I'll actually be able to get served.' She unloaded my drink and poured herself a glass of rosé.

Jade and Mike sat on the squashy sofas across from us, her face red and leaning towards him. They were clearly in the middle of some intoxicated deep and meaningful. He pulled her into a tight hug. 'You're special, Jade,' I heard him shout over the music.

I turned my head away. If Mike was going to try to crowbar

in one last nostalgia shag with Jade after the way he'd treated her, I didn't want to watch it play out. He'd, predictably, lost interest in Jade after taking her virginity at Reading. What we weren't expecting was him to lose interest so quickly. He had a new girlfriend within a week.

The music was too loud, combined with the yells of hundreds of sincere and insincere goodbyes occurring around us. It got to the point where Jessica and I were spending our last night together sitting in total silence, sipping our drinks. We stood at various points, to hug various people we didn't know or like that much, trading promises to always stay in touch. Jade got a phone call that pulled her from Mike's grip. He then spied Karly, a girl he'd had a thing with a few months ago, and vacated the sofa immediately, his arm already around her, steering her to the bar. I watched Jade's eyes follow him and I hoped so much that she'd find someone to fall in love with up in York when she started, someone who would appreciate how amazing she was. I knew she'd wish the same for me. Manchester and York weren't that far away, so I was looking forward to us visiting each other.

Jade hung up and returned to us. 'That was Sally,' she yelled. 'She's having a packing crisis and can't make it. Do you mind if I go over to say goodbye?'

'Not at all!'

She shook her head. 'This is too weird. I can't believe you're leaving tomorrow, Fern. TOMORROW.'

'You're only three weeks behind me, and then you're leaving too. York has such a late starting date.'

'I'm not leaving,' Jessica reminded us, pouring herself another glass of wine.

'We know,' I said, straining a smile. 'You're in charge of going to London first and setting up a wonderful life for us after graduation.'

'Right, I better go to Sally's.' Jade swung her bag over her shoulder. 'OK. This is it.'

We gazed at one another. 'This is goodbye, I guess,' I said. A tidal wave of grief and fear crashed around me as I stared at my friend, reflecting on how different we were likely to be when we were reunited.

'Only for a few weeks before I visit,' Jade reminded me. 'Oh my God, it's so WEIRD! Next time I see you, we're going to have all these new friends, and lectures and stuff.'

'Friends for life,' I joked, and Jade laughed. We'd been taking the piss for weeks now about the pressure to meet your 'friends for life' at university.

'Excuse me,' Jessica raised her arm in the air, 'I think you'll find you already have some of those.'

We pulled her into a hug, shoving her head into our armpits. 'Of course!' I reassured her. 'I'm going to hate everyone at uni for not being you.'

Jade and I hugged multiple more times, both crying a bit, before she finally dashed out of the door, glancing once more at Mike, who didn't even wave goodbye. Jessica and I turned to one another and shared a sheepish smile. It suddenly felt so desperately awkward with her. We both craned our necks around, taking in the symphony of surrounding goodbyes. I noticed Liam and his bandmates in the corner. He caught my eye, raised his hand slightly to say a small hi and bye, and I waved back. Then his eyes drifted to Jessica and his face hardened into a sneer, and I saw him mouth *'Yoko Bitch'* –

her new nickname. She must've caught my reaction, because she twisted her head and sighed when she saw Liam. 'Shall we go?' she asked, mouthing *'Fuck you'* back at him, while he flipped her off.

Jessica and Liam's break-up two months ago had erupted fault lines through our friendship circle. Even though Liam had dumped her because they were *'too young to feel like an old married couple'*, Jessica had come out the villain. She'd got wasted and rebounded with Phil from Mike's band in the back of his car, ruining the potential merger of Mike's band and Liam's. They'd been planning to form a 'superband' called 'She Screams', but the idea lay in tatters now. Jessica had gone from 'Slutty Jessica' to 'Perfect Girlfriend' to 'Yoko Bitch'. Not that she appeared to care – shrugging it all off whenever I brought it up.

'Shall we just go on a drive?' she said, turning away from Liam. 'You and me? Like old times?'

'That sounds perfect.'

It took half an hour to actually leave the pub. I did my rounds of hugging everyone goodbye, promising to stay in touch, swapping numbers with people I'd never really been friends with. Then we were free. Without saying it, I knew exactly where to take us. Up up up the giant hill, to the viewing spot. During the day it was packed with families clad in walking boots, bearing picnics and designer dogs. But, at night-time, the viewpoint car park was ours, and so was the view stretching out beneath us. I pulled up my hand brake and we smiled at one another. We'd been coming here at night ever since I passed my driving test. Jessica passed me a cigarette and we clambered out into the sticky September night, walking to the marble viewpoint. Our home town sprawled out below us in a sea of orange blobs. She passed me her lighter and we started smoking, not saying anything as we stared out at it all, both of us aware of the huge cusp of change we were perched on. This town. All I'd ever known was this town. Whereas tomorrow my parents would drive me for four hours up the M1 and spit me out in Manchester – a sprawling concrete mass of a city where nobody knew anything about me. If I kept my scars hidden, they'd never be able to guess who I'd been before. And Jessica wouldn't be there . . . For the first time in years, my identity wouldn't be linked to hers – endless comparisons where I fell always short. It was terrifying and wonderful to consider in equal measures.

'This town,' I said, breathing menthol smoke over the view.

'This fucking town.'

'I don't know how I'd have survived it without you.'

She lay her head on my shoulder. 'Ditto.'

We smoked our cigarettes into stubs. Reached into her packet and plucked out new ones. The thoughts we were having too big to be unaccompanied by cigarettes.

'I can't believe that this time tomorrow I'm going to be there,' I said. 'At university! What if nobody likes me?'

Jessica looked at her flip-flops. 'Everyone will love you. People always do. You've always made friends so easily.'

'They won't be you though.'

She batted the compliment away. 'They'll be nicer. Less complicated.'

'Shut up! You're irreplaceable, Jessica.'

She finally looked up at that, met my eye, her face bathed in silver moonlight. 'Really? You mean that?'

'Of course. Oh my God, the things we've been through together.'

Her pointed teeth shone as she smiled. 'I mean, it's going to take someone quite extraordinary to outdo the things we've done.'

'Nobody else has done a tap dance in a kebab shop, that much I know for sure.'

We laughed and coughed at our bizarre shared memories that nobody would understand but us, until a sadness laid itself over us like a quilt.

I put my fag down. 'Are you sure you don't want to go to uni?' I tried again. I twisted towards her, watched her face for reaction, and she shook her head as if she was tired.

'Nah.'

'But now you and Liam have broken up, there's nothing keeping you here. And you got such good grades. Without even trying, I may add.'

At that, she laughed. 'I mean, the fact I didn't try probably means I shouldn't be getting into shitloads of debt for academia. Anyway, uni! How would I even get there? My mum doesn't drive. Dad wouldn't give me a lift.'

'I'm sure he would! Or there are trains . . .' I wasn't sure why I was having this debate with her now, when it was too late, even for clearing.

'I've got this temp job starting in a few weeks. It's seven pound fifty an hour. So it won't take long to save enough for a deposit to move to London. Then I'll be in London. Stupid

Liam and his shit band won't be holding me back, so it's going to be even more fabulous.'

That's all her plan was. *London*. Go there. Be in London. She got annoyed if you pressed her for details.

'Yeah, I know, I know.' I lit my fourth cigarette. 'I guess we wouldn't be at the same university anyway.'

'And I'm going to come visit you all the time.'

'You better! Honestly, Manchester. It's so huge. I'm scared I'm going to drown . . .'

She reached over and pulled me into her. 'You won't,' she soothed, and I could tell she meant it. 'You're so much stronger than you ever give yourself credit for. Think of how many amazing people you're going to meet. And you get to read loads of books, and do loads of writing. It's going to be brilliant.'

'I hope so . . .' I looked out again at the sea of illuminated dots of life below me. 'At least with that many people around hopefully one person will fancy me,' I joked, lamely. 'I may even get to lose my virginity before I die.'

'EVERYONE is going to fancy you. *I* fancy you.'

'Hmm . . .'

'Honestly, you're gorgeous.'

'Hmm . . .' There was so much evidence to suggest other-wise. I figured I had until the end of first year to lose it before it became a bigger problem. Being eighteen and a virgin was pretty bad. I was sure most of the people I'd meet the next day wouldn't be. If I kept quiet about it, I could just about pull it off. But, if I got to nineteen, *twenty* . . . Boys would expect me to be better at sex than I would be . . . bleeding all over their sheets and trying to ensure they entered me at the most perfect point of my virginity-loss playlist I'd made for the occasion. 'It's just all so huge,' I said again, throwing my hands out to the blobs of orange. 'Life, stop being so huge! Like there's all these people out there who are strangers now, but, in time, will be really important people to me.'

I felt her stomach-laugh next to me. 'I can't believe you're this insightful and you're not even high.'

'There was a point when we were strangers,' I pointed out. 'Isn't that mad to think about?'

'Hmm.' She trailed off and ground her cigarette into the dusty ground, wrapping her arms around her chest. A breeze lifted her hair, blowing it across her face, and she fought to push it back behind her ears, lost in thought. I waited . . .

'I never want us to become strangers,' she said finally.

I let out a laugh. 'We won't.'

'Do you promise?'

'Of course.'

'Say it. Say you promise?' She twisted towards me with an almost rageful earnestness.

I held up a guide's promise sign and faked a laugh. 'I promise we'll never become strangers.'

'I promise too.'

Her smile split her face in half and she pulled me in for a final hug. Our last before I'd drive her back to the pub, because she wanted to get half a gram and party the night away.

If I'd known how much everything would go to shit, I would've hugged her for longer.

Thirty-two

I laid my head on my office desk and let the nausea dance up my gullet until my whole mouth tasted of bile.

'Stop this, stop this,' I whispered to the empty desks around me. 'This is self-harm, Fern. Just fucking stop this.'

I took some deep breaths and sat upright in my fancy orthopaedic chair. There, on my work monitor, was Ben and Tiffany's engagement photo once again. A hiccup of sick. My heart tickling the inside of my throat. I wanted to cry. Scream. Both.

Just outside my empty office, I could hear the cackles and jeers of my colleagues drinking in the pub downstairs – their fun floating up through the open windows. Nobody wanted to be at their desk when the weather was this glorious. It was the first proper hot day of the year, and, predictably, everyone in my team had hurtled outside at five p.m., sunburning their noses and guzzling pink cider poured onto ice. Derek had tried to drag me down with them. 'Come on, we should celebrate the traction on your Freud coping strategies listicle,' he'd said, but I'd pretended I needed to finish my stats report. It lay open on my browser, obscured by the engagement picture. My counselling series kept exceeding expectations, but that achievement meant nothing compared to Tiffany's on the screen before me.

A wave of laughter thrummed through the window. I leant forward, putting my face as close to Tiffany's digital one as possible. *Was she prettier than me?* She was definitely younger than me, but only in that photo. In truth, out there in the world, she was two years older than me. But part of what made me so sick was how young and pretty she looked in this image. Her teeth white and straight, no creases around her eyes, camera held at the perfect angle to give her a good jaw, when I knew, from stalking all her other pictures, her jaw was actually quite square. I spent more time torturing myself with how pretty she was than on examining how happy Ben looked, although that was next on my agenda. This woman, smiling out at me, with everything I've ever wanted, spent so much time in my thoughts. Sometimes I even dressed for her. I'd pick out an outfit with her in mind – wanting to out-better and outdo, in case we ever bumped into one another, or if she ever stalked me back. Sometimes I dieted for her too. Every time I stood to one side and bent an elbow to make my arm look slimmer in a photo for my socials, it was for Tiffany. Look at me, winning the thin-arm war, you bitch I've never actually met.

Did Tiffany ever stalk me back?

It would be so totally typical if she didn't – if Ben's ex never once wondered about who he moved on to. Would make it such a giant power imbalance – my obsession compared to her total chosen ignorance of my existence.

Why her, and not me? I thought, peering at the photo again. Why did he propose to her, and why won't he propose to me? It was way past my deadline to not be worrying about it. We'd lived together over a year and a half now. We'd had at least three stilted conversations around the subject, though he'd gone super quiet about it recently. Was he going off me? Surely he had enough information to make an informed decision about whether he wanted to spend the rest of his life with me? How much longer would this audition go on for? I was running out of lines. Going a bit mad. Whenever a wedding came on our TV, I'd stiffen like a rabbit in headlights, moving only my pupils to try to read his expression, because SURELY A PART OF HIM WAS THINKING ABOUT IT? But no. We were so good together. We got on so well. What more would he want? How much more of my life was I willing to waste waiting for him? Was it because he still loved Tiffany? The even crazier part of me was starting to worry it was Jessica's arrival that had derailed him – had made him see how much better other women were out there.

'Has it ever occurred to you that you could propose?' Heather had said, rolling her eyes as I brought it up for a sixth time. 'It being the twenty fucking first century and all.'

'I can't,' I said. 'And before you get mad at me, it's not a feminism thing, but a Me thing. I'm too insecure . . . If I proposed and he said yes, I'd worry for the rest of my life that he only said yes because I'd asked.'

She rolled her eyes harder. 'The dude teaches psychology, Fern. I don't think he's the sort of person who'd say yes to marrying someone to get out of an awkward conversation.'

'You say that, but . . .'

'I mean, if at this point, you're still too insecure to discuss it openly, then why are you even together in the first place? Fucking hell, by date four with Katie, we were discussing who would carry and birth which baby.' Heather looked genuinely flummoxed. 'What does it mean to you, anyway? Like, if you're happy together, which you always tell me you are, why does marriage matter?'

'I don't know. I guess someone proposing to you means being . . .' I tailed off, too embarrassed to say it, especially to her.

'*Chosen,*' I whispered to myself, staring at Tiffany's smug grin. The smile of being chosen.

Three Tube trains went past at Tottenham Court Road before I was able to cram onto a carriage and embrace the sweat of a dozen strangers' armpits. I managed to siphon my way to the open window, and risked lifelong tinnitus by pushing my head out, letting the warm wind lift my hair. I hadn't heard from Ben all afternoon, and worried about it more than I would've done before. He usually went out for a few staff room drinks on a Friday, and his iPhone usually died by two p.m. each day. But it was his turn to cook dinner. It felt wrong, lying about working late, but if he ever discovered the full scope of my insecurity, that would be the end of us. Ben could tolerate my depressive episodes, but I doubt any guy found excessive jealousy attractive.

'Sorry I'm late,' I called, pushing through our front door, sweat beading on my forehead. 'I tried to hack the Central Line by staying an extra hour, but it's like a fucking casino. The house always wins.'

'Come join us,' Ben called back happily. 'We've got margaritas.'

'Who's us?'

'Jessica is us,' Jessica's voice echoed down the hallway as I kicked off my sandals.

Why the hell was Jessica there?

I followed their laughter, and found Bridget on our sofa, lolling like a tiny Marie Antoinette, completely engrossed in her juice box and cartoons.

'Hi Bridget.' She just wiggled her finger in reply. I found them in the kitchen and sensed their shared atmosphere of fun. Jessica leant against the counter in the most glorious summer dress – white and covered in pink polka dots, twinned with a pink ribbon crowning her ponytail. She looked like Zooey Deschanel's hot evil twin. Ben had his shirtsleeves rolled up, a margarita in his hand.

'Hi guys.' I kissed him on the cheek, then scanned the kitchen. The blender was empty in the sink. Had they drunk a whole pitcher together? Without even messaging me? Actual dread started pulsing through me.

'Here, have my drink.' Ben passed over a large glass filled with crushed ice. 'If I have any more, I'll be sick into dinner.'

'Looks like you guys are having quite the sesh.' My voice came out very casual, but I was not feeling casual at all.

Jessica laughed, and I watched her reach out and needlessly touch Ben's arm as she laughed. 'Sorry, Fern, it's my fault,' she said. 'I came over unannounced, and you weren't here. We just got chatting and carried away by the good weather.'

We.

The word hit like a bullet. That wasn't a word for her and Ben.

'Sounds fun,' I chirped, taking a slurp of the green slush.

'Ben's just convinced me to try dating again.'

'Shouldn't she?' he asked me. 'I mean, honestly, what's the worst that can happen?'

'Well, I could marry a narcissistic arsehole who leaves me a single mother, ruined and alone?'

Ben scrunched up his face dismissively and batted the comment away. 'Nah, lightning doesn't strike twice.'

'Ben!' she shrieked. I watched as she mock hit him. More needless touching.

I gulped another gulp. 'Aren't you giving up on all that?' I reminded her.

Jessica nodded. 'I am.'

'Stupid,' Ben said, plucking my drink off me so he could have a slurp. He was high energy for a Friday evening. Had that puppyish bounce he used to have when we were first together. 'You're only, what, Jessica? Thirty-two or something? Life's too long to be alone for ever.'

I took the drink back off him. 'Aren't you scared they'll be put off by her having a kid?'

It was a sour, awful thing to have said. Surprising even myself, but Jessica didn't seem to have noticed. She nodded. 'Exactly. It's not really an aphrodisiac, is it? Motherhood?'

Ben waved a dismissive hand again. 'Ridiculous. Bloody hell, at our age, you assume most people are going to have kids. I was surprised Fern didn't, to be honest. Everyone knows dating in your thirties is second-time-around stuff.'

I twisted to him. 'You thought I'd have kids?'

'Yeah, maybe.'

'And you didn't mind?'

'No! Why would I?'

Jessica pointed at him. 'See! This is what I need! A man who thinks like this.'

Careful, bitch, my brain said. Viscerally. Violently. *Get away from him. Get the fuck out of my house.*

Instead, I laughed shrilly. 'Ben isn't a one-off,' I said. 'But, only date if it's what feels right for you.'

'Maybe if I take a bit more time off. Speaking of which,' she lifted her chin to empty her glass, 'I should probably stop gatecrashing your weekend and actually feed my child.'

'You're welcome to stay,' I offered, hoping she'd say no.

'Bless you, but Fridays are the only night she's allowed potato smiley faces. Bridget will scream the place down if I renege on such a promise.'

Ben laughed heartily and I wanted to smack him. But, instead, made myself go over and hug Jessica. 'Shall we get a coffee or something this weekend?' I offered – mostly out of guilt at my own thoughts.

'That would be lovely, thank you.'

I watched her gather her stuff, and Ben, slightly tipsy, came and held me from behind, kissed the top of my head. The second he did it, I felt much better.

'Right, Bridget, come on, potato smiley-face time.'

Her child arrived so quickly in the doorway she was like a cartoon. 'HOW MANY CAN I HAVE?' she asked, climbing Jessica's limbs, and we all laughed again. Ben remembered it was his turn to cook and started collecting pans out of the drawer, making clattering noises, as I went to walk them out. Just as we got into the communal corridor, a thought occurred.

'Jessica?'

She turned back, Bridget's small hand in hers. 'Yep?'

'What did you want? I mean, why did you come over? Is everything OK?'

And I swear, there was a tiny moment's hesitation. Her eyes went wide as she searched for an answer. One that would've come quickly if she was telling the truth. Instinct curdled my stomach, my hands shaking slightly. Paranoia descending once more. 'Oh, I just wanted to see if you fancied a coffee this weekend.' Her delivery was perfect. Breezy. Seamless. 'But, as you just asked . . . Can't wait. Do you want to try that new place in Hackney Wick where the coffee comes from fermented poo?'

I laughed once more through my discomfort. 'I mean, no, but also, yes.'

'I'll message you.'

As I closed the door behind them, my hackles were up. Ben, oblivious, wrapped his arms around me when I found him in the kitchen. 'That was nice,' he said, neutrally. 'It's good to get to know your friends better.'

He kissed the top of my head. He was right. It should be nice. Why didn't it feel nice? Why didn't it feel like the time we went on holiday with Heather and Katie, and they'd all stayed up drinking without me? I'd fallen asleep smiling, hearing her rant at Ben through the floorboards of the Airbnb, lecturing him on the ethical issues of surrogacy.

I leant up and kissed him back, knowing I'd spend the whole weekend obsessing over this. 'Yes,' I said. 'Really nice.'

Eighteen

September–November 2004

From: FernGully@hotmail.co.uk
To: JessLovesYou69@hotmail.co.uk
Subject: Can't believe I'm a fresher!!!!????

Hi Jessica,
How are you? I miss you! You feel so far away. I sort of
hate it.

Firstly, THANK YOU for taking my mentalist phone
call the other night. I don't know what came over me, I
just got very overwhelmed on my first night here. I'm
not sure how everyone else on my corridor coped so
well! I feel really homesick. But it's only been three days,
I guess, and I'm so glad you took my call, and reminded
me I could just come home if I wanted. I'm going to try
and stick it out until at least Christmas. The girls on my
floor are actually really nice. We went to this bar crawl
last night, which was very intense and busy and sweaty.

This girl, Heather, is my favourite so far. She has all these crazy theories about things.

Anyway, thanks again for being there.

Love

Fern xxx

*

From: JessLovesYou69@hotmail.co.uk

To: FernGully@hotmail.co.uk

Subject: Do you have to wear thick-rimmed glasses everywhere?

FERN!

Any time. I'm always here for you. Glad to hear you're settling in, but also glad to hear you're missing me. I miss you loads!!!!!!!!!!!! Town is so weird without any of you here, but Jade and I are having many adventures before she leaves for York. We got the train to London the other day and got stoned in Hyde Park, and took out one of those rowing boats. Too wasted to row, of course. Just went around and around in tiny circles, laughing too much, and chucking Percy Pigs into the lake because we had a bet about whether or not they could float. (They can't.) Glad your hall is nice and friendly. You'll get the hang of it all soon, I promise.

Sorry such a quick one. Jade outside. We're going to Brighton.

Love

Jessica xxx

From: FernGully@hotmail.co.uk
To: JessLovesYou69@hotmail.co.uk
Subject: Percy Murderer

Jessica!!!!

OMG! SO sorry it's been a while since I've emailed.
Things are SO CRAZY up here. I take it all back. I love
uni! I love Manchester! Everyone is great! I'm having
such an amazing time! I just needed to get over the
huge shock of it all and now, honestly, it's so fun, you
must come visit, you must APPLY TO MANCHESTER and
come next year.

OK OK, so where to start? Right, so my hall are so
great. But what's especially great is this girl called
Heather. She's SO fucking cool. You would love her. She's
a lesbian. She came out to us all last week. Isn't that
cool? Said it's the first time she's been out her whole life,
even though she says she knows she's been gay since
she was, like, a foetus or something. ANYWAY, she is so
smart, Jessica. She's got all these opinions about boys
and girls, and how fucked up everything is. She wants
me to join this 'Feminist Soc' with her, but I'm not sure. I
told her I don't wanna burn my bra and not shave my
legs and she laughed. We'll see. It's all quite interesting.

All of us have been going out most nights, and it's so
fun. Drinks are so cheap! Come to uni! All of us have
bonded so well. They feel like family already. And, even
though I'm drunk most nights, I've not done drugs since
I've come, isn't that weird?

Anyway, the other big news is . . . I HAVE MET A

BOY! An actual boy who I fancy. The only problem is that everyone else in our halls seems to be in love with him too. His name is Danny and he lives upstairs and he is GORGEOUS. Like he has the nicest floppy hair, and really good skin. He's on my course, so we met the first night, and agreed to walk into our first lecture together. Then, when I turned my head, he was kissing someone, and that's basically Danny all over. He can't really go anywhere or do anything without someone kissing him. But he sees me as more than that, I can tell. We have such amazing deep talks when we walk into lectures. Like all about the Iraq War, and Shakespeare, and the poetry he writes. We study in his bedroom together, on his bed, and it's so intense, our feet brushing together and stuff. We end up talking 'til really late about all these deep things. I'm just going to enjoy being his friend and see what happens, but I do really like him. It's so nice to like someone after so long. OMG, I have to go! We are all going to the fancy dress shop for this night out tomorrow. The theme is 'Bad Taste' – how funny is that? I'm going to go as a Hell's Angel. Danny was going to go as a rape victim but Heather had a MASSIVE go at him. That's the weird thing about being her friend – you realise SO MANY things aren't funny!

So, yeah, having the time of my life, Jessica! It's great. Sorry I've been so busy. I miss you of course. Let me know your news. When do you start your job?

Oh my GOD – they're playing the Spice Girls and having an impromptu corridor disco, I have to dash.

xxxx

From: JessLovesYou69@hotmail.co.uk
To: FernGully@hotmail.co.uk
Subject: Wow

. . . it sounds like you're having a great time. That's brilliant, Fern. I'm so happy you're settling in now. I mean, of course you were going to make friends and everyone will love you! You always make friends wherever you go. Heather sounds like someone we all need in our lives. And Danny sounds very good-looking, but also a bit like trouble. Be careful there!

Things have quietened down here. Jade's started York now, so the rest of us are getting used to it being the rest of us. Can't wait for you all to come home for Xmas. I started my job this week, and it's going good. It's just office admin stuff, but it's fun to wear grown-up office clothes, and my manager is thirty, called Ian, and I have a bit of a crush on him. I think he has a crush on me too. It's nice to have a real man in my life. Like, Ian has his own flat he rents, and he brings a packed lunch into work. Can you imagine? My plan is still to save enough to move to London. I'm doing OK. Just miss you! Honestly, Fern, I really do. I miss texting each other the moment one of us wakes up to meet up. I miss getting high with you and having deep chats. I miss dancing like lunatics. I miss going to the kebab shop with munchies and ordering cabbage with our chips and burger sauce to make it 'healthy'. And I miss just you and me driving around in the middle of the night and feeling like we're the only two people left on earth.

Sorry, I'm being a bit sentimental, aren't I? I think it's just taking a while to adjust to being left here. But I'm so happy you're having a good time.

Love

Jess xxxxx

xxxx

*

From: FernGully@hotmail.co.uk

To: JessLovesYou69@hotmail.co.uk

Subject: Oh Danny Boy . . .

Jessica!!!!!! I'm SO SORRY it's taken me SO LONG to reply. I MISS YOU TOO! SOOOOOOOOOOOOO much. It's mad. I miss those things all so much too. It's weird, that life you described feels so far away right now. Happy your job is going well. Please don't get together with a man just because he has a packed lunch though. Surely we must strive for more than that?

OMG, I have so much to fill you in on. SO much has happened. Manchester is still amazing. I've joined the student union newspaper, and I've got my first story!! I have to go interview people about the stress of finding a house for second year. Speaking of which, we've already signed on a giant house of eight – isn't that cool? And guess what? Danny is living in the house next door. How perfect?! We are still just mates, but getting closer each day. We got set our first essay and he invited me to his to study together. We ended up talking about Shakespeare and stuff until we both fell asleep on his bed, SPOONING. It was the best thing that's ever happened to me. I've never had anything like this before. He didn't make a move though . . . I think . . . hope . . . he didn't make a move because I'm more special to him than all the girls he gets with when he's drunk.

Oh shit, I have to go again! We're going to this medics bar crawl tonight and I need to get my costume ready. We're going as all the different stages of Madonna music videos, isn't that so cool? I'm going as her in 'Like a Prayer', but Danny is going as her in her cone bra! So ridiculous but hilarious! I LOVE HIM, JESSICA.

Love

Fern xxxxxx

*

From: JessLovesYou69@hotmail.co.uk
To: FernGully@hotmail.co.uk
Subject: Visit soon?

Wow, Fern, it sounds like you've been really busy. I hope the Madonna night went OK. Do send me a photo when you get the chance. It sounds like there's a lot of group fancy dress at university. What are you going to be tomorrow? The seven circles of Hell? (*You know what? That's quite a good idea, feel free to copy it.*) Things are going OK here. I'm just working all the hours there are to save money, and my crush on Ian certainly helps. But, other than that, yeah . . . not a lot to share. Liam randomly asked me to go to his latest gig which I thought was quite cheeky, after referring to me as 'that Yoko Bitch' for months. The band must be struggling with everyone who normally tolerates their gigs going to uni. My heart bleeds for him . . . NOT!

Please write back when you get the chance. I miss you.

xxxxxxxxxxxx

★

From: JessLovesYou69@hotmail.co.uk
To: FernGully@hotmail.co.uk
Subject: I've got NEWSSSSSS

Hi Fern,
OK, so you've not replied to my previous email, even though it's been two fucking weeks . . . who's counting? Well, me! Until just now, because I can't even be mad at you because I AM SO HAPPY!

Oh my God, Fern, so Ian and I are together! Like properly together. It's going SO fast, but it feels SO right. I've basically moved in with him, which sounds crazy, but he has his own flat, and it's so crammed at my mum's it just makes sense. We were both working late loads, and then, one night, he asked if I wanted to get a drink, and I said yes. Anyway, we ended up wasted and he basically said he's loved me since my first day. And he's only been working late to spend time with me! I AM SO HAPPY! Fern, you will love him. He's started making ME a packed lunch every morning too. Isn't that great? Honestly, Fern, I think he's my soulmate. On that first date, he asked me sooooo many questions about myself, and I found myself telling him everything. All my shit with my dad, and Liam and stuff, and it didn't scare him off! In fact, he just hugged me hard, and kissed the top of my head, and it was so magical. My mum got a bit weird about the age gap, but it's only because she hates everyone who is happy in life. Anyway, Ian says I've got 'an old soul' and I don't seem eighteen at all. I'M JUST SO HAPPY! PLEASE WRITE BACK, I MISS YOUUUUUUUUUUUUUUUUUUUUUUU

Jess xxx

★

From: FernGully@hotmail.co.uk
To: JessLovesYou69@hotmail.co.uk
Subject: WHAT LE HELL?

OMG Jessica! I can't believe it. Woah! You sound really happy. I can't believe you live together already. I'm still a fucking virgin, and you're LIVING with a guy. I must be in the slowest sexual lane possible. I'm, like, fucking *doggy-paddling* down it with some old withered women who have to wear those floats in their M&S swimsuits because otherwise they'll sink from being too frail. And even THEY are probably lapping me, as they no doubt got laid in the war or something, when everyone was so horny from being in the Blitz . . . BUT I DIGRESS!!! Woah. Huge news. I can't wait to meet him when I come home for Christmas. Honestly, so happy for you. Why don't you come and visit and fill me in on everything? I would lovvvvvve to have you up here and show you everything and everyone! I talk about you all the time!

LOL about Liam and his shit band doing shit.

Sorry again it took me so long to email. Things are just non-stop here, but really great. I love my course. I love the creative writing the most. Danny says I'm good. We are STILL just friends, SIGH. But spend so much time together everyone calls us 'The Couple'. I wish he would finally make a move! Anyway, my piece for the paper made it to page seven, which is pretty cool! I like the Me I am up here, if that makes sense? Come visit! I think you'll like her too!

XXXX

*

From: JessLovesYou69@hotmail.co.uk
To: FernGully@hotmail.co.uk
Subject: How's December 5th?

I'm looking at the Trainline and there are tickets to Manchester that are only £7.50 each way. Before then it's too pricey. Would that work? I know it's just before you come home for Christmas, but still . . . Let me know ASAP and I'll book. We have SO much to catch up on, Fern. I can't wait.

xxxx

★

From: FernGully@hotmail.co.uk
To: JessLovesYou69@hotmail.co.uk
Subject: BOOK IT

NOW!!!!
AHHHHHHHHHHHHHHHHHHHHHHHHHH

Thirty-two

'Another bottle?' Ben asked me, grinning over the posh table-cloth. He was wearing the only good suit he owned, but looked hot anyway.

I smiled back, and twisted around to our waiter. 'Go on then,' I told him. 'We're celebrating.'

'I'll bring it right over.' The man gave a little bow then went off to secure more of the second-cheapest wine in the restaurant.

I pulled a sulky face. 'He didn't ask me what we were celebrating.'

Ben laughed as he poured the last dregs of our previous bottle into his glass. 'You just lowered our rank in this place. He must know only plebs come here to "celebrate". Everyone else here is just having a casual dinner.'

'I can be casual. I am so casual.' I lifted my posture and tried to copy everyone around me. We were in a posh 'small plates' restaurant that everyone richer than me kept raving about. I'd never spent so much money to still feel so hungry.

And, though we could just about afford to be there, I still felt very much like Jack in the first-class section of *Titanic*. I held my chin up, and lifted my pinkie on the wine glass, and started talking in a plummy voice. 'I do worry little Henrietta won't take to lacrosse,' I said. 'Also, she wants to come home and actually see us at Christmas, can you think of anything more ghastly?'

Ben let out a burst of laughter, and then sucked his chest in, playing along. 'If only she'd been a boy,' he added. 'I do feel she's done it deliberately, ruining the heirship.'

I lifted my mostly empty glass. 'Well, if the test results come back OK then we can try for another. I can't BELIEVE how weird they're being about us being cousins.'

Ben snorted and I dissolved, and we were still giggling when the waiter returned, with the wine all dressed up in its little napkin scarf. I glanced over at Ben, love heavy in my heart, as he went through the rigmarole of tasting the wine, and nodding, and not knowing what facial expression to make when the waiter poured it. Tonight was just what we needed. Me especially. To get away from our flat, with Jessica always around, and to get out of my head, which was intent on falling into an insecure abyss. Once the waiter left, and we could relax, Ben held up his glass.

'I really am so fucking proud of you,' he said, his face bathed in the subtle golden light of the opulent restaurant.

'I mean, it might all be a total wind-up.'

'Yes, but still . . . I can't believe an agent has been in touch. About a book deal. This is, like, the dream.'

I was so uncomfortable with this strange new plot twist that Ben's words almost felt foreign. 'I mean, the agent could be a total charlatan and the whole thing could be a terrible embarrassment.'

In a mad turn of events, the success of *The Other Side of the Tissue Box* had apparently caught the attention of the publishing industry. Two days ago, a non-fiction literary agent called Lucinda had emailed to tell me I was a genius, that she wanted to be my agent, and that I totally needed to let her take me out to lunch. Earlier that day, she'd taken me to a place even nicer than this to share 'her vision for me'. She wanted me to write my *Gah!* web series into a memoir, exploring my journey from a teenage suicidal mess to 'mental health expert'. Her hands had become more and more animated over the lunch she didn't eat, as she filled my head with the very grandest of notions. '*Going to be huge . . . you've really tapped into the zeitgeist here . . . I predict a huge marketing campaign . . . foreign sales . . . bestseller lists . . . you'll be invited to all the festivals to share your expertise.*'

I think Lucinda's head almost fell off when I'd told her, 'I'd think about it,' rather than signing her contract straight away.

Ben, sensing my thoughts, put his glass down. 'Are you still unsure? It's such a huge opportunity, Fern. Huge.'

I sighed. 'I know we need the money and everything, but I'm not sure I believe it's right, you know? I mean, I'm not even a counsellor yet. I'm years away from that. I don't want to fuck up.'

'I don't want to get all psychology teacher on you, but you know fear is a bad reason to say no to anything.'

I nodded and took a sip of my wine, thinking it didn't taste much better than the six-quid bottles we got from Londis.

'You're right. Maybe it's that. I'm trying to work out if it's that . . .' The waiter returned with some pudding menus. My eyes flicked along the menu, where they explained in calligraphy the precise life cycle of the poached pear – where it grew up, what boarding school it went to – and my finger pointed at the chocolate éclair. The waiter nodded. Ben didn't even look, just asked if they had apple crumble. He nodded again, and was gone. 'I think maybe I just want to focus on being a really good counsellor at the moment,' I said, then sighed again. 'I don't know. I just don't want to be like Stacy, that influencer, you know? Making money by talking about mental illness when I'm not an expert, at least not yet.'

Ben reached over and took my hands. 'Well, whatever you decide to do, I'm so proud of you.' Our eyes locked and I loved him so much. Why didn't he propose, right now? In this gorgeous restaurant we could barely afford? This was so good. *We* were so good. Weren't we? Propose, then I could finally relax. And, as our lovely meal continued, I slowly soured it in my head. I got upset and grumpy each moment Ben didn't drop to one knee. As it became clear, once more, it hadn't occurred to him at all to pick me. *Why not? Why not? Why not?*

Later that night, we were drunk on the sofa, and I could tell Ben wanted to have sex with me. We lay with our legs sprawled over the sofa arm, his hand rubbing my arse through my dress, as we giggled into each other's mouths. I half loved it when he wanted me like this, and half resented him for only wanting me like this, not wanting to commit in the way I needed.

'I love this dress,' he murmured.

He pulled it down, started kissing my boobs through my bra. 'And I love this bra.'

I laughed, pushed his head so he could keep doing what he was doing. We tumbled about on the sofa, clothes pulled up or shed. Drunkenly getting Ben's trouser leg stuck on his foot, and he hopped around to get it off. Then we collapsed onto each other again, our bodies beginning to merge. I pushed my insecurities from my mind and tried to make myself ready.

'Goddammit. I'm dying for a piss.' He pulled back from my mouth and pushed himself off the sofa. 'Sorry. Sorry. I'll be back in a second.'

I laughed as Ben ran away, seeing his erection bulge through his pants.

'Stay just there,' he called back.

'I will.'

While he was gone, I did a quick pre-sex rearrangement. I put my fingers into my knickers to check I was wet enough. Let my hair down. Rearranged myself into a more flattering position, but faux relaxed into it, so it would look like I just naturally and casually displayed myself, like a nude on a chaise longue, with my hair flowing perfectly down one shoulder. I waited.

'Sorry,' Ben called. 'I need to get my erection to go down before I can piss.'

'Hurry up,' I called back, smiling. 'Or I'll start touching myself without you.'

'Fern! You've just made it come back!'

I laughed and plopped myself down on a cushion again. Tried to keep myself in the sexy zone, despite being able to hear Ben's random bursts of restrained piss land in our toilet.

I reached into my knickers, touching myself to keep the mood going, when his phone buzzed, lighting up on the coffee table. I decided to put it screen down, so it didn't distract him. I leant over to turn it around. But, when I saw Jessica's name on his screen, my eyes went to it like a homing missile.

Jessica.

Then his phone went again. And again. More and more messages flooding in from her. At gone midnight. So many of them, his phone's lock screen wouldn't let me see any of them, just that she'd messaged him five times in quick succession.

I started shaking, half naked on the sofa. I didn't even know they'd swapped numbers? I'd never gone through Ben's phone, no matter how tempting it could occasionally be. I always refrained, but Jessica . . . I reached out and punched the home button, breaching a cardinal relationship rule. Only the first message would show.

Jessica: Got something to show you xxx

The toilet flushed and I dropped it to the table, my hands still shaking. I tried to replicate my relaxed sexy pose, but my body was riding an adrenaline surge. Every possibility ran through my head as Ben thudded barefoot back to me. Why did he even have her number? What was she showing him? What did the other messages say? Are they meeting up without me? She was around constantly . . . Oh God, Ben had arrived. That look in his eye. Sex on the cards. I couldn't be less turned on. I was too busy free-falling.

'Now,' he said in a deliberately cheesy voice, leaning towards me. 'Where were we?'

I tried to kiss him back. I tried to trust him. This man, who'd spent the whole night telling me how proud he was. I trusted Ben. Didn't I? Shouldn't I?

I broke off for a second, put on a coy grin. 'Your phone was going nuts,' I said. 'When you were in the loo. Someone might be in trouble or something?'

A flash in his eyes, or was I imagining it. 'Did you see who it was?'

'Yes,' I deadpanned. 'I went through your phone. Read all the messages. I can't believe you're fucking cheating on me with five other women. Aren't you exhausted?'

The joke was a test. I scrutinised his face for a reaction and Ben passed. Maybe he passed? Because he grinned, not flinching at all. 'I don't use them all for sex,' he said. 'Some of them fill the emotional void you leave in me.' He twisted over and picked it up. I wanted to hold a magnifying glass to his face as he read Jessica's messages. I could make nothing out though. He didn't reply, just punched the message away, and returned, grinning, to me.

'Anything important?'

'Nah.' He shrugged and moved to kiss my neck again. I could think of no way of stopping the inevitable sex – not without making it clear how much I was freaking out. So I went onto autopilot, faking moans and sighs, while, on the inside, I dived head first into how bad it'd been when this last happened.

Eighteen

November 2004

It just *felt* like an important night. I couldn't place it, but, in my bones somewhere, there was a deep tingling. And, by some grace of the universe, I happened to look effortlessly good for the occasion.

'I don't understand how you look so hot,' Heather said, when she'd walked into my uni room wearing a ballerina tutu. 'You look about twelve years old, and you also look super hot.'

It was particularly impressive considering I was dressed as Avril Lavigne. I'd straightened my hair so it fell like two rulers either side of my face, and wore a stripy tie as a necklace over a Motorhead T-shirt, twinned with the knee-high socks I wore under my mini-kilt. I also had on enough eyeliner I could probably eat it and survive for three days if I ended up stranded in a desert.

'I don't understand it either! But I'm not going to complain.'

It couldn't be more perfect, as I was spending the evening at Danny's side. As if on cue, he thrust my uni door open, playing air guitar, and yelling the lyrics to 'Sk8er Boi' at the top of his lungs, eyes closed as he started jumping around my room. He was an equally cute-sexy hybrid. He'd gelled his hair into spikes, decorated his arms in flannel wristbands, and wore a dog collar necklace, giant baggy jeans, and a Blink 182 T-shirt. He leapt onto my single bed and took a giant sideways jump off, before landing at our feet, finally taking us in.

'Holy fuck, Fern, you look hot,' he said, sounding genuinely surprised.

'Doesn't she?' Heather agreed. This was the first time we were fully assembled in our group fancy dress, and we all squealed at how awesome we looked. Heather's tutu wafting up and down as she jumped in the air. My door went again, and Monique entered wearing a cheerleading outfit and balancing drinks on her arm.

'I've got shots . . . oh my God, you guys look AMAZING.' She almost dropped her tray of Apple Sourz.

Heather pointed to one of her ballet shoes. 'He's a punk, I do ballet, what more can we say?'

'I can't cope. This is too good. Oh my God, I have to take a photo.' Monique carefully put the tray down on my cluttered desk, and took out her tiny digital camera. 'Right, cram together. Danny, you go in the middle, as you're the Sk8er Boi.'

Danny pulled me into his side, his hand snaking around my waist, setting every atom of my skin on fire, tickling me to make me smile.

'Say "TEENAGE KICKS",' Monique said, holding her camera up to her eye.

'TEENAGE KICKS,' we chanted. And, maybe it was wishful thinking, but Danny took a while to let me go.

Pre-drinks were held in the halls bar, which was packed with other friendship groups dressed for the same theme night. I was at Danny's side, perched on his knee, as there wasn't quite room on the sofa. His physical proximity made it very hard to concentrate on the giant game of *Never Have I Ever* happening around me. I was sitting in a circle of goths, and pink ladies, geeks and punks, new romantics and grungers. Everyone downing drinks and boasting about all the crazy sex they'd had. The shots I'd done upstairs backstroked around my head, and I zoned out like I always do whenever we played this fucking game. Oddly enough, there was never a round saying, '*Never have I ever sat alone in a corner at a house party while everyone else got off with each other.*' So I always ended up sober and socially anxious. I shifted on Danny's lap and almost fell off. He cheered and pulled me back up, before chugging his drink because he'd been naked in public before. This was news to nobody, as Danny was prone to getting his arse out on most occasions, especially if he felt he wasn't getting enough attention in that particular moment. He'd been removed from the student union twice for just bending over and getting his butt out in the middle of the dance floor. I knew, on paper, he was a ridiculous person to fancy. But, when it was just me and him, walking to our lectures, or him lying on my bed, doing our seminar reading together, he was different. Wise, considered, dry, sometimes even quiet. I'd fallen asleep on his bed twice now, both of us waking up spooning and sheepish, poised potentially on the cusp of something, but he never made a move. I wondered if tonight meant anything – us coming in a joint costume. 'Just what we'd expect from The Couple,' Monique had said, as we roped Heather in to be the third person in our Sk8er Boi love triangle. I was mulling it over so much that I'd tuned out the drinking game, and, without thinking, I reached over and took a sip of my vodka lemonade. The table erupted around me.

'Oh my God, Fern,' Peter, a medic from downstairs, yelled. 'Who would've thought?'

'Huh?' I looked around, and everyone was cheering me in disbelief, while a few others gregariously slurped from their drinks.

'When did *YOU* have sex outside?' Monique shouted, as I realised what I'd mistakenly admitted to.

'What? I . . . sex *outside*?' I was about to correct the mistake, but, for the first time ever, I was the focus of our uni group's attention. And, from the corner of my eye, I saw Danny looking at me.

'I am shocked,' he said, with his hand over his mouth. 'Very fucking shocked, Fern.'

I'd instantly become socially relevant. Noteworthy, rather than the quiet girl who always wore long sleeves. I sat up straighter, the power sucking my posture in, pushing my shoulders back. Danny's impressed gaze giving me confidence. I put my straw in my mouth and found myself performing a role, a fake coyness to cover my fake promiscuity. I shrugged and said in a voice that very closely resembled Jessica's, '*What can I say? I grew up in the suburbs. There were a lot of fields.*'

'WOAHHHHHH.'

'WHOOOOOO.'

'WHAT THE HELL, FERN?'

'IT ALL COMES OUT.'

I'd never been more popular. As the game continued, I added further embellishment to my imaginary sex life. Would Fern have had a threesome? No, I didn't think so. But, yes, Fern had *totally* said the wrong name in bed. ('WOAHH WHOOO'.) And, I guess I could've had a Friend With Benefits – why the hell not? After I downed my drink to admit I'd joined the Mile High Club, I found myself talking utter rubbish in my new Jessica voice. 'It's amazing what you can cover up with one of those thin woolly blankets they give you,' I said, while two people high-fived me.

'Oh my God, who did you shag on a plane?' Danny whispered, pulling me tighter.

I grinned. 'Just some guy called George I met on holiday in Greece.'

I was wasted by the time we left for the club. Danny helped me stand, holding me steady as I stumbled. 'I don't think I know enough about you,' he said, tilting his spiked hair to one side. I felt an edge there that hadn't been there before.

'You only needed to ask,' I said, winking.

The nightclub queue was long and throbbing and none of us had brought coats.

'I'll keep you warm,' Danny said, noticing my knees knocking under my kilt. He hugged me from behind, and I seeped into his body, inhaling his scent.

'How about me?' Heather demanded in her flimsy leotard. She'd been giving me funny looks since we got out of the taxi.

'Come on in,' he beckoned, and Heather's tutu scrunched

against us. 'Gotta keep my love triangle happy.' His hand reached down and grazed my arse. I looked up, caught his eye, and Danny grinned. Giant fireworks of lust and hope exploded through me. So overwhelming that, when we did eventually get into the packed and sweaty club, I went straight to the bar and ordered two double vodka lemonades in one pint glass. It was empty by the time I found our group mushed on the main dance floor.

The vodka infused my system, mixed with all of it already in there. It made me daring and funny. I felt so confident of my sex appeal, just by *pretending* I'd had sex. Our gang kept being stumbled into by even drunker groups of freshers. My arm was burnt by a lit cigarette. A girl in stilettos stepped on Monique's foot. More shots, brought over by Danny, half-spilt on a tray. Throwing them down my neck with a wince. Perching over a sodden toilet seat in the packed girls' loos. Getting lost every time I left the group. Sweat dripped from the ceiling. Everyone screamed like the Queen had turned up when 'Hey Ya' came on. Everywhere I looked, people copulating. Tongues in mouths. Girls pushed up against quiet corners, hardly conscious, with boys they'd just met putting their hands into their knickers. Nobody batting an eyelid. All totally normal. In fact, I laughed. It was funny. Stuck my tongue out at my friends. Look how blue it is from the aftershock. Where's Monique? Oh, she's being sick in the toilet. Who's going to take her home? Not me. Not when Danny has hardly left my side. Not when he's looking at me like this.

Danny vanished for a while and the night was temporarily ruined.

'Where did he go?' I screeched in Heather's eardrum.

'Are you OK?' she asked back. 'You can hardly stand.'

'But where did Danny go?'

'Do you mind that he's got his hands all over you?' Her eyes were wide, concerned. 'Tonight is going so off-piste.'

I grabbed her shoulders. 'I really fucking like him,' I told Heather. The first person I'd told other than Jessica. 'Like, I think I'm falling in love with him.'

Her eyes got even wider. 'What the hell. Fern. Really?'

I nodded so hard my eyes rolled around my head. 'I think we'll be really good together. Don't you? He's different when it's just us.'

'Umm . . . I mean, Danny's funny, and I know we call you "The Couple", but that's a joke . . . be careful, Fern. He's just a boy enjoying his first term of uni. . .'

'You think I'm too ugly for him? That he wants someone else?'

'Fern, it's not that. I just . . . Oh, here he comes.'

We looked over. Danny was squeezing through the dense crowd like a calf being born. His spikes had wilted and he looked so damn cute. He smiled at me. At me.

'WAIT FOR IT!' he said, instead of hello. He fell onto me and I had to hold him up, his eyes unfocused but excited.

'WAIT FOR WHAT?'

The song ended and Danny was already jumping into the air. It took a second for Heather and me to get the beat. Then we screamed as Avril's voice filled the air. Could she make it any more obvious? Our friends went mad and cleared a space for us to perform the song. More people made room when they saw our costumes matched the song. I was being watched by hundreds of people, but I didn't care. I *was* Avril. I was playing air guitar, so fucking brilliantly. Heather flounced around me in her tutu as she adored Danny from afar. Then he became a superstar, and Danny slid on his knees towards me on the filthy dance floor. I pulled him up and we jumped in the air. Then we were kissing. Full-on grabby kissing as people cheered us, thinking it was part of the act. I couldn't believe I was finally kissing Danny. His hands were all over my back after pulling me in by my tie necklace. The song finished, but we kept kissing. Gasps from our friends. '*Oh my God.*' '*It's about bloody time!*' '*DEVELOPMENTTTTTTTT.*'

I can't remember much from that point onwards . . .

Can't remember leaving the club.

Can't remember being in the taxi.

Blackness until I was in Danny's room. Where all I remember is fragments . . .

'Your room's always so disgusting.' I'm laughing 'til I fall off the bed. Piles of clothes and shit everywhere.

Danny laughing too. Joins me on the floor. We keep kissing.

My legs wrapped around his back, his hands feeling up my body.

It feels glorious. It's enough like this. I am happy for it to stay like this.

Danny isn't.

Lifts my tie necklace over my head. Then my top. In my bra. Never been in my bra in front of a boy before. My scars. I open my mouth to try and explain them. But *shhh* with his mouth. He hasn't noticed. Or doesn't care.

I want him to notice and to care but also not care, if that makes sense?

Memory fades again.

We're on his unmade single bed. Where so many girls have been before me. Only in my knickers. How did the rest of my clothes come off?

'Danny?'

'Hmm?' Through kisses down my stomach I'm not sure I'm ready for.

'Do you like me?'

'Of course.'

Need more than that. Need a Mr Darcy-style declaration, preferably. *I've always seen you as more than a friend* would be a good starting point. *Too scared of my feelings, you see. You don't know how beautiful you are. Wasn't expecting to meet the love of my life in my first year of uni. Did I ever tell you how, out of all the girls I've even seen in real life, you are somehow the most gorgeous, with the best body and face and sense of humour and laugh and hair and personality and spirit and fashion sense and there is something so so special about you, how can you not realise, Fern, just how special you are? I think I'm falling in love with you. Is it too soon to say that? We don't have to rush, you know? I'm willing to wait.*

Instead, he says, 'Are you on the pill?'

'No.'

'Bollocks. Hang on . . .'

Rummaging around in his top drawer. I twist my head. See a row of foiled condoms. The top three have already been ripped open for girls that aren't me. Girls Danny doesn't see again. I won't be one of those girls, will I? Not when we've had so many talks about poetry? Not with the spooning sleepovers.

I'm not sure I even want to have sex.

I'm a virgin.

If I have sex with Danny, I will lose my virginity.

That's quite a big deal. God, my head is heavy.

'Hey hey hey, are you falling asleep?'

I jerk up. 'No. Just having a rest.'

Danny is naked. I can sense it rather than see it. I'm too scared to see it. I've never seen a naked male body before. I want to run away from it. Aren't I supposed to lust for it? What's wrong with me? I glance over. Fucking hell. What the actual HELL is sticking out of him? Oh my God, is that what an erect penis looks like? It's insane! How do men cope with having one of those? What the fuck am I supposed to do with it? I don't want this. I want Danny to have the body of a Ken doll, and for us just to smush against one another like plastic toys.

I'm.

So.

Drunk.

Can't be scared of it. Jessica isn't. I'm so behind. I reach out and prod it, like a child trying to learn how to pet a cat. Danny lets out a sigh, even though I'm quite sure that's not how you toss someone off or whatever the fuck I'm supposed to be doing in this messy unmade single bed with the first man I've ever seen naked.

He pulls me to him. Kissing me. He pulls my knickers down.

I don't want this.

I just want to kiss.

I can't say no though.

I can't reveal my inexperience. Maybe, in time, once we

fall in love. But, for now, I need to stop being scared. Look what happened with Liam. I've learnt from my mistake. You let them do the things they want and then they love you. Especially when you're eighteen.

Can't remember much else. Only that, because it hurt so much, I concentrated instead on the song that was playing through Danny's MacBook.

It was 'She Will Be Loved' by Maroon Five, ironically.

I was woken by the thudding thwack of a fire door closing as some student made their way to breakfast. I lay naked, next to Danny, feeling overwhelmed at the memories surging in, trying to fill in the blank spaces. I started to cry, and, not wanting to wake him, I stumbled into my Avril costume and tiptoed to find the bathroom to have a little cry in peace. The boys' toilets were predictably gross. It burnt as I peed. When I wiped myself, I found blood. I shook my head and wiped my tears away. I was being dramatic, as usual. It was just sex. And I'd lost my virginity to someone I really cared about. Not many people could boast that. Danny and I would get better in time. We were both drunk. He hadn't known I was a virgin. He was such a good kisser. Sex would get better.

He was still zonked when I got back to his room, and I watched him sleep unashamedly. God, he was beautiful. Like a sexy porcelain doll. I couldn't believe I got to see him like this. What a privilege, what a . . . *holy fuck*, I'd bled onto his sheets.

Danny woke to the vibrations of me frantically dabbing at his bed with a damp tissue.

'What's going on?' he asked through a thick layer of sleep.

I stuffed the bloody tissue into my bra and lay over the wet patch. 'Morning.'

'Morning.' He leant over and kissed me on the lips, and momentarily everything was amazing again. He was kissing me like last night was real. He groaned and stretched his arms over his head, still naked. His nakedness was still quite ground-breaking to me. I couldn't quite cope with it yet. Maybe I needed to build up to it a bit more slowly over time, like exposure therapy? One bollock at a time, or something? 'Christ, my head hurts.'

'Mine too.' My vagina also hurt. Quite a lot. All rough and bruised and raw.

He pulled me into him and dozed off again, his breathing slowing to a snore. I tried to sleep, but my body was itching in anticipation. I passed half an hour just looking at him. Feeling surging through me as I examined his face. I reached out and touched his cheek to check he was real.

He stirred and frowned himself awake. When he looked over, his face was different. Blocked somehow. My stomach sensed it straight away. 'Y'all right?' he asked.

'Yeah, sorry. It's just, you know? A bit weird, isn't it?'

'Yeah, I guess.' He shrugged sleepily. 'It doesn't have to be weird though, does it?'

No point there really being a question mark there, when it was such a clear instruction.

'I mean, I guess not.' My eyes fell to the sheet, my heart going like a jet engine about to take off.

'Are you OK? You're not upset or anything, are you?'

'Why would I be upset?'

His voice has an edge of irritation that he was trying to

hide. He reached out and pushed my chin up, forcing me to look at him. His face was smiling and kind as he delivered all the next blows. 'I really hope last night doesn't make things weird between us,' he said. 'I really value our friendship.'

It was going so wrong. I'd read it so wrong. My heart was screaming, but I smiled. 'Oh yeah, me too.'

'I mean, Fern, I really like you. We obviously really click and stuff . . . But, well, I'm sure you can tell that I'm not in a *"relationship place"* right now, you know? We're freshers. We're never going to have this opportunity again, are we? To be this free? Have this much fun? I know if I got into a relationship with anyone right now I'd regret it. Resent them. You would too.'

Breathing was so very difficult. Tears so very hard to contain. I managed a nod.

'. . . I mean, if I was looking for something like that, you are exactly the sort of girl I would choose.'

Even though he was being a total dick, the fact he'd said that still meant so much. I looked up at him, blinking. 'Really?'

'Of course. You're smart and funny and pretty and caring. Like, of course I have feelings for you . . .'

'You do?'

'Yeah. I mean, I've loved getting to know you this term, but it's always felt a bit . . . intense between us, hasn't it? Like it could be a big deal? I sensed you were the kind of girl who would only want something serious, and so I held off, as I'm just not in that place at all right now. But then, last night, hearing you play *Never Have I Ever*, I realised I'd got you wrong.'

He hadn't got me wrong. I'd got me wrong. Oh God, what had I done? I focused on breathing without choking.

'. . . it's great we've been able to . . . you know . . . and it not mess up our friendship. I mean, we're still mates, right?'

'Yes.'

He kissed me on the forehead, smoothing my hair down each side of my face as he did so. Kissing me like a child. 'When I'm ready for a relationship,' he said, 'you're the first person I'm going to call.'

They have the girls they fuck and the girls they fall in love with.

And I found myself thanking him. *Thanking* him.

'Hello, Fern?' Jessica's voice was sleepy over the line.

'Jessica.'

'Are you OK?'

'I lost my virginity last night.'

'What! Oh my God!' Her voice was initially excited, expecting squealing and debriefing and gossip and so exciting. 'Tell me everything . . . Oh my God, what's wrong?'

I could only sob until my phone ran out of credit. She had to ring me back. And, with my back propped against the wall of my uni room, where I'd never, ever felt lonelier, I choked out the story.

She said all the things we are programmed to say for such inevitable let-downs. Gave me all her best *what an arsehole*s, *you are worth so much more than that*s, *I'm so sorry*s, *I love you*s, and *it will be better next time. You will find someone who deserves you*, she promised.

'I'm up in a few weeks. We can kill him together.'

'We can't. I still really like him. God, I'm so pathetic.'

'You're not pathetic.'

'I'm sorry.'

'Fern, it's going to be OK. I'm going to come up and I'm going to make it OK. You've got me, remember?'

I sighed. 'Thank fuck I've got you.'

Thirty-two

It fell apart cliché by cliché. All the tropes were ticked off, one by one.

I'd decided to surprise Ben by coming home early.

I wanted to treat him to a silent apology for all the crazy thoughts I'd been having about him. To atone for the psychological sins he didn't know I'd committed. So, when our office's internet went down and nobody could do any work, I saw my chance. After three hours of IT people swearing while their arses disappeared under desks, we were sent home. No point staying. Thank God we were off deadline. Go home, enjoy the weather. It will be sorted by tomorrow. Most of my team descended on the nearest park with cans of pre-mixed G&T.

'You coming, Fern?' my editor, Derek, asked me, as we all left the building with a frothing bunking-off energy. 'Just for one?'

I shook my head. 'Ben's just finished for summer, so I'm

going to go home and surprise him.' I smiled. 'We'll probably go get a picnic in the park or something.'

'Well, isn't that romantic?'

'Let's hope so.'

Eighteen

November 2004

Jessica sent the message a week before she was due to visit me in Manchester.

Jessica: Ian is a lying dickhead. He's had a gf THIS WHOLE TIME. She lives in Spain. Are you around for a call?

I rang her immediately, tucked up in my hoodie, having a disco nap before we went out that night.

'Oh hon, are you OK?' I asked, breathless.

She wasn't crying. 'He's not worth the tears,' she kept saying, and I could picture her on the other end of the phone, her jaw set and resolute. Grasping desperately to any power she had left by not showing how hurt and humiliated she was. She relayed the details of how she found out like it was the shipping forecast. The girlfriend was having a year abroad for work. Jessica had found a stash of their framed photographs in his bottom drawer. The week he'd had a mates' holiday, he was really over in Spain, seeing her. He hadn't expected to fall in love with Jessica. He'd only flown to Spain to break things off with Kerry, but he couldn't follow through with it. Could Jessica please let him know if she was going to forgive him or not, because, if she didn't, he thought it was still worth trying to make things work with Kerry instead.

'I honestly don't know what to say,' I told her, which was true. 'Are you OK?'

'Yeah,' she replied sharply. 'Why wouldn't I be?'

I'd winced at her tone down the line, thinking, *You asked me to call you, Jessica.* I took a breath, working out what to say next. She was at her worst like this. Blunt. Closed off. A fortress of a woman.

'I mean, anyone would be upset.'

'He's not worth it.'

'OK . . . well, it's going to be amazing when you come up here.' I tried to cajole her. Once she saw Manchester, she'd realise how limited her life was, and grow. 'We'll have a proper girls' night out. I'll show you all the best bars. You're going to LOVE Heather. She's the best person to talk to about boy stuff. She has all these academic theories about them that make you feel so much better.'

'Who's Heather again?'

'You know? My housemate.'

She paused. 'Oh, yeah. Cool. I remember. It's going to be great, you're right. How many grams shall I bring up?'

'Oh.' I bit my lip, searching my uni wall for inspiration on how to handle this. I'd made a massive corkboard montage, and a picture of Jessica and me was right in the middle, next to a cartoon Danny had drawn of me in a seminar that I still looked at for at least five minutes every day. 'Umm . . . about that . . . Would you mind not bringing any drugs? We can drink and stuff. But none of my friends up here do drugs, and I think it could make them uncomfortable.'

The longest, coldest silence.

'Are you still there?'

'Yep. No coke. No worries. Look, I have to go now, Fern. I've got to get my stuff from his before he's back from work. Plus, now I have to look for a new job obviously.'

'Are you sure you're OK?' I pressed.

'Yes! I'll see you next week.'

Thirty-two

I leant my head against the bus window, smiling as London smeared past me in a haze of sunshine. I'd messaged Ben to see where he was.

Ben: Sat in front of the fan, eating a twister. It's too hot. xxx

Through the glass, I passed school kids on their lunch break, licking ice lollies. Mums pushing buggies with other mums. A queue outside the ice-cream van in the park. A heavily sunburnt man padded past in flip-flops and no top on. The heat hit me as the bus hissed and spat me out into the village. I put my sunglasses on and it felt like being on holiday. I'd go to the shop and get some bits to take to the park, maybe get a can or two of Ben's favourite beers. I said hello to the men in Londis; we commented on how hot it was. I grabbed a basket and flung houmous and bread, olives and stuffed vine leaves into it. I added strawberries, and melon sliced into cubes and put into plastic. A case of beers for Ben. Two pink G&Ts for me. I was excited to get home.

I couldn't wait to see his face when I walked through the door.

Eighteen

December 2004

It was so surreal, seeing Jessica in Manchester. The combining of my two lives, two selves. I grinned and waved madly as she pulled a little suitcase towards the train barriers.

'You're heeeeeeeeeerrrrrrrreeeeee.' I flung myself at her, made her drop her suitcase handle.

She laughed. 'I'm here.'

'Was your journey OK?'

'Yeah, fine. Fine. It didn't actually take that long.'

She had a new winter coat. This huge Cruella de Vil fur one that looked sensational. In fact, everything about her looked sensational. Her make-up was perfect, hair in a complicated up-do. I felt suddenly frumpy in my jeans and University of Manchester hoodie. I'd forgotten how much effort she made, how much I used to make fruitless attempts to catch up with her.

'I can't wait to show you everything. OK, right, so this is the train station. Obviously. And it's right next to Canal Street, which is full of these amazing gay bars. The music is always epic. And this is the bus station . . . Do you have any change? It's OK. I'll pay. It's only 50p. It's so cheap up here, honestly. You can get drunk on, like, a fiver.'

As we got on the bus, my unsolicited personalised tour continued while Jessica just stared out of the window, quiet.

'So, that, over there, you see that door? Monique vomited all down it in Freshers' Week, it was hilarious. Her puke was purple. Like if a magical dinosaur vommed. That's what we call her now. *Barney*. Hang on . . . right, you see that building? That's where I have my lectures. Right, so we're coming up to the Student Union. We're going there tonight. What do you think? Do you like it?'

Jessica turned away from the glass. 'Yeah, it's great. It's . . . big.'

'You get used to it. I got lost so many times in my first week. But now I know it really well.'

When we got to the halls, my nerves ramped up. I so desperately wanted her to approve of it all.

'Here's my corridor. Oh, here's Heather! Heather, this is Jessica. My best friend from home.'

Heather was in the middle of carrying a giant bowl of 'grub' to her room and had toothpaste on three spots, but smiled warmly, and held out her spare hand to wave.

'Hi Jessica, I've heard a lot about you.'

Jessica put on a smile. 'You too.'

'You coming out with us tonight? It should be fun. We may end up in the Union because it's a Saturday. All the fucking residents are out in the clubs at the weekend.'

She nodded again. 'Yep. Great.' She said nothing else. Filled no silence whatsoever, so I stumbled into it.

'This is Heather's grub,' I explained, pointing to her giant bowl of food that looked like sick. 'She makes it whenever she can't be bothered to cook. Heather? Explain what's in it?'

She held it up to Jessica to see, who peered at it half-heartedly. 'Couscous. A can of tuna. Kidney beans. Rocket. And some salad dressing.'

'Isn't that disgusting?' I asked Jessica, who just smiled again.

'Hey, I won't be hungry for hours. Right, I better eat this and finish my lab notes before tonight. Nice to meet you, Jessica.'

'You too.'

As Heather kicked her fire door shut, I frantically filled Jessica in on more needless details. 'Isn't she great? I'd say she's my best friend up here. She was really nice during the Danny stuff too. Kind of there, without being there too much, if that makes sense? Isn't her grub hilarious? She eats it about five times a week. She's a medic, so she's quite good on nutrition. She wants to be a gynaecologist and knows so much about the pill. Did you know it can change who you fancy? Right, so here's my room.' I unlocked the door and beckoned her in. She dropped her suitcase and stared around, and I tried to see it through her eyes. Taking in my posters, my corkboard – hoping she'd notice all the photos of us up there. Her eyes found it and her whole demeanour softened.

'Oh my God, I can't believe these have been up on your wall this whole time?' She walked over and examined them. Then pointed to one of my favourites. She stroked it lovingly, while I joined her side. 'I can't believe this one is up.'

'Of course. It's the best photo ever taken.'

'What must your friends think of me?'

It was a photo we'd taken one day when we'd got spectac-ularly day-drunk in the sun. During a dreamlike trip to the local Morrisons to pick up more to drink, Jessica and I got obsessed with watching this toddlers' car ride in the entrance hall. We'd decided to get in, and Jade took the photo of us crammed into this tiny yellow car, limbs escaping out of the windows, both our knickers on show, our heads thrown back in laughter as the ride bumped us around. What really made the photo was the security guard in the background, making his way over to chuck us out. The dramatic irony was sheer perfection. It was taken literally two seconds before we were carted away.

'They, quite rightly, think we are both legends.'

'I love this photo.' She stroked it again. When she turned back to me, I could see Jessica was over her weird mood. 'I've really missed you, Fern.'

'I've missed you too!'

She hugged me, then broke away, opened my computer, and put on a track.

'That's better,' she said, starting to dance. 'Right. We've got a lot to catch up on.'

Thirty-two

It couldn't be more daytime television. I got a funny feeling when I put my key in the lock of our front door. There was music playing, so my entry went unnoticed. A weird instinct hit me, telling me not to call out 'hello'. I saw shoes that weren't mine by the door. Designer sandals. No children's shoes – just hers. Already I was thinking, *He didn't tell me she was around*, and, *he said he was just sitting in front of the fan*. Already I knew. Had always known, from the second I let her back in my life. But in that moment, when I was quietly sliding my sweaty feet out of my sandals, I dared hope I was wrong. This couldn't be happening again, surely? I heard laughter. Then voices over the music. I recognised Jessica's flirtatious voice . . .

It wasn't coming from the living room either. But our bedroom.

I couldn't breathe. Could hardly walk. My knees disintegrated as I tiptoed through my own house. I was going to be sick. I was going to be sick on the floor. I paused outside, wanting to enjoy these last seconds of naivety . . .

Then I pushed open the door and it creaked.

Ben and Jessica were sitting on the bed. Their eyes widened at my arrival, their heads twisted around, gasps flew out of their mouths. They sprang apart, but a split second before they'd been sitting right next to each other, their heads so close they were almost kissing, and the shock on their faces . . . I knew. I knew so clearly I'd walked in on something. The end of my life. The inevitable.

'Fern?' Ben's shocked voice.

'Fern!' Jessica's frantic eyes.

I turned and fled.

Eighteen

December 2004

Jessica pulled two bottles of wine from her bag like a magician doing a trick. 'Look what I've brought,' she sing-songed, holding them up. 'Do you have any glasses?' Without asking, she rummaged around and found two dirty mugs. She swilled them with water using my corner sink, and filled them to the brim.

'Jessica, it's only four o'clock.'

'Come on. It's my weekend away. Help me experience being a student properly.'

And when had I ever been able to say no to her?

We started drinking and chatting, and the walls of my unfamiliar life faded away and it was just us again. Jessica pulled up a new song while draining her third drink. 'This is the song we both need right now.'

'I Hate You So Much Right Now' by Kelis blasted out of my speakers – her anger visceral and familiar – and we both laughed.

'We should request it tonight and sing it to that Danny guy while kicking him in the balls,' she said.

I stopped laughing and perched on the side of the bed. 'Yeah, about that.'

Jessica came and joined me. 'About what?'

'The Danny thing. I know he behaved like a dick, but I've been thinking about it, and maybe I gave him the wrong message? Like, I never admitted to him how I really felt. I just went along with the "fuck buddy night" storyline. I'm hoping maybe . . .' I felt the wine hit my bloodstream. With the winter sky black outside, it didn't feel like late afternoon. '. . . maybe if I was honest, maybe we could get together? Like, he's still so sweet to me, and still asks me to study with him all the time. What if I've just given the wrong impression?'

Jessica tilted her head as she thought about it. 'I don't know, Fern. It was pretty cold, what he did.'

'But he didn't know I was a virgin. He thought I was happy doing something casual.'

'Hmm.'

'I still really like him, Jessica.'

'Hmm.' She drained her mug of wine and wouldn't make eye contact.

'You get to meet him later,' I said, grabbing a straw. 'He's got tickets to the same night. Maybe you can analyse him for me? See if you think he has feelings for me?'

She nodded. 'And, if he doesn't, I'll kick him in the balls.'

'No, you can't. Nobody knows how I feel about him. They all think it was just a mutually casual one-off.'

'I'll pretend I've kicked him in the balls by accident.'

'What are you going to do? Cossack dance?'

Jessica smiled. 'Yes, how all good plans start.'

The wine bottles emptied and we danced around my room,

shrieking. For an hour or so, it was just our own perfect little bubble. We kept hugging, saying how much we'd missed each other and then hugging again. But as it got darker, we got drunker.

'Oh my God, Monique,' I yelled, when she knocked to ask to borrow my hair straighteners. I gave her a tight hug and pulled her inside. 'This is Jessica, my friend from home.'

Jessica waved, but then started laughing at nothing.

'You have to dance with us,' I said, trying to unplug my hair straighteners. They were too stiff in the socket, and I fell backwards yanking them out, to more splutters from Jessica.

'Are you guys drunk already?' Monique asked, eyeing the empty wine bottles on my desk.

'We're reminiscing,' I explained. 'Please dance.'

'Umm, maybe later?' I saw the look on her face. Mildly bewildered. Slightly judgemental. A panic overcame me.

'It's just we loved these old songs,' I explained, speaking much too fast. 'Back when we were kids.' Monique was a new friend and I was suddenly worried she thought we were weird.

'They're not old songs, they're the ONLY songs,' Jessica yelled behind me, still dancing, and I cringed at how drunk she was as I handed over the straighteners.

'OK, OK, I believe you. Anyway, thanks for these.' She held the straighteners up. 'I'll bring them back. We're meeting downstairs at eight, right?'

I nodded, trying to appear more sober. 'Yep, eight it is.'

She still had a slight look of judgement on her face and I wanted to stand in front of Jessica, who'd put on 'Nobody Wants to Be Lonely' and was trying to get me to sing along.

'She's a bit drunk,' I whispered.

Monique slow-nodded again. 'I can see that. Tonight should be fun.' She waved the straighteners again and left us to it.

'We need to get ready,' I said, but Jessica held out her hands, yelling along, and wouldn't let me do anything other than scream along with her.

Thirty-two

I pelted down the hallway and pushed my feet into some ballet pumps.

'Fern?' Ben called from the bedroom. The sound of them whispering. Figuring out their story. Oh my heart, it hurt so much. I couldn't . . . think. Just needed to run.

Jessica's face around the door. 'Fern!'

I was out in the hall, hurtling down the stairs, slamming through the doors out into the summer air.

Their faces.

My best friend.

Ben . . .

I ran so fast through the village I was probably a cartoon ball of dust to the sunburnt groups drinking Aperol spritzes on the pub tables outside. My feet hurt as they hit the hot pavement. My lungs were already at capacity from the unexpected cardio.

I got to the park, and the full force of the heartbreak hit

me then. *Ben* . . . I loved him and I couldn't believe he'd . . . she'd . . . I *knew* it. I knew this was going to happen . . .

I stumbled onto the grass, weaving my way through circles of hipsters drinking and playing Mölkky. Then I came to a small overgrown area and bent over on the edge of it, thinking I was going to puke. My chest heaved, back arched, tears fell into the dust. I hacked up spit and phlegm and pieces of my broken heart as this new reality sank into my bones.

I was *so* stupid. So stupid to let Jessica back in. The rage arrived. The rage I'd worked so many years to push down. The rage I'd ignored when Jessica turned up all those months ago. I let out a groan of emotion, fists clenched. Tears streaming down my face. Incapable of anything other than bending over in the vortex of feeling. I spat again. Cried again. Then I heard . . .

'Fern?'

My body was allergic to her voice. I rippled at my name. Wiped my mouth. Stood up. She'd caught me up. I turned around. Jessica's eyes were the widest they'd ever been.

'Fern, please, just listen to me.'

Eighteen

December 2004

Jessica, as usual, looked a million times better than me. She wore a silk cami top, piled with loads of pearls and eye make-up, paired with this perfect pair of tight pedal pushers and some great heels. I felt basic and dumpy in my dropped-waist miniskirt and thick-strapped top.

'*Ta-da!*' Jessica turned around to reveal her finished face, make-up brush still in hand.

'Oh piss off, you're too pretty.'

She laughed and didn't deny it. 'I just wish we had coke,' she sighed. 'Imagine how much fun we'd be having with coke right now.'

I blinked blearily. This was the third time she'd brought this up since we'd finished the wine. She'd complained so much about the night being 'too tame' that I'd even run down to the halls bar and brought up another bottle. I was already exhausted and vexed by her. More friends had tried to come in and say hi, but seemed taken aback by how drunk we were. Jessica hardly acknowledged them. There had been more than one weird look, and I panicked that my carefully curated new life would crumble if Jessica carried on being like this.

We eventually congregated downstairs, and I introduced Jessica to everyone else. She only brought out her dazzle when some of the boys arrived, asking them about their courses, sticking her chest out.

'Fern's my best friend in the world,' she told Heather, as we piled into various taxis to take us into town. It was the first time she'd spoken to any of the girls. 'You get her on loan, you understand?'

I laughed, almost awkwardly, while Heather smiled, raising both eyebrows at me as Jessica struggled to get into the car.

Time blurred once we got to Vodka Revolution. Everyone ordered planks of different flavoured shots, and, after my third or fourth, I stopped babysitting Jessica, and let myself enjoy the night. She was on shot five or six, and sat next to me, looking bored and bewildered, as we all had conversations she couldn't join in with.

'Oh my God, the medics bar crawl. Do you remember when Joe was sick on Pete's head?'

'It was funnier because they were both dressed as giraffes from Noah's Ark.'

'Look! Over there! It's Creepy Chris from Freshers' Week.'

I laughed, the table laughing with me. And with the music so loud, and the city still so new and exciting, and with my new friendships still needing a lot of work to be fully forged, there wasn't space for Jessica that night. I'd made a mistake inviting her. I didn't want to miss one second of bonding with this group of people. They were still shiny and exciting, whereas Jessica was drinking too much and not being friendly, when I knew she could be. Why couldn't she embrace my new life? Try with my new friends? Why was she determined to drag me back into the role of Old Fern, from home? I started to feel a bit resentful. I'd cleaned myself up in Manchester, and I'd been able to bloom away from Jessica's shadow. I wasn't awful. I tried. I kept asking her if she was OK. I tried to explain the background details of stories we were sharing, so she'd understand them. But, as we all got drunker, I admit I probably did go twenty minutes just chatting with my new friends, telling myself Jessica would be having a good time, that she was capable of making small talk . . . ignoring the fact that all of us were still socially anxious freshers, who didn't want to be lumbered with this random drunk girl from Fern's home town, no matter how pretty she was.

'Remember the traffic light party?'

'When that boy, Roger, wore brown, because he didn't know if he was ready to cheat on his girlfriend from home yet?'

'What a gent.'

A girl sat next to me who I recognised from lectures.

'Do you do Creative Writing too? Oh my God, isn't our lecturer the best? We should totally get coffee after our next lecture. That's great.'

I tried again, holding up Jessica's floppy arm. 'This is my friend from home, by the way,' I told Beth, my new potential friend. 'Jessica.'

'Oh, hi, Jessica,' Beth said, looking slightly thrown.

'Hey.' Jessica would hardly make eye contact. She seemed bored. Her arms were crossed now. I felt another pinch of annoyance.

'What uni do you go to?' Beth asked, trying to be friendly. 'Is it nearby?'

'I don't go to uni,' Jessica replied, sticking out her chin. 'I work in an office. Well, I did until I shagged my boss before finding out he has a girlfriend in Spain.'

Beth's mouth formed a small shocked 'o'. 'Right,' she said. 'Umm, that's . . . oh well.' She turned away and my annoyance throbbed.

'Are you OK?' I whispered to Jessica.

'Can't we just go back to your room?' she replied, sounding like a tired child. 'Find some weed from someone and watch films, just us?'

'We've got tickets to the Union,' I reminded her.

'So?'

'So, it's a really good club night, and it's hard to get tickets. You're going to really enjoy it once you get in. I promise. It's a cheese night. They play Disney songs.'

'Hmm.' She plucked a shot off a plank, one that wasn't hers, and threw it back. I looked around to check nobody had seen her, doing a quick table scan, and that's when I saw him in the doorway.

'Oh my God,' I said, grasping her hands.

'What is it?' Jessica, noting my anxious jolt, sat up with me.

'Danny's just arrived,' I whispered, pointing under the table to his group of approaching friends.

'Which one's Danny?'

'The one with the brown floppy hair, on the left, wearing the stripy blue shirt.'

Danny spotted our table, held his hands around his mouth, and made a dinosaur calling noise that made everyone laugh.

They headed over while I became instantly aware of each placement of my hair, whether or not my breath smelt, if my mascara had got blobby, if my stomach was poking out in my top. 'God, he is quite good-looking,' Jessica said.

And, I think I knew then, exactly what was going to happen.

'Remember to analyse him to see if he likes me,' I reminded her.

'Of course.' Though I watched her watch him as Danny diverted to the bar, returning laden with more trays of shots. 'For the table!' he announced. 'Sorry for being late! We were at the football social.'

He started hugging and high-fiving us in a row, and Jessica and I were last. I anticipated contact with him, hungry for the touch of his skin.

'Fern!'

'Hi, Danny Boy.' The smell of his neck was so intoxicating, I didn't want to let go of our hug.

'And who's this?' he asked, pointing to Jessica, who had sat herself up, pulled her hair to one shoulder, leant herself over so her top was lower.

'This is my friend from home, Jessica.' I reluctantly introduced them.

'Jessica, nice to meet you.'

'You too.' She gave him her grin back.

Danny pulled up a chair and turned right into us. 'So, OK, Jessica, I want to know everything about my English buddy over here,' he said, leaning in and whacking me on the back. 'What was Fern like in school? What was her worst fashion disaster? Did you guys ever make out at a girly sleepover?'

'Danny!' I shrieked – half delighted he was taking such an

interest in me. Maybe he was in love with me and wanted to get my best friend onside? For a second, I thought everything might come together. Maybe I could talk to him later that night? Tell him how I felt? But then I saw Jessica do the grin again and look Danny right in the eye. The way she'd done, all those years ago, in McDonald's, sipping her milkshake, flirting with Matt from school . . .

'I mean,' she said, in a sexy but innocent voice, 'all girls do at sleepovers is wear tiny pyjamas, have pillow fights, and practise kissing on each other.'

Danny raised both eyebrows. 'Fern, your friend from home is great,' he told me. 'Bring her every weekend.'

Their eyes locked once more.

No.

This couldn't be happening. Not again.

Thirty-two

I stood up to face Jessica. The hatred zinging through me, souring my tongue. Over fifteen years of resentment and jealousy, passes and forgiveness dissolved in my stomach, and I said what I'd always wanted to say, needed to say, almost glad I could finally say it.

'You fucking slut.'

'Fern! Please. Just listen. I know what it looks like.' She held up her arms, trying to step towards me.

'NO!' I screamed. The pain coming out. Humiliation coming out. Shame coming out, but only making me want to double down and make it worse. 'I hate you! You're a pathetic fucking whore and I hate you. Every woman who has ever known you fucking hates you because of what you are.' Once it was out, I felt as if I'd lost a stone, I'd said it all. I'd finally told her what I thought.

She stopped, her mouth dropping open. She held her stomach as if I'd shot her.

'Is that seriously what you think of me?' She dared to look

upset, when she was the one who had taken and taken, the one almost kissing my boyfriend on my bed while they thought I was at work.

'How can I *not* think that? Oh my God, Jessica! I'm such an idiot.' I started cry-laughing. 'Kim and Amy were right about you. All those years ago, when you bloody got with Matt. They told me not to trust you, and they were right.'

Tears started leaking down Jessica's face. Surprising me. Making me angrier. How dare she cry?

'Matt?' She took a step backwards into the undergrowth.

'You knew how much Kim liked him, and you got with him right away.'

She started to protest, but I raised my hand to stop her. 'And you knew how much Jade liked Mike, but in you went. And you knew how much I liked George on that trip to Greece.'

'What the fuck . . . who?'

'YOU KNOW WHO.'

'Fern!'

'No! And then Liam. LIAM. You had to go fuck Liam, didn't you? And I forgave you. Kept forgiving you, and then Danny . . .'

Jessica's fists clenched. She dared to look angry back. 'I don't have to listen to this,' she said. 'I came here to explain.'

'The truth hurts, does it?' I yelled at her back as she turned to duck out of our little hidden patch of undergrowth.

She stopped and twisted her neck around. The hatred on her face was everywhere, like well-applied foundation. I'd never seen someone hate me so much. How could she be the one mad at *me*? Not when Ben . . . *Ben* . . . I still couldn't believe Ben. Oh God, my heart.

'Yes, Fern.' She wiped a tear away. 'It really does. I can't believe . . . you said . . .' She made a guttural yell and threw her arms to the air, scattering birds before facing me again, her voice thick with emotion. 'Like, those boys. Basically all of them took advantage of me! Of how drunk I was, or vulnerable. Like Matt . . . Fern, I could hardly stand that night. I thought you understood that? And as for that guy George, I only kissed him. That was for ever ago. I'd forgotten he even existed. I wish I could say the same for Mike, who pressured me to do these fucked-up things, spread rumours about me, and called me "Slutty Jessica", to my face, and I had to laugh. *Laugh.* And Liam? Fern, you never told me you still liked him and, holy fuck, did you dodge a bullet. You *know* what he made me do at Reading. *Brown wings . . .*' She hack-laughed and sniffed. 'He held me down and made me do it, but what could I do? He was my boyfriend and he was in a band and nobody would believe me anyway because I was, as you say, such a fucking slut.' More tears fell as my heart slowed down, no idea what to make of any of this. 'I thought you understood, Fern,' she said, staring right at me. 'We've talked so much about things since. Maybe you didn't understand so much then, but at least now . . .'

Eighteen

December 2004

The cheese pumped through the Union speakers. Arms flew into the air. Drinks spilt onto strangers by people who didn't say sorry afterwards. Shoes stuck to the floor. Students piled into the bar, waiting to be served. Couples groped in the darkness. It was the same Saturday night at the Union it always was. My new friends' arms around my shoulders, jumping up and down, making me sing along. The way you couldn't do the Macarena without feeling a little bit dead inside. Bumping into people from your course and chatting, only to ignore each other on Monday. All the same, except that my best friend in the world was kissing the boy I lost my virginity to in the corner. The boy I'd told her only hours ago that I really liked. I'd finally reached my limit. I was done.

'Are you sure you're OK?' Heather asked, for the millionth time, her breath made totally of vodka.

I nodded and gave a giant grin. 'Of course! Why wouldn't I be?'

She yelled into my ear. 'Well, I know you and Danny had that night . . .'

'It was nothing. Just a one-night stand.'

'Still though . . . Are you not at least a bit pissed off that she's supposed to be catching up with you?'

I tipped my head back to finish my drink. 'Nah. This is just what Jessica does.'

I was drunk almost to the point of numb. A weird calm around me, as I realised the inevitability of this. It hurt. Oh, by God, it hurt so much. But I felt almost . . . free to be cruel now. A coldness in my blood. A relief almost, that I wouldn't have to have Jessica in my life any more. Wouldn't have to defend her. To others, to myself. To always be the ugly one next to her. To always be eclipsed by her.

She'd been kissing Danny basically since they arrived. She honestly acted like nothing had ever happened from the second he started chatting her up in Vodka Rev. I watched her turn her seduction switch up to eleven, watched her challenge Danny to do a tray of shots each, almost too shocked to do anything but watch. Watched their heads get closer together. Watched their hands brush each other in the queue to get into the Union. Watched her stumble on the way to the club and have him collect her up, laughing, and hold her to him. And then watched them find a quiet corner and gyrate against the wall together, him practically holding her up with his body. I looked over and saw they'd vanished. She'd be going back to his room, being better at sex with him than I had been. With my inexperience, and shit self-confidence that I had from all those years being rejected, because I was stupid enough to be friends with her.

I leant over to Heather and yelled into her hair. 'Can we have a sleepover in your room? Stay up all night? Watch all of *Pride and Prejudice* or something?'

She eyed me curiously. 'What about your friend?'

'She's at Danny's now. And she's got a key to my room.'

We recruited Monique to join us as she said she felt sick. The rest wanted to stay 'til closing. 'Set You Free' came on, just as we were threading our way through the dance floor, and everyone started jumping around as if they were on a sunset beach in Ibiza rather than a cramped darkened room that was a coffee shop during the day. I kept up my pretend fine-ness in the cab home. Grinned as we queued for a chip butty. Smiled as we agreed to take a ten-minute break to get into our pyjamas, and get ready for the sleepover. Then, after I'd washed off my make-up and climbed into my nightclothes, I hummed to myself as I packed up Jessica's things that were discarded all over my room. I zipped up her bag, then left it on the end of my bed for her to find later.

I didn't speak to her again until the night she came to the book launch.

Thirty-two

I looked at Jessica's tears falling, in disbelief still. Still not used to seeing her cry. I'd hardly taken in a word she'd said.

'I can't believe you're trying to make yourself the victim in this,' I said, stunned. 'Literally, right at this moment.'

'Oh, you can talk about being the fucking victim,' she spat back. So loud, that a mother pushing a toddler looked over at us and rushed by. My phone started vibrating in my pocket. Ben, I guessed. Trying to find out where I was, where Jessica was. Now he'd had time to figure out his lies. Or maybe he wouldn't even bother. Maybe Jessica was about to tell me they were moving in together or something.

'What are you talking about?'

'Please, Fern. You only ever see things from your perspective. God knows why you think you'd make a good counsellor, when you're the most self-obsessed person in the world.'

'Excuse me?'

Jessica's whole face was sour. I'd spewed out what I'd needed to – now, it seemed, it was her turn, no matter the circumstances. 'Everything just *happens* to you, doesn't it, Fern? You're so obsessed with how life is so hard for you, you never think to consider what's going on . . . Like, when we were younger, you had parents that loved you, friends, money. Money! Oh my God, so much fucking money. But, all you did was bitch and whinge about being sick, not having a boyfriend.'

'I tried to kill myself!'

'Yeah, well, maybe so did I, did that ever occur to you? Did it ever even fucking occur to you what it was like to be me? Why I got so wasted, let boys do those things? Yeah, so you had scars all down your arms. I get it. But what about my scars? My way of self-harming? Just because I wasn't bleeding, doesn't mean I wasn't bleeding. And you just . . . left me, Fern. You just packed my bag and cut me out.'

'After WHAT YOU'D DONE.'

'I was too drunk that night in Manchester to be doing anything other than be taken home by my friend. I know I flirted with him because I was mad at you for ignoring me, which is shit, but that's all I was going to do. But that's all I really remember. I was so drunk I got with a boy my best friend liked. Doesn't that make it clear how wasted I was? And I apologised to you, about the Danny thing. I emailed you and you never replied. And where was my apology? For letting some random guy I didn't know take me home after about ten shots, and then fucking dumping my stuff into a bag?'

I threw my arms in the air. 'I can't believe you're doing this. After what I've just seen! Ben . . . Ben is everything to me, Jessica, and you . . . you . . .' I start wailing again. Huge guttural sobs of pain catching up on me.

'. . . Ben is planning to propose to you,' Jessica said quietly.

Hang on. Hang on. Hang on.

I looked up.

'We're not sleeping together, for fuck's sake. I've been helping him pick out a ring today. He was checking it looked shiny enough before we found a good hiding spot in the bedroom. I'm the one who made him realise he's being an idiot by not proposing to you.'

'What?'

She started walking backwards, her face stained with tears. 'I can't believe you thought I'd . . .'

'Jessica! Hang on! What . . .'

'No. Fuck you. I never should've let you back into my life.'

She stepped out into the sunshine, wiped under her eyes, set her chin in a way I'd see her do a million times before. Determined. Steely. And she walked away without looking back.

Eighteen

December 2004

The next morning, her bag was gone.

Thirty-two

I stared at the spot in the bushes where Jessica had been – my life, my memories, my insecurities, rearranging themselves in the air around me. I'd just found out Ben was about to propose, and yet I felt utterly sick. The shock collapsed my knees and I found myself sitting in the dust, wiping tears away as quickly as they fell, shaking.

Until, of course, Ben called again.

'Fern? What the hell? Where are you? Are you OK? You just ran off.'

Immediately I started sobbing. The hugeness of my misjudgement, and its implications, ripping through me.

'Jessica and I . . . we had a fight . . .' I managed, before another wave of sobs hit me.

'A fight? About what? Where is she? She just ran after you? Seriously, Fern, I'm worried about you. What's going on? Where are you?'

His concern added to my heartbreak. If only he knew: how little I trusted him, what I hid from him, the mess he thought he was in love with. I didn't deserve this man, especially if I kept lying to him.

'I thought you might be sleeping together,' I half whispered. 'You and Jessica. I accused her of having an affair.'

'What the fuck?'

'. . . because, Ben, I am an insecure, jealous mess and I try to keep it from you because it's disgusting and pathetic, but it's the truth. I thought you definitely wouldn't want to marry me once you'd met Jessica. And I also think it's because you're still in love with Tiffany, or maybe you just don't love me enough, but I've been going crazy for months because I am crazy and . . . and . . .'

. . . and then I couldn't speak any more. I was crying too hard. The relief at finally having said it all, combined with the self-disgust, and the knowledge that saying it would definitely ruin everything.

I expected the phone to go dead. Ben didn't speak for a very long time, as I howled, alone, in my mess on the ground. Until, finally, he sighed and said, 'Fern, I'm worried about you. Please come home so we can talk.'

And a tiny shred of light broke through the undergrowth and shone on my face.

Thirty-two

Ben sat against the bed on the floor; he shook his head again. 'I still can't believe you thought I was cheating on you.'

'I know, I'm sorry.' I closed my eyes, dropped my head. We'd been talking it out since I came home, covered in tears and guilt. The sun gently baked our flat as I told my boyfriend everything, finally. My insecurities. My jealousy. My paranoia. And everything that had happened between Jessica and me. We'd started talking in the bedroom, moved to the kitchen, cried together in the sitting room, but now we were sprawled on the floor by the bed, and in a completely different place.

'I was doing the opposite of cheating on you.'

'I know. And I should've trusted you but . . . I'm . . .' God, this hurt. All this telling. I thought of the ring he'd hidden somewhere in this room, and wondered if he'd ever give it to me now he knew who I was. I'd told him I'd understand if he didn't, though it had broken my heart to say it. And it had broken it even more when he didn't rush to reassure me he would. 'It's just . . . so much happened between her and me.

And I've tried to make myself forget it all. But, when she came back, it all rushed in and was so overwhelming, and I should've told you about our past. I know I should've. But I was . . . ashamed.'

'Ashamed of what?'

I looked up at this man who had been planning to propose to me. If I loved him as much as I claimed to, it was better to tell him, better to show him who I really was. 'Look, it's hard having a friend like Jessica. Being close to someone that beautiful, who is so good at getting on with men. You never want to admit out loud that you're the ugly awkward friend.'

'But Fern, you're gorgeous.'

'Not next to Jessica, I wasn't. I was invisible. She got chosen over me again and again, and it made me ashamed and bitter and . . . cruel. Ben, I've been awful to her.'

'You haven—'

'I have. I . . . I . . .' Jessica's words and revelations haunted me in whispers. The things that were done to her. The things I was sick enough to be jealous of. Maybe my invisibility has been more of a blessing than a curse? 'I . . . didn't protect her. I was so convinced I was the victim that it never occurred to me she was a victim too. I've let her down so badly . . .' I started crying again. 'You must hate me. You must think I'm the worst person ever.'

Ben, exhausted, pulled me into him and let me cry into his shoulder. He hushed me and patted me and, most importantly, didn't leave me. Didn't call me a psycho. He laced my fingers with his and I let out a deep sigh from my lungs, at this act of forgiveness and repair. 'You can trust me, you know that, right?' he said, forcing me to look at him. 'I know you're not feeling great about yourself right now, but I still love you, Fern. All of you.'

'You do?'

'Yes. But you've got to trust me.'

'I do.'

'Really, seriously, you have to trust me.'

I looked at him and made myself feel the urgency of his words. I realised I hadn't trusted him, not until now. I'd spent the last six months lost in memories about Jessica, and reflecting on all the things she had done to be deemed untrustworthy, rather than reflecting on all the things boys and men had done to me, and the women I knew, to make me not trust them. The hurt came from them, not Jessica. Never Jessica. She had just as many scars as I did, if not more. I blinked through wet eyelashes, at this man in my life, who I believed to be different . . . better . . . or so I told myself. I realised I had to trust him, in order for this to work. But *that* should've been the bigger leap of faith. Not trusting my best friend, who understood it all in a way Ben never could.

'I trust you,' I said.

I *finally* trust you.

Then Ben kissed me. Even though I'd given him a glimpse behind the curtain, he still kissed me. I whimpered in relief, falling into his mouth, crushing him into a hug, promising myself to let go from this moment. To believe. In him. In myself. If only it wasn't too late for me and Jessica.

Thirty-two

Fern: Jessica. I am so, so, so sorry. I don't have the words, apart from sorry ones. Please call me. xxx

Fern: Hey, thought I'd give you a few days to let things settle down. But just sending a message to say that I am thinking of you, and our fight, and I'm sorry again. Here whenever xxx

Thirty-two

My parents had, thankfully, bless them, gone out. I'd decided to go home for the weekend, in a blaze of *'I want to repair everything with everyone'*, but, after one full Saturday with them, I was regretting booking a Monday morning train home and not a Sunday one. However, they had 'a commitment to meet the Hogarths for lunch', and I was alone in their house, still in my pyjamas, wondering if it would ever feel like my family home. Nursing a cup of tea, I climbed the stairs to my 'bedroom', which was essentially the guest room except it had all my childhood crap stuffed into one cupboard. I sipped and blew the steam off my drink, staring at the cupboard door for a very long time, wondering if I'd ever feel up to this. Ben had warned me not to 'torture myself' about my friendship ending with Jessica. But, if she was going to ignore all my calls and messages, I wanted to mark the termination of our friendship somehow. To say goodbye, even if it was just to a ghost. I heaved a deep sigh, placed my mug on the bedside table, and sat on the floor, yanking open the cupboard door, my childhood falling out on top of my lap.

A flood of physical memories engulfed me. Two shoeboxes stuffed with keepsakes slid onto my knees, and I put them on one side, and dug about in the cupboard, releasing another pile of boxes that fell onto the carpet. This door must not have been opened since I stuffed everything in here, years and years ago, in a rush as I was still too upset at my parents for selling our childhood home. I lifted the lids off the boxes and peered inside, trying to date them. The first appeared to be things from my early childhood – blotchy paintings of rainbows, exercise books of wiggly handwritten stories about total nonsense, a Pez dispenser in the shape of Minnie Mouse. I gave myself half an hour or so of self-indulgence, allowing myself to look through and remember how cute I was. But that wasn't why I was here, so, eventually, I closed the lid and riffled through the boxes until I found the one I was looking for.

My Jessica box.

It wasn't technically just that. It was actually dated 2000–2005, but those were my Jessica years, and, as I took the lid off, it may as well be dedicated to her. A harsh smell hit my nostrils, and I winced, searching through the wads of paper and other junk, until I found the source right in the bottom corner. A withered old spliff, with the words 'in case of emergency' written in Jessica's handwriting. As I picked it up, it unravelled and erupted ancient cannabis dust onto my hand, making me swear and dash to the toilet to flush it all. I laughed out loud on my return, shaking my head at her. I started riffling through properly, past stacks of old photographs of

Amy and me, with Kim lurking at the side, replaced with photos of Jessica and me, and the years we discovered baggy jeans and eyeliner. I traced her face with my finger. God, she really had been beautiful. But, as I held a photo at arm's length, I realised for the first time that so had I. The girl smiling anxiously next to her wasn't an ugly friend. She certainly didn't match the way I remembered looking, which was pudgy and plain. I was never going to get model scouted outside the Oxford Street Topshop, but I was pretty. How hadn't I seen it at the time? I dropped the photographs and started rifling around the box with more urgency, not even sure what I was looking for. I found Jessica's old breakfast bowl. I found the azure friendship bracelet. I found the chopped plastic strip of the Reading musical festival wristband. Then I found a stack of papers, all with Jessica's handwriting. Notes she'd passed me in lessons, 'spells' she had created for us to do at the weekend, and, at the bottom, a letter I'd completely forgotten about. My mouth fell open as I unfolded the A4 sheet of paper. I'd found it the morning after our psychic sleepover. The night I'd finally opened up to Jessica and told her all about my mental health struggles.

• *Fern's Reasons To Hold On For Tomorrow*

Hi Fern,

I'm going to leave this under your pillow like a CREEP but I really hope you read it. Thank you for being so honest with me last night. I've decided to write a list of ten reasons why you should NOT DIE, just in case you ever feel like that again.

1) Jessica would miss you very much otherwise

2) You won't get to find out what JK Rowling has written as the final chapter of Harry Potter and hidden in a cave

3) . . . or get to watch the Harry Potter movie

4) What will happen to your Sims if you die? One is about to be an astronaut!

5) You don't want to die a virgin, remember?

6) We won't get to go to college together and reinvent ourselves as very cool people

7) What about our plans to go on a road trip around America, and find movie-star husbands in LA?

8) Ditto to go interrailing around Europe and find sexy tanned boyfriends called Julio?

9) No offence, but your school photo this term was terrible because of the frizz-rain situation, and this is the photo they would use in all the newspapers, so you may as well hold on for another year until you can get a better headshot

10) Whenever you feel like you want to die, tell me, AND read this
list. Add to this list whenever you think of a reason to stay alive,
until it's so long that you'll always want to stay here and hold on
for tomorrow. ALWAYS HOLD ON FOR TOMORROW, FERN. I
love you xxxxx

The note fell to the carpet. How could I have forgotten? Oh
my God. I was awful. This note . . . I remembered it so vividly
now. Finding it the next morning. Smiling with every inch of
my body. Treasuring it always. Feeling seen and loved and
understood for the first time in my whole life. How had I
blocked out that Jessica was the one who inspired my Hold
On For Tomorrow blog post? The blog post that gave me my
life, my job, that helped me find Ben? Had I really disasso-
ciated that much since I so ruthlessly cut her out? Christ.
What must she think of me?

Then I remembered what she'd said, when she'd turned
up at my event all those months previously.

*'Your blog post was amazing . . . I sent you an email, saying
how proud I was . . . you never replied though.'*

I got myself off the floor, dashed downstairs, and retrieved
my laptop from my rucksack in my parents' kitchen. I entered
my password incorrectly twice before I got access, and then
kept mis-clicking as I tried to pull up my archive folders,
wondering where I'd stored all the emails I'd downloaded
when everything took off. Finally, I found it, and typed in
Jessica's name, holding my breath, and it pinged right up.
Unread. The olive branch she'd given me years ago. Ignored.
Unseen. I opened it up, and read it in tears.

From: JessicaT@USAMail.com
To: HoldOnForTomorrow@GeeMail.com
Subject: You remembered!!

Dear Fern,

Sorry, that's a weirdly formal way of starting an email, isn't it? I have to say I'm a bit overwhelmed after seeing you ON THE NEWS with this amazing project you've started. It's amazing. You are amazing. You've always been amazing, but this is super amazing. I can't believe my stupid note has inspired something so huge. And it means so much to me that you've been thinking about me too. Honestly, Fern, my fingers are shaking as I type this email. I really hope it's OK that I've got in touch, and I hope I've not read too much into this. I'm scared that I'm just desperate and lonely and miss you. Firstly, I really need to say how sorry I am for what happened. For all of it. I don't know why I do the things I do. I think I need to figure it out though because, the truth is, I'm so unhappy, Fern, and losing your friendship is the worst thing that's ever happened to me. I actually live in America now. Can you believe it? I've married this man and we've even had a daughter together but nothing feels right. I feel so alone over here. And I thought I was so in love, but my husband is being weird and off, and I don't have any friends and . . . fucking hell . . . sorry . . . I don't know why I'm typing any of this. You must think I'm crazy! Honestly, I've never had anyone I can talk to, truly talk to, since we fell out, and just feeling able to

email you is unleashing all this stuff. I really hope it's
OK that I've emailed. How are you? Things look like
they're really crazy right now, but I pray so much that
you're happy. You've always wanted to be a writer and
now your blog post is EVERYWHERE and it means the
world to see you doing all this. Please do write back if
you get the chance. I can imagine you're swamped
right now, but I'm happy to wait. Hearing back from
you is MY reason to hold on for tomorrow.

So much still needs to be said, I know. But the only
words I have right now are I love you and I'm sorry.

Jessica xxxx

Voicenote:

*So, hey, OK. I'll stop after this, I promise. I just . . . well . . .
messages always sound so shit, don't they? It doesn't feel right
saying how sorry I am over a message. But I really am sorry,
Jessica. For so much that I don't even know where to start. I
just read the email you sent me all those years ago and God . . .
I can't believe I didn't see it. If only I'd seen it . . . I really am
so sorry. I'm not trying to make excuses, but, I've been thinking
so much about us growing up and what we went through, and
I think we were all messed up by it more than I thought.
Anyway, again, I'm sorry. I am fucked up. I see it. I should've
said sorry. I should've been a better friend. Back then, and now.
You were right . . . you weren't to blame, and I'm sorry. It's
so weird walking around Victoria Park. It's been months now,
and I keep wondering if I'm going to bump into you and I
wish we were just friends again. But better friends. Free from
all the shit we've been carrying. But yeah, I can't make you*

forgive me, and I don't want to pester you. But . . . I'm sorry. What I said was terrible. I hope you and Bridget are OK. I wish you every single happiness. I'll stop now . . . Thanks for listening to this.

Thirty-three

A month later, I came home from work and found the flat filled with candles. Ben stood amongst them, weeping before he'd even got down on one knee, still wanting to marry me. I cried with him, hugging on the floor, in an ocean of light. The happiest moment of my life. If only I could've told her about it, even though she knew it was coming.

When he put the ring on my finger, she was the first person I wanted to tell.

Just as she was the first person I had wanted to tell when I really fell in love for the first time in my third year of university.

And how she was the first person I wanted to tell when he broke my heart two years later because we couldn't make the long distance work.

She was the first person I wanted to tell when I got my first proper job.

She was the first person I wanted to tell when my blog post took off.

When I finally got my first good job, it was her I wanted to call.

Every time I heard the word 'azure'. Every time a Disney song or Carole King played. When I saw online people from school who I didn't like have nice things happen to them, and people from school I did like have horrible things happen to them.

When I finally met Ben, I wanted to tell her about him so much.

Then she came back. Then she left.

And, when I found my wedding dress, she was the first person I wanted to tell. And when I got accepted onto my Level Four counselling course, it was her I wanted to celebrate with. And, when my period was late, and Ben and I had to have these weird, initially petrified, and then giddy talks about what to do, she was the first person I wanted to tell. And when that period came seven weeks later, including a cluster of cells that should've been our baby, she was the first person I wanted to tell.

Because she was the only person who ever truly knew me, and me her. Who understood what we'd shared, how we'd laughed, the jokes we'd made, haircuts we'd seen, growing up-ness we'd done. The pressures we were under – both visible and less visible. Some getting better, some worse, as the world changed and us with it. A man can't ever understand a woman like another woman can – especially the women who knew you as a girl.

I wanted to tell her everything, every day, especially how sorry I was . . .

But she didn't want to be told.

Thirty-three

I look for Jessica everywhere. Every time I see a nice dress, or a cool coat, or a good fringe, my heart ignites. But it's never her. I can't walk past the part of the park where we fought. My shame is scorched into the earth there, leaving me with intense self-loathing about the things I'd said.

'To some degree, I get it,' Ben has reassured me. 'I mean, you shouldn't have said the stuff you said,' he continued. 'But you know that, that's why you've apologised. And, considering the things that happened when you guys were younger, I can sort of understand why you'd be suspicious.' He'd leant his forehead against mine. 'No need to worry about anyone leading me astray though,' he'd said. 'I hope you know that, Fern.'

'I do.'

We'd kissed, and, what was so strange, was that, now I knew I had him for sure, I finally believed him. Finally fully trusted him. All the edginess and worry vanished the second he got on the ground and got out a ring. I'd been picked. Finally. I stopped stalking his exes online. I relaxed. Laughed more. Ate more. Drank more. Ben kept saying, 'I should propose more often, I love this side of you,' almost as a joke. And it infuriated me because I would've been like this all along, if only he'd made it clear he was picking me earlier.

In fact, after I said yes . . . After the initial flurry of telling people, and intense love-making, and wedding planning, and ring-showing, I'd had a mild panic for a week or two about whether or not I actually picked Ben back. I watched him sleep and sometimes thought, *'Oh my God, is this it? Him? Really? Are you sure it's him?'* Our whole relationship had been such a rollercoaster of waiting to be chosen, of being the person onstage auditioning, that I'd not really considered if I wanted the part now that I was being offered it. But, after a week or two of mental processing, I fell in love with Ben in a different way. A less puppy-dog way. A considered way. I was finally myself in love, rather than the darkest parts of myself wanting to be loved . . . And now, when he looks at me and holds my hand, it's the happiest I've ever been. Well – would be the happiest if, on the day I finally got the love of my life, I hadn't lost my other one.

It's spring again. The blossom peaked last week and is starting to fall. Trodden into mush underfoot on the paths. I have a coffee in my hand – trying to enjoy the small things I can enjoy now there isn't a baby inside me any more. My foot slips in the magnolia mulch and I let out a small squeal and almost drop my cup. My hand goes to my stomach protectively before I realise there's nothing there to protect any more, and I take myself to a bench to collect myself, staring down at the rotting blossom.

I hear the joyful noises of children in the playground over
the fence. I wince. I've been avoiding this section of the park.
But never the best at impulse control, I get up and watch the
mayhem taking place. The small pudgy bodies running from
thing to thing, yelling *'follow me'* or, *'this is MY stick'* and,
'watch what I can do'. Their primary-coloured clothes, and
random tutus or Spiderman costumes they insisted on wearing
that morning. The energy of the packed swing set, the squeak
of butts travelling down the slide, the spinning chaos of the
merry-go-round. I watch and let myself smile. *It's OK that
this is not part of my life now*, I tell myself, rather than letting
myself get jealous of the surrounding parents.

And that's when I see a girl almost too pretty to be real.
In a sunflower playsuit teamed with red sunglasses, long dark
hair flowing down her back, digging curiously in the sand.
My heart soars in my throat and I scan the benches trying
to find Jessica. I scan again, and then gasp, because she's on
a bench in the corner, reading a book. My old best friend,
but she's not the Jessica I know. No stylish haircut, no make-
up, no curated outfit. She wears leggings and a long T-shirt
with some trainers. She still looks beautiful – she will always
look beautiful – but she's not trying any more. I sway on my
feet and deliberate whether to go over. I can't not. The pull
is so magnetic. I'm smiling before I'm even at her bench. My
body is heavy with missing her. I dodge the chaos of children
running around my thighs and my body casts a shadow on
her book. She looks up.

'Hi,' I say.

'Oh. Fern.' She's shocked, closes her book, crosses her
arms.

'Umm, can I sit?' I wait for the rejection, am ready to cry. I shouldn't have done this when I'm still so fragile. But she gives a small smile.

'I guess.'

'Thank you.'

I sit as far away on the bench as I can, to be respectful. We don't look at each other. A minute passes. Two. Three. Five. In total silence. I'm already crying. There are so many things to say and yet none of them feels right. So I open my mouth and say the only thing I know for sure is real and right.

'I love you,' I tell Jessica.

A gasp. She's crying too. I feel her shoulder jolt next to me. 'I love you too.'

Then we are hugging, getting tears on each other's shoulders, as a game of *What's the Time, Mr Wolf?* echoes behind us.

'I'm so sorry,' I say into her T-shirt. 'Honestly, for what I said. For everything. I'm so sorry.'

'I'm sorry too.'

The sun brightens, makes my face glow from its warmth; the backs of my eyes turn from pink to red. We laugh once we break apart, reach into our bags and get out tissues. A small awkwardness lingers in the air, both of us knowing the conversation that needs to come.

'It's been ages,' I tell her.

'I know. I'm sorry I never replied to your messages.'

'I get it. I was awful.'

'Yes, no. That wasn't why I didn't reply. I needed . . . time . . . I guess. Then it got too long and I didn't know what to say.' She looks over at my decorated finger. 'So you said yes,' she says. 'Congratulations.'

'I have you to thank for such a nice ring.' I'd had so many compliments about it when we'd announced the engagement.

'It was my pleasure, really. I always remember you saying that you wanted an emerald engagement ring. Green, because your name is Fern.'

I'd known she'd remembered when Ben presented it. It was part of the reason I'd cried so hard when I said yes.

'It's perfect. Thank you.' A quiet moment, as we both watch the kids get closer to Mr Wolf, them trembling with the antic-ipation of being chased. Bridget isn't playing with them though. She's still completely engrossed in building an elab-orate sandcastle. One that's so enticing, another girl, wearing a pink Disney costume, tentatively joins her. Bridget allows her to join in, pointing out instructions about where the next turret should go.

'How have you been?' I ask, turning my body to face her on the bench. Taking in her new look, still not sure what I make of it. 'You look . . . different,' I add. 'Not bad, but, you know . . . more laid-back.'

When Jessica smiles, she does it without trying to hide her pointed teeth. 'I'm not sure how I feel about it yet,' she admits. 'I . . . well . . . I started a degree in September.'

'That's amazing.'

Her smile grows wider. 'Yeah, I thought it's never too late, you know? And I had the money from the divorce and everything.'

'What are you doing?'

God, her whole face is a smile. '*Gender studies*, if you can believe it. I'll never get a job, but holy fuck, am I loving it.'

'Oh my God!' I clasp my hands together. 'I love this. I absolutely love this.'

'Me too. Your friend Heather inspired me, at that dinner party. It's been like therapy or something. I'm a mature student, of course. So I thought I'd be this weird old lady who everyone ignores. But my classes are amazing, and, from week one, they were telling me stuff about ageism in women and stuff. They're . . . well . . . I think young people have it a lot more sussed out than we ever did.' She tugs on her T-shirt. 'Anyway, I thought I'd try a week or so without all the . . . effort. See how I feel. Try and figure out if I do it for me, or something else.'

'You look beautiful,' I tell her. It's true.

'Hmm . . . I'm not sure. We'll see.'

'This is amazing.' I'm being too enthusiastic in my desperation to make amends, and we both know it. She allows it though.

'Thank you. Anyway, how about you? How's the book going? Is it coming out soon?'

I laugh, and sigh. What a long time ago that feels. 'No. It's not coming out at all.'

'What?'

'I turned down the offer with the agent,' I explain. Oh, I've wanted to tell her this for so long. 'I mean, on one hand, it was stupid, because I need the money to pay for my new course. But that's what I'm focusing on. Becoming a counsellor.' I still smile whenever I say it. 'I want to qualify and then specialise in helping young women who've been messed up by men.'

'Oh Fern. Wow . . . I don't know what to say. I mean, you'll be amazing, but I'm sure you'd have written an amazing book too.'

I shake my head. 'I don't know. I certainly wouldn't have until I sorted myself out a bit more.'

'You'll be an amazing counsellor . . . I know what I said . . . but I only said it to hurt you. I really think you'll be great.'

Her words are medicine. Her opinion one of the only few that matter. 'Thanks. I've got a long way to go . . . Also . . . double bonus . . .' I start picking my nail, wondering whether to go there, address it. 'I've now got to have two years' compulsory counselling as part of the course. I thought I'd had enough therapy as a teenager, but, considering I was accusing my best friend of sleeping with my boyfriend, I think we can both agree I really need some more.'

I do a loud, false laugh, to let her know how I'm sorry but trying to make it better. I expect her to join in, but Jessica doesn't. She looks at her lap, picks her own thumbnail.

'I did flirt with him,' she said quietly.

'Oh.'

'I mean, it was pointless, as he's so in love with you anyway. And I never would've gone there, but . . . you weren't going totally mad. I did try . . . a bit . . . with Ben. To see if he fancied me . . . It's wrong. I know it was wrong. Even though it was nothing, I shouldn't have even tried. That's part of why I've not seen you . . . I needed to figure out why what you said hurt so much.'

I take a breath. 'And?'

'And, well, I think there's a part of me that's always been angry at you. Jealous of you.'

'Jealous of *me*?'

'Yes. Of course. For how easily you make friends. How girls always like you. Girls always *hate* me, but I've always found it easy to make boys like me . . . I think, if I have to admit it to myself, I cling to what I can do to men. It's the only power I've ever had . . . but the things they did to me revealed I never had any power to begin with.' She sniffs hard and wipes her eyes. 'You've always had so many girls to turn to, to talk to when things go wrong. Whereas, with me, Fern . . . you're the only girl friend I've ever had. It hurt, what you said, what you believed, after everything I'd told you . . . but it hurt the most that part of you was right. I couldn't help myself. With Ben. Even though I promise it was just useless, pathetic flirting.'

I let out a sigh and close my eyes for a second, letting the sun warm my eyelids, and letting myself feel all the things her admission makes me feel. The anger comes roaring out but is doused almost instantly with a calm, blue under-standing. Because, what she'd said about me, not so very far from here, had hurt me a lot too. And the truth of it was what had burnt the whitest scar. My utter incapability of seeing it from Jessica's point of view. How I had judged her, from that first party. Even though I'd never said anything out loud, she must've felt it. As she got used, and recycled, and shamed, and discarded, when the boys just kept on using and recycling and shaming and discarding, I should've tried to protect her. Instead I made it about me.

'Thank you for saying that.' I look her right in the eyes. 'I'm not angry.' I smile. 'I'm not, but I'll appreciate it if you try not to do it again.'

She laughs. 'Never. I promise.'

'And, hey, what you said . . . you were right. I have so much to be sorry for. I . . . I can't believe how much I let you down. How self-obsessed I was. How jealous I was, of something nobody should be jealous of. I've been thinking so much about what you said, and I'm trying to be better.'

'Thank you for saying that,' she echoes. 'Honestly. It means a lot. Though I can't believe you were jealous of *me.*'

'And I can't believe you were jealous of me!'

I edge my butt closer to her on the bench. She giggles, and inches closer too. I inch again. She copies. We collide arses and fall into our first proper laugh together since the day we burnt it all down. We embrace again, and cry again. For the years we've lost, the pains we've suffered, for how much we adore each other.

'Your degree sounds so cool,' I say when we break apart again, laughing as we wipe under our eyes.

'Oh my God, it's *so* cool. You should meet some of my friends on it. I mean, I'm in the slow lane. I'm only just learning about how men aren't very nice to women, but they're already trying to tell me that gender doesn't even *exist*, that you can be whoever you want, change your mind about it even . . . I feel very old . . . and very jealous. I mean, can you imagine how much easier life would've been if we'd known stuff like that in our day?'

I reach out and squeeze her hand, and remember everything we've lived through together. The normal things we endured as we grew from girls to women. The days in school where boys would line us up in order of our fuckability. The parties where it was normal to lie on top of a semi-conscious girl, do things to her, then call her a slut afterwards. A Christmas number-one song about a pregnant woman being stuffed into the boot of a car and driven off a bridge. Laughing when your male friends made rape jokes. Opening a newspaper and seeing the breasts of a girl who had only just turned legal, dressed in school uniform to make her look underage. Of the childhood films we grew up on, and loved, and knew all the words to, where, at the end, a girl would always get chosen for looking the prettiest compared to all the others. Reading magazines that told you to mirror men's body language, and hum on their dick when you went down on them, that turned into books about how to get them to commit by not being yourself. Of size zero, and Atkins, and Five-Two, and cabbage soup, and juice cleanses and eat clean. Of pole-dancing lessons as a great way to get fit, and actually, if you want to be really cool, come to the actual strip club too. Of being sexually assaulted when you kissed someone on a dance floor and not thinking about it properly until you are twenty-seven and read a book about how maybe it was wrong. Of being jealous of your friend who got assaulted on the dance floor because why didn't he pick you to assault? Boys not wanting to be with you unless you fuck them quickly. Boys not wanting to be with you because you fucked them too quickly. Being terrified to walk anywhere in the dark in case the worst thing happens to you, and so your male friend walks you home to keep you safe, and then comes into your bedroom and does the worst thing to you, and now, when you look him up online, he's engaged to a woman who wears a feminist T-shirt and isn't going to change her name when they get married. Of learning to have no pubic hair, and how liberating it is to pay thirty-five pounds a month to rip this from your body and lurch up in agony. Rings around famous women's bodies saying *'look at this cellulite'*, oh, by the way, here is a twenty-quid cream so you don't get any. Make sure your drink doesn't get spiked. Don't drink too much to make yourself vulnerable. Make sure you don't get an unlicensed cab. Don't let yourself get picked in the wrong way. Look at this woman in the papers who has had more than three boyfriends – the slut. A guy grabbing your arse in the club is a compliment. A guy telling you you're ugly is actually him saying he likes you. Do you know how many men are falsely accused of rape? Isn't it disgusting? Don't ever lie about something so terrible. We won't believe you anyway. Go to a festival and see no women onstage, but try to have fun, when it's not safe to be near the front. You're so basic to put a flower in your hair. Go to the cinema and see men grow, and women help them grow while wearing next to no clothes and then getting raped and dying. Give it an Oscar. Fuck like a porn star. Make me a sandwich. Stop being difficult. Shut up. Put up. Use this anti-ageing cream. Nobody wants to fuck you any more, Karen. Oh, come on, it's only a joke.

I look out at Bridget, getting her dress covered in sand. She and her new friend are engrossed in their sandcastle project, their heads so close they're probably giving each other nits. The castle is taking up most of the sandpit now. It's turned into an impressive project – some of the other children are noticing, chewing on their bottom lips, trying to work out how to join in. The two girls are concentrating too hard to notice them noticing. I wonder how many precious years they have left until they start noticing the noticing. Until the noticing means they change how they play, what they make, how they view each other. I want the world to be better for these girls. I am scared for them. Bridget really is astoundingly beautiful. My eyes skim over the rest of the playground, landing on the small group of Good Dads in the corner. With their babies in slings on their chests, and their paternity leave, and good for you, what heroes. They stand together like celebrities often do, and speak in deep voices about their sleep deprivation. It's a start. I guess we should be grateful for the start. But, as they talk, I see where their eyes land, and it's on Jessica's beautiful daughter.

They watch her.

So I hold hands with my best friend in the world, and imagine what we could've been without it all. How I've wasted so much time and stress on the attention of men, when my relationships with them will never be like this because they'll never be able to understand. I reflect on how, the only times I felt myself, and safe, and safe to be myself, was when it was just us. With women. With Jessica.

'Young people definitely have it easier,' I say, looking out at the bustling playground.

'Yep. So I keep telling them.'

'I worry there's still quite a lot of work to do.'

'That, there definitely is.'

'So much. But less, I hope. Less . . .'

I glance down at Jessica's hand in mine, and marvel at the beautiful friendship we've managed to just about keep going, under the never-ending gaze and pressure of what we're supposed to be, and do, and behave, and look like. Taught that our greatest allies, the ones who get it, are our competition and enemy. And how incredible it is that we're able to still be there for each other, still holding hands, under the crippling pressure of that.

'I know I've said it already, but I love you,' I say again.

'I love you too.'

I rest my head on her shoulder, as she asks me about the wedding. I invite her to the hen do. She smiles and says yes.

We squeeze each other's hands and watch her daughter play.

Acknowledgements

This isn't the book it was supposed to be, written in a year that was definitely not supposed to be. When my editor and I discussed my plan for this novel, over afternoon tea in a packed restaurant in early 2020, it was the last time we'd see each other for almost two years. Like the rest of the world, we were enjoying our last weeks of life before a deadly worldwide pandemic – blissfully unaware about how everything was about to change.

Before 2020, I'd spent most of my career fighting against another, less-newsworthy pandemic – the pandemic of violence against women and girls. And, yet, in the years leading up to COVID-19, those of us in this field had witnessed what can only be described as a global awakening. This devastating issue was finally being taken seriously. Women were starting to speak out, and, even more encouragingly, they were being believed. There was a giant wave of energy and mobilisation – a sense that the time had finally come for things to change, and I watched in awe as women and allies marched across the world, shared their trauma on the MeToo hashtag, and, most surprisingly of all, saw perpetrators being held accountable. One of my last memories before the world closed down was of the seemingly impossible conviction of Harvey Weinstein. I remember watching the news and feeling this jubilant sense of justice and triumph, before the headlines switched to news of the coronavirus travelling to Europe, of impending lockdowns, stories of whole cities in China and Italy being locked in their houses. And then COVID-19 hit England, and, for those of us lucky enough to not be key workers, we were all shut inside. Shut inside, with all the time in the world to think and reflect.

Something strange happened to many women during that time. Something that I found wasn't discussed publicly, but whispered on WhatsApp conversations while we all checked in on each other. As we learned how to Zoom or make banana bread, to fill the endless time we now had on our hands, I found that lockdown was also a time where past experiences women had been avoiding, or normalising, or out-running, eventually caught up with them. It was a time where memories resurfaced. Where they realised that 'The Thing' that happened to them when they were younger maybe wasn't OK. That maybe it was even a crime. A trauma. Speaking to a friend who works at a rape charity, she confirmed they were having a surge in calls about incidents that happened five, ten, twenty years ago. We'd been woken up but then driven inside our houses to remember and realise and get angry. And, me, trying to write a novel while the world outside my window was changing forever, I too found history catching up on me – memories of growing up that I saw in a new light. And, thus, this novel became something different and darker from the initial celebration of female friendship I'd plotted. A total shift from the plan. This manuscript became an unwieldy *purging* of some kind, one that I only finished once the world started to unlock again.

I want to thank my glorious editor, Kimberley, for having such an unwavering faith in this book's total detour. This wasn't the novel we excitedly discussed over scones and naivety about '*that virus in the news*'. But this is a book I am so proud of, a book I'm glad exists, and it couldn't have gotten here without her total confidence in the strange process I went through writing it. To my editor, April, in the US too, for also guiding and steering me through Fern and Jessica's journey. Thanks to Madeleine Milburn, who never doubts me no matter how determined I am to doubt myself. Your confidence keeps me brave. And to everyone who works at the MM agency, at Hodder, and at MIRA in the US who champion my books. I adore and need every single one of you.

It's still my greatest pride to be an ambassador for Women's Aid, a charity that was needed even more urgently in lockdown. Thank you for everything you do to protect women and children from violence, and thank you to everyone who works in this sector. One day, hopefully, we will find the vaccine that solves this issue. But, in the meantime, thank Christ you exist.

The pandemic reminded me just how dear my loved ones are to me. Thank you to my wonderful parents and sisters. And, to W – the man who has morphed from beloved boyfriend, to husband, to father, over the journey of writing this novel. Truly the light in my darkest times. I love you.

Thank you for always encouraging me to be brave in my writing, for always believing in me, and for putting up with my obsession with discussing hugely dark topics over dinner. You are everything. And to little C, I hope we can make the world better and easier for you.

And, finally, thank you to all my girl friends. My insides. My support networks. My pillars of wisdom. My walks around the park. My senders of eight-minute-long voicenotes. My mirrors. The funniest, most brilliant, bravest, women in the world. Rachel, Emily, Emma, Lisa, Becky, LorLor, Ruth, Sara, Tanya, Lucy, Katie, Krystal, Alywyn, Sam, Nina, Claire, Sophie, Louie, Alexia, Christi, and everyone else who has brought nothing but pure joy and solidarity into my life. I adore you all, forever.

For more information and advice for those affected by rape or sexual abuse, contact Rape Crisis or Women's Aid – both of which are national organisations offering free and confidential support to those in need.

Rape Crisis
Helpline: 0808 802 9999
More information: rapecrisis.org.uk

Women's Aid
More information: womensaid.org.uk